T0274303

SHADOWS OF TRUTH

ALSO BY ASTRID SCHOLTE

League of Liars
The Vanishing Deep
Four Dead Queens

SHADOWS OF TRUTH

ASTRID SCHOLTE

ALLEN&UNWIN
SYDNEY·MELBOURNE·AUCKLAND·LONDON

First published by Allen & Unwin in 2024

Copyright © Astrid Scholte, 2024

All rights reserved. No part of this book may be reproduced or transmitted in any form or by any means, electronic or mechanical, including photocopying, recording or by any information storage and retrieval system, without prior permission in writing from the publisher. The Australian *Copyright Act 1968* (the Act) allows a maximum of one chapter or ten per cent of this book, whichever is the greater, to be photocopied by any educational institution for its educational purposes provided that the educational institution (or body that administers it) has given a remuneration notice to the Copyright Agency (Australia) under the Act.

Allen & Unwin
Cammeraygal Country
83 Alexander Street
Crows Nest NSW 2065
Australia
Phone: (61 2) 8425 0100
Email: info@allenandunwin.com
Web: www.allenandunwin.com

Allen & Unwin acknowledges the Traditional Owners of the Country on which we live and work. We pay our respects to all Aboriginal and Torres Strait Islander Elders, past and present.

 A catalogue record for this book is available from the National Library of Australia

ISBN 978 1 76106 889 8

For teaching resources, explore allenandunwin.com/learn

Cover design by Debra Billson
Title design by Theresa Evangelista
Cover images from Shutterstock & Adobe Stock
Text design by Eileen Savage
Illustrations p5, 287 & 375 by Astrid Scholte
Set in 11.25/17.5 pt Adobe Caslon Pro by Midland Typesetters, Australia
Printed and bound in Australia by the Opus Group

10 9 8 7 6 5 4 3 2 1

The paper in this book is FSC® certified. FSC® promotes environmentally responsible, socially beneficial and economically viable management of the world's forests.

Everyone who followed me here...
this book is for you.

Telene Government Hierarchy

THE REGENCY

Regency General

Regency Agents

VARDEAN

Telene Herald

VIOLENCE AT VARDEAN LEADS TO PERMANENT LOCKDOWN OF FACILITY

Tulla Lunita

PRISONERS involved in a riot at Vardean have been returned to their cells after creating a 'violent brawl' that took both Vardean guards and Regency agents to control.

Approximately fifty inmates were returning from their nightly meal when the disturbance broke out. Reports claim the riot began in response to a newspaper article that insinuated Regency corruption in the legal system. However, no copy of the article has been found, and its origins are unknown.

The inmates refused to return to their cells and fought back against the guards. There were numerous injuries on both sides, but no fatalities reported.

The Regency has released a statement that no lawyers or even guards are to return to Vardean. For 'Telene's safety' the Regency has locked down the facility and is investigating security breaches, with its agents to replace the Vardean guards. The riot has been blamed on a lack of proper security detail and the superintendent has been dismissed. The *Telene Herald* reached out to both the superintendent and Regency General for comment, but received no response.

THE REGENCY: FRIEND OR FOE?

Barlor Grotherman

AFTER the recent change in law, where no court cases will be tried, one might begin to question the Regency's approach. Public outcry has demanded a return to the ways of old; where citizens of Telene are provided a fair trial before sentencing. Now, even non-edem crimes won't go before a judge, and the perpetrators will be locked in Vardean for the fore-seeable future.

Will this increased level of penalty deter future crimes? Or is Telene on the verge of a civil war?

You can trust in the *Telene Herald* to bring you the latest information as the situation develops.

Keep vigilant and stay safe.

CHAPTER 1

NARENA

N arena didn't know how to tell Cayder's story.

Where would she begin?

Did the story start when Cayder planned to break his sister Leta free from Vardean? Or weeks earlier, when Leta had been arrested for allegedly starting a fire that destroyed the entire town of Ferrington, killing over 300 people?

Or did Cayder's story actually start seven years ago in Ferrington, when his mother was killed in an edem – extra-dimensional magic – incident?

Narena's fingers hovered over her typewriter. She had been tasked by the *Telene Herald*'s editor-in-chief, Barlor Grotherman, to write Cayder's story.

When did the story truly start? What led to his disappearance?

After Cayder began working as a legal apprentice at Vardean, he had begun to question whether his mother was actually killed by edem that night. He had wondered if the Regency was responsible for her death, as they had framed Leta for the fire in Ferrington, and been involved in the king's disappearance nearly two months ago. Not to mention, they had covered up the existence of the creatures known as the hullen that Narena had seen with her own eyes.

Narena's fingertips glided lightly over the keys; the pressure not enough to push the ink onto the paper.

More importantly, Narena thought, *how did the story end?*

The last she'd heard from Cayder was almost a week ago. He was shadow-bent on his ridiculous plan to break his sister out of prison. Narena had tried to talk him out of it, but it had been pointless. After Leta was poisoned by the Regency and almost died, Cayder would stop at nothing to free his sister. Including becoming a criminal himself.

But his plan had been to break his sister out of Vardean and be pardoned by the princess, not disappear without a trace! There were no details on who had started the riot that night or signs of any inmates who had escaped. Surely, if Cayder and Leta were free, the Regency would have plastered the town with their faces.

Still, Narena hoped Cayder had been successful.

Then the Regency announced that rebels had infiltrated the castle isle and murdered the king and the princess in their beds. Without the royals, the future of Telene was fragile, so the Regency claimed, and they had set sail for its neighbouring nations to sign a treaty to reopen the borders and reinstate trade.

Four days had passed since the prison riot, and Cayder and Leta had not resurfaced. Narena began to fear the worst. She had visited all their usual haunts, including the pub, the Belch Echoes, and the library; she even made the trolley trip out to the burned fields of Ferrington. She had hoped to find Cayder and Leta hiding out somewhere, but had found no sign of them.

'Well?' a voice asked.

Narena glanced up. A girl leaned over her desk to see the piece of paper stuck in Narena's typewriter; her long auburn hair danced along the keys as she tried to read what was on the page.

Narena pushed back from her desk. 'Do you mind, Farrow?'

'I do, actually.' Farrow straightened and scrunched her nose. 'Your page is blank. You're supposed to submit five hundred words in...' she glanced to the clock hanging on the brick wall, '*one* hour.'

'That's not what I meant.'

Farrow acted like she was Narena's superior simply because it was her second summer working at the *Telene Herald*; despite the fact that they were both interns and the same age. *And* that Narena had spent more than half her life inside the walls of the *Telene Herald* while her mother, Tulla, finished her latest article. The *Telene Herald* newsroom had been Narena's second home; she'd been raised by the stories forming around her with the typewriters' staccato rhythms. When Narena lay in bed at night, the beat of the keys was the soundtrack to her dreams, as though her thoughts were being recorded for future reference.

After Cayder's disappearance, Narena's mother had insisted her daughter work where she could keep an eye on her for the summer. Apparently working at the library with her father wasn't 'safe' enough. However, Narena was more concerned about her mother: the Regency had visited their home, threatening her life unless she stayed away from Leta's case.

3

Narena needed to keep Cayder's plan to escape Vardean a secret to keep her mother safe. Which was why she couldn't write the article that was due in an hour.

'Well?' Farrow asked. 'Get typing!'

Narena twisted two sections of her thick black hair together. 'I don't have anything to write about.'

She wished that were true. She knew too much – that was the problem. The Regency was in charge of Telene and their power seeped into the far corners of the nation like a dark shadow. The Regency was dangerous; accusing Leta of *their* crime was proof enough.

The truth itched behind Narena's fingertips, desperate to be freed.

Could writing this article be a way to find out the truth of Cayder's disappearance? And hold the Regency accountable?

No one is going to believe a seventeen-year-old high-school student over the Regency, she thought bitterly. *I'm also Cayder's best friend.*

'You're Cayder's best friend,' Farrow said.

Narena glanced up. Had she said the last part out loud?

Farrow narrowed her eyes at her. 'If you didn't know what he was up to, then who did?'

After the riot, Cayder and Leta's father, Alain Broduck, demanded the Regency tell him what happened to his children. When they failed to offer an answer, or allow him back inside Vardean, Alain went to the papers to place a missing persons ad.

Mr Grotherman had approached Narena for an insider's perspective. As Cayder's best friend, *she* was the best person to write the story. Mr Grotherman even stuck Cayder's missing

MISSING

Cayder Broduck
Age 17 years

Missing from: Vardean
Hair colour: dark brown
Eye colour: golden brown
Height: 6'0

Last seen inside Vardean before the riot and subsequent lockdown. He was wearing a white shirt and blue pants and jacket.

Any information that leads to his location will be rewarded justly.

Contact Alain Broduck on 64284

person ad on her cubicle wall as 'motivation to write the article'. As though she needed motivation to find him.

'Cayder had secrets,' Narena said to Farrow. 'He told lies.' She pushed up off her chair. 'There's nothing I can write that will help his father find him.'

If she could, she would have already done so.

Farrow followed Narena into the kitchen. Narena let out a not-so-subtle sigh.

'You have a deadline,' Farrow said. 'You have to write something.'

'What's the worst that can happen? I get fired? I'm not even getting paid.'

'But you want to, one day. This is your dream, right?' Farrow gestured to the rows of typewriters before them, and the journalists typing frantically as their end-of-day deadline loomed.

Narena wasn't sure how Farrow knew that, but yes, being a reporter was her dream. She would study journalism after high school and follow in her mother's footsteps. She was born to do this. Born to tell stories, reveal the truth and crack open cold cases that everyone else had left dead and buried.

But now…without Cayder, what did her dreams matter? The truth was merely words floating out in the ether. Nothing of consequence. What she really *wanted* to write, she couldn't.

'Dreams change.' Narena poured herself a cup of coffee and took a long sip. She hated the taste, but this was what reporters did. They drank coffee to fuel their stories and meet their deadlines.

When Narena was younger, she used to pour herself a cup of hot torlu tea when her mother would grab a mug of coffee and settle in for the night. Narena would feed a piece of paper into the typewriter and begin clacking away at the keys. While her mother wrote reports on the latest edem crimes, Narena wrote hard-hitting exposés about cockroaches and how they were the most misunderstood creatures.

Narena never could have imagined that years later, she'd be sitting on the biggest story Telene had ever known. If she wrote what was burning up inside her, she could become the most famous journalist in the nation before she graduated high school. Her career would be set.

She might also be thrown in Vardean for treason. Or worse.

Narena took another sip of her bitter coffee and let the liquid warm her chest. She hoped that, wherever Cayder and Leta were now, they were safe. She hoped she hadn't heard from them because they were lying low, and not because they were both stuck in Vardean.

'I don't believe you,' Farrow said.

Narena leaned her hip against the kitchen counter. 'That's fine with me.'

Farrow pursed her lips and something stirred in Narena's mind – that little voice that she had heard since she was a kid. The niggling feeling that there was a story here. Something unsaid. Some truth Narena needed to uncover.

Narena placed her coffee mug down on the counter. 'Why do *you* care so much?'

'I don't. I was just trying to help.' Farrow crossed her arms over her chest. 'One intern to another. We should stick together.'

'Now, *I* don't believe *you*.'

Farrow huffed. 'Fine, don't hand in your article. See if I care.' She turned on her heel and stomped off.

Farrow was definitely hiding something, but Narena had been suppressing her insatiable curiosity since Cayder disappeared. She had promised her friend she'd keep out of trouble, and Narena had learnt the hard way that digging up secrets often led to dangerous answers.

Narena's deadline came and went. She pushed away from her desk. Despite what she had said to Farrow, she *did* hate to miss a deadline. She looked for Farrow's flash of auburn locks and found her green eyes fixed on her own. Farrow raised one brow, as though challenging her.

That niggling voice came back, but Narena pushed it down and glanced away.

No investigating. No stories. Keep yourself out of trouble.

That was what Cayder had said the last time she saw him. She never thought they'd be his final words to her.

Narena headed to the Belch Echoes after work, in case Cayder showed up as though he'd merely been cramming for a test all week and had forgotten what day it was. She climbed the rickety stairs to the table they used to frequent.

How could this place look the same, when everything else had changed? Cayder's disappearance, the death of the king and the princess, and the Regency's new laws. While most people shied away from edem and the prospect of spending their lives in Vardean without a fair trial, others had become incensed. People picketed the streets, demanding the Regency rethink its new laws. A swell of unrest was building in the city streets of Downtown Kardelle – a bubble soon to burst.

Narena took a large gulp of her torlu tonic and nibbled on fried fowl strips with traditional Meiyran spices. She wasn't sure how long she would continue to wait for Cayder. Hopefully, he wouldn't test her commitment to its limit.

Narena took out her notebook and flicked through the pages that detailed everything she knew about the Regency, Leta's case and the hullen. If she gave this to Mr Grotherman, would he be able to do something with it?

You have no proof, she thought. *They're just words on a page.*

'Did Mr Grotherman fire you?'

Narena startled. 'What are you doing here, Farrow? Did you follow me?'

Farrow shrugged and slumped into the chair opposite her. She snagged a piece of fowl from Narena's bowl and bit into it.

'Go ahead,' Narena muttered, placing her notebook safely back in her bag. 'Help yourself.'

'Well? Did he?'

'You'd like that, wouldn't you?'

Farrow scrunched her freckled nose. 'I told you. Us interns need to stick together.'

'As long as I do what you want me to do.'

'Then he didn't fire you? I really thought he was going to. You did miss the deadline after all. You've missed *all* the deadlines this week. That's an important part of this job. You know, *deadlines.*' She crossed her ankles and for the first time Narena noticed she wore mismatched coloured socks under her long black skirt.

'Yes,' Narena said. 'I'm well aware of that.'

'Why don't you write what Mr Grotherman asks? Don't you want to find Cayder?'

'Of course I do!' Why was this girl hounding her?

'Then why not tell the truth?'

Farrow raised a curved eyebrow, making Narena jealous. She had always wished she could raise one brow at a time. It was a perfect interrogating technique: question your subject without a word. Which was exactly what Farrow was doing. Narena was being interrogated. By an intern. And from reading Farrow's articles, not a very good intern at that.

Narena let out a breath before repeating the line she'd said dozens of times over the last week. 'I don't know what happened to Cayder on Monday night. I wasn't there.'

'I believe you,' Farrow said.

Good. Now go away.

'But I do know where you were the night before Cayder's disappearance. You were at the *Telene Herald*.'

Narena's mouth popped open before she could stop it. 'What? *No* – I wasn't an intern until after Cayder disappeared. I was working at the library.'

Part of that was true.

'You were at the *Telene Herald* the night before Cayder disappeared.' Farrow tossed an auburn curl over her shoulder and gave her a cunning smile. 'I'd forgotten my bag and when I returned to collect it, I saw you.'

'So?' Narena asked. 'I was helping my mother with something.'

'Helping her with *this*?' Farrow pulled a piece of paper from her bag and placed it on the table. It was the article that Narena had written for Cayder.

The air between them grew heavy.

'I don't know what that—'

'Don't even try to deny it,' Farrow said.

Narena's stomach lurched. 'My mother had nothing to do with that.'

'But you did.'

'You have no proof that *I* wrote that,' Narena said. 'It's your word against mine.'

Farrow cocked her head. 'Who do you think people are going to believe wrote this article that ended up in Vardean? Me, who has no connection, or Cayder's best friend?'

She was right. Narena was implicated the day she agreed to take the stand on Leta's case – and step into the Regency's line of sight.

'Do you work for the Regency?' Narena asked. Even though Narena didn't end up taking the stand, perhaps they had been spying on her.

A flush of red burned across Farrow's cheeks. 'I would never.'

'Then what do you want?'

'The truth,' Farrow said earnestly. 'You started to tell it, why did you stop? Why not share this article with all of Telene?'

'Why do you care?'

Farrow leaned back in her chair. 'I have my reasons.'

'Well,' Narena said, 'I have *my* reasons to keep the truth to myself.'

'If you're such a believer in the truth, why would you give up on it?'

'It doesn't matter.'

A fierceness flashed behind Farrow's green eyes. 'You don't believe that.'

Of course Narena didn't. 'There's nothing I can do to help Cayder.'

She couldn't find him. She couldn't expose the Regency. She couldn't write the truth.

No investigating. No stories. Keep yourself out of trouble.

'I'll help you,' Farrow said. 'First, tell me everything you know.'

'And why would I do that?' Narena asked.

Farrow picked up the article and waved it around.

'Because if you don't, I'm taking *this* to Mr Grotherman.'

CHAPTER 2

LETA

Ever since Leta was young, she had imagined what life would be like on the other side of the veil. She envisioned all sorts of far-fetched locales, fantastical creatures and fanciful people. After her mother had died, Leta imagined she would be waiting for her there, holding out her hand, her long black hair trailing behind her like a cloak made of midnight. It was a world Leta would never want to leave and where dreams were made into a reality.

When Leta had accidentally used edem in Dr Bueter's office, resulting in his body dissolving in front of her, she thought she had been wrong. Edem was nightmare fuel and everyone was right to fear it.

Then, when Leta had found Dr Bueter alive at Vardean's Regency headquarters, she learned edem did not equal death and destruction, and her mother could still be alive. Leta, Cayder and the others had jumped through the veil, hoping to escape the Regency.

For that brief sliver of nothingness between Telene and the world on the other side of the veil, Leta wondered which of her theories was in fact correct: was the other side a dream world, or a nightmare?

Either way, there was no going back.

She imagined a world of night-time, where the skies were so thick with hullen, the stars were masked from view. However, as soon as she arrived on the other side, she was blinded by a brilliant yellow light. With Telene's sun obscured by the perma-cloud, she'd never seen a sky so intense. But that wasn't her biggest concern.

She was falling.

Fast.

Leta wasn't sure who screamed first, but it triggered a scream of her own. And now she was screaming, she couldn't stop. The freezing wind lashed at her hair and clothing. This was not the dark world of Leta's dreams.

She had jumped through the veil holding onto Cayder and Jey, but Cayder was gone. She wanted to call out to her brother, but his name was caught in the turbulent breeze. She managed to find Jey's face in the luminous haze. His dark eyes were filled with windswept tears. His hand was slipping through her grasp.

'No!' she cried.

But she couldn't hold onto him any longer. Their connection broke and Jey was ripped away. Leta looked around wildly, tearing at the empty air. She tumbled towards a restless ocean of deep purple, almost black, water.

No, no, no, no, no!

She slammed back-first into the water, knocking the air from her lungs. She sank, unable to move – her body stunned from the collision. Jey submerged not far from her. He plunged below the surface then kicked back up.

Leta wanted to reach for him, but her muscles wouldn't obey. She opened her mouth to scream but it only let the salty water into her lungs. She gagged, screaming in her mind.

A dark cloud appeared overhead, blocking the light filtering from above as she sank into the depths. Was it death?

She wanted to laugh at the absurdity of it all: she had broken out of Vardean only to drown seconds later. She would never see her mother again. And her father would never learn the truth.

A large shape burst into the water and something wrapped around her waist. A talon.

The hullen!

Of course! Cayder had summoned two of the feathered creatures at the Regency headquarters to help them battle the Regency agents.

The hullen pulled her from the ocean and back into the light. While Leta's body still wouldn't cooperate, she was able to cough the liquid from her lungs.

'Jey—' she croaked at the creature. 'Save Jey!'

Jey was bobbing up and down in the water below.

'Hey!' He threw up his arms. 'Over here!'

The hullen collapsed its translucent wings and dove towards Jey, scooping him out of the water with its free talon.

'Are you okay?' Jey twisted in the hullen's grasp.

Leta nodded. Her body was starting to obey her again. 'I got the wind knocked out of me.'

The hullen flapped its expansive wings and soared across the water.

'Stop!' Leta pulled at the claw hooked into her clothing. 'We need to save the others!'

The scaly claw didn't budge. There was no use in fighting against the creature. Its grip was like iron.

'Hey, you giant bird-thing!' Jey shouted up into the belly of the beast. 'Help them!'

Another squawk sounded from above.

The other hullen!

Leta tried to find her brother in the midnight purple sea, but she could only see the rolling waves.

'Don't worry,' Jey said. 'The other creature will find them.'

Leta wanted to look the hullen in the eye, but she couldn't see anything but its silvery translucent feathers over her head.

The hullen continued across the water and Leta spotted an island rising out of the waves. Off to the right side of the island, it looked as though someone had taken a giant brush of white paint and swept it across the horizon. But it wasn't a cloud. It was the absence of anything and everything.

The purple waters blended to turquoise waves that lapped against the shoreline. Leta had never seen such a brilliant colour, but there was something wrong about the way the water moved. The foam of the waves had broken against the rocks, then surged back out into the ocean and rose upward.

It's going backwards, Leta realised.

The hullen veered through a deep, wide fjord. Sheer cliffs banked either side of the inlet. Black, jagged spires punched out from the tops of the cliffs towards the bright sky. A snow-capped mountain range glimmered in the distance.

'Where are you taking us?' Jey asked the hullen.

The creature twisted and turned through the ravine until it reached a landing on one side of the cliffs. The hullen lowered them towards the ground before unceremoniously dropping them both to the earth.

The hullen had deposited them within a rocky clearing surrounded by a dense forest of warped black trees. The trees leaned in like curious shadows.

'Nice landing, mate,' Jey said. He helped Leta up. 'You okay?'

'Peachy,' she said. 'You?'

He grimaced. 'I'm alive.'

The hullen landed in front of them with a *thwomp*.

The hullen looked different on this side of the veil; its horns were spiralling silver and its moonlight eyes glowed with intelligence. The scales across its snub-nosed face looked like polished flat pearls and its feathers were like petals of crystal. The wings appeared to be made of a thin, silvery spun silk.

'Thank you,' Leta said to the creature.

'Is that its ribcage and heart?' Jey pointed to the creature's translucent body.

While it wasn't exactly like the magical creatures Leta had imagined when reading stories of the veil, it wasn't a monster either.

'What's your name?' Leta asked.

The creature cocked its head in response.

'I don't think it can talk, Nettie,' Jey said.

'Maybe not, but I think she's trying to communicate.' She held her hand out as though she were approaching a horse. 'What are you trying to tell us?'

Jey laughed. 'Since when did our captor become a "she"?'

'Captor?' Leta scoffed. 'She saved us!'

Jey raised an eyebrow. 'That has yet to be determined.'

'Jey!'

'Fine,' he said, holding his hand to his side. 'I suppose a *thank you* is in order.'

As if perturbed, the creature turned and headed into the surrounding forest.

'Should we follow her?' Leta asked.

Jey glanced back to the inlet. 'I can't believe I'm saying this, but I think we should wait for your brother.'

Leta followed his gaze, waiting for the other hullen to appear.

'Huh,' Leta said, realising the sky was an even, bright-yellow canvas. 'Where's the sun?'

'Hasn't anyone ever told you it's dangerous to look directly at the sun?' Jey asked.

'But... The sky is so bright! How can there be no sun?'

Jey shrugged helpfully.

The hullen let out a hooting call, as though it was trying to get their attention.

'Come on.' Leta pulled on Jey's arm. 'We have to go.'

Jey let out an exhausted groan. 'Sure. Why not? Let's follow the magical mystery bird into the dark forest of dead trees. What's the worst that can happen?' Leta opened her mouth to reply but he tutted. 'Don't answer that.'

They trailed after the hullen as it clicked and clacked across the rocky ground.

'What do you think happened to the trees?' Jey asked. The branches were jagged, as though they had grown around an object that was no longer there.

They reminded her of the photographs of the burned and blackened trees of Ferrington. 'It looks like there was a fire.' Leta and Jey locked eyes.

Leta approached one of the trees and touched the bark. 'Ouch!'

'Still hot?'

'No.' She tapped the trunk with her knuckles. 'Cold. Like ice.'

'This place keeps getting weirder and weirder,' Jey said with a shake of his head.

They continued following the hullen. Jey was dragging his feet like a petulant child, while excitement propelled Leta forward. She was close to her mother; she could feel it.

The hullen kept its silken wings close to its body to move through the forest. The creature hadn't turned back around to acknowledge them.

'What do you think it eats?' Jey asked. He looked like he was close to falling asleep. It had been a long night.

'I don't know.' Aside from the rocky ground and the icy tree spindles, there didn't appear to be anything else *living* here.

Was the hullen actually alive? Or were the creatures the ferrymen of the dead? Which would mean—

'Jey—' Leta said. 'Stop.'

'What is it?' His handsome face formed a frown.

Leta reached out and placed her hand on his chest, holding her breath.

'Nettie—'

'Shush. I'm listening.'

'For what?'

She could feel it, the reassuring thud under her palm. 'You're alive.'

Jey blinked. 'I would sure hope so.'

'Let's keep going.' Leta pushed thoughts of the afterlife away.

The trees began to crowd in on each other, their branches tangling together to form a web above them. Leta could barely see the sunless sky. Darkness fell over them in cool shadows, but unlike Telene, here there was nothing moving in the darkness. No edem.

It was cold enough in the light; in the shadows, it was freezing. Leta's teeth began chattering.

'It feels like it's about to snow,' she whispered.

'Why are we whispering?' Jey whispered back.

'I don't know.'

Something about the place seemed sacred. Perhaps only because she had dreamed of it since she was a child. Finally she was here, walking through her childhood fantasy.

Jey placed his arm around her. 'I'd offer you a jacket, if I had one.'

After a while, the trees parted to reveal a grand waterfall spilling from a cliff above. The hullen stopped beside the pool, tipped its head back and let out a hoot.

Leta placed her hands into the crystal blue water. 'Do you think it's safe to drink?' She was so thirsty. She couldn't remember the last time she'd drunk something. She took a sip. It tasted like water from home.

The hullen let out another hoot and raised its nose to the waterfall.

'Weird,' Leta said, realising the water was running upward instead of down.

Through the curtain of water, Leta could see a dark opening. A cave.

'I think she wants us to go in there,' Leta said. 'What do you think, Jey?'

'Nettie…' Jey was slumped over.

Leta ran to his side. 'What's wrong?'

He sagged against her. 'I—' He wheezed a wet cough.

Leta guided him over to a fallen log, her hand against his back. When he was seated, she lifted his hair from his face, smearing red across his forehead.

What the—? She checked her palms and noticed they were stained red.

Blood red.

'I'm sorry,' Jey said. 'So sorry.'

When he straightened, Leta saw that the front of his stolen grey Vardean uniform was dark. Almost black.

Leta stared at her red-tainted palm in realisation.

Her palms were covered in his blood.

CHAPTER 3

CAYDER

The wind had separated Cayder and Leta the second they'd launched through the veil. And although he couldn't see her, he heard her scream as she vanished from sight.

Cayder tumbled through the clouds, unsure what was up and what was down. Bright light burned his eyes like sharp chemicals in the air.

A figure fell towards the water, long hair floating behind her like a golden cape.

The princess.

Somehow, she managed to look graceful.

Cayder threw his arms out like the wings of a bird and steadied his descent. He spotted Leta crashing into the deep purple waves below.

He tried to call out to her, but his voice was a whisper against the deafening wind.

Something silver sped by. Followed by the sound of a screech. The hullen pulled Leta from the water.

Cayder glanced around as he heard the flapping of wings.

The other hullen!

The creature sank its talons into Cayder's belt, halting his descent. Its claws caught the skin at Cayder's waist and he hissed in pain, but after everything he'd been through, he could survive a few scratches.

He'd never been this close to a hullen, even when he had summoned them to attack the Regency headquarters. He could hear the creature's heavy breathing above him, but rather than the warmth of a red-blooded creature, a chill of shadows radiated from its translucent body.

Leta's hullen had pulled Jey from the water and veered to the left. Cayder's rescuer took off after it.

'No!' Cayder pointed back to where he last saw Kema and the princess. 'Help them!'

The hullen swooped in the direction Cayder indicated and caught Elenora in its free claw; she still had her grip on the edem-fuelled weapon she'd stolen from the Regency and used to decimate their headquarters – not to mention shooting Dr Bueter. Her grey eyes were large and her cheeks had been roughened by wind.

'Cayder,' she said, breathless. 'Thank you.'

'It wasn't my choice.' Cayder searched for Kema's figure in the water below. 'It was the hullen.' He knew it was a horrible thing to say.

The princess didn't respond.

Let her be upset. Let her feel a taste of the betrayal he'd felt when she turned them in to the Regency. Let her feel as though their promises to look after each other had meant nothing.

Cayder finally spotted Kema below them. The hullen closed in on her when—

BAM!

The hullen shrieked, jostling Cayder and Elenora in its grasp.

'What was that?' Elenora asked.

BAM!

Something whizzed by.

'We're being shot at!' Cayder yelled.

The hullen let out another shriek, but this time it sounded mournful. Silvery liquid oozed from one of its wings. The hullen attempted to fly but it couldn't remain upright. They tumbled back towards the water. Elenora let out a cry as she lost her grip on the gun and it fell into the ocean.

'Let go!' Cayder said to the hullen, trying to prise the talon from his belt. The creature could do nothing for them now; Cayder didn't want to hit the water with it attached to his back. 'Drop us!'

The hullen finally let them fall into the sea.

Without any passengers, the hullen glided along the surface of the water and out of sight. Cayder didn't have time to worry about its fate.

The water was freezing. The first wave drew him up towards the sky, while the next wave tossed him backwards, then forward again then back again. The waves were moving *against* each other, forming a foamy mess. And Cayder was trapped in the middle, tossed around like a doll.

The weight of the water pulled at Cayder's guard uniform, threatening to drag him under.

'Take off your shoes!' the princess instructed.

'What?' Cayder spat out, along with some salty seawater.

'Your shoes will weigh you down!'

Cayder ducked his head under the freezing water and untied his laces. His shoes sank like stones. Cayder kicked his feet to keep afloat. But it was a battle he was sure to lose over time.

Kema appeared on the horizon. 'Hey!' she shouted.

'Kema!' Cayder shouted back.

She rode the top of a wave over to meet them. 'What happened to the hullen?'

'Shot,' Cayder said.

'By who?' Kema asked, glancing around.

'I don't know.' Thankfully, the shooter had disappeared along with the hullen.

'And the others?' Kema asked.

'The other hullen took them that way.' Cayder pointed to the sky, as though it looked different to any other part of their surroundings.

Kema trod water beside him. 'I don't see any land.'

Neither did Cayder. Was this world purely ocean and sky? Where did the hullen live?

The Regency General had made this world sound like it would be full of displaced people and things – anything that had been impacted by edem. Cayder wasn't expecting *this*.

'I saw something on the water when I was falling.' The princess nodded behind her. She looked strangely calm. 'Something silver.'

'I didn't see anything,' Cayder countered. He didn't want to swim in the wrong direction only to find more open water.

'And we don't know who or what was shooting at us. We can't risk it. We need to continue east – where the other hullen took Leta and Jey.'

'East?' Kema asked. 'How can you tell directions in this place; there's no sun!'

He gestured to more of the deep purple ocean. 'Our left.'

'Land could be hundreds of kilometres away,' Kema said. 'I'm a strong swimmer, but not *that* strong.'

'What I saw wasn't as f-far.' The princess's lips were starting to turn blue. Cayder's fingers began to prickle and burn.

They had to get out of the ocean.

He spat out some salty water in the princess's direction. 'What did it look like? Land? A boat? A weapon?'

'I don't know,' she said. 'You'll just have to trust me. There's something out there.'

'Trust you?' He scoffed. 'After what you did? I'll *never* trust you.'

The princess glanced away as though she'd been slapped in the face by a wave.

'Now's not the time,' Kema reprimanded Cayder. 'I say we head for whatever the princess saw. It's the best option we have. Our only option.'

Cayder's arms and legs were already beginning to tire, and he couldn't feel his feet anymore. 'Well, I say we swim in the direction of Jey and my sister.'

'Go then,' the princess said. 'I'm getting out of this water as soon as possible. Who knows what creatures lurk below?'

The princess starting swimming in the other direction.

'Creatures?' Kema asked. 'I didn't sign up for more creatures. Wait up, Princess!'

'Edem be damned!' Cayder cursed. He wanted to locate his sister; they had just found their way back to one another. But he couldn't go off on his own. He was in a strange world, full of strange things. He had to play this smart.

Safety in numbers.

CHAPTER 4

JEY

Jey had never liked improv. In drama class, he wanted to know the backstory, the details of the scene: where he was supposed to stand, what he was supposed to say and how the audience was supposed to feel. Jey craved order, not chaos. Even though some might argue that Jey invited chaos into his life. He did, after all, rebel against his father's desire for quiet control, fall in love with the rebellious spirit that was Leta Broduck, get himself arrested for his father's 'murder' – to cover for Leta – then join a coup to break out of prison. Not to mention jumping through a portal to another world.

Despite evidence to the contrary, Jey liked order.

As soon as Leta and Jey had been rescued by the hullen, Jey wanted to know what was next. Following a semi-translucent bird that was straight out of a nightmare was not a plan. And yet he couldn't fault Leta, even though all he wanted was to rest. After everything that had happened in Vardean, surely they were owed some respite. A little lie down, for half an hour. Tops. Then Jey could forget the throbbing in his side and the reminder that he'd been shot...

Jey had been somewhere in the void between Telene and the next world when he felt the lick of flame against his side. Of course, he'd been worried at the time, but then he was falling from the sky, and that took precedence.

From Jey's prior experience with edem weapons, people disintegrated after being hit and were sent to *this* side of the veil – like his father, Dr Bueter. But Jey was *already* on this side of the veil, so he didn't need to worry about disintegrating, right?

He'd thought he was out of the woods – figuratively, and certainly not literally, until he became increasingly lightheaded. His shoes were squelchy with sweat, and – Jey feared – blood.

He'd decided it was a good idea to take off his shoes, but when he bent down to untie them, he couldn't straighten back up.

That was when Leta noticed he was wounded.

'I'm sorry, Nettie,' he said again. 'I didn't want you to worry.'

'Are you kidding me?' Leta demanded, even though her eyes were full of concern. 'We're in this together, Jey! You can't keep things from me. Did we learn nothing from Ferrington?'

Jey knew she was right. Leta was always right.

'I'm too shot to argue with you,' he said.

She unbuttoned his guard uniform to reveal a garish wound on his side. Around the wound, black veins spiderwebbed across his torso. Rivulets of sweat ran tracks down his neck and shoulders and onto his arms and bare chest. The movement made his fake echo marks appear as though they were alive. Jey squeezed his eyes shut.

Not today, death. Not today.

'When did this happen?' Leta asked, her voice shaking.

Jey tried to shrug but his arms were made of stone. 'Between worlds.'

Leta scrunched his shirt into a ball and pressed it to his side as Jey hissed in pain.

'I'm sorry!' Leta said. 'I don't know what else to do!'

But Jey did. They had to stick with the plan – or the loose plan of a plan that they had.

'You have to keep going.' He nodded towards the waterfall and cave.

Leta jutted out her chin. 'I'm not leaving you here.'

Jey tried to push himself up but fell back to the log.

'You can't carry me,' Jey said. 'And *I* certainly can't carry me.'

'Then she will.' Leta turned to the hullen, but the creature merely hooted in response.

'The hullen can't fit into the cave. And that's where you need to go.'

Leta squatted beside him so they were face to face. Her large brown eyes burned. 'I'm *not* leaving you.'

Jey gave her a small smile; anything more was too much effort. 'You don't have a choice.'

She shook her head. 'There's always a choice.'

'Nettie. I think this is pretty bad. And if I'm right, I won't survive this—'

'Don't say that!'

He let out an exhausted breath. He couldn't feel his body anymore. Which was a blessing. The pain had melted away. And soon his consciousness would follow.

He bit the inside of his cheek to keep the darkness at bay.

'*Leta*.' It was rare he used her real name, but she needed to know how serious he was. 'Keep going. Find help. I can't – I can't go with you.'

He didn't think they would be parting again so soon, but if she didn't get out of here, they might be parting forever.

His eyelids were heavy. And sleep too appealing.

Sleep. Blessed, blessed sleep.

'Jey!' He could hear the tears lining her voice. 'Get up!'

Her hand was warm in his, but as he began to drift away, her hand felt elusive. No matter how hard he tried to grasp onto her and stay awake, he couldn't. She was drifting away like the remnants of a dream, moments after waking.

He thought he was fine, that he would *be* fine, but this wasn't fine.

He forced his eyes open. One more time.

'*Go*,' he said. 'Find your mother.'

He saw tears fall from Leta's eyes as he closed his.

CHAPTER 5

ELENORA

Elenora swam at a steady pace, even though her freezing extremities were screaming at her to move faster and escape the glacial water. But she knew she needed to reserve her energy if she wanted to find whatever she'd spotted out on the indigo ocean.

Elenora was familiar with the sea. Aside from living on a small coastal island her entire life, she spent her summers in the water to escape the stuffy castle. Despite four years separating the two royal siblings, Erimen would challenge Elenora to race around the isle while their parents cheered them on from the pebbly beach. Even though Elenora had never caught her older brother, their competitions had made her a strong swimmer.

After their parents died, Elenora would sneak out of her bedroom at night and float on her back, enjoying being weightless in a sea full of stars. On a quiet night, she imagined her parents existing in a similar place, not part of the living world, but also not forgotten. Suspended in the dark. An in-between life.

But this ocean was different. The waves were shadow-bent on pulling her forward then dragging her backwards, and the temperature was icy, despite the severe sky. She ducked down to swim under the waves; it was the only way to keep from being tossed about, but she had to come up for air every now and then.

'Do you see anything yet?' Cayder asked from behind her.

As much as she wanted to turn around, Elenora kept to her steady strokes. Changing her pace would only make it more difficult to start up again. Elenora had to be machine-like. Steady. To ensure fatigue would not win.

Now that she knew Cayder was behind her, she was more determined to lead them to safety. She needed to prove she could be trusted and right her wrongs. Even if Cayder never forgave her. Even if he hated her forever.

And yet, if she hadn't betrayed Cayder and the others, she wouldn't have found out the truth about Erimen and the other side of the veil. And Cayder never would have discovered his mother could still be alive.

And Elenora had helped them escape; Cayder and Leta would have most certainly been captured by the Regency.

Kema glided along the top of the water, working out the pattern to the strange tide by crisscrossing from wave to wave. The guard was strong, her muscular brown arms slicing through the water like blades.

Elenora wasn't sure how long they'd been swimming; she'd lost all feeling in her arms and legs, which was making it difficult to move. She was tempted to give in to the numbness and allow the water to drag her down to oblivion. Perhaps she'd find her parents there…

She shook herself free of such thoughts. She had to keep going. For herself. For Erimen. For her people.

Elenora dove back under and pushed forward. While the water was clear, Elenora couldn't see far out in front of her, although she thought she saw the movement of small shiny fish.

'There!' Kema called out when Elenora surfaced for another breath.

A wave lifted Elenora up and she could see where Kema was pointing.

A glimmer of silver glistened on the horizon. It looked like a line of heat haze, except it shifted. Elenora was pushed under the waterline and when she kicked back to the surface, the glimmer was gone.

'Where?' Cayder asked Kema.

Kema shook her head. 'It was there a moment ago.'

'I see it!' Elenora said. The shimmer of silver was clearer than before, and closer. Much closer.

'How did it move so fast?' Cayder asked, dumfounded.

'These currents are unpredictable,' Kema said. 'Unnatural.'

Elenora gasped. 'It's a boat!'

A silvery vessel with half a dozen pearly-white sails appeared ahead. However, it was sailing off to the right and away from where they trod water.

'How do we gain their attention?' Elenora asked. They'd never be able to catch up to the boat; they needed the boat to come to them.

'Take off your clothes,' Kema said. 'I have an idea.'

Elenora struggled to take off her prison guard uniform while staying afloat. When she tried to unbutton her shirt with her numb fingers, she slipped underwater.

'Cayder!' Kema ordered. She had already pulled off her uniform. 'Help her!'

'I'm f—' Elenora had wanted to say *fine*, but she dipped under the water again.

A strong arm encircled her waist and lifted her above the surface.

'Th-thank you,' Elenora said, working on her buttons. Cayder didn't respond, although his weary breaths panted into the back of her neck.

She tried not to think about how warm Cayder's body was against hers. Luckily, he couldn't see her blush as she stripped down to her underwear.

'You're next,' Elenora said, holding out her arm for him to take. She felt much more buoyant now that she'd freed herself from her wet clothing.

Cayder dropped his arm from around her. 'I can do it myself.'

He disappeared under the water and when he resurfaced, he had his shirt and pants in his hands, leaving him in a white T-shirt. Through the wet shirt, Elenora could see a large echo mark on his back.

Kema took the clothing from Cayder's hand and tied their garments end to end, while Cayder helped her stay afloat. 'Take one end,' she said to him. 'We're going to send them a signal.'

Cayder grabbed the cuff of his pants and Kema allowed the waves to pull her further away.

Their clothes only made a stretch of around six metres of

fabric, which wasn't much, but it would catch the eye more than three heads bobbing in the water.

'Now we wait,' Kema said, pressing her blueing lips together.

The silver vessel sat several storeys above the waterline; it made the small boats that travelled to and from the castle isle look like bath toys. Its sails appeared to be made of a material spun from translucent silvery thread and the hull of the boat reminded Elenora of the slick grey pebbles that she and Erimen used in their skipping-stone contests.

The boat was undeniably beautiful. A vision sent to save them.

If only it weren't about to run them down.

'Umm...' Cayder said. 'I don't think our signal worked.'

'Hey!' Kema shouted, waving her hands around. 'Down here!'

'Help us!' Cayder followed Kema's plea. 'Stop!'

Cayder bobbled in the water, throwing his hands in the air as the ship bore down upon them. Perhaps it was the cold, but Elenora couldn't find any words or the energy to speak. Everything was heavy.

'The boat's not stopping,' Kema said. 'We have to get out of the way. Swim. *Now!*'

Kema took off in one direction and Cayder in the other. Elenora continued to bob in place.

'Princess!' Kema yelled. 'Get out of the way!'

But the vessel was too fast.

Elenora couldn't will her muscles to move. The glimmering ship had bewitched her body and mind. How could something so beautiful be deadly?

She could hear Kema and Cayder yelling and screaming at the

vessel to stop but their voices seemed distant and unimportant.

The current pulled Elenora towards the hull. She couldn't have fought it if she'd tried. The ship blocked the vibrant sky from view and Elenora was sucked underwater. Her nose and mouth filled with salty brine and her chest heaved. Her lungs burned for oxygen.

She braced, waiting for her body to be dragged under the hull.

She waited...

And waited...

Until the darkness claimed her.

———

'Princess.'

'Princess.'

'—Elenora!'

Elenora stirred and opened her eyes.

Kema hovered over her; her dark eyes full of concern, her white-blonde hair dripping rivulets down her brown face. 'Are you all right?'

Elenora pushed herself upright. She was in a room with arched metal rafters, as though she had been swallowed and found herself inside the belly of some terrifying steel beast. The water around her was being drained away through a grate in the floor. She twisted to see a flap close to the bright outside world.

The silvery vessel *had* swallowed them.

'Where are we?' Elenora croaked.

Before Kema could reply, another voice replied, '*Levisial.* But more importantly, *why* are you here?'

Behind Elenora were hooded figures in black cloaks that fell in watery waves around their bodies. Elenora had never seen a material like it; it was some combination of liquid and fabric.

'Get up,' one of the cloaked figures ordered with a low rasp.

Kema helped Elenora to her feet. *Where is Cayder?*

She found his sullen face; the man with the raspy voice had his hand around Cayder's arm.

'We don't wish to cause you any trouble,' Elenora said with a cough.

'Who are you?' the man asked. 'Are you with the radicals? What are you trying to steal from us this time?'

Radicals?

'We're from Telene,' Elenora corrected.

The man growled. *Wrong answer.* 'You create weapons that will destroy us all.'

Kema placed her hands on her hips. 'No.' Even in her under-clothes, she was imposing. 'We're not part of the Regency.'

He pointed to Kema's arms. Her brown skin was lined with fragmented echo marks, which Elenora had never noticed before. 'You're all alike. You want what you can't have. What doesn't belong to you.'

'Why did you save us then?' Cayder asked, wrestling against his captor.

'She demanded it,' he replied simply.

'Who?' Elenora asked.

'Take them to her.' He nodded to the other guards. 'The queen will decide their fate.'

38

CHAPTER 6

CAYDER

Cayder and the others were escorted by the guards through the insides of the *Levisial*. Their captors had provided them each with a black cloak.

'Just stay calm,' Cayder whispered to Kema. 'We'll find a way out. We always do.'

'No talking,' the man behind Cayder grunted.

Their captors weren't much friendlier than the Regency. Cayder hoped that wherever Leta and Jey were, it was somewhere safe.

The crew of the *Levisial* stared as they walked along a metal gangway through the middle of the ship. Some watched with interest, others scowled as they passed. Cayder wanted to explain that they weren't connected to the Regency; they had come for salvation, not damnation.

The gangway led to a curved wall that hung beneath the deck. There were no doors or windows. The gruff man pressed his hand against a panel on the wall. The wall rippled.

Edem, Cayder mouthed to Kema and she nodded.

The wall slid to the side, creating an opening into the room. Cayder wondered how they had managed to harness edem, before he received another sharp shove between his shoulder blades.

'In,' the hooded man ordered. 'All of you.'

They entered the circular room while their captors remained outside. The door sealed shut behind them.

Great, Cayder thought. *Another prison.*

The room was dim; a small amount of illumination filtered in from a window in the ceiling. Through it, Cayder could see more cloaked figures up on the deck, working the masts of the boat. An ornate four-poster bed with black satin sheets sat off to the side of the room.

'At least we'll be comfortable,' Kema said with a grim grin. 'It's better than a cell in Vardean.'

'What do we do now?' Elenora asked. Her fair brows were pinched together.

Cayder was tired of plotting and planning; the responsibility weighed heavy in his bones. He needed something to go his way. Just once. He didn't know why the others looked to him for answers; every plan of his had gone sideways. First Leta's case. Then escaping Vardean. Now this.

'I don't know,' he admitted. 'I thought we were going to meet their queen.'

'You are,' a voice said. It sounded like a sigh mixed with the rustling of leaves on a windy day. 'I am the Shadow Queen.'

Cayder spun around, peering into the dark. The queen's voice came from the right of the room but he couldn't make out a form, a figure, anything.

'We've come from Telene,' Cayder said. 'We're not here to cause any trouble.'

'Why *are* you here?' Now her voice seemed to be coming from the left.

'We had nowhere else to go,' Cayder admitted. 'We were at the Regency headquarters when—'

'*The Regency.*' The word thundered throughout the room and the darkness vibrated.

There was something there, in the shadows. The back of Cayder's neck prickled in warning.

'You have come to destroy us,' her voice was as hard as stone.

'No,' Cayder said. 'We're not with the Regency!'

'All you want is my power – you always have. You are all the same.'

The darkness in Cayder's periphery shuddered and shook.

'All the same.'

The shadows twisted around each other like tendrils of seaweed caught in a whirlpool. Faster and faster the shadows spun. Cayder couldn't see who was controlling them. His cloak rustled as the shadows swirled around them, creating a black vortex; they were caught in the middle.

'We're *not* the same!' He shouted over the roar of the swirling dark. 'I am not like the Regency! I'm not like the Regency General!'

The shadows stopped, hovering around them. 'The Regency General?' the queen asked, her voice cold as ice. 'What do you know of him?'

'I know that he has been using edem – your magic – to create weapons. He is ruthless. He will do anything to control Telene, and the rest of the world. And he will hurt anyone who gets in his way. *We*,' Cayder gestured to Kema and the princess, 'do not follow him.'

Cayder exchanged a glance with Kema and she nodded; the queen needed to know the truth if she were to trust them.

'And he's here,' Cayder said. 'He was shot by one of his own weapons.' Best not to tell the queen that it was Elenora who pulled the trigger and the reason he once again walked this realm. 'The Regency weapons displace people from Telene over to this side of the veil.'

The shadows swarmed to the centre of the room and smothered all light from view. The tendrils of black wove themselves together, tighter and tighter to form the outline of a woman. Her dress was made of billowing darkness, her hair a length of curling black smoke, her skin an ash grey. And her eyes glinted like moons – like the hullen. A crown made of weeping shadows sat upon her head.

The queen hadn't been hiding in the shadows, controlling them. She *was* the shadows.

'Come.' She beckoned with an outstretched hand, shadows trickling from her fingertips.

Cayder swallowed sharply and took a step forward.

'If what you say is true,' the queen said, 'then you must help me. Help my world and yours.'

'We will help in whatever way we can,' the princess said, her voice resolute.

'Then you must find him,' the queen said simply, closing her moonlit eyes for a moment. 'The Regency General holds the key to our future – and why your world and mine will be nothing but darkness.'

The princess might be royalty back in Telene, but that didn't mean she was in charge here. And as much as Cayder didn't like Dr Bueter, they weren't about to go on some sort of quest for revenge. They had barely escaped with their lives the last time. Cayder only cared about finding Leta and reuniting with their mother. Everything else was secondary.

'Their edem weapons,' Kema said. 'They're hurting your world, aren't they?'

'It's not just the weapons. Every time edem is used in Telene, it drains my world of power, obliterating sections of my world bit by bit. But yes, if the Regency set off their weapons, it will destroy what remains here.' The queen sighed and it sounded as though hundreds of people sighed along with her. 'I thought I had prevented such catastrophe; alas, the future seems more certain with each passing day. I know the Regency General well: I see his face behind my world's destruction. I used to see a fleet of royal vessels, heading to the other nations to discuss reconciliation. But now, I see the fleet packed with Regency agents and their weapons armed.'

They hadn't stopped anything by destroying the Regency headquarters. 'You can see the future?'

'I see all.' She gave Cayder a sad smile. 'Past, present and future.'

'How long do we have?' Cayder asked.

The queen closed her eyes. 'The vessels are preparing to set sail. They will reach both Delften and Meiyra in just over a week.'

'Dr Bueter must have instructed the Regency to set sail before he disappeared,' the princess said, her mouth twisting in anger. 'They're using the royal fleet under the guise of diplomacy!'

'We don't know where Dr Bueter is,' Cayder said, interrupting the princess before she could make any promises.

'You saw the general come through to this side of the veil?' the queen asked.

'We—' He glanced at the princess. 'We saw him get shot but jumped through the veil before he completely disappeared.'

'Then you know where he is.'

Cayder shook his head, not understanding. 'We don't.'

'You know where to start looking,' the queen said, unperturbed.

He looked at Kema and she merely shrugged.

The edges of the queen's hair dispersed as she moved. 'Our worlds were once one. One land. One people. *My* people.' She twisted her hands around and around until a dark sphere hung between them. 'My parents were the reigning king and queen of Telene. It was clear from the moment I was born that I was different; I was born with shadows in my veins and a connection to the dark. My parents blamed my "affliction" on being born during a total solar eclipse. They hid me from the world, and hid my face behind a luminous mask in hopes to conceal the dark patterns across my skin.'

Elenora gasped, touching her own face. Was she thinking about the royal mask she used to wear?

'I was all alone, not allowed to be a part of the world. I spent much of my time daydreaming, and that was when I learnt I could control shadows, and bring forth objects from the past, present and future. The shadows were my connection through time.'

The ball continued rotating in her grey hands. 'I was a lonely child, watching life pass by from my tower – my prison. I tried to bring life to me – like the birds I saw flying through the sky. But when they arrived in my room, they did not appear as I had expected. They had been corrupted by time, and my power.'

'The hullen,' Cayder said.

The queen nodded. 'My parents grew increasingly afraid of what I could do, while others saw the opportunities to use my power for their own gain. They wanted me to build cities from the future, cultivate crops – create more hullen to protect them. The more I used my power, the weaker I became. I begged my family to allow me to be free. To live.

'At night, I foresaw my destruction, and the world's, because of my power. But my parents would not listen. They couldn't see beyond their own greed. I did the one thing I could do to save everyone: I stripped my power and everything I had created from Telene.'

The queen pulled her hands apart and the shadow sphere fractured in two. 'I created this world – based on what I'd seen of Telene. A place where I would be safe. And I formed a barricade to prevent anyone from coming through.'

The Shadow Queen had created the veil!

'Centuries passed and as this world evolved, so did I.' She held up her grey hand. 'My humanity faded away and I became my real self. And where light in your world brings life, darkness – and my power – sustains life here.' The two balls shifted away from each other. 'Telene forgot about me – or so I thought. A small group of people passed down the truth of the past and my existence; they were adamant to return to the ways of old and spent decades trying to breach the veil. Eventually, they succeeded.'

The princess gasped. 'The Regency!'

The queen nodded. 'And once the tear was formed, my power, and the darkness of this world, began draining through the veil and into Telene. Over the years, my world has lost all darkness, and its life source. Little remains alive. And without night, I am trapped within my own vessel. I cannot leave here and travel through the tear to stop your people from using my power. Nor can I create new life. And the further away my power is used, the more unpredictable and dangerous it becomes – for both sides.'

They didn't need the queen to tell them that. Cayder, Kema and even the princess had experienced the unexpected consequences of using edem.

'The closer you are to the source,' the queen spread out her arms and the shadows fell from them, appearing like wings, 'the more control you have.'

That explained why Cayder was able to call the hullen and have them do his bidding; he was at the precipice of the veil. And close to the queen.

'And the opposite is true,' she said. 'As a child, I had never left Telene's shores, so I had no knowledge of the world that existed beyond it. This world,' she gestured to the smaller floating ball, 'does not exist beyond my replica of Telene. And when the Regency weapons are detonated far from Telene's shores, in a place that does not exist here, the results will be catastrophic. Both our worlds will implode.'

Cayder ran a hand down his face. No wonder the crew of the *Levisial* hated echo marks – they were a reminder of their coming demise.

And we are the harbingers.

'I'm sorry,' Cayder said. 'We didn't know.'

The Shadow Queen let out a quiet laugh that sounded like chimes in the wind. 'How could you? Your history has been hidden from you.' She clasped her hands together and the spheres disappeared.

'By the royal family,' the princess said. '*My* family.'

The queen lowered her head. 'And mine.'

'My brother, Erimen, was displaced by an edem-fuelled weapon and sent here. Have you seen him?'

'I have not,' the queen said. 'But I would like to meet him. You are both family.'

'What about Maretta Broduck?' Cayder asked.

'I don't know of her,' the queen replied. 'As my power diminishes, so do our resources. What remains here is a world that few can survive.'

The princess's face fell. Cayder understood her disappointment; he had hoped his mother was alive on this ship. But he wasn't giving up hope yet.

'If we promise to find Dr Bueter for you,' Cayder said, 'will you let us go?'

The queen tilted her head, a smoky tendril of hair falling over her shoulder. 'Let you go?' She blinked her moonlit eyes. 'You are not held captive here.'

'Could have fooled me,' Kema murmured.

'The Regency General is the key,' the queen said. 'He knows how to move back and forth between the worlds – he can alter his weapons to work in the opposite direction. Once he sends us back to Telene, I will close the tear in the veil – preventing any further edem, as you call it, from seeping through and saving both our worlds.'

'What about the Regency weapons?' Kema asked. 'How will we reach the boats if they've already set sail?'

The queen's eyes sparkled and in a blink she disappeared and then reappeared across the room. 'I will take care of that. But I need you to find him – I cannot leave this vessel.'

'Where do we look?' Cayder asked. The general already had more than an hour's head start.

'I thought you understood – I based this world on Telene – or the parts I'd seen of it. Our air is the same. Your castle—' she nodded to Elenora, 'was once *my* home. Wherever the Regency General disappeared; he will have appeared *here*.'

'Dr Bueter was shot at the Regency headquarters,' Cayder said.

'That building does not exist here,' the queen said. 'He would have fallen into the ocean – like you.'

Then he's likely dead.

'And what if we can't find him?' Kema asked, shooting Cayder a concerned glance.

'Then we will all die.'

———

Cayder, Kema and the princess were shown to their sleeping quarters while the *Levisial* sailed to where Vardean *would* exist in this world. After showering and dressing in some spare clothes the guards had given them, Cayder sat next to Kema in their small cabin. The princess was next to head into the shower.

Kema was inspecting the jagged echo marks on her hands and arms. 'I was hoping they would disappear,' she said.

'I think they look cool,' Cayder said.

Kema smiled, although her eyes were tight. 'Thanks, Boy Wonder.' She ran her fingers through her short, bleached locks.

'You hanging in there?'

'We just found out our entire history is a lie and that this place,' she gestured around us, 'is an offshoot of Telene. But yeah, I'm fine.'

Cayder let out a terse breath through his teeth. 'I know how you feel. It's definitely not what I was expecting.'

Cayder felt more isolated than ever before. He was never the believer. He wasn't Leta. He wasn't his mother. And now, everything he knew about the past had been a lie.

Cayder didn't know what to think. First his belief in the legal system had been torn apart, now his views on his entire world had completely crumbled. He felt like he was still in the ocean, tumbling around, weightless, confused, scared and angry.

The royals had no right to steal their history from them.

If Leta hadn't sought out the truth behind edem, they would never have discovered the knife's edge that Telene, and the entire world, lived on. They never would have known the real dangers of continuing to use edem.

Cayder would bring Dr Bueter to the queen and he would fight: for his friends, his family and his home.

'Are *you* okay?' Kema nudged Cayder with her shoulder. 'If you pull any harder, you'll rip a chunk out.'

Cayder lowered his hands from his hair; he'd been unconsciously tugging at the ends.

'What if we can't find Dr Bueter?' he asked. 'What if his team already found a way to return him to Telene?'

A crease appeared between Kema's brows. 'Surely the Shadow Queen would have seen that happen. She said he's not on board the boats.'

'Right. And what if we find him but he won't help us?'

'He *has* to. He's not going to condemn the entire world and himself. The general wants power. There'll be nothing for him to have power over if he doesn't stop what he's doing.'

'Do we tell everyone back home what we've learnt? That our history is a lie?'

'Whoa.' Kema placed her hand on his; he hadn't realised they were trembling. 'One step at a time. We focus on finding Dr Bueter—'

'And Leta and my mother—'

'And Erimen,' the princess added. She was standing behind them, her borrowed cream shirt hanging off her petite shoulders. Her lips and cheeks were flushed crimson from the heat of the shower.

She's stunning.

He banished the thought as soon as it arose, turning his head so she couldn't see how he'd admired her beauty.

Just a pretty surface. I won't let her fool me again.

'Of course,' Kema said, breaking the terse silence. 'We find *everyone*. And it's not our job to tell, or not tell, Telene the truth.'

'It's not,' the princess agreed. 'It's mine.'

'Of course, Princess,' Kema said. 'You can make the decision when the time comes.'

'She's no princess here,' Cayder reminded Kema.

Kema heaved a heavy sigh. 'How many times does she need to apologise?'

'It's not about that. *Her* people,' Cayder pointed at the princess, 'are the reason we've been kept in the dark. The royals took away our history and then punished anyone who dared try to uncover the truth.'

'That's not true,' the princess said.

'Isn't it?' He approached her, trying to ignore the heat emanating from her dewy skin. 'They abused the Shadow Queen's power and then covered up her existence. They pretended they were better than everyone else. They outlawed edem and set up Vardean as a deterrent so we wouldn't uncover our past.'

'What else could they do?' the princess's fair brows knitted together. 'Using edem *is* dangerous and it will lead to the end of both our worlds.'

'They should have told us the truth!' Anger flamed through his veins and rushed to his cheeks. 'If they had, Leta would have never been out in the field searching for answers. The Regency probably wouldn't even exist! I thought the Regency were the ones to blame, but no, it's the royals. It's you.'

'Stop it.' Kema placed her palms in the air. 'This is not the princess's fault, and you know it.'

He barked a harsh laugh. It felt good to let his frustrations out. The legal system was a farce. The royals were a joke. 'Who should I blame then?'

'No one.' Kema turned to the princess. 'Don't mind him; he's just stressed about being separated from Leta.'

'He's right, though.' The princess's voice was so quiet, Cayder could barely hear her.

'What?' Kema asked, her dark eyes large. 'No, he's—'

'I should have told you my plan from the start,' she said. 'I'm sorry, Cayder.' Her grey eyes locked on his; they were dull and flat. 'I truly am. I should have trusted you. And yes, the royals kept secrets, but they kept them from me too.' She bit her lip. 'I wish I could say that I would have made a different decision, in my ancestors' shoes, but look at what I did to you. To us.'

Us. There is no us.

And yet, Cayder's chest ached at her torn expression.

A tear ran down her cheek. 'My ancestors didn't trust our people to make the right decision, and I didn't trust you. And I'm sorry for that. I'm really, truly sorry.'

She turned on her heel and retreated to the bathroom. Soft sobs seeped from under the door.

Kema shot Cayder a cold look. 'What is wrong with you? That girl has been through enough over the past few months! Her brother disappeared and she was blamed for his death and then locked away in Vardean with no one but herself to rely on. Can you blame her for being cautious? And you've just proven that you can't be trusted!'

'What do you mean? Of course I can.'

I haven't done anything wrong, he thought.

'Look at the way you're treating her! You turned against her at the first opportunity!'

'She turned *us* in!' he hissed. 'Have you forgotten? She wanted to sacrifice Leta's freedom for her own desire for revenge!'

'You have to let that go, Cayder. She was doing what she thought was right. For *her* family. Can't you see? You're the same.'

Cayder shoved his hands into his cloak's pockets. He wouldn't have sacrificed another person's freedom for Leta.

But he knew he was lying to himself; he would do anything for his sister. Just like Elenora would do anything for her brother.

Kema was right.

'Should I—?' he gestured to the bathroom.

'Not now,' Kema said. 'Give her some space.'

'Okay.'

Kema reached up to pat his head. 'Good, Boy Wonder.'

CHAPTER 7

LETA

'Jey?' Leta's breath caught in her chest. *'Jey!'*

He can't be— He can't leave me.

Leta placed a shaking hand to his neck. She wasn't ready to say goodbye. She'd never be ready.

'Thank the shadows,' she whispered as his pulse thudded against her echo-marked fingers. After spending many evenings with her hand lying against his chest, Leta knew the beat of Jey's heart as well as she knew her own. The rhythm was off...

Perhaps he needed to rest?

Leta laughed sourly. He'd been shot. She should have paid better attention and realised something was wrong, but she'd been selfish and cared only about what she wanted, what she needed. Here she was again, barrelling headfirst into a situation without a second thought for Jey, just like she had when she'd stolen into Dr Bueter's office. And when she'd travelled to Ferrington without telling him.

Had she learnt nothing from Vardean?

Thankfully, Jey's wound didn't appear to be expanding like Dr Bueter's. Which meant what?

Jey's forehead creased and his eyes twitched behind his lids.

'What do I do?' Leta brushed her fingers through Jey's dark locks. If she stayed with him, he would definitely die. If she left him, he might die. Alone.

Tears pricked at the back of her eyes.

'Urgh!' Leta scrubbed her hands over her face. This wasn't what was meant to happen. They were supposed to escape to freedom.

The hullen hooted once more, startling her.

'Can you help?' She pointed to Jey. 'Protect him?'

The creature pointed its snout to the waterfall and the cave behind it. That wasn't a yes, but it wasn't a no either.

Leta had to be resilient. For Jey.

'I'll get help.' She hoped he could still hear her. She pressed a kiss to his burning forehead and headed towards the waterfall.

She refused to look back. If she saw Jey's prone form, she'd rush to his side and never leave.

The water misted the air as she approached the rock face. The cliff receded behind the waterfall and the cave entrance was hidden behind some boulders. When she hesitated, the hullen hooted behind her.

'All right, all right,' she muttered. 'I'm going.'

She climbed around the boulders and into the mouth of the cave.

You're doing the right thing. You're doing the right thing. You're doing the right thing.

She would say it for hours if she had to. She would say it until she believed it.

———

The cave wound deep into the cliff-side until no light was visible from the outside world. Leta kept her hand to the rough stone as she took each step. The chill from surrounding walls sank through her soaked guard uniform and into her bones. It was strange to be surrounded by the dark and see nothing but black.

The further she travelled into the cave, the colder it became. The rock walls had given way to slick ice and a set of stairs was carved into it. She continued downward carefully, somewhat reassured by the stairs being human-sized. She wasn't prepared to come face-to-face with any other creatures.

Leta recalled a story her mother used to read to her at bedtime, of a spindly creature that left a trail of gold coins in a forest, leading poor unsuspecting people to its lair. The creature would then appear and devour them whole. The lesson was about greed, but it wasn't the best night-time tale. And certainly not one to remember while exploring an unknown land in the dark.

Leta's terrified panting echoed around the cavern. Surely the hullen wouldn't have brought her here to be devoured by some beast. Not after saving her multiple times.

Leta stumbled forward, catching herself on the ice walls and scratching her palms on a sharp edge. She had reached the end of the staircase!

'Hello?' She peered ahead. Her entire body shook from fear and the chill of the room.

A light swung in her direction, pausing on her face.

Leta squinted and shielded her eyes. 'Who's there?' she asked.

The reply came quickly. 'How did you find us?' The light didn't shift. 'What do you want?'

Leta felt like she was back in Vardean, being interrogated by the prosecution.

'The hullen brought me here,' she replied, trying desperately to see something other than the light. 'Who are you?'

The man holding the torch moved closer. Heat licked her skin. '*Who* are you?'

'Leta Broduck. Please! I need your help!'

The light faltered on her face. 'Maretta's daughter?'

A breath caught in Leta's throat. 'You know my mother?'

The man surprised her by laughing. 'Of course!'

The light switched off. A moment later, a series of lights flicked on in the ceiling, revealing a low cavern chiselled into what looked like black ice.

A man who was as tall as Jey and a woman who only came up to his shoulder stood in front of her. The man had a boyish face with a smattering of freckles across his creamy skin, a mess of red curls upon his head.

'King Erimen?' If Leta hadn't been so shocked, she would have bowed.

'Just Erimen will do.' Beneath his coat, he wore a torn white shirt and worn grey pants – hardly an outfit befitting royalty. 'And this is Chemri.' He motioned to the woman beside him with thick brown curls and wide hazel eyes under dark brows.

'Is my mother here?' Leta asked.

'I'm afraid not,' Chemri said.

Leta wilted like a parched flower, drooping to rest her hands on her knees. She let out a frosted breath.

We were wrong. Mother is dead.

'No,' Erimen reiterated. 'Maretta's out right now. We were awaiting her return.'

And just like that, energy returned to Leta's body, zapping beneath her skin.

'She's alive?'

Erimen grinned, looking like the twenty-three-year-old man he was, rather than the crowned king of a struggling nation. 'Very much so.' He held his arms wide. 'She built this place.'

A collection of blankets, backpacks, ropes, boots, a pickaxe – all kinds of supplies – lined the walls of the cavern.

'Where is she?' Leta asked.

'Out collecting supplies.' Erimen nodded towards the ice stairs. 'You know what she's like; can't stay still for long.'

Leta pressed her hand to her thrumming heart. No one had spoken about her mother as though she was alive for *seven* years. And the king of Telene spoke so casually, as though she might walk in from the next room and offer a pile of deebule pastries.

Royal etiquette be damned.

Leta flung her arms around the tall king.

Erimen froze, then patted her back. 'Maretta will be thrilled to see you.'

Tears filled Leta's eyes. 'Thank you!'

'We should be thanking your mother,' he said, and Chemri

nodded. 'Without her, we would have nothing. She is our true leader. She saved us.'

Leta *knew* Dr Bueter was a liar! Her mother was a good person. She didn't build Regency weapons to destroy entire cities. She helped people.

As tempting as it was to collapse in relief, she needed to remain strong. 'My boyfriend has been injured. He needs medical assistance.'

The boyish grin disappeared from the king's face. 'What happened? Where is he?'

Leta pointed up the icy stairs. 'He was shot by an edem weapon as we escaped through the veil.'

'You *jumped?*' Chemri asked. She looked shocked and impressed at the same time.

Leta nodded. 'We didn't have a choice.'

'I'll go find him.' Chemri grabbed a bag from the supply wall. 'I'll bring him back.'

'I'm coming with you,' Leta said.

'Wait—' Erimen placed his hand on Leta's shoulder. 'You look like you're moments from collapsing.'

'Nah-uh,' Leta said before she could stop herself. This was the king she was speaking to, not her brother. 'I'm coming.'

Erimen stooped so that they were eye to eye. 'When was the last time you slept, Leta? Ate? Drank?'

Before Cayder had broken her out of her cell. Although she had been poisoned and hadn't been able to keep anything down, so it would have been some time before that...There was that mouthful of water she'd had outside the cave. Did that count?

'Well, I—'

'Exactly,' Erimen said. 'You rest here and we'll help your boyfriend. Don't worry.'

He directed Leta towards a bench cut into the black ice and gently pushed on her shoulders. Her body was more than happy to comply and crumpled down. Luckily, the bench was covered in a thick woven blanket to prevent the chill from radiating into her body.

In the back of her mind, Leta knew she had something important to tell the king. Something about his sister... but the seat was comfortable enough that her mind began to wander.

I just need to rest. For a little bit...

CHAPTER 8

NARENA

Narena headed to Farrow's house the day after she was blackmailed by the infuriating auburn-haired intern. She'd been awake all night trying to think of a way out this mess. It wasn't until the early hours of the morning that she realised the only evidence Farrow had was the copy of the article. If Narena destroyed the piece of paper, there would be no proof that either of them had even been at the *Telene Herald* that night.

Now, Narena just had to fool Farrow into thinking she was actually helping her, long enough to get her hands on the article.

Farrow lived in an apartment complex not far from the markets of Penchant Place. A sense of desperation permeated the air, along with the pervasive metallic tang wafting across the Unbent River from the power plant in the industrial district on the other side.

The Regency had been on a recruitment drive since the closure of Vardean, hiring new agents from laid-off prison workers and anyone out of work due to the Ferrington fires. The influx meant new Regency agents were ever-present, on every corner. Narena skirted around the agents working the market, moving quickly to Farrow's apartment. She knocked on the red door, sending fragments of paint to the floor like crimson snow.

'Coming!' a voice called.

Footsteps thundered down the stairs and Farrow flung the door open.

'Hi!' Farrow's pale skin was flushed, her auburn curls twisted above her head in a bun. Farrow usually wore a simple blazer and long skirt to work, but today she wore cropped jeans and a floral blouse.

Narena smoothed her hands down her wrinkled shirt, which she hadn't thought to iron this morning. 'Hi.'

'Come on in.' Farrow pulled Narena inside and slammed the door behind them as though Narena might have been followed.

The Regency *could* be trailing Narena's every move. After all, she'd been a person of interest in Leta's case. She doubted she'd fallen off the Regency's radar that quickly.

You're not doing anything wrong, Narena reminded herself. *You're catching up with a friend from work.* At least, that was what it would look like. As far as Narena was aware, no one but Cayder and Farrow knew of her involvement in the Vardean riot.

And it needed to stay that way.

Rickety stairs led up to Farrow's top-floor apartment. The paint inside the building's stairwell hadn't fared any better than the front door. If anything, it was worse. Sections of wallpaper had been shed – or ripped off in chunks. Rather than remove the layers and start again, a fresh covering of wallpaper had been plastered on top – leaving the walls a blotchy, bubbly mess.

Narena had to restrain herself from poking one of the bubbles to see what would happen.

'My mother's out at the market,' Farrow said. 'We have the apartment to ourselves for the morning.'

The apartment was in disarray; in the living area, books sat on almost every surface. Some books were split open as though their reader had fled mid-paragraph, while others were tabbed with hundreds of colourful stickers. Narena was somewhat familiar with this frenzied state – after all, she frequented the library during exam time, and the study hall often looked in a similar condition.

Many of the books Narena recognised; she'd done similar research for Cayder before they headed to Ferrington. It hurt Narena's heart to see some of the books had the Downtown Kardelle Library sticker of on the front, while stuck under a bowl of greasy noodles.

'Sit here.' Farrow pushed books to the side to reveal a round dining table that overlooked Penchant Place. It was a good view, considering the size of the apartment.

'I'm sorry,' Farrow said as Narena took the seat opposite her.

'That's okay.'

'These are all I could find.' She gestured to the books around her.

Narena had assumed she was apologising for the mess; if anything, she looked proud of her mountains of books.

'I think you've got the entire veil theory collection out on loan,' Narena said.

'The library stopped me from taking out the same books over and over again.' She shrugged. 'So I didn't take them back.'

Farrow had stolen them?

'I'll give them back one day,' Farrow said, picking up on Narena's concern.

Narena nodded. 'Why do you need me then?'

'Your article spoke about the hullen like they were real. Are they?'

Narena would never find her article in the mess surrounding her. She needed more time.

'I'll tell you,' Narena said. 'If you tell me why you care so much.' Was she merely a conspiracy theorist?

Farrow thought her offer over before replying. 'Do you know my last name?'

'Um,' Narena thought back to when she'd first been introduced to Farrow earlier that week. 'Tember?'

'No.'

It wasn't like Narena to forget something like that. 'Sorry. I thought you said—'

'Tember is my father's name, who left before I was born.'

That was strange. Why would Farrow have used a different name? 'Are you sure you're not a Regency spy?'

Farrow clenched her fists on the table, scrunching the page of one of the library's poor books. 'I'm no spy.'

'Who are you then?'

Farrow let out a long breath. 'My grandmother was Elorian Pedec – do you know her name?'

She didn't. 'Should I?'

'That would depend on who told you about her.' Farrow brushed a loose curl back from her forehead. 'My grandmother's parents owned a fishing trawler and they lived in one of the few houseboats out on Lake Rusterton. Despite her parents working on the water, they made her promise to never go swimming in the lake. She was told creatures had lived in the shadows of the water for hundreds of years – before the veil appeared. As a child, my grandmother believed in those tales and never swam in the lake.'

Superstitions weren't anything new in Telene; after all, there had been tales of creatures in Ferrington for decades. She knew not to immediately dismiss Farrow's story.

'When my grandmother was a teenager,' Farrow said, 'she realised the stories were simply meant to keep a young child from entering the water before they were a strong enough swimmer to handle the unpredictable currents. A cautionary tale, nothing more.'

Narena leaned forward. The books that covered every surface of this apartment indicated that this was not a mere cautionary tale.

'My grandmother was not like me,' Farrow said, a frown pulling at her mouth. 'She was adventurous and beautiful.' Farrow pulled a black and white photograph out of a box. Narena scrunched her nose in confusion; the girl in the photo could easily have been mistaken for the girl sitting opposite her.

'During the summer break, my grandmother was tempted by the water. She didn't see the harm; she was a strong swimmer by that point.' Farrow said. 'And the summer heat was unbearable. She could handle the currents.'

'Could she?' Narena asked. She wanted Farrow to hurry up and give her all the information; Farrow appeared to like to take her time and set the scene. Tell a story.

'There were no currents.' Farrow lowered her voice as though someone might overhear.

'What do you mean?'

'My grandmother jumped into the lake that summer, prepared for the pull that might drag her under.' Farrow shrugged. 'Nothing happened. The water was cool, but relatively still.'

'Currents change depending on the weather or season,' Narena recounted what she'd learnt in school. She couldn't help but wallow in the dire thought of returning to Kardelle Academy in a few short weeks without Cayder.

Focus. Now was not the time for a pity party.

She saved those for the early hours of the morning when she woke with a start, imagining Cayder and Leta's lifeless and waterlogged bodies washing up onto Telene's shores.

Had her article got Cayder and Leta killed?

'That's what my grandmother thought too,' Farrow said. 'She spent many days that summer in the lake whenever her parents headed into town to sell their haul at the markets.' Farrow cocked her head to the window and the sound of hagglers outside. 'My grandmother relaxed; she got *too* relaxed. She invited friends over to the houseboat for her seventeenth birthday party.'

Narena found herself once again leaning forward. She wanted to take notes, knowing something was coming, but she didn't dare pick up a pencil and break the spell that Farrow had cast over her.

Farrow matched Narena's posture as though they were exchanging secrets at Belch Echoes. 'Her friends were all strong swimmers; most had been on the school's swim team that year.

My grandmother would never have done anything to endanger them, but it was a ridiculously hot day and the humidity was unbearable. You can imagine; the reddish water right there, sparkling like a ruby, begging to be touched.'

Narena could imagine it all. What she couldn't understand was why Farrow's articles were so dry when the girl could clearly tell a story.

'They were swimming, playing in the water, goofing around,' Farrow said with a shrug. 'They weren't drinking, which is what the Regency later claimed. My grandmother swore no one had touched a tonic before entering the lake.'

Narena believed Farrow; whether her grandmother had told the truth was a matter for later consideration. She tucked that thought into the back of her mind.

'It happened so quickly,' Farrow said. 'One moment, her friends were all in the water and the next minute, Cass – my grandmother's best friend – was screaming.'

Narena held her breath; if she leaned forward in her chair any further, she'd faceplant onto the table.

'My grandmother swam towards Cass, terrified.' Farrow's expression was strained as she relayed the story. 'Cass was bobbing up and down, her face as white as fresh snow. My grandmother looked her over, searching for wounds, but she couldn't see anything. Cass was fine.'

'Why did she scream?' Narena managed to find her voice.

'Because of her boyfriend, Krenin. Cass hadn't wanted to get her hair wet so Krenin had placed her on his shoulders. The water wasn't that deep, you see. But then he dunked her into the water and she was furious! She thought it was a prank. But when she surfaced, she couldn't find him.'

'Did he get sucked down by a current?'

'No. The water was still that day.'

'He just disappeared?'

'Cass said she saw something shadowy in the water. But there were no shadows.'

Narena worried her fingers together. 'And the Regency thought it was due to intoxication?'

Farrow nodded. 'They couldn't find a body and my grandmother couldn't prove what had happened. The Regency said that Krenin must have gotten into trouble while swimming and drowned.'

'What about his girlfriend's testimony?' Narena asked. 'Surely the Regency had to believe Cass about the shadow?'

'The Regency found nothing in the lake, but my grandmother didn't give up. She continued to investigate what happened for years. She contributed to this book.' Farrow placed a book open that displayed a creature lurking in the water underneath a boat. It was the same book Narena and Cayder had read on their trolley ride to Ferrington.

'The Regency publicly humiliated her,' Farrow said. 'They wrote an article for the *Telene Herald* that claimed the entire book was a bunch of stories from uneducated simpletons. They even suggested that my grandmother was a "person of interest" in Krenin's disappearance. After that, everyone in Rusterton refused to do business with the Pedecs. Friends abandoned her, even Cass. My grandmother lost everything.' Farrow wiped a tear with the back of her hand. 'A few years later, she ended her own life.'

Narena sucked in a shocked breath. 'I'm so sorry. That's horrible.'

'That's the power of the Regency,' Farrow snarled. 'They force people to believe whatever propaganda they want to spread. My mother was only a baby when my grandmother died, and still, she inherited my grandmother's tainted legacy. I use my father's last name so that I am not painted with the same brush.'

'What can I do?' she asked. How could she not? Farrow was no blackmailer. She was someone who needed help. Someone who had been wronged by the Regency. Someone like Cayder.

Farrow leaned forward, grabbing Narena's hands in hers. 'Help me take the Regency down. Write an article exposing their lies for the world to see. Help me clear my grandmother's name.' Her touch was like a spark to Narena's chest. Her breath caught in her lungs.

But it wasn't that simple. Even if she wrote the same article she had for Cayder, it didn't mean people would believe it. After all, the *Telene Herald* had printed exposés in the past, but most people trusted the word of the Regency; why would they change their minds now? With the king and princess gone, the people of Telene were more vulnerable and uncertain than ever. And the Regency promised security.

If Narena was truly to expose the Regency, they needed more than hearsay. Narena would have to prove that they were lying to the nation before she could overturn their hold on Telene. Perhaps then Cayder and Leta would come out of hiding.

'You know what we have to do,' Narena said.

Farrow shook her head, her fingers lingering on the photograph of her grandmother.

'We need evidence that your grandmother was telling the truth,' Narena said.

Farrow rolled her eyes. 'If I had that then you wouldn't be here.'

Narena tried not to take that personally. 'It's time to go on a road trip.'

They needed to find out what lurked at the bottom of Lake Rusterton.

CHAPTER 9

ELENORA

Elenora wandered the *Levisial* with one of the queen's cloaked guards walking behind her like a shadow. Elenora didn't want to see the burning hatred in Cayder's golden eyes. The queen's revelations were seen as a deception perpetrated by the royals, and the reason he had lost the people he loved most.

Had Erimen known the truth? Had her parents? The Shadow Queen was their long-lost relative, after all.

Or had her parents died before they had a chance to reveal the truth to their children? If they had, would Elenora have thought any differently about edem and its role in society?

She didn't think so. As she had told Cayder: she didn't trust easily. Being part of the royal family meant that you couldn't always trust someone's intentions.

Elenora headed back to the queen's chamber.

'Can I speak with the queen?' Elenora asked the guard posted by the door.

The man nodded to the panel in the wall. 'Ask, and she will decide.'

Elenora placed her palm to the panel as she'd seen him do earlier. For a moment, nothing happened.

Please let me in, Elenora thought. *I need to speak with you.*

Until she found Erimen, the Shadow Queen was the closest person she had to family.

The wall in front of her rippled and the door opened.

'Hello?' Elenora stepped into the room. 'Shadow Queen?'

A dark mass lay atop the four-post bed. The shadows knitted together to form the queen.

'Myrandir,' the Shadow Queen said, sitting up from her bed. 'Please call me Myrandir.'

Elenora stepped into the room and the door closed behind her. 'I'm sorry for disrupting your rest, Myrandir.'

'Keeping a human form,' Myrandir said with a shrug, 'or close to a human form, wears me out. I fear the day I am unable to pull myself together and stand in this world – or any other.'

She is dying, Elenora realised.

'I promise to help.' Elenora bowed her head. 'The people of Telene – *my* people – will do the right thing if they know about you and this place.'

Myrandir moved from the bed to stand in front of Elenora, her dress made of shadows flowing behind her like silk. 'They knew before and they did not.'

She was right. The royal family had known of her gifts and had abused them. Myrandir had never been able to be herself. Much like Elenora had never been anyone but the royal spare, trapped within the castle with no real friends and only Erimen for family.

'I will ensure they do,' Elenora said. 'Times have changed. Telene does not need your power – our city is developed, we are self-sufficient. We have everything we need.'

'If that's true, then why does the Regency head to their neighbouring shores, intent on domination?' She let out a smoky breath. 'People always want more.'

Elenora wondered if Myrandir considered herself to be one of them – human. Or did she think she was something else entirely?

'What has your life been like?' Myrandir asked. 'Has your world treated you fairly?'

Images flashed in Elenora's mind. The Regency General's face. Her brother disappearing in her arms.

'I see,' Myrandir said with a sigh. 'Nothing has changed.'

'*We* can change it.' She wished she could take Myrandir's hand in hers, but she was worried her fingers would slip through her grasp. 'Together.'

Myrandir gave Elenora a sad smile. 'I see much of myself in you. You want to change the world for the better, but instead, you are told what to do and who to be. A pawn rather than a queen.'

That wasn't Elenora's experience. While she had never been in charge, she lived her own life.

Didn't she?

'You are requested on deck, my queen,' the guard said, appearing behind them.

'Thank you,' Myrandir said to the guard.

She turned to Elenora. 'Come – let us change the world.'

———

When Elenora reached the deck, she saw Kema and Cayder huddled together. Cayder gave Elenora a sheepish smile when they locked eyes. It was the most warmth she'd seen touch his face since she betrayed him.

The queen moved to stand between the silvery sails; the harsh light leaching the dark from her shadows. Black wisps of her hair lightened, her grey skin paled, her dress stilled. In the light, Myrandir became human.

She turned and Elenora saw her eyes still glowed. Raised black veins crisscrossed her face and neck. She looked at once young and ancient. This was the face that her parents tried to hide.

'I cannot remain here long,' she said. 'A shadow cannot survive in the light.'

'How do you?' Elenora asked.

'My power keeps me alive,' the queen replied. 'But my crew is human, like you.' She pointed to the bow of the boat. 'When I created the two worlds, I brought over a few people that supported me.' She gestured to the crew around her. 'The *Levisial* draws water into the belly of the ship, capturing fish and seaweed for the crew to eat while we monitor the veil and are away from the city and our crops.'

'That's how you rescued us,' Cayder said.

'It is,' Myrandir replied with a smile. 'Although we did not intend for you to be our next meal.'

'Thank shadows for that,' Kema said.

The *Levisial* cut through the water like a blade. The wind whipped Elenora's hair around her face. The last time she'd been on a boat was after the General had arrested her, transporting her to Vardean. A bag was over her head so she couldn't seek out edem and use it to escape. Not that she'd been in any state to do so – watching her brother disappear in front of her eyes had shocked her into catatonia.

Elenora squinted, her eyes watering from the wind and bright sky. This journey could not be more different. Even with Myrandir's warning about the future of their worlds, Elenora was hopeful. A new world lay out before them, and the chance to see her brother was on the horizon.

Even Cayder appeared more at ease. He stood with Kema, whispering. For the first time in a while, Elenora didn't think they were talking about her.

A set of pearlescent stairs led up to the captain's bridge. There, Elenora found a woman at the helm. In her hands were two maps layered on top of each other. The woman flipped between the bottom page, which appeared to be a map of Telene, and a topology drawing. Someone had marked an X on the water towards the coastline where Vardean should have been.

'Hello,' Elenora said. 'I'm Prin – I'm Elenora.' Best not to mention her connection to the people who had imprisoned Myrandir.

'Kioral,' the woman said with a curt nod, not shifting her eyes from the ocean ahead. The golden ring through her nose complimented her amber complexion. Rather than turning the wheel, she slid her hand across the surface of a circular stone plate.

Elenora watched in wonder. 'How are you controlling the boat?'

'Our queen created the *Levisial* using her power, pulling the vessel from the future. Because it was created from edem, we can control the ship by touch.' She moved her hand to the left of the wheel plate and the *Levisial* slowly turned, cutting across the swirl of waves.

'You make it sound so easy,' Elenora said with a sigh. 'Back home, edem – that's what we call Myrandir's power – can't be controlled.'

Kioral's mouth set in a twisted sneer. 'That's because that power does not belong to you. It belongs here. With us.'

Elenora understood that now. 'We will tell everyone the truth. They will know their actions are hurting people here.'

'Why would they care? If you tell them there is a world where this magic can be controlled – won't they want a part of it?'

'Perhaps.' Elenora wasn't sure what their response would be. Or the rest of the world's. 'Do you wish you lived in Telene?'

Kioral pursed her lips. 'My family have sought to protect this world and our queen for generations. Your people have always been seen as the enemy.'

Elenora understood what Kioral was saying. 'We are all a product of our upbringing. We believe what we believe because of what we're told.' Elenora gestured to the glittering violet seas before her. 'I never knew this place existed. And you have always been told that we steal your magic for personal gain.'

'Is that not the truth?' Kioral cocked an eyebrow.

'The truth lies somewhere in between, I think. At least, that was what my mother used to believe.'

'My mother fell to her death after a section of land she was standing on shifted to your world because someone used the queen's power,' Kioral said bitterly, then glanced away. 'We see things differently.'

The wind picked up, lashing Elenora's hair across her face. The *Levisial*'s silvery sails flapped like clipped wings attempting to take flight.

'Drop the sails!' Kioral bellowed to the crew. *'Now!'*

The crew scattered across the deck; their arms outstretched to reach the masts.

The boat tilted; Elenora screamed as she went sliding across the deck. She slammed into the railing and hooked her arm around it, to avoid going overboard. The ocean surged below her. While she had survived the waters once before, she didn't want to try her luck a second time.

Kioral spun her hand around on the wheel. 'Hold on!'

'What's happening?' Elenora stayed crouched to the ground as the sails retracted and disappeared into the masts with a ripple of edem.

'The weather is unpredictable here,' Kioral said as she fought to keep the ship upright. 'The queen pieced this world together using her power of accessing the past, present and future. Sometimes we get caught in the collision of different sections of time.'

That explained why the waves were so erratic!

'As the queen's power drains to Telene,' Kioral shot Elenora an accusatory glare, 'time becomes more muddled and the conditions are harder for us to survive.'

Elenora pulled herself to her feet. She couldn't help but seek out Cayder down on the deck. He gave her a quick nod. He was okay. Both Cayder and Kema gripped onto the side of the vessel. Myrandir stood in the middle of the deck, her arms spread wide, shadows extending from her fingers.

'What is she doing?' Elenora asked.

'Trying to control the wind,' Kioral replied. 'But her power is diminished in the daylight.'

'Left!' the queen shouted to Kioral. 'I can feel a stable gap of time.'

Kioral brushed her hand across the plate and the vessel lurched.

The waves on one side of the boat launched up towards the deck. Elenora threw her hands up over her head, ready for the water to crash down upon her. When she remained dry, she glanced up.

The waves had frozen on either side of the boat! In between lay a calm stream of water for the *Levisial* to sail through.

'Raise the sails!' Kioral shouted and her crew rushed to the masts, placing their hands upon the metal to release the material once again.

As the *Levisial* passed through the water tunnel, Elenora saw sea creatures trapped in the static waves around them.

'How long will it last?' Elenora asked in awe.

Kioral shrugged. 'Hopefully long enough for us to pass through.'

Myrandir met the captain's gaze and they exchanged a knowing nod.

She had saved them.

Again.

———

The *Levisial* manoeuvred between gaps in time, zigzagging its way across the ocean. Occasionally the vessel was outmatched by the weather and a wave would dump onto the deck and everyone on board. The water fell straight off Elenora's cloak, leaving the clothes underneath bone dry.

'We're here,' Kioral said, slowing the vessel.

As expected, no towering structure rose out of the water.

'Send someone into the depths,' Myrandir ordered from the deck. The black veins around her eyes looked like spiderwebs. 'See if there are any remains.'

Remains? Elenora thought this was a rescue mission.

Elenora peered over the edge to watch as two of the crew removed their cloaks to reveal diving suits beneath. They jumped into the water. Elenora joined Cayder and Kema down on the deck.

'I hope they find him,' Elenora whispered.

'Mm-hmm,' Kema murmured in agreement.

'I don't,' Cayder said.

They turned to him in surprise.

'You hope Dr Bueter is alive?' Kema asked.

'Dr Bueter isn't the problem.' The wind had ruffled his dark brown hair and Elenora's fingers twitched, wanting to tame the strands. 'The Regency is.'

'After everything he's done, I thought you would be happy to never see him again,' Kema said.

'The Shadow Queen might be able to stop the boats, but we need someone to shut down the Regency for good,' Cayder said. 'And only someone in power can do that.'

Someone who's not me, Elenora thought. And she couldn't blame him for thinking that way. With the royals gone, the Regency held all the power in Telene.

Cayder was right. They needed Dr Bueter alive.

———

After a day of exploring the depths, Myrandir called off the search. There were no signs of the general; he may have made it to shore. The *Levisial* headed to the closest dock so that the search could continue on foot.

Steep mountains rose from either side of the water as they neared land, casting shadows across the boat. Myrandir tilted her head back and sighed as she merged with the darkness, her moonlight eyes like stars in the night.

A metal dock stretched out from the island; at the end of it stood a black statue of the queen, her arms held out wide. The expression on her face was not one of welcome, but of warning. At the other end of the dock, in between the valley of the mountains, was a small cluster of buildings made of silver and glass and sharp as a blade. Elenora had never seen anything like them.

'That's our city,' Kioral said as she docked the vessel. 'Or what is left of it.'

'Sadly, I cannot come with you,' Myrandir said. 'However, the head of my Shadow Guard, Rusteef, will assist you on your journey.'

The gruff man in the hooded cloak that they had met earlier stepped forward. 'I will keep you all safe.'

'Safe from what?' Kema's shoulders were square, ready to fight off any incoming danger.

'We are not a united people,' Myrandir said with a sad smile. 'Those who come from Telene fight for our food and supplies. They have stolen precious grain and keep it for themselves.'

'Is that who shot down our hullen?' Cayder asked.

Rusteef exchanged a glance with Myrandir and she nodded. 'You must find Dr Bueter and bring him to me so that we can return to Telene.'

'We will do our best,' Elenora said.

'If we cannot stop the Regency,' Myrandir gazed up to the sky and the visible tear in the veil, like a bleeding black wound, 'then our worlds are doomed.'

'If you can see the future,' Cayder said, 'can't you tell us where to find him?'

Myrandir shook her head; her hair of shadows whirled around her like a dissipating haze. 'I cannot see where he is, only that his next course of action triggers the end of days.'

'We will find him. You have my word.' Rusteef bowed his head. 'Stay among the shadows, my queen.'

'Be quick in the light,' she replied.

Elenora was hit with an intense pang of grief – Rusteef's admiration for his ruler reminded her of her family's trips to the mainland before the death of her parents. The people of Telene had always welcomed them.

What would her parents have thought of this place?

Rusteef escorted them down the dock and into one of the silver buildings. Inside were two land vehicles that looked like small gondolas from Telene, but without glass on the roof or sides. The cabin had two seats and sat on four large wheels.

'These vehicles are from the future,' Rusteef said, pulling down his hood to reveal a bald head and a warm brown complexion. His eyes were kinder than Elenora expected, although his thick eyebrows were drawn low. 'We'll take two crawlers and scour the land closest to where your Vardean was built. You will need to separate.' He gestured to the crawlers. 'They only hold two people each.'

Kema nodded to Rusteef. 'I'll go with Mr Shoves-a-lot.'

'My name is Rusteef.'

'Of course,' Kema said with a thoughtful nod. 'I'll go with Rusteef Shoves-a-lot.'

Cayder approached one of the vehicles and examined a smooth panel along the front. 'How do we drive these things?'

'Like this—' Rusteef climbed into the crawler's cabin and pressed his hand against a panel. The panel shifted underneath his touch and a lever rose with a shimmer of edem. 'You push down for speed, right or left for directions and back to slow.'

Cayder jumped in the other vehicle and brought the lever into position. It was strange to see edem used so casually, and without repercussions. Elenora joined him in the cabin and Cayder pushed the lever down. The crawler lurched forward, sending Elenora whipping back into her seat.

'Sorry!' Cayder exclaimed, his tan cheeks darkening with embarrassment. He immediately let go of the lever and they jolted to a stop.

Elenora quickly clasped the safety buckle across her chest. 'That's okay.'

'Careful,' Rusteef ordered, scooting his crawler around theirs to take the lead. 'You do not need to be so rough.'

'Right,' Cayder said, setting his jaw. 'I've got this.'

Elenora recognised his look of determination – she'd seen it many times when he visited her in Vardean. And she couldn't stop the responding hope that bloomed in her chest. Hope that they *would* save this world. Hope that she would find Erimen.

And hope that Cayder would look at her like he once had.

———

The crawler hurtled across the rocky ground that wound around the side of one of the sheer mountains. Elenora had to admit she was enjoying herself, and Cayder kept fighting the tug at the corners of his mouth. She understood his desire to stay focused on the task at hand, but after everything they'd been through, was it so wrong to enjoy the moment? To smile?

Not in front of me, she thought.

Cayder had made it clear he didn't trust her, even if he had decided not to punish her anymore. Meanwhile, Kema was openly hollering up ahead, despite Rusteef telling her to be quiet. It only made Kema shout louder.

Cayder drove over a bump in the ground, sending the crawler into the air and lifting Elenora out of her seat. She let out an involuntary *whoop*. Cayder glanced over at her and grinned, before realising and quickly shutting the smile away. But it didn't diminish her mood.

Erimen would love this.

He had wanted to fly as fast as the stones they skipped across the ocean when they were kids.

Imagine the feeling! he would say. *Dancing along the top of the water.*

A trolley was the fastest-moving vehicle in Telene and it came nowhere near the speed of the crawler.

Elenora gripped onto the side, closing her eyes and imagining Erimen sitting alongside her. He would have ruffled her hair and whistled a ridiculously bawdy song he'd heard one the of guards sing.

While everyone saw Erimen as a strong and serious type, upholding the laws their parents had set, Elenora saw only the brother from before the rebels had attacked and killed their parents. The brother who was adventurous and lighthearted.

After he was crowned, Elenora only saw glimpses of who her brother had been. Elenora didn't know if Erimen had worn a mask to conceal his true nature, or whether he'd been forever changed by their parents' passing.

As the years went by, Erimen had become more and more of a mystery to her.

But soon they would be reunited and there would be no more secrets between them.

CHAPTER 10

CAYDER

Cayder followed Rusteef's crawler as they careened around the mountain. The road was carved into a sheer rock face while water crashed against the cliff below.

Elenora had closed her eyes as they travelled, allowing Cayder to look at her without her knowing. The flaming anger he'd felt in her presence was beginning to subside, and he wasn't sure how he felt about that.

Was Kema right? Should he give Elenora another chance?

He smirked. Kema was always right. He thought of Kema as an older, and much wiser, sister. And, even though he hadn't wanted Kema involved in this mess, he was glad she was here. It was almost like having Graymond guide them through the unknown.

Cayder's stomach lurched, but it had nothing to do the crawler bouncing over another bump in the ground. Did Graymond realise Kema was missing? Or would Vardean keep Graymond in the dark about what had happened to his daughter?

There wasn't much Cayder could do about that now. Not from here.

Elenora's long blonde hair blew around the open cabin. Occasionally a lock would touch his neck, and it was like a bolt of lightning to his heart. Cayder hated the hold she had on him. He wouldn't allow her to sink back under his skin. He had to stay focused.

Find Dr Bueter. Find Mother. Shut down the Regency and go home.

Home – what was happening back in Telene? He hoped the riot in Vardean would cause some change, but he doubted it. While it had only been one day since they'd jumped through the veil, it felt much longer, and home was becoming a distant memory.

The road ahead stopped abruptly, as though the mountain had been cut with a giant knife. Cayder expected Rusteef to halt his crawler, but the vehicle continued forward and dropped over the edge.

'Kema!' Cayder cried, lifting up out of his seat.

Elenora grabbed his arm then swiftly withdrew it when he turned to her.

They cautiously approached the ledge. Cayder hadn't heard the sound of the vehicle crashing to the ground.

'Hurry up!' Rusteef called from below.

The pressure on his chest lifted. They were all right. Kema was all right. As much as Kema had insisted she come along, Cayder felt responsible for her well-being. He wouldn't let anything happen to her.

Cayder gradually pushed the lever forward and the nose of the crawler tilted downward. They teetered over the edge. The mountain had given way to a sprawling glacier. Rusteef's crawler was idling at the bottom of the steep, icy slope.

The crawler needed only a little nudge as it rolled over the precipice. Cayder clenched his jaw, feeling as though his teeth might crack as they rolled down the frozen cliff. The ice crunched under the tyres but they didn't slip; the vehicle must have been built for unexpected changes in terrain.

Cayder pulled up next to the others. Rusteef and Kema climbed out and Cayder followed suit. The water of the ocean lapped against the sleek slab of turquoise ice.

'We used to have a port here.' Rusteef nodded to the abrupt change in terrain. 'But the weather changed suddenly, and half of the mountain collapsed. We lost many people that day.'

'The captain's family,' Elenora said, nodding sagely. 'She told me about it.'

Rusteef raised his thick eyebrows slightly. 'I'm surprised; Kioral doesn't usually talk about that day.' Rusteef gestured out to the ocean. 'If the Regency General survived the fall, this is the nearest entry point to land.'

'Dr Bueter has been here before,' Cayder said. 'He knows how to survive.'

'He would need supplies.' Rusteef sounded angry – though Rusteef always sounded angry.

'Where would he find them?' Elenora asked.

'He could be working with the radicals.' Rusteef said, shielding his eyes against the glare from the glacier. 'They have a hideout somewhere, although we've never found it. They scour the land for supplies that cross over from Telene and stockpile them for themselves.'

'Sounds like the Regency,' Kema said with a roll of her eyes. 'All for one, and all for them.'

'What's the plan now? There are no footprints,' Cayder stamped his foot on the ice. 'Nothing to indicate he made it to shore.'

Perhaps Dr Bueter *had* died out in the ocean. Were they searching for a ghost?

'We split up and search for the radicals' hideout. Little remains of this world that isn't ocean.' Rusteef pointed to the white void on the horizon. 'Then return to this location in three days.'

'Sounds like a plan,' Kema said, heading back to her crawler.

But that would mean he would have to ... 'Wait—'

Kema turned to look at him, a warning in her eyes. She knew what he was about to say: he wanted to ride with her. *Three* entire days with Elenora was too much, too soon.

Kema gave him a small shake of the head.

'Good luck.' Cayder offered a smile that felt more like a grimace.

Rusteef handed Cayder the maps. 'You need these more than we do. You head east,' he tapped the map, 'we'll head west.'

'What about the north?' Elenora asked.

Rusteef shook his head. 'No one goes to the mountains. The terrain is too dangerous.'

Cayder rolled the maps together and placed them inside his cloak.

'There are supplies in the trunk of the crawler,' Rusteef said. 'You'll have everything you need.'

'Be good!' Kema said cheerfully as they departed.

———

As they headed east, the glacier turned into a block of dry earth. Shards of ice stuck up from the ground like giant splinters and Cayder had to carefully manoeuvre around them. Gone was the thrill of speeding across the landscape. One advantage was that he had to focus on driving; he could ignore the fact that Elenora was sitting so close beside him.

The earth shuddered and a gash opened in the ground ahead. Cayder twisted the lever and the crawler sprang around the hole.

'What was that?' Elenora asked.

Cayder shook his head and the dark strands of hair away from his eyes. 'I don't—'

Another crack appeared ahead. This time, something sprouted forth. A brown pillar tunnelled up to the sky and then split into a canopy of green.

A tree!

Cayder turned the crawler to avoid slamming into the trunk when another crack materialised.

'What's happening?' Elenora cried as cracks appeared all over the field as though someone had taken a hammer to a sheet of ice.

He didn't have time to respond. He steered the crawler as more saplings sprang from the earth and evolved into mature trees in the blink of an eye.

Just as quickly, the trees began to wither, raining leaves down upon them.

The crawler's back wheel clipped one of the trunks.

'Would you like me to drive?' Elenora asked.

'You think you can do better?' Cayder snapped, and instantly regretted it.

Elenora turned away, her cheeks flushing.

They didn't speak for hours.

———

Cayder grew tired, and he hadn't spotted anything resembling a building or shelter or whatever the radicals' hideout might look like.

'We should stop for the night,' Elenora suggested, breaking the silence. They were driving through a field of blooming red flowers. The crawler rolled over them, leaving a bloody trail behind.

Cayder looked up at the bright sky. 'It's not night. It's never night here.' His voice was rough from disuse and lack of hydration.

'We still need to eat and sleep.'

'We're fine.' He didn't want to stop. He wanted to find Dr Bueter so he could get back to what he really wanted to do: locate his mother.

'Shit,' Cayder said as he clipped a rock.

The crawler tilted up onto two wheels. Cayder twisted the lever to try to right the vehicle and the crawler slammed down. The wheels spun, failing to find traction on the earth. Elenora squealed as they skidded across the field, sending flowers flying.

Shit shit shit.

The world around Cayder blurred until the back of the crawler slammed into a tree. He was jolted from his seat and smashed his forehead into the console.

'Cayder!' Elenora cried. 'Are you okay?'

Even though they had stopped moving, his head still whirled.

'Fine,' he muttered. Something hot trickled down his forehead.

'You are *not* fine.' The cautious tone she'd been using with him fell away. She had a small cut on her cheek.

I did that, he thought, feeling sick. Actually, he was going to *be* sick. He leaned over the side of the crawler and vomited. There wasn't much in his stomach, just a bit of water.

Elenora freed herself and rushed to his side. 'We need to get you out of here.'

'Is the crawler damaged?'

'Is that all you care about?' She held out her arms for him to take.

No. It wasn't. 'Are *you* okay?'

'I'm unhurt.'

He knew that wasn't entirely true. Still, she was helping him rather than worrying about herself. She pulled him from the cabin and he sank to the ground, leaning his back against one of the crawler's wheels.

'I should have listened to you,' he said. 'I should have stopped driving hours ago.'

'It's hard to know what time it is here.' She raised her face to the bright sky above, which highlighted the gash on her cheek.

'We should clean that. Make sure it doesn't get infected.'

He tried to rise, but she pushed him back down. '*I'll* get the supplies.'

He didn't have the energy to argue with her.

Elenora carried a box from the crawler's trunk over to him. He could see it was heavy by the way she struggled with it, but she didn't complain. She rummaged through the contents.

'Sleeping bags, a tent, a cooking pot, pouches of fish stew… *Ah!*' She pulled out a smaller box. 'A medical kit.'

A thought stirred in Cayder's mind but it was too fuzzy to grasp onto.

'Here—' She pressed a cotton pad to his forehead and he hissed. 'Sorry!'

'It's okay. You're just trying to help.'

They both stayed quiet as Elenora cleaned Cayder's wound. Her hands were gentler now, moving across his skin with a feather-light touch. She smoothed a bandage onto his forehead while he studied the ground, not wanting to get caught in her grey eyes.

She was close. Too close.

'Drink this.' She pressed a water pouch into his hands.

Cayder did as he was told. His head cleared a little as he sipped the water. 'How much do we have?'

'Enough for a few days, I think.'

Cayder nodded. 'Your turn.'

'My turn?' Her brows pulled together. He pointed to her cut cheek. 'Oh!'

Cayder squeezed some water on a pad and leaned over her. Unlike Cayder, Elenora didn't flinch, her eyes watching his every movement. He let out a heated breath and Elenora's eyes fluttered shut.

It was easier then. He held her chin in one hand and gently wiped with his other. He tried not to think how she managed to look pretty with blood and grime on her face or how easy it would be to lean in and close the small distance between them. The last time they were close like this, she had kissed him.

Why couldn't he banish that kiss from his mind?

'There.' His voice was gravelly and he immediately moved away from her. 'Done.'

Elenora opened her eyes and there was some kind of emotion there that Cayder couldn't decode.

'It shouldn't scar,' he said, in case that was what she was worried about.

She pushed to her feet. 'We should set up camp here. I'm exhausted and you need to rest.'

Cayder was not going to disagree this time. The thought of climbing back into the crawler sent a shooting pain through his forehead.

They set up the tent, hammering the pegs into the crumbly earth.

'I'll sleep outside.' Cayder nodded to the narrow shelter. While there was room for two people, it would be tight. Driving with Elenora next to him had been difficult enough. Elenora handed him a sleeping bag without comment.

Cayder had never slept outside, but how difficult could it be? The field was fairly soft and there didn't seem to be anything alive out here. No animals. No bugs. Nothing to keep him awake. Besides, every time he blinked, he was closer to sleep.

Elenora pulled out two fish stew pouches and a cooking pot. 'I'll make us some food.'

'How are you going to heat it?' Cayder asked.

'I'll figure it out.' She wasn't short with him, but it was clear something had shifted; she wasn't tiptoeing around him anymore. She seemed more herself. And more capable than he was. For a sheltered princess who rarely left the castle isle, she moved around the campsite with ease.

Elenora pulled out another metal contraption from their supply box and unfolded it onto the ground. It had a sharp spike beneath it and a space for the pot above.

'I wonder…' she said, mostly to herself.

She started twisting the sharp point into the earth until a black smoke seeped out. She flicked a switch on the side and a black flame sprang to life. Her face was lit with wonder, as though she had discovered something truly magical.

'Edem lies beneath the surface,' she said.

'Not for long,' Cayder countered.

Once the stew was heated, they ate in silence, looking anywhere but at each other.

After their dinner, Elenora headed to the tent.

'Are you sure you'll be all right out here?' she asked over her shoulder, her golden hair contrasting against her black cloak. 'It's awfully bright.'

Cayder slipped into his sleeping bag. 'I'll be fine.'

'There's room in the tent.' She pointed to her temple. 'You could have a concussion; I should keep an eye on you.'

'Go to sleep.' He set his jaw. 'I'll wake you in a few hours.' They couldn't rest longer than that.

Cayder drew his sleeping back up and over his head to block the light from his eyes.

He hoped that wherever Leta was, she was doing better than they were.

CHAPTER 11

LETA

Leta had always felt more at home in the darkness than the light. In the dark, she could pretend her mother wasn't dead; that she was sitting at the edge of her bed, running her fingers through Leta's hair while singing Delft folk songs about travelling the seas. Songs about the ocean were as foreign to Leta as the Delft language itself. Leta had never travelled to Delften to visit her mother's family, as all other nations had refused Telenians entry for over a decade – until the spread of edem was under control. The only boats Leta had ever seen were the small charters to and from the castle isle.

To Leta, the ocean was a vast, mythical place where anything was possible – an unexplored universe that separated nations from each other. Leta's grandparents had often explored places to the west of Delften – far from Telene. They never worried about 'edem polluting their shadows'. And much to their confusion and chagrin, Leta's mother had decided to study in Telene to be close to the veil.

Leta's grandparents had pleaded with their daughter to return to Delften after she graduated; however, she had already met Alain Broduck and set her sights on joining the Regency. Like her mother, Leta had considered herself blessed to live in Telene, with its connection to edem. Leta had inherited far too much of her mother's curious spirit and she pitied her cousins who lived in drab Delften, where their only concern was the change in seasons.

The Delft songs Leta's mother used to sing floated in and out of Leta's consciousness as she slept. When she woke, she wished to linger in the restful haze. She wanted to cling to the sound of her mother's voice and the ghost of her mother's hand resting on her arm.

But all good dreams must come to an end.

Leta opened her eyes, recognising the black icy ceiling above her as the underground settlement she'd discovered. The final notes of the Delft tune hung in the air as the last of Leta's dreams fell away.

Leta blinked at a blurry figure. A woman sat at the edge of her bed, her black hair braided and tied around the crown of her head. She wore a silvery feathered coat over a beige dress with a simple corded belt, her feet bare. Her mother – just as she had appeared in her dreams, aside from the grey twisting through her black locks. Around her mother's hazel eyes were deep-etched lines and her warm olive skin was pale and sallow. She looked like an old, faded photograph come to life.

This wasn't the mother from her dreams. The mother she'd lost. *This* woman was older.

Everything the king had told Leta flooded back to her.

'Mother!' Leta leaped from the bed, throwing her arms around her. 'You're here!'

She was warm. Solid. Real. Even a faded version of her mother was more beautiful than Leta remembered.

'I am,' her mother replied. Tears lined her voice.

Leta wasn't used to her mother crying; Maretta Broduck was known for the sound of her laughter as it echoed through the hallways of Broduck Manor. Even when times were tough, like when Leta's grandfather, Dapi, passed away and the family were unable to travel to Delften due to the border restrictions, her mother had remained resolute. She wanted her children to understand that Dapi would want them to celebrate his life. She held a party in his honour, and they ate all of Dapi's favourite Delften foods and danced to old Delften songs.

Leta, however, had never been good at controlling her emotions.

'I missed you!' Leta pressed her face into her mother's neck.

She smelled the same: like Leta's childhood and dark fairytales.

'And I you.' Her mother gently pushed Leta's shoulders back so she could study her. Leta covered her flushed, splotchy face with her hands but her mother prised them away. 'Don't hide from me,' she said while studying her. 'My beautiful baby girl.'

My mother. Here. Alive.

And seemingly well. In all of Leta's hopes and dreams, she could not have imagined a better moment. And yet, someone was missing.

'Where's Cayder?' Leta asked, wiping her cheeks. 'Did the other hullen bring him here?'

Her mother's forehead creased, falling into a well-worn wrinkled pattern that Leta hadn't seen before. This version of her mother frowned, and often.

'No, he's not here. What happened? Clearly, you've been through an ordeal. You've been asleep for more than a day; I didn't want to wake you.'

A day?

Her mother ran her fingertips along Leta's hands, tracing the death echo. The underside of her palms had been bandaged. Leta remembered scraping them on the rock, and her blood mingling with Jey's.

'Where's Jey? King Erimen said he was going to help him.' Leta stood but slumped back on the bed as the world swayed around her.

'Take it easy, Nettie.' But the nickname only made Leta more determined.

'Jey was shot by one of the Regency's weapons!'

Her mother placed a gentle but firm hand on Leta's shoulder. 'Have something to drink.' She raised a cup to Leta's lips.

As Leta drank, her mother said, 'Jey is here.' Concern crossed her features. 'He's resting.'

'I need to see him.' A fresh set of tears ran down her cheeks.

'He's stable. First, you need to tell me everything that happened to you and your brother. As much as I love seeing you, I never wanted to see you *here*.' She shook her head sadly. 'How did you end up here? Where is your father?'

It was a long story, and one that began seven years ago when her mother first disappeared. Leta told an abbreviated version of everything that had happened and what led to her jumping through the veil.

They were both in tears by the time Leta finished the story. They cried for the years they had lost, what happened in Vardean and the joy of finding each other again.

'We're together now,' her mother said, as though reading Leta's mind. 'And we *will* find your brother. The hullen never fail.' She wiped the tears from Leta's cheeks and then from her own. 'We will be reunited soon.'

———

Even though Leta had been resting for over a day, she was still unsteady on her feet. Her mother held onto her arm as they headed to Jey's room. Leta had been changed into some dry clothes while she was unconscious and given a coat to combat the chill of their icy surrounds.

A series of tunnels connected the underground chambers, with lights plugged directly into the black ice walls, no wires to be seen.

Maretta Broduck had always seemed like some kind of mythical creature to her daughter, and seeing her mother seemingly float through the corridors in her floor-length dress only fortified the thought.

'Edem runs through every living thing,' she explained to Leta. 'It provides power for the lights and nourishment for crops – or at least, it used to.' She tapped the frosty wall. 'We built this place below the ground as there's still some untapped edem down here. But it's only a matter of time before there's nothing left to extract.' She nodded to a darkened corridor on their left. 'As time goes on, we lose more and more power and we have to conserve what's left.'

'Who's *we?*' Leta asked.

'Anyone from Telene that ends up on this side of the veil.'

'Like you,' Leta said. 'And King Erimen.'

She nodded, short and sharp. 'And others. The hullen usually find anyone who crosses over who needs help and brings them to our compound.' She smiled. 'Like they found you and your brother.'

Except Cayder wasn't here. 'How did they know where I was?'

'It will be easier if I show you. But first—' She directed Leta into another small room. 'Please don't fret when you see him.'

Her mother stepped aside to reveal Jey lying on a narrow gurney. His shirt had been stripped off, leaving his tattooed arms and chest bare. A tube with black liquid was inserted into the inside of his left elbow. The veins that travelled up his arm to his shoulder were raised and dark, as though someone had traced them with a black pen.

Leta ran to his beside. 'What did you do to him?' His wound had been covered in a white bandage, but Leta could see the laceration festering beneath. 'Jey! Are you all right?'

He didn't move; not even his eyelids flickered.

'Erimen and Chemri found him passed out by the waterfall,' her mother said. 'He hasn't woken yet.'

'What are you pumping into him?' Leta wanted to yank the needle free.

'He was shot by one of the Regency weapons. The only way to counter the effects of edem is *with* edem. We're trying to slow the progression.' Her mouth pressed into a sad line. 'We're trying to stop time.'

Jey's usual warm tawny skin was ashen and dark shadows circled his eyes. He didn't look injured. He looked like he was dying.

'Slow the progression,' Leta repeated. 'Will it heal him?'

'I'm afraid not.' Her mother pulled back Jey's bandage to reveal an ugly gash. At least it wasn't bleeding anymore. 'We can stop the wound from further deteriorating, but we haven't been able to reverse it. We can only hope that Jey's body will do the rest.'

Hope. That wasn't enough.

'We have to get Jey back to Telene.' Leta was prepared to throw him over her shoulder and carry him out of there. 'We have to get him to a *real* hospital.'

The equipment in the room looked like it had been cobbled together from bits and pieces of busted machinery. Desperation clutched at her chest.

'I'm sorry, Nettie,' her mother reached for her hand, 'but there's no way home.'

Leta sidestepped her mother. 'That can't be right. The Regency General was displaced here and was able to go back to Telene using one of his weapons.'

Her mother gave her a kind, understanding smile – the smile Leta would receive when she was explaining one of her childish theories on the veil.

She's humouring me.

'If that was possible,' her mother said, 'don't you think I would have come home?'

'I *saw* the Regency General disappear with my own eyes. And he's here now. If we find him, he can bring us all home.'

'And why would he do that?' Erimen stood in the doorway. 'The man had me killed.' He shrugged. 'Or at least, he tried to.'

'I'm sorry, Nettie,' Leta's mother said. 'I've spent years trying to get back. Our resources are scant. We scavenge what we can when something is displaced from Telene, but I can't create a way home.'

'Can't? Or *won't*?' Leta asked. 'Dr Bueter told us everything, Mother. He said *you* created the edem-fuelled weapons. Surely you can create ones to send us home.'

Her mother placed her hands over her mouth, but she didn't deny her involvement.

'Maretta?' Erimen's face fell. 'Is that true?'

Leta remembered that her mother once revered the royals. Was that why she had kept this secret from the king?

She turned to Erimen, her shoulders hunched. 'It was an accident. I was trying to harness the power of edem. But all I achieved was displacing an object in time.' She glanced at Leta, her eyes imploring. 'I was only doing my job.'

'That weapon you created killed hundreds of people in Ferrington,' Leta said. 'And I was blamed.'

Her mother's voice was quiet and broken when she replied, 'I know.'

'How?' Her mother had been here for seven years. How could she have known what had happened only a few weeks ago?

'I'll show you.'

———

Leta didn't want to leave Jey, but she couldn't wait by his bedside and do nothing.

Erimen remained quiet as they journeyed through the underground tunnels. Passers-by bowed their heads in respect. Everyone was wearing equally tattered clothes and coats; nothing was new here, it appeared that everything had come from Telene.

'Maretta,' another passer-by murmured, lowering their head.

They weren't bowing to the king; they were bowing to her mother!

Leta wondered how many people were here because of the edem weapons. Were the people of Ferrington walking these hallways? Did they know Maretta Broduck had created the weapons that had destroyed their lives?

They entered a large room carved into the icy walls with a patchwork metal globe in the centre. A woman was studying the globe, jotting down notes as two rings touched with a gentle clang. She acknowledged Maretta's entrance but didn't seem concerned or interested in Leta, as though she was used to new people coming and going.

'You made an edemmeter?' Leta asked, approaching the shifting globe. The map carved on the spherical surface matched that of Telene. On top of that surface was another layer, which had geographical markings that Leta didn't recognise.

'It took me many years to piece it together.' Her mother gestured to a metal rod that burrowed into the black ice beneath their feet. 'This world reacts when edem is used in Telene. From the seismic activity, we can monitor where the temporal shifts occur.' She pointed to where the two rings had crossed. 'Large disturbances indicate an increased level of edem activity. As you know, that often results in displacement from Telene. We send our team out to the areas mapped that match the location,' she tapped the globe, 'and help anyone who has arrived here.'

'You found the people from Ferrington,' Leta said in understanding.

'Yes. They didn't know what had happened or where they were. And we were there to help.'

'It was a difficult time for everyone.' It was the first time the king had spoken for a while.

'I'm sorry, Erimen,' Leta's mother said.

Erimen nodded. 'We all make mistakes.'

'I didn't know he would continue without me,' she said, rubbing the bridge of her nose.

He being Dr Van Bueter, of course.

'Did you know Dr Bueter wants to force the borders to reopen?' Leta asked. 'That's why he's pushing for the creation of these weapons. He's going to start a war if the neighbouring nations don't give him what he wants.'

The woman who had been studying the globe glanced up.

'Can you please give me a minute, Erithe?' her mother asked. She was clearly in charge here, but how many people knew the truth about her past?

'I did what I was told,' she said once Erithe had left. 'My role was to investigate and control edem. I thought I was helping; if we could control edem, then there wouldn't be as many injuries and deaths.' She let out a tired breath. 'If I had known what I would end up creating, and the damage it would cause, I would have stopped. I would have stopped Van.'

'No one blames you,' Erimen said. 'We can't change the past. We can only move forward with the knowledge we have now and vow to do better.'

Leta was surprised by his considerate reaction. Telene was *his* nation. And Maretta had created a weapon that had ultimately ended his reign, and separated him from his sister—

'Elenora is here,' Leta said, remembering that she hadn't told the king this vital piece of information. 'She was arrested by the Regency for your disappearance and suspected murder.'

'My sister?' Erimen sounded much younger. 'How?'

'The children escaped Vardean via the veil,' Leta's mother explained. 'Princess Elenora, Leta, Jey, my son, along with a family friend.'

'Why didn't the hullen bring them here?' Erimen raked a hand through his red curls. 'Where are they?'

'That's what I'm trying to figure out.' She picked up a notepad and flipped back a page. 'The edemmeter showed a great deal of edem usage two days ago.' She tapped a point on the edemmeter. 'Right at the Regency headquarters.'

Leta recognised the structure of Vardean etched on the globe. 'That was us,' Leta said, remembering she had been asleep for more than a day. 'Cayder called the hullen to him so that we could escape. Once we arrived here, the hullen grabbed us from the ocean – how many are there?'

'The hullen? Not as many as there used to be,' her mother said. 'As edem and this world disappear, they have less to survive on. That's why they have been spending more time in Telene over the recent years.'

'What happens if they don't have edem?' Leta asked.

'What happens to everything else in this world.' Her mother clasped her hands together. 'They die.'

'Why can't the hullen take us back through the veil?' Leta asked. 'They easily move back and forth.'

'The hullen are made of edem,' she said. 'And only edem can travel back to Telene. The veil is a one-way ticket, I'm afraid.'

'But edem is keeping Jey alive, right?' Leta asked and her mother nodded. 'If we run out of edem here...' She couldn't finish that sentence.

Her mother pressed her lips together in a tight line. 'We will find a way. Right now, there is enough edem to keep Jey stable and protect the entire compound.'

Leta's heart was pounding in her chest. She didn't want to ask, but she knew she had to.

'For how long?'

Her mother exchanged a look with Erimen and he nodded.

'A few years,' the king said. 'Maybe even a decade. We don't know.'

A few years.

That was all they had.

CHAPTER 12

NARENA

Narena had always had a great relationship with her parents. She'd never given them a reason not to trust her: she didn't come home late and was always where she said she would be.

Every Sunday afternoon, she would help prepare the traditional Meiyran meal of fish and potato dumplings. Narena's job was to debone the fish, while her parents made the dough. Her father would sing old Meiyran songs while both Narena and her mother would tell him to stop. No one in the Lunita family could hold a tune, although that never deterred her father.

There wasn't a single Sunday afternoon Narena could remember where she hadn't helped prepare the meal. But today was different. Narena had found a stray thread in Farrow's story, and she would pull on it and see where it would lead.

Narena wasn't a great liar. A stone sat in her stomach as she considered various excuses to get out of their Sunday ritual. Travelling to the houseboat and back again would take the entire day. Narena couldn't think of anything that would explain her absence for that length of time. And since Cayder's disappearance, her mother had been watching her more closely.

The stone in her stomach grew heavier and heavier until Narena felt like she might be sick – which gave her the inspiration she needed.

'I don't feel good,' Narena said, stumbling into the kitchen on shaky legs.

Her father was sitting at the table, reading the newspaper while eating breakfast. He placed his thick-rimmed glasses on the top of his balding head. 'Oh no! Come here, Re-Re.'

Narena dragged her feet and slumped into the chair beside him. He pressed his hand to her moist forehead.

'You're burning up!' He retracted his hand quickly, fearing he'd catch it.

Good, Narena thought. She'd stuck her face in a sink of steaming hot water with a cloth over her head for fifteen minutes, until she was on the verge of passing out.

'I should stay in my room.' Narena pushed herself to her feet slowly. 'I don't want to make you both sick.'

Her mother was strangely quiet, watching her from the bench as she peeled potatoes.

Narena shuffled back towards the stairs when her mother called out. 'Wait!'

Oh no.

If her mother questioned her, Narena was sure to crumble.

'Take this—' Her mother handed her a mug of ginger root tea. 'I made a pot this morning. It will help with the fever.'

Narena nodded and took the mug in her hands. 'Thank you, Me-Me.'

'I'll bring you up some bone broth at lunchtime,' her mother said, brushing a sticky strand of Narena's hair away from her face.

'No!' Her mother snatched her hand back. Narena quickly clarified, 'I need to sleep. Please don't wake me.' Narena forced a yawn. 'I'm tired. So so tired.'

Her heart hammered in her chest as her mother's eyes roamed over her.

'My poor darling,' she said finally, taking Narena's free hand in hers. 'You're shaking.'

Shaking from fear and guilt.

'Stay in bed.' Her mother decided with a nod, as though she was the one who had suggested it in the first place. 'If you need anything, give me a yell and I'll come to you.'

'Would you like me to sing for you?' her father asked. 'It might help you fall asleep.'

Her mother scoffed. 'That's the last thing she needs, Laino. The poor girl is already feeling unwell.'

Her father shrugged and went back to reading the newspaper. 'Just trying to help.'

Now Narena had to work out how to climb out of her second-floor window without breaking her arm, her leg or her neck. She should have paid more attention when Leta shared stories of sneaking out of Broduck Manor.

After changing out of her pyjamas, Narena placed some pillows under the blankets, in case her mother decided to check in on her. Hopefully, her mother would want to stay clear of Narena's 'bug' and not come too close.

Narena wasn't sure what the day would bring; she wore her pink gumboots, just in case, which was the first thing Farrow commented on when they rendezvoused at Downtown Kardelle Station.

'It's thirty-five degrees out,' Farrow said. 'Why, are you wearing those?'

Narena was perfectly aware of how hot it was. She felt as though there were puddles *inside* her boots.

'I thought we might go in the lake,' Narena said, her cheeks flaming.

Why had she thought this was a good idea? She was in way over her head.

Farrow narrowed her green eyes. 'You have a twig in your hair.' Farrow pulled the object from Narena's black braid.

Narena had managed climb out her bedroom window without incident. Mostly. She had stumbled into a bush after losing her footing in the garden bed.

'Thank you.' Narena's cheeks were now scorching embers.

The two girls boarded the trolley out to the south coast and the seaside town of Rusterton. Narena took a seat and Farrow sat opposite, propping her feet up beside Narena.

'How did you get out of the house?' Farrow asked.

'I told my parents I was sick and snuck out.' Best to keep to the short version. Farrow didn't need to know how long it took her to take the first step onto the window ledge.

Farrow crossed her feet at the ankles. 'And here I was thinking I'd be travelling alone.'

'You didn't think I could do it.' It wasn't a question; the answer was written all over Farrow's proud face.

'That's not it.' Farrow placed her bag on the table between them. 'I didn't think you *would* do it.'

Something hot twisted inside Narena.

Narena had never had a large circle of friends; she was the daughter of a librarian and a journalist and her best friend was focused on his studies and his future, rather than being interested in attending social events. Narena knew she wasn't popular, and had never cared. Yet, sitting opposite Farrow, wearing her bright pink gumboots, she found she did.

'You forget,' Narena said, '*I* was the one who snuck into the *Telene Herald* to write the article that inspired the biggest riot in Vardean's history.'

That shouldn't be something to boast about, but she wanted Farrow to see her as more than the bookish friend of Cayder's. She had been brave too.

Farrow grinned, her eyes sparkling with amusement. 'Oh, I haven't forgotten. That's why we're on this adventure together.'

Narena raised her eyebrows at that. 'We're on this "adventure" because you blackmailed me.'

Farrow waved off her comment.

Also, Narena was fairly certain that Farrow would rather be here with someone else, *anyone* else, but she needed Narena. Being *needed* was different from being *wanted*. Aside from her parents, Cayder and Leta were the only people who had truly wanted Narena around.

Narena busied herself with her backpack to distract herself from the pinch in her chest.

'What's the plan, then?' Farrow asked.

Narena took in a steadying breath before glancing up. 'We go to your grandmother's houseboat and see what we can find.'

'And if we don't find anything?'

Narena had hoped she wouldn't have to answer that question.

———

It was a short one-hour trolley ride to the southern coast of Telene. Narena and Farrow disembarked at Rusterton's station. Everyone around them appeared to be set for a day at the beach; families were loaded with bags full of towels and toys. A few children giggled at Narena's gumboots. While everyone headed through the seaside town and down to the beach, Farrow and Narena headed away from the water.

'Did you ever come here as a child?' Narena asked as they travelled along a dirt road that wound its way through the bush. Rusterton was the closest beach to Kardelle; Kardelle only had steep rocky cliffs down to the water.

Farrow shook her head, her auburn curls bouncing. 'Never. My mother didn't want to return after my grandmother...' Farrow's brows pulled together.

'Oh,' Narena said. 'It happened at the houseboat?'

Apparently, it was also too painful for Farrow to say out loud; she merely nodded.

Narena swallowed down the lump in her throat. This wasn't just the investigation of what had happened decades ago to Farrow's grandmother's friend, but Farrow facing the place her grandmother had taken her final breaths.

There was one question Narena needed to ask.

'Your grandmother,' Narena started, her voice soft, 'are you sure she wasn't, um, hurt in the same way her friend was years earlier?'

'Yes, I'm sure.'

Farrow turned away from Narena and quickly wiped tears from her eyes.

'If you don't want to continue on,' Narena said, 'you could wait in town. I'll see what I can find.'

Farrow looked Narena up and down, and Narena waited for her smart reply.

'No,' was all she said.

———

By the time they reached the long driveway that wound in and around the brush towards the lake, there were no signs of other people. The only noise, aside from the crunch of their shoes against the dirt path, was the call of birds.

'My grandmother didn't like crowds,' Farrow said, breaking the silence. 'After her friend disappeared, her parents moved closer to Kardelle. But when she turned eighteen, she moved back here. The houseboat was just as they'd left it – her parents couldn't sell the property after the accident.'

Narena wasn't used to the quiet. Living in Kardelle, she was familiar with the ever-present hum of the trolleys, the bustle of the markets and people squashed into close quarters. The capital had been overpopulated ever since the veil was uncovered. Many felt safer closer to Vardean, and Kardelle's city centre.

'My grandmother was hoping her friend, Krenin, would turn

up one day.' Farrow worried a bracelet around her wrist. 'She wanted to be here in case he did.'

'That's so sad.' Narena knew what it was like to be haunted by the past. She had seen it with the Broducks.

What if she never found out what really happened to Cayder that night? What if she never saw him again? Narena could imagine Cayder with her right now. He would be peppering Farrow with questions, determined to help bring about justice for Farrow's family, his dark brows low over his ochre eyes. The image was so real, she had to peek over her shoulder to check he wasn't walking beside her, a ghost haunting her waking days.

'That's it!' Farrow pointed to some wooden beams visible through the brush. 'The houseboat!'

Farrow took off, leaving Narena stumbling after her.

Narena reached the bank and stopped beside Farrow. At the end of an old mooring was the houseboat. Or what was left of it. The structure had crashed into the side of the mooring, tilting it towards the reddish water. Narena remembered reading that the suburb of Rusterton was named after the lake, which was the colour of rusted metal.

'What happened to it?' Narena asked.

'What does it look like?' Farrow snapped.

Farrow's walls were back up.

'I'm sorry.'

Farrow gave Narena a hard look. 'Don't apologise – you didn't do this. It must have crashed into the mooring during a storm. Come on.'

A few of the planks on the mooring had rotted away and were lost to the water below. Narena couldn't help but think they were playing some kind of morbid hopscotch as they leaped from plank to plank to avoid falling into the lake.

'What are you planning to do?' Narena asked once they reached the end. The front door had been pushed into the side of the mooring; the entrance was blocked.

'Find another way in,' Farrow replied. 'I didn't come all this way to stare at the outside of the house.'

'I'm coming with you.'

Farrow merely shrugged in response. 'Do whatever you want.'

Narena held her breath as Farrow stepped onto the house-boat's pontoon. The structure swayed a little, but didn't sink.

The paint on the wooden walls had faded and flaked away; the house appeared to have once been a sunny yellow. Narena followed Farrow as she gingerly stepped along the side to reach one of the windows. Farrow attempted to slide the window open. It didn't budge.

'It's jammed,' Farrow said.

'Maybe there's another way in?' Narena didn't like the thought of jumping into the lake before they knew more about what they were getting themselves into, but if there was no other option...

Smash!

Farrow kicked the window in. Narena couldn't see anything inside, only the darkness waiting for them.

Farrow climbed through the window and disappeared from view.

Narena could barely catch her breath; Farrow was moving at a frantic pace.

'Are you okay?' Narena asked.

'Fine. Your turn!'

Narena didn't want to go inside, but she also didn't want to wait by herself. If there was any evidence of the Regency's involvement in Krenin's disappearance, then she needed to find it.

Narena ducked inside the windowsill. She still couldn't see Farrow. Her foot landed on something uneven and she stumbled into the dark.

Two arms encircled her. 'I got you.'

Farrow's face was close to Narena's. The green in her eyes sparkled in the light filtering from the broken window.

She's so beautiful, Narena thought.

Narena righted herself as her cheeks warmed. 'Thank you.'

She knew her entire face would be red, but the darkness would conceal it. Edem swirled in the shadows, shifting around like lurking creatures. Narena had never seen so much of it. She hugged herself, scared to accidentally touch it.

A beam of light broke Narena out of her thoughts. Farrow wielded her torch around the room. Edem fluttered away like a flock of frightened birds.

Narena glanced to the window behind – a portal back to the light, and safety.

A wicked grin spread across Farrow's face.

'Let's go explore.'

CHAPTER 13

ELENORA

Despite being awake for days now, Elenora couldn't sleep. The tent was nice and dark and cool, despite the perpetual daytime. And while Elenora's body yearned for sleep, her mind stubbornly turned everything over and over. Especially the look in Cayder's buttery-gold eyes as he leaned in close to clean her wound.

His hold on her face had been unexpectedly soft; his gaze too. It was almost like going back in time when he looked at her with such care. Her heart took flight with hope and happiness. Finally, she wasn't alone any longer. She had closed her eyes to hold on to the moment, knowing that his walls would soon be back up. He was injured. Tired. He wasn't himself.

Or, Elenora thought, *he was* more *himself. He was too tired to keep his walls up.*

Which meant what? That Cayder didn't hate her?

Although Elenora had grown up surrounded by palace staff who cared for her and met her every whim, she had always felt an emptiness. A space for friends – for people who truly knew her for who she was, and not the title she held. That emptiness grew after she lost her parents.

Elenora had hoped Cayder could be a friend – possibly more – but she had ruined it.

She could still feel the warm press of Cayder's lips against hers when she had said goodbye – pretending to give herself up to the Regency. She hoped there would be a time when that decision didn't feel like an unrelenting weight upon her shoulders.

She wished Erimen was here. While Elenora never talked to her brother about boys, he had always dispensed good advice. He had walked the line that their ancestors had set out before them. He had been born to rule and easily bore the weight of sovereignty. And he had done so with honour and grace.

Where in this world is he?

Elenora rolled onto her side. Outside was quiet; she had forgotten what restful silence sounded like. She had been raised in a cacophony of noise. Erimen had been a noisy child, running through the corridors of the castle singing silly songs at the top of his lungs, waiting for his father's booming reprimand, which would only make him sing louder. Their parents would throw parties for dignitaries that filled the stone halls with raucous music and even more raucous laughter. While Elenora's parents believed in upholding the traditions of the monarchy, they did things their way: with a touch of frivolity and fun. A playfulness that Erimen had inherited.

When Elenora was older, Erimen would encourage her to join his quest to annoy their father, to stir and play and be free – as much as two royals could in their closely controlled world.

She would play Erimen's games, but she had always been quieter. More cautious. Different.

While Erimen easily befriended the children of the castle staff, Elenora kept to herself. She wanted to make her own friends and forge her own way in the world. She had plans of attending the university on the mainland, where she would study everything and anything she could. It was unlikely she would ever take the throne, and therefore, she could make a life of her own. Away from the castle isle.

Then their parents had been killed and a quiet spread through the castle like a disease. Erimen and Elenora were the source. Whenever a staff member passed in the hall, they would stop what they were doing or saying and place their hand to their heart in respect. Erimen stopped singing his silly songs and shunned his friends, throwing himself into his royal duties. Their parents' deaths had created a hardened version of the boy Erimen had once been.

Back then, Elenora would sleep with the window open, in all seasons, in order to hear the waves crash against the rocks and push out the quiet. But while in Vardean on the top floor, she had learned to appreciate and value silence and the time it gave her thoughts to breathe and take shape in the dark.

What would Erimen's advice be now? Should she give Cayder his space? Or continue to chip at his walls?

How could Cayder forgive her when she hadn't yet forgiven herself?

———

Elenora eventually fell asleep. Her dreams were tangled fragments from the past few days: Dr Bueter's face after she shot him, Cayder's expression when she betrayed him, the queen appearing out of the shadows, the crawler spinning across the ground, the tent shaking in the wind...

Elenora woke with a start. That last moment hadn't happened.

She peered into the dim, trying to place where she was. The wind howled outside, shaking the tent from side to side.

'Elenora.' It was Cayder. 'Can I come inside?'

She sat upright, pulling her sleeping bag up to her chin. 'Yes.'

Cayder unzipped the tent. His almost-black hair was dusted with sand. He shook his head and ran a hand over his face.

'I can't breathe out there.' He coughed, proving his point. 'It's some kind of sandstorm.'

More unpredictable weather.

'There's plenty of room in here,' Elenora said, her voice tentative from sleep and unease.

Cayder zipped the tent closed and placed his sleeping bag next to hers. He lay on top of it and stopped moving, as though he had immediately fallen asleep. But his breathing gave him away. His chest rose and fell rapidly, in time with the beat of her heart.

He was so close to her, maddeningly close. If she moved her hand to her side, she could brush her fingers against his.

She didn't move, following his lead by also pretending to be asleep.

The wind continued to howl, shaking the tent. Luckily, Elenora had buried the pegs deep. When Elenora and Erimen were kids, they had often camped out at the edge of the castle isle, pretending they were far from home. They would camp outside for days, until they ran out of food and reluctantly returned to the castle and daily royal life.

The tent wobbled around her, but Elenora didn't fear the wind. Only the boy beside her. And her own heart.

Try as she might, she could not fall back asleep. Not with Cayder so close and the storm raging outside. It sounded like sand being blasted against the tent.

This was ridiculous! They knew they were both awake but would not admit it to each other.

Being together as the sand whirled outside the tent made the moment feel more intimate, as though their secrets were trapped in with them. Elenora waited for Cayder to say something, *anything*. She needed him to break the silence. She needed him to *want* to speak with her. Being shunned in the dark would hurt more than it would in the harsh light of day. There was no one here but the two of them. It was more personal. More painful.

Elenora squeezed her eyes shut, begging sleep to take hold. But the more she wanted it, the more it eluded her.

'Rusteef didn't warn us about pop-up forests and sandstorms.'

Cayder's comment was so sudden and soft, Elenora wasn't sure if she'd imagined it.

'No,' she replied as softly. 'He didn't.'

'Although this tent appears to be built for such weather.'

Her breath left her in a whoosh. She hadn't imagined his voice after all.

'Yes,' she said. 'It does.'

It was short and awkward, but it was something. A hand held out in the dark.

Elenora felt her body relax. Perhaps she could sleep after all.

Then Cayder shifted. When he spoke again, his voice was closer to her ear; he had moved onto his side.

'I wonder what else we can expect,' he said. 'What else this place has in store for us.'

Us.

'I don't know.' Elenora's heart thudded in her chest. She had no chance of falling asleep again now.

The warmth of Cayder's breath brushed against the side of her face. She desperately wanted to turn and see his expression. Instead, she forced herself to stare up at the shaking tent.

'I'm sorry,' Cayder whispered, barely audible over the storm. 'I'm so sorry, Elle.'

Elenora's breath hitched. He hadn't called her Elle since she betrayed him. She found herself turning towards him, her body automatically moving closer. She could see the outline of his face: the sharp cheekbones, the flash of his golden eyes, the set of his full mouth.

'No,' she said. '*I'm* sorry. I betrayed you. I betrayed—' she swallowed hard, 'I betrayed *us.*' *And who we could have been.*

He let out a breath, warming her face. 'I understand why you did it. And I forgive you.'

As much as she longed for the words, she could hardly believe what she was hearing.

He forgives me. 'Thank you. I know I don't deserve it—'

'You do. You deserve so much better than the way I have treated you. I hurt you...' His fingertips brushed across the bandaged cut on her cheek. His warm touch seared down her veins and fluttered through her heart to her stomach.

'I've treated you terribly. Worse than I've treated anyone. Only because—' She heard him swallow. 'Only because I cared so much about you.'

Elenora's heart pinched. *Cared.* Past tense. He didn't care for her anymore.

'I understand.' She tried not to let her voice quiver. 'I would have felt the same way.'

He huffed a laugh. 'You would have handled it with much more grace.'

'All is forgiven.' She gave him a small smile that she hoped he could see.

He moved his hand to rest on the side of her face and shifted closer, his lips a whisper from hers. He paused, his gaze flicking up from her mouth to her eyes. He waited for her response.

She gently pressed her lips to his then pulled away. It was a short kiss, but the action stirred something inside her. She wanted more of him, but she wasn't sure if—

He tangled his hand into her hair and pulled her towards him. He kissed her deeply, opening his mouth to meet hers. Elenora gasped, her entire body tingling from the contact. She gripped onto the front of his cloak, pressing her mouth where his sharp jaw met his neck. He smelled like the salt of the sea and smoky campfire.

'I'm so sorry,' he whispered against her skin.

'Stop apologising.' She pulled his mouth back to hers.

Her entire body flushed hot and she climbed out of her sleeping bag. She had stripped down to her undergarments before going to sleep and she immediately regretted it, trying to cover herself.

'We can stop.' Cayder registered her hesitation. 'If you want?'

Elenora had never been semi-naked in front of a boy. She had imagined what it would feel like, but nothing had prepared her for this. Her thoughts battled between debilitating shyness and burning desire. In the end, desire won out.

Elenora shook her head.

The left side of Cayder's mouth lifted and he ran his hands down her bare arms. She slipped Cayder's cloak off his shoulders and helped pull his shirt over his head, revealing his skin and echo-marked shoulders beneath. She traced the lines down his back.

'What does it look like?' he said, his voice husky.

She trailed the smoky marks of his skin. They looked like feathers. 'Beautiful.'

She wrapped her arms around the back of his neck to pull him even closer. Cayder hissed, but it wasn't a sound of pleasure.

'What is it?' Elenora asked, releasing him.

'I don't know.' Cayder touched the back of his head.

In the dark, Elenora could see his fingertips were darkened with blood.

'I must have cut the back of my head when I crashed the crawler.'

'I'll get the medical kit.'

But Cayder held onto her hand, his eyes wide. 'I'm so stupid.'

Elenora chuckled. 'It wasn't your fault. You were tired.'

'No – it's not that.'

'Oh?' She hoped he wasn't referring to *this*. To being together.

'Dr Bueter,' he said. 'We didn't see him actually disappear, right?'

'No...' Elenora tried to catch onto his train of thought. 'But the results of the edem weapon can't be stopped. Once someone is shot, they will eventually disappear. Like my brother.'

Cayder pointed at her. 'Exactly.'

'I don't understand.'

'Your brother was shot and had time to go back to the castle isle and find you, which means Dr Bueter would also have had some time up his sleeve.'

Elenora didn't understand where he was going with this.

'Where else would he go if he needed medical help?' he asked.

Oh. 'Kardelle County hospital?'

'Yes!' Cayder searched the tent for his cloak. He pulled out the map that Rusteef had given them. 'And when the doctors failed to help him – as they no doubt would have – then he would've disappeared there.' He pointed to the hospital on Telene's version of the map.

Elenora finally understood what he was trying to tell her. She grabbed the other map and placed it on top. 'Which means he would've arrived in the same spot *here*.' She tapped the mountain range. 'He didn't disappear from the Regency headquarters. He didn't fall into the water.'

Cayder grinned, a dimple flashing. 'No, he didn't.'

CHAPTER 14

JEY

Jey's eyelids felt glued shut. He remembered trying to escape weapon-fire. From the burn biting his side, it appeared he was not successful.

The bad news: he must have passed out, and left Leta all by herself in a strange new world.

The good news: his side ached like a hot poker had been punched through his flesh.

Pain equalled life, right?

Jey forced his eyes open. He was in some kind of room that was painted dark blue – almost black. It was cold, really cold. And for some reason, he had lost his shirt. He tried to roll onto his side and immediately regretted it. A searing pain shot from his side to his chest.

He couldn't remember anything else except Leta's pale face watching over him, his blood on her hands.

'Nettie?'

'She's not here,' someone replied.

Jey tried to turn his head and groaned.

'Relax,' the voice said.

'Sure, mystery man.' Jey's voice was rough from lack of use. 'I have no idea where I am and I've been shot. Relaxing is not exactly the first thing on my mind.'

'I'm not a man,' the voice said calmly. 'I use they/them pronouns.'

'Sorry,' Jey said. 'I shouldn't assume.'

Jey tried to bring his hand to his burning forehead but found it was tied to the bed. Yep, he was right to be on edge. 'Why am I tied up?'

'We have you restrained for your own safety as you were thrashing about in your sleep.'

'Sure. That's what every good abductor says. And by good, I don't mean like, *good*.'

They huffed. 'Stop moving before you hurt yourself.'

'That ship already sailed,' Jey said. 'I've been shot.'

'I'm well aware.'

'Where am I? Where's the girl I was with?' Jey needed to know Leta was okay.

'We found you alone with one of the hullen.'

Jey wasn't sure if that was a good thing or a bad thing. Leta had planned to come back for him; hopefully she was safe.

Finally, the person approached Jey's bedside. They were tall and narrow, with short-cropped white-blonde hair, frosty-blue eyes and cheekbones as sharp as a shard of ice. They wore a white cloak. They looked like a ghost.

Not a practical colour for someone planning to maim and torture.

'I'm Dezra,' Jey's abductor said. 'Your doctor.'

Jey noticed a thin tube of smoky black liquid inserted into his left arm. 'What in burning shadows are you pumping into me?' He wrestled to get free, but his bonds wouldn't let him budge an inch.

Dezra placed a pale hand on Jey's shoulder. 'It will stall the progress of the wound from your Regency weapons. It's the only way to stop the edem infection from spreading.'

Jey gritted his teeth. 'I'm not with the Regency.' Now was certainly not the time to mention that their leader was his father . . .

Dezra assessed Jey with cool eyes. 'I was told you came through the veil. Only the Regency has access via their headquarters. They want to destroy this world.'

A rough laugh burst out of Jey's chest. 'Clearly, I'm only good at destroying myself. I got shot trying to escape from the Regency, not by helping them.'

'If you say so.'

'What is this edem infection?' Jey looked down to ensure he was all still there.

'Your weapons—'

'Not my weapons,' Jey corrected.

Dezra didn't look convinced. 'The *Regency's* weapons, or any edem usage for that matter, displaces objects between the two worlds.' Jey nodded; his father had been shot and had started to disintegrate in front of his eyes, for the second time in Jey's life. 'You were shot before arriving here, correct?'

Jey nodded. 'I got hit on my way through.'

Dezra's eyes brightened with interest as though Jey was a fascinating specimen. 'We've never seen anyone like you before.'

'That's not the first time I've heard that.' Jey grinned, but even that hurt.

Dezra ignored Jey's smug remark. 'Because you were between worlds, edem doesn't know where to displace you to.'

'Okay...What does that mean?'

'Edem will continue to try to relocate your body, causing your corporal presence to break down.'

'My what?'

'Your physical body.' Dezra gestured to Jey's prone form. 'It will be pulled towards two different places until it's torn apart.'

'*What?*'

'Don't worry,' Dezra said. 'Feeding you more edem will stem the process and keep you in one place.'

'If you're trying to help me, then why the bonds? Am I a prisoner or a patient? Because right now, you're sending me very mixed signals, Doc.'

'I help whoever comes through my doors, regardless of their allegiances.'

Jey glanced around the room and realised that what he thought was paint on the wall was the deep blue-black of ice. 'I don't see any doors.'

Dezra sighed, closing their eyes. 'Theoretically speaking.'

Jey was used to that sigh – one he'd often heard from his father. 'You don't believe me?'

'I think the others believe your story, and Leta's. I am undecided. You don the Vardean guard uniform after all.' Dezra gestured to the Vardean emblem on Jey's pants.

'Wait – Leta is here?'

'She is.'

'Talk about burying the lede, Doc! Where is she?'

'With her mother.'

Jey blinked. 'Her mother?' Her mother that was supposed to be dead?

'Leta Broduck is with her mother, Maretta Broduck,' Dezra said, as though Jey had taken a hit to the head rather than being shot in the side. 'Maretta is in charge here.'

'And where is *here*, exactly? In case I get lost and need to find my way back.' Jey gave Dezra a rueful grin.

'The underground compound.'

Jey remembered the hullen gesturing towards a cave behind the backwards-moving waterfall. 'You live in an icy cavern?'

'Only if we want to survive,' Dezra said.

'You're awake!'

Leta flew into the room. She grabbed Jey's right hand in hers. 'I was so worried! You've been out for days!'

Jey shrugged, ignoring the pain that seared through his left side. 'You know me; I'm harder to kill than I look.'

Leta's brows pinched together. 'You *look* dreadful.'

'Way to boost my ego, Nettie.'

'Mother—' Leta held her hand out to a tall woman who was lingering in the doorway. 'Come meet my boyfriend, Jey.'

Jey grimaced and whispered to Leta, 'Do you think we could remove my bonds first?' He didn't want to meet another member of Leta's family while restrained – it was becoming a weird tradition.

'Of course,' Leta said, kissing his cheek. She undid the right buckle and Dezra untied the left, although they gave Jey a wary look.

Once Jey was untied, he sat upright, careful to not pull out the needle in his left arm.

Maretta looked like a painting come to life with dark greying hair, light eyes and a warm olive complexion. Jey could see where Leta had inherited her beauty.

'It's very nice to meet you, Jey,' Maretta said. Jey noticed she shared the same smile as her daughter. 'I'm so glad my little girl had someone looking out for her while I was gone.'

'It's nice to meet you too, Mrs Broduck. And I can't really take credit for that; Nettie looks out for herself. And, of course, there's Cayder... *Wait* – did the others turn up?'

'Not yet,' Maretta said. Concern was etched in the lines of her forehead. 'But we have a team out searching for them.'

'Where do you think they are?' Jey asked.

Dezra raised their pale eyebrows and Maretta set her jaw. Jey knew that expression; he'd seen the same ferocity on Leta's face whenever she was angry.

'We believe they might have been intercepted by a group we've clashed with in the past,' Maretta said. 'They refuse to share food and supplies with us.'

'Why?' Jey asked.

'It's their belief that we are to blame for the state of this world,' Maretta explained. 'While most of us here were born in Telene, they have always lived on this side of the veil. They see us as a danger, even though we are simply trying to survive. But we have formed a tentative truce: we steer clear of them and they steer clear of us. And if we broach their settlement, then we're breaching the truce.'

'Would these people hurt Cayder and the others?' Leta asked.

Maretta rubbed the back of her neck. 'I would hope not.'

'That's another reason why we live underground,' Dezra said. 'Protection.'

'How are Jey's vitals?' Maretta asked Dezra.

'Stable,' they replied.

'Come now, Doc,' Jey said. 'No one likes a liar.'

Leta gripped Jey's hand in hers. He could barely feel his fingers. 'Nettie, I need those,' he said, prying her away gently.

'The wound has stopped responding to edem,' Dezra said. 'All we can do now is wait and see how Jey's body reacts.'

'Thanks, Doc. Then can we remove this—' Jey gestured to the needle in his arm.

'I'm afraid not,' Dezra said. 'If we remove the intravenous drip, the wound will continue to deteriorate.'

And Jey would be torn apart.

'Are you saying I need to keep myself hooked up to this stuff for the rest of my life?' Jey didn't want to play the martyr, but it was hardly the future he envisioned for himself.

He saw Leta and Maretta exchange a knowing glance. They were hiding something. Jey could feel it like a splinter under the skin.

'Am I dying?' Jey asked.

Leta climbed onto the narrow bunk and pressed her forehead against his temple. 'You're absolutely *not* dying.' But her voice was unsteady. Leta was never good at hiding her emotions. She would be a terrible actress.

'That sounds like something someone would say to someone who is dying,' Jey argued.

'You're not dying,' Maretta agreed, patting Jey's leg. 'You just need some help. Think of this as a medicine.'

Medicine that needed to be shoved into his veins twenty-four seven?

'Once we get back to Telene,' Jey said, 'will I still need this medicine?'

'Well—' Maretta began.

'We don't know,' Leta interrupted. 'We'll have to wait and see. But hopefully not.'

Jey looked between mother and daughter. Much had happened in the days since he'd seen Leta. Much she hadn't told him.

'We should leave Jey to rest,' Dezra said. 'We should not worry him with this.'

'Should I be worried?' He looked between Dezra and Maretta. 'You look worried.'

'The doctor is right.' Leta avoided his gaze. 'We should let you rest.'

'I was just unconscious for—' he raised an eyebrow at Dezra in question.

'Three days,' Dezra offered.

'Three whole days,' Jey said with a nod. 'I'd say I'm well rested.'

Jey could match Leta's stubbornness – there was a reason they had both ended up in Vardean.

'There's nothing you can do right now,' Maretta said gently. 'You look after yourself and we'll figure out the rest. It's not worth getting worked up over.'

'No offense, Mrs Broduck. But this is not me worked up. I'm only around a two of a possible ten.'

'I see,' Maretta replied, a smile curling the corners of her mouth.

'Come on now, Nettie,' Jey urged. 'I thought we promised not to keep secrets from each other.'

Leta pointed at his bandaged side. 'I thought so too.'

'Fair point. But I told you eventually, that's what matters right?'

Leta studied his hand in hers. 'Right now, you need to get better.'

Jey jerked his chin at Dezra. 'Doc says I can't get better. So why don't you tell me what's really going on.'

Leta and her mother exchanged another look and Jey groaned. That couldn't be good.

'Fine.' Leta sat upright. 'There isn't any way home, and this place,' she gestured around them, 'is a sinking ship. The world is literally fading away into nothing. And if we don't find our way off this ship in the next few years then we go down with it.'

'Not the best news,' Jey muttered. 'But my father got himself out of here, so there's hope, right?'

'Always,' Maretta replied with a wan smile. 'But as I told Leta, we don't have any weapons here that can transport us back to Telene.'

'Then we need to find my father.' The plan seemed simple enough to him.

'Dezra, can you please give us a moment?' Maretta asked.

Dezra nodded. 'Don't remove that.' They gestured to Jey's edem infusion.

Jey saluted with his free arm. 'Got it.'

Once Dezra left, Maretta confessed, 'I've been testing a theory.'

Leta spun to look at her mother. '*What* theory?'

Maretta held out both palms defensively. 'There's so much I don't yet know – I've been working on something over the last year, as edem usage has increased in Telene. But I didn't want to get anyone's hopes up.'

Jey could use some good news. 'Go on. Humour us.'

Maretta pulled a small table over to the side of Jey's bed and pulled a tattered notebook from her pocket. She found the page she was looking for and bent the spine so the book would stay open in place.

An image of the edemmeter had equations written all around it. Jey had seen similar images strewn around the apartment when he'd lived with his mother.

'Ahhh,' Jey said. 'Sorry Mrs Broduck, but I don't speak genius.'

'Call me Maretta.' She ran a finger around the globe sketch. 'I built this edemmeter during the first few years of being here.'

'Were you alone back then?' Leta asked.

Maretta shook her head. 'Many people had already been displaced here. I was just the next in line.' She gave a rueful smile. 'The people before me helped me understand what had happened, and how I'd arrived here. I decided to build our own edemmeter so that we could track the usage of edem in Telene to locate resources to survive. But I always had other plans. I wanted to go home.' She smiled at her daughter. 'I missed my children. My family.'

Leta reached over and grabbed her mother's hand. Jey smiled, but his chest ached. He missed his mother. He missed being a part of a loving family.

'Over time, I began to notice a trend,' Maretta said. 'I believe, although I don't have any proof, that the seismic changes this world encounters when edem is used is actually the thinning of the veil, and that when someone uses edem – on this side or the other – a weakness is created.'

'Another tear?' Leta asked.

'Not quite,' she replied. 'But it's as though our two worlds grow closer.'

'Are you saying we can return to Telene when someone uses edem?' Jey asked.

'Not exactly,' Maretta said. 'My hope is to use the edemmeter to detect when a large amount of edem is being used in Telene, and then use edem on our side of the veil in the same location in hopes of creating a tear from *here* to *there*.'

'And then we can walk on through,' Jey said with a nod.

'That is my hope,' Maretta said, 'yes.'

'That's it?' Leta demanded. 'That's your theory?'

'I continue to monitor and test—'

'It's been seven years,' Leta interrupted, folding her arms over her chest. 'You've been testing for *seven* years.'

'Nettie—' Jey started.

She held up a hand. 'Don't *Nettie* me. This ship is sinking, remember? And you're tied to it.' She gestured to the edem infusion in his arm.

'I know.' He was painfully aware.

'We keep trying,' Maretta said. 'That's all we can do.'

'It's not enough.' Leta jumped up from the bed. 'I'm not going down with ship, and neither is Jey.'

Jey watched her storm out of the room, desperate to follow her.

CHAPTER 15

LETA

Leta had always been good with directions. She found her way back to her mother's lab with ease. There had to be something here that would help them go home. She was not going to watch Jey slowly slip away.

The lab assistant, Erithe, was studying the edemmeter when Leta stormed in, her brown eyes whipping about the room as though the solution to all their problems was lying in plain sight.

'Leta.' Erithe acknowledged her with a nod. 'Are you all right?'

Erithe was a similar age to Leta's mother, with short greying blonde hair and a freckled complexion. According to the calendar scratched into the rock wall behind Erithe's desk, she had been here for two years.

Leta pulled out one of her mother's notebooks and began flipping through the pages. 'I'm fine.' She knew it was an insult to think she could find a way out of here in mere days, when her mother had been searching for seven years, but as her mother used to say, 'A busy mind is a constructive mind. A bored mind falls easily into traps.'

'The transition here is always difficult,' Erithe said. 'It took me months to come to terms with my new reality.'

Leta wouldn't be here for months – she *couldn't*.

Flipping through her mother's notebooks and seeing her familiar handwriting was like falling into the past.

Her mother had always carried a notebook with her, capturing her thoughts as she wandered from room to room in Broduck Manor. The book was filled with secrets and songs and sayings. When Leta first learnt to write, she would shadow her mother around the house with her own notebook. Leta crammed hers full of crude sketches of the world as seen through her imaginative childish gaze. Pies growing from trees. Birds with leaves for wings. Cayder without a mouth so he couldn't tell her what to do.

Back then, Leta had wanted to peek inside her mother's notebook, inside her mind, but the notebook was always kept out of reach. As Leta flipped through it now, she understood why. Sketches of machines and weapons cluttered the pages.

Her mother's secrets laid bare.

'Erithe—' Leta's mother had entered the lab, but Leta did not turn around to acknowledge her. 'Can I please have a moment with my daughter?'

'Of course, Maretta.' Erithe hurried from the room.

'Nettie,' her mother began, sitting beside her. 'I wish this place was more than a half-life, but we do have time to figure this out. And I know with your bright mind, we will.' She curled a lock of Leta's short hair behind her ear.

Time to figure this out? 'A few years, right?'

Her mother pressed a kiss to her temple. 'Hope is all we have.'

'Is that what kept you going for the last seven years?'

Her mother's face crumpled into that worried look of hers. 'I didn't have any other choice.' She grabbed Leta's hands. 'I wasn't sure if I'd ever be able to come back to you, but I did try.' Her grip tightened. 'And we will find Cayder, I promise you. We will all be together.'

'I don't think I can live here,' Leta whispered. 'I mean, I don't *want* to.' Tears stung the back of her eyes. 'I want to go home.' She'd never thought she would, but she missed Broduck Manor. She missed the stomp of her father's footsteps around the house. She even missed his bellowing frustrations.

'Oh, honey.' Her mother encircled her in her arms. 'I know. I know.' Maretta wiped the tears away from Leta's cheeks. 'Do you want to help me run a test? A busy mind is a—'

'Constructive mind,' Leta finished with a nod. As much as she didn't like leaving Jey alone, she wanted – *needed* – to do something productive. And there was already a team trying to find Cayder and the others.

Maretta brought a tree branch to the workbench. 'I have to be careful with how many branches I use.'

'Why?' Leta had seen lots of trees on the surface, although they were black and icy.

'The ground isn't the only thing that holds edem. Here—' She handed Leta a small hand saw. 'I'll monitor the edemmeter.'

'Okay...' Leta began sawing away at the tree branch. The silence hung heavy in the lab as the branch snapped, releasing the edem inside. Leta forced herself not to shrink back.

'Ready?' her mother asked.

Leta hadn't used edem since the incident with Dr Bueter. 'What do you want me to do with it?'

'Edem controls time.' Her mother held out a small seed. 'You don't need to fear it here.'

Leta took the seed in her echo-marked fingers and touched the shadowy substance before she chickened out. Her mother gave her a reassuring nod. 'Tell it what you want.'

Leta closed her eyes and whispered, 'Grow.'

Edem rippled around her skin. What was once smooth and opaque became hard and granular. Darkness rained down from Leta's hand and hit the benchtop with a *hush*.

'Soil?' Leta asked, confused.

But the edem hadn't finished restructuring. A section of the soil shifted and a pop of green emerged, revealing a vine. It grew out of the soil and twisted towards the ceiling of the lab before drooping to the side. A bulb bloomed from the end of the vine, swelling until a flower appeared with a flash of red and white.

'A blooming heart!' Leta nudged the silky flower with her fingertips. It was as real as the air they breathed. 'Did that register?'

She knew the answer before her mother shook her head. The rings on the edemmeter hadn't budged.

'It's not enough,' her mother said.

'How much edem do you think we need to use to create a tear from this side?'

'More than we have, I fear. The more I take, the less we have to survive on.'

'Isn't it worth the risk? If we use everything available then we could go home.'

'*Could.*' Her mother shook her head. 'We have to think of the entire compound. There are more than four hundred people who rely on me to protect them.'

'What about your family? *We* relied on you. You could have come home years ago if you tried harder!' Tears sprung angrily into her eyes. She was *their* mother – wasn't that more important?

Leta had been right when she imagined a nightmare world on the other side of the veil; this was far from the fanciful place she'd dreamt about when she was younger. Cayder was lost and she would lose Jey – forever.

'I couldn't drain our supplies and sentence everyone here to a slow and painful death of starvation. The less I use for my tests, the longer we can survive here.' Her mother crossed her arms over her chest. 'It was not an easy decision, Nettie, but it was the correct one. And I continue to make that decision every day. Let me show you around. It will help you to see the life we have built here.'

Leta didn't want to see the rest of the compound. She didn't want to get comfortable. She wanted to keep pushing forward.

'No,' Leta said. 'Let's run more tests.'

———

Leta found herself enjoying working with her mother, despite the situation. When Leta had last seen her mother, she was too young to recognise her as anything other than that – a mother. Always full of sunshine smiles with gentle, healing touches and a story on the tip of her tongue. If she had grappled with the weight of her job and what Dr Bueter had asked of her, she had hidden it from her family. Perhaps too well.

Had Alain Broduck known the truth about his wife and what she did every day? Or had he also been in the dark? Leta had never known them to argue, unless it had been behind closed doors while their children slept.

Leta could appreciate her mother's intellect, even if it had been used to create weapons. And if they found a way home, they could undo the damage of Ferrington, and all those who had been impacted by edem and found themselves on this side of the veil.

Leta refused to leave the lab, only returning to Jey's side at 'night'. She didn't want to see this place as anything other than a stopover. She wouldn't allow this reality to become her future, despite her mother pleading with her to see more of the compound and understand their way of life. Leta preferred to stay focused on the task at hand. And staying busy kept her mind off Jey's condition and the fact that Cayder still hadn't turned up.

Leta was eating another dinner with her mother in the lab when Erimen entered with an update.

'The team have returned,' Erimen said. He didn't need to tell them they'd been unsuccessful, the disappointment was written all over his face. 'We'll continue to search. We won't give up.'

Her mother remained silent, placing her hands on Leta's in reassurance.

Leta studied the edemmeter and the geography of this new world, wondering where her brother could be. The dreamer in her wanted to be out there exploring, but she was no longer a little girl who believed in fairytales.

She walked to Jey's room after dinner, feeling the icy ceiling of the compound press down upon her. Her mother walked alongside her, a spectre brought back to life.

'Goodnight,' Leta mumbled, her focus on the frosty floor.

'Nettie,' her mother said softly.

Leta glanced up. Her mother gave her an understanding smile. 'I know you're worried about Cayder, but we *will* find him.'

Leta was worried about everything.

'It's my fault he's here,' she said. 'If I never went to Ferrington, I wouldn't have been arrested for the fires and he wouldn't have tried to break me out of prison.'

'Then we wouldn't be here together now.' Her mother placed her hand on the side of Leta's cheek.

Leta nodded, but she still felt uneasy. Yes, she was reunited with her mother, but not for long. And Leta wanted more than the time she had promised. She wanted more for Jey, for them all. And her father deserved to know what had happened.

'Come out flying with me tomorrow,' her mother said, her expression wistful. 'It will make you feel better.'

'Maybe.'

But Leta had no intention of leaving the lab until they found a solution.

'This isn't your burden, Nettie,' her mother reminded her. 'You're not alone.'

She wrapped her arms around her mother, relishing in the fact that she could once again breathe her in.

—

Jey was already asleep when Leta slipped in beside him. Dezra had told her that they would sedate him at night to help his body recover quicker. But Jey didn't look any better than when Leta had first seen him in this bed. And his black veins were spreading across his body like wildfire.

Leta pressed a kiss to Jey's temple and attempted to fall asleep to the hum of the hospital machines.

But like every night since she'd jumped through the veil, she didn't dream.

For she was already in a waking nightmare.

CHAPTER 16

NARENA

The houseboat creaked as Narena and Farrow explored its underbelly. While the place smelled of mildew, Narena was relieved to find it dry inside. They carefully stepped away from the window and across the tilted room. Each step they took sent off a series of splintering *cracks*. Narena imagined a spiderweb of fractures forming under her feet, and if they were to join, the entire floor would give way.

Farrow flashed her torch on some chairs and a table, which were slammed into the far wall. 'This is the living room.'

Narena wasn't sure where Farrow planned to go, so she followed closely behind, ignoring the edem swirling in her periphery.

Aside from leaning to the side, tossing everything about, the houseboat seemed well preserved. From the undisturbed layers of dust coating the floor, it was clear no one had been here for a long time.

Narena winced as something tore underfoot. Anything could be valuable, especially when they weren't sure what they were looking for.

'What is it?' Farrow asked.

Narena blew decades worth of dust off a framed image. 'A painting,' she said, flattening the ripped canvas. 'I'm sorry, I didn't see it.'

Farrow shone the torch onto the destroyed surface. A girl with bright green eyes and red hair looked back at them.

'That's my grandmother,' Farrow remarked.

'She looks so much like you.'

'My grandfather was a painter,' Farrow said. 'He must have painted this while they were still together.' Her mouth twisted sourly. 'He hated her obsession with the accident and hated this house.'

The tear Narena had created in the portrait went through Farrow's grandmother's forehead. As though she was split in two. Forever scarred.

'Do you want to keep it?' Narena offered it to Farrow. 'I'm sure we could get it mended.'

'I'm not here for keepsakes. I'm here for the truth.'

She sounded so much like Cayder; Narena's stomach contorted.

They continued on, sifting through the items on the floor. Narena was careful to step only where Farrow did, not wanting to destroy anything else.

Attached to the living room was a small kitchen. All its glasses, crockery and cutlery had fallen from the shelves. Broken glass and pottery covered the floor. Narena squatted to take a look at the broken shards, to see if she could piece anything together, but they were the size of small pebbles.

'I don't think we should go in there,' Farrow said.

Narena agreed, but part of her mind lingered behind, even when they moved into the adjoining room.

'This must have been my grandmother's bedroom.' Farrow nodded to a mouldy mattress slumped against one wall. She hesitated before crossing the threshold.

Narena held onto the doorframe to stop from skidding into the slanted room and into Farrow.

'Why did your mother never come here?' Narena asked; clothes were strewn about the room as though someone had started to pack in a hurry then abandoned everything.

'She was only a baby when her father – my grandfather – took custody of her. The Regency had done such a good job of publicly tarnishing my grandmother's entire family, it didn't matter where she went. My mother tried changing her name to her father's, but it was too late. Everyone knew who she really was.'

Narena crouched to comb through the dresses of faded yellows and soft pinks. They didn't look like the clothes of a haunted woman.

Farrow moved over to a small wooden desk that had been bolted into the wall and hadn't moved when the houseboat collided with the mooring.

'Can you help me?' Farrow pulled at the desk drawer. 'It's stuck.'

They jimmied the drawer open and the contents tumbled to the ground.

'Bills—' Farrow shifted letters to the side with large red writing on the front.

OVERDUE.

FINAL NOTICE.

'Looks like your grandmother had money troubles,' Narena noted.

Farrow rolled her eyes. 'That's what happens when your husband takes your child away and leaves you to rot. Grandmother sold her story to whoever would buy it, but otherwise, she had no money coming in. No one would hire her. They thought she was crazy. Or worse: a murderer.'

'How can people be so cruel?'

'Rusterton has always been a tourist town. Did you know the royals used to vacation here by the lake?'

Narena hadn't known that.

'But after Krenin's disappearance, no one wanted to come to the place where someone had disappeared under such strange circumstances. The local businesses suffered so they spread a rumour that my grandmother had killed her friend. That was more acceptable. Only then did tourists return to Rusterton and businesses kept their doors open – at my grandmother's expense.'

Narena could understand everyone's desperation, but to ruin a person's reputation – someone who was already struggling – was despicable.

Among the unopened overdue bills was a leather-bound book.

Farrow flipped through the pages. 'It's my grandmother's diary.'

Narena shuffled closer and looked over Farrow's shoulder as she read aloud.

Monday.

I felt its presence again. The best way I can describe the feeling is as though someone is sitting behind you, watching over your shoulder, breathing down your neck. And yet, when you turn around, no one's there.

This time I moved quickly, throwing on my bathing suit and diving off the back deck into the water.

I would catch it this time. Then everyone would believe me.

The two girls locked eyes.

'Something *was* here,' Farrow said, nodding to the water beneath them.

The ramblings of Farrow's grandmother weren't evidence of that, but Narena held her tongue.

Farrow flipped to another page.

Tuesday.

I went into the water while the baby slept. I swam to the spot where Krenin was last seen. Three years since he disappeared, and the weather was just as it had been on that day. I waited in the water. As usual, the permacloud prevented any direct sunlight. No edem shimmered below.

Was that what happened? Krenin used edem and somehow made himself disappear? But that doesn't match Cass's story of something moving in the water.

I wrote to ask her to join me, but she refused. She will never return to Rusterton.

I know she's scared, but giving up is giving up on Krenin and the truth.

I'm no fool. He's likely long dead, but I need to know what happened. My mind won't rest until I do. This town won't forgive me. And I won't forgive myself. I had invited Krenin over. I insisted we swim in the water, against my parents' warnings.

If I could take back that day, I would.

Today, I remained still in the water, holding onto the pontoon; I thought if I blended with my surroundings, the *thing* that took Krenin might make itself known.

I waited in the water for over an hour, until I heard the baby wake and start crying.

I know this is unhealthy. I know I need to let go, like Cass has. Like all my friends. But I cannot. And I will not. I need to clear my name.

Even though the Crown Court threw out the case due to lack of evidence, my name is mud in this town. Everyone views me as a killer. To them, I am the woman who ruined their businesses, their lives.

But what about me? What about my life?

No one cares. Not even my husband. He grows more distant with each day. I can see that look in his eyes when I tell him what I feel about this place. He used to urge me to leave. But now, I can see he wants to leave. Me.

I thought he understood. He used to be the one person who stood by my side when my parents and friends turned their backs.

But I am alone. Still, I will not give up.

Narena's heart fractured for Farrow. Her grandmother had clearly been crying out for help and no one had been listening.

'Should we continue searching the house?' Narena suggested.

But Farrow kept reading passages, her hands clutching the book tighter and tighter as though the words she read aloud were being pulled from her own body, against her will.

Narena realised Farrow *could* have written these words herself. As well as Farrow's mother. Three generations shared this dark legacy that they couldn't shake. And each refused to give up. They continued to search, even if what they were gripping onto were mere shadows of truth.

Farrow continued reading aloud from the journal.

Friday.
My hand is shaking as I write this. The baby is safe. She is safe. I need to keep reminding myself of that. That is important. But not the most important thing.
     It came back.
     After all these years. I always knew it would. I could not explain why. But I knew.

Farrow paused as her hands shook.

'Do you want to leave?' Narena asked.

Farrow ignored her, as though she hadn't even spoken. As though she was reading from her grandmother's journal to some unseen audience.

It was night-time when I felt the presence return. Something lurking underneath. The baby was asleep in her cot so I slipped into the cool water in my nightdress. The porch lights were on, pointed at the water to keep edem away, as always.

I swam to the place where Krenin disappeared, but I didn't have to wait long. Something touched my foot. At first, I thought it was a reed, but then it wrapped around my ankle.

I barely had time to take a breath before I was pulled underwater. My eyes were wide open, but I couldn't see anything around me. I reached for my leg to pull myself free but there was nothing there. Whatever had caught me seconds earlier was gone.

I pushed up to the surface of the water, the porch lights stinging my eyes. I couldn't see the creature Cass had described. That was when I heard the baby cry. I turned to look back at the house and all I could see was darkness. The windows and the sides of the house were covered in black. The creature was going inside. It was going for my baby.

I swam to the ladder, grabbed the fire poker from the fireplace and rushed into the baby's room, ready to attack.

But the creature - or whatever it was - was gone.

I grabbed the baby and fled onto the pier, where the lights were even brighter.

I don't understand. Why go for my baby only to disappear? What was it trying to do, aside from scare me?

Unless that was the point. The creature had scared me away from my home.

But I won't stay away. This is my home. Not theirs.

'This must have been close to when my grandfather took my mother away for negligence,' Farrow said. 'My grandmother didn't live for much longer after that.'

Narena had her hand pressed over her mouth. It was all so horrible.

'The creature—' Farrow looked up from the book. Unshed tears were in her eyes. 'That sounds like the hullen.'

Narena shook her head. 'Cayder didn't think the hullen were dangerous. We saw one in Ferrington. It didn't hurt us and it saved Leta.'

'Just because the hullen didn't hurt you, doesn't mean one didn't stalk my grandmother.'

'I suppose not.'

'There could be a bad hullen, right? Like there are good and bad people?'

Narena wasn't sure. Perhaps Cayder had been hurt by a bad hullen, like Krenin had.

All she knew for certain was that she wanted to get out of there.

154

'Come on.' Narena stood and held a hand out for Farrow. 'We should get going.'

As they walked back through the house, Narena saw the glass fragments lying around the kitchen.

'Oh!' The part of her mind that had been mulling the scene over had finally pieced it together.

'What's wrong?' Farrow asked.

'I don't think the houseboat was knocked into the mooring during a storm.'

'What do you mean?'

Narena gestured to the scene around them. 'Something struck me as strange when I first saw the kitchen. It didn't look like the plates and glasses had simply slipped from the shelves as the boat tilted. The damage here is worse than that.'

Farrow narrowed her eyes. 'What are you saying, Narena?'

Fear tickled the back of her neck.

'I think whatever was haunting your grandmother destroyed her house.'

CHAPTER 17

CAYDER

Cayder and Elenora waited for the storm to pass before dismantling the tent and heading back to the crawler. Cayder let out a relieved sigh when the lever rose from the console and the engine started; he hadn't done any permanent damage to the vehicle.

He pushed down on the lever and the crawler took off, throwing his body back into the seat. He winced; his shoulders were bruised. He hadn't realised it earlier in the tent, not when Elenora's hands were on him.

The tips of Cayder's ears warmed and he kept his focus on the field ahead. He hadn't been embarrassed, but now, with her beside him in the bright light, he was unable to look at her.

He wasn't sure how to react after such a kiss. He hoped she didn't regret it. But after how he'd treated her, he wouldn't be surprised. They were both tired, scared and stranded in a peculiar land. They had needed comfort and found it in each other.

He had been contemplating joining Elenora in the tent – to *sleep* – before the dust storm hit. He'd been dreaming about her and for the first time in a long time, he didn't want to get her out of his head.

Cayder chewed on the inside of his cheek as they traversed the blossoming fields. Elenora hadn't said anything for a while. The longer the silence endured, the more difficult it was to break.

Cayder wished Kema was here; she always knew what to say.

He peered at Elenora out of the corner of his eye; she was clutching her hands together. She looked nervous and confused. She looked like he felt.

Cayder didn't need Kema. He knew what to do.

He reached out with his free hand and took one of hers.

She smiled, and the anxiety that had tumbled around inside him melted away.

———

It took a day to reach the lower slopes of the mountain. The tyres crunched against the rocky ground as the crawler progressed up the incline. The slope grew increasingly steep, until the crawler's wheels could do nothing but spin on the slick surface.

Cayder pushed the lever forward one more time, just to hear the wheels whirl and send a shower of loose rocks down the mountain.

'Looks like we'll need to travel the rest on foot,' he said.

Elenora jumped out of the crawler. 'I wish I still had my weapon.'

'Weapons don't help with climbing.' He smirked.

Elenora nudged him with her shoulder. 'I know that.'

'But seriously. We need Dr Bueter alive.'

Concern crossed her face. 'I'm worried what he might to do to us if we don't have any kind of protection.'

Oh, Cayder thought. *She's scared.*

'We'll protect each other,' Cayder said with a nod.

'Okay.'

His heart leaped at her smile. It felt good to be the one making her smile again. He'd missed it and how it made her entire being shine.

Cayder gestured to the crawler. 'Do we take the tent?'

Elenora shaded her eyes as she studied the mountain ahead. 'I doubt there will be anywhere to pitch it. Let's take the water, food, rope and sleeping bags.'

They crammed their supplies into a backpack that Cayder offered to carry.

'Jey would love this,' Cayder muttered as they began to climb, rock by rock.

'Do you think they're all right?' Elenora asked. 'Leta and Jey?'

'Everything we know about the hullen has to do with protection,' he said. 'I have to believe they're fine.'

She gave him a reassuring smile. 'I'm sure you're right.'

That would be a first.

———

They climbed for hours, until Cayder's hands were slippery with sweat. They'd ditched their cloaks into the backpack after Elenora's had snagged on a rock and nearly pulled her off the mountain.

'Can we rest for a moment?' Cayder asked, puffing. He ran a hand through his locks, and brushed the perspiration from his eyes.

Elenora's cheeks were flushed pink; she wasn't looking at Cayder's face, she was studying his chest, visible through his damp shirt. 'Okay,' she said quickly, turning away from him.

The look on her face didn't help him cool down.

Cayder had never felt like this before; he'd never been popular among the girls at school. Those who weren't put off by his stint at Vardean's reform school had assumed that he and Narena were together. That had never really bothered him, as a relationship was the last thing on his mind. Until he met Elenora.

And for her to feel the same way? It was truly unexpected. And very distracting.

'Can I have some?' Elenora asked.

Cayder blinked. 'What?'

Elenora had been talking and he'd been staring at her like a fool.

'The water,' she said with a chuckle.

He turned away as she drank from the pouch; the image of her was far too befuddling and he could easily slip and fall down the mountain.

Focus, you fool. This is not a date.

Cayder took in the scene below them. The ocean was visible on the horizon like a purple bruise against the yellow sky. The port was a glimmer of silver to the right and to the left of the island was – nothing. A vast white emptiness. Like when a photo shifts during the developing process.

The edge of the world.

Elenora sat beside him; he could feel the heat radiating off her.

She lifted the hair from her neck and started plaiting it. 'It's so hot. But strangely, I'm not getting burned.'

'No sun,' Cayder said. 'No sunburn.'

Elenora nodded to the empty white space to the left of them. 'No life.' She pressed her lips into a grim line. 'When we find Dr Bueter and the others and return to Telene, the Shadow Queen will repair the tear in the veil and Erimen will ensure no one tries to use edem ever again.'

'What about you?' Cayder asked. 'What will you do when we get back?'

Elenora pulled her knees to her chest and wrapped her arms around them. 'I will help my brother in any way I can.'

'But how will Erimen prevent anyone – like the Regency – from creating a new tear? Even with the knowledge that this world is on the brink of collapsing – people might want to continue to use edem for their own gain.'

'I don't believe that.' She shook her head. 'People are inherently good.'

Cayder didn't necessarily think people were 'good' or 'bad', and using edem wasn't a sign of one or the other. *He* had used edem to bring the hullen to their aid; that didn't make him a bad person. And if he hadn't, they would be locked up in Vardean right now. Or dead.

'What about the people who won't listen?' Cayder considered out loud.

'We will need to put some kind of deterrent in place,' Elenora said. 'To ensure people do the right thing.'

'Like Vardean?' Cayder laughed humourlessly. 'Isn't that

exactly where we are right now? How can we stop people from doing something that helps them but hurts others? Especially if they don't see that hurt first hand.'

She studied the crumbling grey rocks at her feet. 'I don't know.'

He sobered, noticing the downturn of her mouth. 'I'm sorry, Elle. I didn't mean to put this all on you.'

She lifted her gaze and her grey eyes were sad, defeated. 'I know, but you're right. People use edem all the time, knowing the results are unpredictable. It doesn't stop them. This world,' she gestured around them, 'is outside what they can see and comprehend. Why would they care about its protection? Even the threat of the end of our own world might not be enough. The growing dark streak across our sky doesn't deter everyone – nor does Vardean.'

'We'll figure it out,' Cayder insisted. 'You're not alone in this.' He wished he hadn't brought it up.

She nodded but didn't smile.

CHAPTER 18

ELENORA

Elenora knew Cayder hadn't meant to be hurtful; after all, what he'd said was true. She felt the weight of the situation resting on her narrow shoulders. It might not be fair, but it was her burden. For every luxury she had been given, for every beautiful dress, every fantastic feast, the counterbalance was the responsibility of being a royal, and that was to safeguard the health and well-being of her people. While Elenora had not been crowned queen, she took her responsibilities to heart.

She wanted to make her parents proud. Like Erimen had.

Elenora and Cayder returned to their climb. The surface wasn't easy to scale; some sections of rock were sharp like shards of ice; others were soft and crumbled underfoot. Elenora's hands were cut and bleeding and her feet were sore, but she didn't stop. Each step higher brought her closer to finding their way back home.

And she had to admit, watching Cayder climb was not the worst way to spend her day. While he didn't have the cultivated bulk of Jey, Cayder's body was muscular, lithe and narrow.

As they climbed, the sweat on Elenora's skin cooled her body, until her teeth began to chatter. She thought it was because they neared the top of the mountain, then something icy splatted onto her cheek.

Snow.

A white mist moved across the mountain, cutting Cayder off from view. As Rusteef had warned, the weather had gone from blisteringly hot, to freezing.

'Cayder!' Elenora called above her. 'Where are you?'

'Don't move,' he replied. 'Let the storm pass!'

Elenora nodded, her teeth chattering. She gripped the rock with freezing fingers as a flurry of white fell from the clouds above.

This is not good, she thought. It was difficult enough clinging to the sheer wall without adding slick ice to the equation.

Elenora's knees started to shake, her lips cracked and her eyes stung as the blizzard whirled around her. She desperately wished she still had her warm cloak on. She closed her eyes and thought of warmer places to stop the shaking in her legs, which were bound to send her sprawling to the ground.

My cloak. A fire. The tent. Cayder's embrace.

It wasn't working. Her legs were trembling.

'Are you all right?' Cayder called down.

No. 'Y-y-yes,' she stammered.

She wanted off this mountain. *Now.*

The blizzard pulled at her clothing and lashed through her hair, releasing it from her braid. The wind howled and the mountain creaked and cracked around her.

'Cayder?'

She couldn't hear his response over the storm, or perhaps he hadn't heard her.

She waited for what felt like hours. Her clothes were saturated from the snow, and she could no longer feel her legs. While she was no longer trembling, she knew this wasn't a good sign.

She needed to move – she needed to bring some warmth back into her bones.

'I'm coming up!' she announced, and carefully reached for a rock above her head. White had clustered around her eyes – her lashes were frozen.

She grabbed the rock with numb fingers and pulled up, lifting her leg to another foothold. When she shifted her weight to it, the rock shattered underfoot.

Elenora screamed as she tumbled, sending a shower of snow and rubble down the mountain.

'Elle!' Cayder yelled from somewhere in the frosted haze above.

Elenora scrabbled for purchase, but she was moving too fast and the snow made everything too slick.

She fell until she struck a large rock, taking the impact on her arm. A white-hot pain lanced through her, and she let out a piercing scream.

Tears mingled with ice and snow as she pressed her forehead to the cliff face. She was safe. She was alive. But she couldn't move. She had prevented her fall, but at what cost?

Elenora glanced up to see the bright yellow sky above. The blizzard had disappeared as quickly as it had arrived. Her body instantly felt warm and sticky from sweat. She should have waited it out – like Cayder suggested.

'Elle!' Cayder scrambled down the mountain. 'Are you okay?'

This time she wouldn't lie. 'No.'

He reached for her. 'Give me your hand.'

Every muscle inside her body screamed. 'I can't.'

'You have to.'

Elenora heard the worry in his voice. She glanced beside her and realised why. She was a breath away from a vertical drop. If she moved slightly, she'd fall hundreds of metres to the ground.

She shook her head. 'I can't,' she repeated. 'I can't move my right arm.' It was still propped up by the rock she had collided with.

Cayder's dark brows pinched together as he studied her position. She recognised that look on his face; he was trying to solve an impossible problem.

She gritted her teeth through her tears. Everything about her arm felt wrong. If she tried to move it, her muscles felt as though they were being ripped from the bone.

'I think I dislocated my shoulder.'

'That's okay,' Cayder said, sounding forcibly calm. 'Keep breathing.'

She sucked in a wobbly breath and then let it out through her teeth. Snow and debris hailed down from above and scattered in her hair.

'Cayder, I'm scared.'

'I know. But I've got you.'

Even though she didn't mean to, she shifted her weight. The rock shelf popped and splintered underneath her. Elenora let out a shriek. Sections of it fell into the chasm below.

This was bad. She couldn't move her right arm to grab Cayder's outstretched hand, nor could Cayder move onto the shelf to grab her – they'd both go down with it.

'What if I...?' she tried to shimmy along the shelf towards him but the chunk of rock between them crumbled. A slab came away from the mountain and smashed into millions of pieces – a preview of what would happen if Elenora were to fall.

'Don't move.' Cayder assessed the gap between them.

'But I thought you said to—'

'I know.'

'Maybe a hullen will come along if I fall?' Elenora said with a nervous laugh. 'Like last time.' It was the only hope she had.

'You're not going to fall.' His eyes burned into hers and she believed him.

'What do we do?'

'We protect each other,' he said with a succinct nod.

Her chin wobbled, and while she felt as unstable as the rock shelf beneath her feet, she forced herself not to crumble.

'*Elle.*' His voice was firm.

Elenora locked eyes with him and she knew: he had a plan. She also knew that whatever he was going to do next, it might fail. Fear was written all over his face, despite his attempts to sound reassuring.

'I'm going to grab your right arm,' he instructed, 'and you're going to jump to me.'

Elenora looked at the space between her and where Cayder stood. It wasn't a large gap, but she suspected the shelf beneath her would crumble if she pushed off it.

'But,' she winced at the thought of it, 'my arm.' She still hadn't moved it. The pain had made her feel lightheaded and disconnected. Perhaps this wasn't really happening. Perhaps she was still asleep in the tent and Cayder had never come to join her.

'I know, Elle. It's going to be very painful.'

She squeezed her eyes tight and let a fresh wave of tears run down her face.

'Don't move until I have a hold on you, okay?' He was already shifting closer to the gap between them.

'Wait!' Even speaking caused a ripple of pain across her shoulder and down her arm. Her chest was tight. 'I don't think I can do this.'

'You can. I know you can. You took down the Regency headquarters, remember? All you have to do is push off once I have a hold of you.'

She *had* to do this. She couldn't die here, not before finding Erimen. 'Tell me when to jump.'

She studied Cayder's face in case he was the last thing she'd ever see. She hoped he could read everything she was too scared to say out loud.

He gave her a short nod and reached across to grab her injured arm by the wrist.

Pain ricocheted through her body. A scream built within her lungs. But she didn't move. She didn't breathe.

'This is going to be the worst part,' he said.

She wept at that. The touch of his skin on hers was enough to make her want to pass out. She couldn't handle any worse.

'I've got you.' He leaned as close as he could. 'Now jump!'

Elenora pushed off the shelf with both feet. The rock crumbled beneath her. But she didn't have time to look down. All she could do was scream as Cayder used her injured arm to swing her body towards him.

She saw the terror written all over his face as she slipped in his grasp.

In a world of light, darkness came calling.

CHAPTER 19

JEY

Jey wasn't going to let the end of the world get him down. Or his injury. Or rather, he wasn't going to let it show that it was getting him down. He was used to suppressing his true feelings. His father never wanted to talk at dinnertime, preferring Jey to stay silent while he read over his reports.

Had his father known that his weapons were destroying this world? Did he care?

Jey was never much for wallowing, even with his own death staring him in the face. It didn't help to dwell on it. It certainly wouldn't fix the situation. Allowing Leta to work with her mother rather than worry by his bedside suited them both. Jey could pretend he wasn't dying as his veins began to turn black, one by one, and Leta could spend quality time with her mother.

Leta, being Leta, had taken it upon herself to find a way back home. She had made it very clear that Jey was to stay put.

Jey had tried to relax, but how could he when the needle sticking into his arm was pumping him full of edem and the only thing keeping him alive? It wasn't like the fate of the world was waiting for Jey to regain his strength, but he wanted to do something useful. He felt somewhat responsible: it was because of his father that this world was rapidly declining.

Back at the Regency headquarters, Jey had been prepared to let his father go, releasing all the resentment, hurt and anger that had tied itself tight around his heart. But now, Jey knew he couldn't turn away. While he couldn't help Leta and her mother – he wasn't a scientist – he *could* try to reason with his father. But not while lying in this bed. He had to get out of here.

Which meant tricking his babysitter/doctor.

'Hey, Doc,' Jey said. 'How many people live down here?'

Dezra turned their pale eyes towards Jey. They looked annoyed; Jey didn't blame them. 'We currently have four hundred and twenty people in our community.'

'Wow.' That was more than Jey expected. 'Four hundred and twenty people who were killed by edem.'

'No one was killed,' Dezra said. 'This isn't the afterlife.'

'I would hope not. I always imagined more crusty bread and fewer debilitating injuries.'

Dezra looked like they were going to crack a smile but then thought better of it.

'When edem affects a person in Telene, the magic tries to return here, and it drags the person back with it.' Dezra gestured to the carved black ice around him. 'But they get stranded, as living matter can't travel back through the veil.'

'No living matter?' Jey asked.

Dezra shook their head. 'No animals or humans.'

'Why is that?'

'We're not sure,' Dezra said. 'Only beings made of edem – like the hullen – can move back and forth.'

'Interesting,' Jey said, although this was not why he had started the conversation. 'Do you have any other patients? Like me?'

'I have an expectant mother and a patient who broke their wrist on a resource expedition.'

'An expectant mother?' Jey saw the opportunity he needed. 'Surely she needs more care than I do. I'm not dying. At least, not today.'

'We have someone looking after her. *You* are the most injured here.'

Great. 'A talented person like you, Doc, must have better things to do than babysit me, right?'

Dezra raised their white eyebrows. 'You are my patient. It's my job to ensure you rest and recover.'

'Look—' Jey raised his left arm. 'I'm strapped to this thing. What trouble could I possibly get into?'

'According to Leta, a lot.'

Jey laughed. 'She's a sweet girl, but she exaggerates. Plus, I'm hungry.'

'I'll ask someone to get you some food from the canteen.'

'Come on, Doc! I want to see the rest of this place. If you tell me to be careful, I will.'

Dezra studied Jey's face and Jey did his best impression of someone innocent and trustworthy and not someone planning to flee.

'Fine. But I'll go with you.' Dezra removed the pouch of edem from the machine and handed it to Jey. 'Don't drop it.'

Jey cuddled the pouch to his side. 'Not planning on it.'

People gawked at Jey as he walked through the icy corridors of the compound; he wasn't sure if it was his tattoos or his veins turning black. Or both.

'I should have put on a shirt,' Jey said to Dezra. 'I don't think this place is ready for—' he gestured to his chest, 'all this.'

'Your clothes were destroyed.'

'Rude,' Jey remarked.

'They were covered in blood and bore the mark of Vardean's guards. We thought it was best to get rid of them. But I can take you to the supply room for a new outfit.'

'Lead the way, Doc.'

Dezra nodded to a woman passing by; she was carrying a pail of bright red apples.

'There are few trees remaining that produce food above ground,' Dezra explained as Jey eyed the apples hungrily. 'We have one apple tree.'

One tree to supply food for four hundred and twenty people – now four hundred and twenty-two? No wonder the situation was bleak.

The supply room was another sad state of affairs. A few backpacks hung on hooks with some rope and nets.

Jey had been hoping to scope a way out of this place, but so far, none of the rooms led up to the surface.

Dezra searched for clothing in Jey's size – apparently, they didn't have many options to fit his six-foot-three frame.

'This is the largest we have.' Dezra handed over a black jumper.

'I can make this work,' Jey said, throwing the jumper over his head. The sleeves were too short and the hem showed a sliver of Jey's inked skin.

Dezra escorted Jey to the canteen next. Jey was starting to feel like a pet being taken for a walk; the tube in his arm was his leash.

'Take a seat.' Dezra nodded to one of the stone benches. 'I'll get some food.'

Jey didn't argue; he was starting to feel lethargic. Perhaps he *should* have stayed in bed like Dezra and Leta had wanted. Or maybe he needed sustenance.

The canteen was full of people; if Jey were to guess, about half the settlement was here. It must have been a mealtime, although Jey couldn't determine whether it was breakfast, lunch or dinner. His stomach didn't care; he was hungry enough to eat whatever was put in front of him.

Jey wound the extra length of the translucent tube around his tattooed wrist, as though it was some kind of bracelet. He knew he should be more concerned about the raised black veins running up his arm, but as long as he was alive, he'd deal with it.

Dezra returned to the table with a bowl of cooked grains and a rosy red apple.

'Thank you,' Jey managed to get out before he started spooning the grain mix into his mouth.

A few people gawked at Jey, while others whispered to each other behind their hands.

'I would have thought they'd be used to new people dropping by,' Jey said.

'Not people who have used edem,' Dezra said. 'Or *look* like they've used a lot of edem.'

Jey tucked his hands into his too-short sleeves. 'Then they're not admiring my beauty.'

'Some people believe we shouldn't be using our edem stores to heal you.' Dezra gestured to Jey's side. 'They believe it should only be used to sustain the few crops we have. They wanted to leave you as you were.'

They wanted him to die.

'Ouch,' Jey said. 'That hurts almost as much as the wound.'

'They were not happy when they learnt your last name. You're lucky Maretta runs this place.'

Jey felt blood rush to his face.

Another world and yet another place I'm unwanted. It was starting to get old.

'So,' Jey said, changing the topic, 'where does this delicious meal come from?'

Dezra pointed to a door behind them. 'We prepare all meals in the kitchen. It's connected to the entryway to allow for ventilation to the surface.'

The surface! Jey controlled his expression so he didn't give his plan away.

'Ah,' he said nonchalantly. 'And the food?'

Dezra's eyes lit up. 'I'll show you.'

———

Around the corner from the canteen was a vast dome chiselled into the black ice. A handful of fruit trees and crops were planted in the ground where a shadowy liquid coiled along the bottom of the plants. The top of the dome was the crisscross of roots from the forest trees above.

'The crops need some light to survive,' Dezra said, nodding to the light filtering through the roots that formed the room's latticed ceiling. 'And edem provides nourishment.'

'What *is* edem, exactly?' Jey asked as they walked through the orchard.

The leaves of the trees were a vibrant green, lush and glossy. Jey had never visited a farm, but he knew what the trees in Telene looked like, and whatever was happening here bore little resemblance to what he used to climb as a kid.

'Edem is a natural element of this world,' Dezra said, rubbing their hands along the branches of a torlu tree, flush with purple berries. 'It's present in everything that originated here. Although, I've found traces in the blood of my patients.'

'People born here?' Jey asked.

'No.' A smile lit Dezra's face. 'It's in blood – everyone's, both in Telene and the people who live here.'

Jey glanced down at the pouch of smoky fluid plugged into his arm. 'How?'

'I'm not sure, but I believe eating the food that is grown using edem leaves a small amount in the bloodstream. Or perhaps it seeps into our cells from the shadows in Telene.'

'Creepy.'

'Not really. Edem is merely the control of time. That's why it's helping you fight off further deterioration of your wound. And that's why it helps the plants grow from seedlings.' Dezra gestured to the orchard. 'Everything here has a level of edem in it. In Telene, it lingers in the shadows; I believe that echo marks are formed because using edem brings what's already in our bodies to the surface.' They pointed to Jey's chest.

'Oh, this? They're just tattoos. I've never actually used edem myself.'

Dezra's brow furrowed. 'Why would you want to appear like you had? Is it no longer a crime in Telene?'

'That's a long story. And while I love telling a good story, I'm not sure you'll enjoy all the nuances. But yes, it is still a crime to use edem.'

Dezra cocked their head to the side as though Jey was a puzzle to figure out. Jey merely shrugged, then winced as the needle in his arm tugged.

———

After the tour, Dezra led Jey back to his room. The pain in Jey's side had decreased – was that from eating the apple and the lingering edem within its flesh?

'Any chance I can see Leta?' Jey asked.

He had promised not to keep her in the dark anymore. And he'd meant it. Even if that meant Leta trying to stop him from escaping this place.

'Rest and I'll see how your vitals look in a few hours,' Dezra said.

Once under the sheets, Jey removed the stolen apple he'd nicked from the orchard.

He'd need more supplies if he planned to go to the surface and search for his father.

Jey's father had avoided him for his entire life, but that was soon to end.

CHAPTER 20

LETA

It had been almost a week since Leta arrived in the underground compound. She was preparing to run another test in the lab when the rings on the edemmeter swirled across its surface.

'Someone's using edem?' Leta asked, approaching Erithe, who watched the rings move with equal parts excitement and trepidation.

Erithe nodded.

'Quickly,' Leta's mother said. 'Let's go run some tests.' She bundled the branches into her rucksack.

She paused at the doorway. 'Coming, Nettie?'

Leta chewed on the side of her mouth. 'I shouldn't leave Jey.' She hated that she had essentially locked him in the recovery room, but she needed him to focus all his energy on getting better.

'What would Jey want you to do?' her mother asked.

Leta didn't even need to think about it.

'Let's go.'

Leta hurried through the cave – drawn to the light in the distance. She sidestepped the waterfall and sucked in a deep breath. While Leta had only been underground for six days, her lungs heaved with relief, as though they had been suppressed this entire time.

One of the hullen was standing by the side of the pool. Leta's heart leaped.

'It's not Cayder's hullen,' her mother said with a sad shake of her head.

'How can you tell?'

'They have different markings on their horns.' She pointed to the creature's horns and the silver streaks that wound around them. 'I was flying this hullen when you were brought in.'

They hadn't talked much about Cayder this past week, preferring to stay busy running their experiments, but Leta needed to know. 'Do you think he's still alive?'

'Yes.' She didn't hesitate.

'How can you be certain? And don't you dare say "hope".'

Her mother's hazel eyes glistened with tears, but she was smiling. 'Why did you investigate my disappearance?'

There were many reasons, but mostly, Leta felt like she would know if her mother was truly gone. She had attended her mother's funeral, stood beside her casket and felt an emptiness. Leta placed her hand to her heart. 'I still felt you.'

'Exactly,' her mother said. She placed her hand over Leta's.

'Cayder's stubborn,' Leta agreed. 'He wouldn't give up without a fight.'

Her mother grinned. 'Sounds like someone else I know. Now, come—' She led her over to the hullen. The creature lowered its head. 'This is my daughter, Leta.' She placed her palm against the side of the hullen's scaly face and closed her eyes.

When her mother dropped her hand, the hullen let out a keening noise and knelt to the ground.

'What did you do?' Leta asked.

'I told it where to take us,' she said. 'Like edem, the hullen communicate via thoughts and touch.'

'You ride them?' Now that the creature had knelt to the ground, she could see a harness strapped on its back.

'It's more comfortable than being carried in its talons,' her mother said. 'Go on!'

Leta approached the hullen warily. Even though she *had* been carried by one before – twice now – she still was cautious around the creature. She found it difficult to see beyond its razor-sharp claws.

Leta gripped the saddle's handle and pulled herself up onto the hullen's back. The creature bristled underneath her; translucent feathers shifting and twitching as though it had an itch it could scratch . . .

Me.

Her mother climbed onto the saddle behind her with ease.

'Here we go!' she whispered into Leta's ear.

The hullen pushed to its feet and sprang into the air like no bird Leta had ever seen – as though it defied gravity. Leta gripped onto the saddle as she slid around. With every beat of its wings, the creature launched higher and higher. Leta wasn't exactly thrilled to be back up in the air, hundreds of metres from the ground. But wasn't this what she'd always dreamt of as a child? To live in a fairytale, her mother alongside her?

But Leta wasn't a little girl anymore; she knew all too well what it felt like to fall, and she wanted to keep her feet firmly on the ground. She squeezed her eyes shut. Her mother, however, let out a *whoop*, clearly enjoying the ride.

'Isn't this wonderful?' her mother asked. 'I fly as much as possible!'

Even though Leta knew her mother had been trying to find a way home, the comment struck her in between the ribs. While Leta and her family had mourned her absence, she'd been here, exploring a new world and enjoying the freedom of flight.

Leta felt the plunge of their descent in her belly, but kept her eyes shut. When the hullen landed, she dared to open her eyes.

Her mother slid off the hullen first and helped Leta down. Leta's knees knocked together as her feet touched solid ground.

'How was that?' her mother asked; her cheeks were flushed and she looked younger, similar to how Leta remembered her.

'Good.' Leta turned away so her mother couldn't see her sour expression.

The hullen had taken them to a clearing between two mountains. Thousands upon thousands of tree stumps were strewn across the valley.

'Is this where you got the branches from?' Leta asked. 'For your tests?'

Her mother nodded.

She had decimated the valley.

'What's that?' Leta asked, pointing to an odd-shaped lump on the horizon.

'Let's find out.'

When they reached the lump, Leta shook her head in confusion. It looked like the sky had opened and delivered a shower of books. Hundreds of them were scattered across the clearing: hardcovers, paperbacks, textbooks and colourful children's tales.

Leta bent down to pick one up; ironically, it was a children's book on myths about the veil – the same book her mother used to read to her at night-time.

They got it all wrong.

'Something must have happened at the library,' her mother said. 'Edem be damned!'

Leta was confused by her disappointment. 'What's wrong?'

'We're too late,' she explained. 'The objects have already been displaced. We need to use edem on this side of the veil while it's weakened.'

Leta nodded to the branches in her mother's pack. 'Should we try? Just in case?'

Her mother shook her head. 'It will be a waste of our supplies. We need to do it at the same time as edem is being used in Telene.'

But how was that possible? Unless someone used edem at the same location as the compound, it would always take them too long to arrive.

That's why it's been seven years, Leta thought miserably.

Leta looked at the books. 'Should we take them back to the compound?'

'No,' her mother replied. 'They're useless.'

'Useless?'

Her mother, the scientist, who had studied two degrees at the same time because she wanted to learn as much as possible, had just called books useless.

'We need food,' her mother explained. 'Machines. Resources. Technology. Even clothes would have been better than this.'

'You're going to leave them here?'

'They might shift back.' Her mother gestured to the bags on either side of the hullen's saddle. 'They're not worth the weight.'

'You used to read this book to me when I was little.' Leta wanted to keep this memento of her old life as a reminder that she could one day return to it. She had spent her entire childhood longing to be reunited with her mother, and now she was, she would give anything to be back at Broduck Manor.

On the front of the book was a faded *Kardelle Library* sticker. It reminded Leta of the hours she'd spent scouring the library for additional information on the veil. Narena would give her a heads-up whenever there were new volumes added to the shelves.

Leta hadn't thought about her friend in some time. She wished she could send a message to let her know she was okay. She glanced down at the book in her hands.

Perhaps she could…

'Do you have a pen?' Leta asked her mother.

'Yes, why?' Her mother pulled one out from her jacket pocket.

'You said only objects move back and forth through the veil, but what if we alter the object?' Leta opened the book to the blank first page and folded down the corner. 'What would happen to the book?'

Understanding illuminated her mother's face. 'It would return to Telene altered.'

'If we wrote a message in this book, could we send it to Telene?'

Her mother looked at the books lying around them. 'There's no way to determine who the message would be received by. If I could have, I would have sent a message to your father seven years ago.'

'Isn't it worth trying? What's the worst that can happen? Someone thinks it's the ramblings of a conspiracy theorist?'

That was what Cayder had always thought about Leta's findings; the Regency had their grip too tight on society to allow for any freedom of thought.

Her mother nodded, considering the idea.

'We can write a message to someone who will believe us,' Leta suggested. She ran her fingertips over the library sticker. Narena was the only other person who knew the truth about the Regency *and* Leta's case. She had also seen the hullen with her own eyes. *She* would believe the message. 'Narena is working at the library over summer,' Leta said, hope igniting within her veins. 'She will be there when these books return!'

The crease between her mother's brows began to ease. 'Narena won't be able help us, but she might be able to find us someone who can.'

'Who?' Leta asked.

'Your father.'

'I don't know about that,' Leta disagreed. Her mother hadn't spoken to her father in seven years and much had changed with Alain Broduck – none for the better. 'He's never believed in anything beyond the veil. How can he help?'

'He doesn't have to believe,' her mother said. 'He just has to do what I tell him.'

'And what's that?'

'Create another tear.'

'How can Father do that?'

Her mother looked uncomfortable. 'The edemmeter is based on an old design: the first Regency machine – the one that created the original tear.'

Leta wasn't surprised to find out the Regency had created the tear in the veil; she had suspected as much back at Vardean.

'But Ferrington is gone.' Waking up in the annihilated town had been the horrifying way Leta had found out. 'And nothing remains of the Vardean headquarters.' The princess had made sure of that.

Her mother gave her an ashamed smile. 'I know, honey. But there's an old base – built years before I joined the Regency – before I was even born. The base where the first weapon was constructed to create the tear.'

'There's a weapon there?'

'A faulty edemmeter,' her mother said with a nod. 'It was the first prototype, but it failed. But I think I know how we could fix our weapon – if your father changes a few settings, I think we could create a new tear.'

Our weapon? Leta wasn't sure she would ever get used to the idea of her mother working for the Regency General.

'I know you don't like the idea of using weapons, Nettie, but it's our best chance to create a doorway home.'

It wasn't so much the weapons Leta was concerned about, but her mother's involvement in their creation.

'How will a new tear help?' Leta asked. 'Don't we need the tear to be created from this side?'

'We do. But if there's a tear we can easily access, we can use all our edem supply in the same location and punch a hole through to the other side.'

Finally, her mother was willing to risk it all.

'Let's do it,' Leta said.

Her mother grabbed a book and began writing.

CHAPTER 21

NARENA

That night after visiting the houseboat, Narena's mind was tangled in a web of darkness and shadowy creatures – creatures that had existed in Telene *before* the veil. *Before* the Regency. But how could that be?

Farrow had been quiet on the trolley ride home, absorbed in her grandmother's diary, running her fingers over the words as though it would help her understand what had really happened. Even though the diary had offered more questions than answers, Narena was happy her friend had something of her grandmother's to hold on to.

Friend – was that what Farrow was now?

Narena hoped so. Farrow wasn't the brash, selfish extortionist Narena had previously thought her to be. And Narena now understood why Farrow had some rough edges; the girl had been through a tremendous amount. Narena was determined to prove she was not like the friends who'd abandoned Farrow's grandmother, or the people who shunned the Pedecs based on the name alone.

When Narena had climbed back into her bedroom later that afternoon and headed down to dinner, her parents only commented on how she appeared to be unsteady on her feet. Narena *had* been exhausted from the day's events. Her mother had sent her straight back upstairs with some bone broth. Narena was thankful that her parents cared so much about her. She couldn't imagine what Farrow's childhood must have been like with the shadow of her grandmother's tragedy trailing her. A tragedy that ran in her veins – in her bloodline – that could never be erased, much like a death echo.

The darkness that tarnished Farrow's childhood was not dissimilar to Maretta Broduck's death, which had forever marred the Broduck family. It had led to Leta's ruin, and ended up bringing her brother down with her.

Narena hoped Farrow wasn't heading for a similar fate.

'What would you do, Cayder?' Narena asked to her quiet bedroom.

But she already knew. Cayder would help. He would seek out the truth, no matter the cost.

———

Narena's father was in a state of panic the next morning after receiving a call from the assistant librarian. Apparently, a vandal had broken into the library overnight.

'I need your help to reshelve the books,' her father pleaded with her at breakfast. 'No one knows the classification system like you do, Re-Re.'

Narena reluctantly agreed, although she wanted to see if Farrow had found anything useful in her grandmother's diary.

When they turned up at the library, the assistant, Marlianne, awaited their arrival. She held a stack of books against her hip like a mother holding her child.

'What's the damage?' Narena's father asked.

Narena struggled to keep up with him as he thundered through the bookstacks.

'I'm sorry, Laino,' Marlianne said. 'A light went out in one of the hallways—'

Narena's father gasped. 'Someone used edem in here?'

Marlianne shot Narena a strange look – one that Narena couldn't decipher. While the two of them had never been close, they had made a good team over the summer. Or so Narena had thought.

'Show me.' His earlier panic was transforming into anger.

They made their way through the library until they reached a roped-off hallway. The light in the ceiling was still out and it was dark. Narena could see edem curling in and around the books like a black sea serpent.

'Why hasn't the light been replaced?' Narena's father asked.

'The Regency hasn't arrived yet to investigate,' Marlianne said with a shrug.

'Why not?'

'Word on the street is that they've been slower to arrive since the riot in Vardean,' she replied. 'Perhaps they're low on agents?'

That didn't make sense; there were agents everywhere these days.

Narena's father pointed to the darkened corridor. 'I'm not going in there until they get here.' As much as Narena didn't trust the Regency, she agreed.

'I think you should go *before* they get here, Laino.'

'That's not normal protocol,' he disagreed, his ears turning red at the thought.

'Trust me. You *need* to go in there.' Marlianne sent Narena a sidelong glance.

What's going on?

Narena's father gazed into the dark and took in a deep, steadying breath.

'If I must.' He stepped over the tape. 'For the library,' he said as though he was walking into a battle.

'What is it?' Narena whispered to Marlianne.

Marlianne frowned at her. 'Why don't you tell me?'

Narena blinked in confusion. 'I—'

'Narena Tanla Lunita!' her father yelled from the shadows. 'Come here. Now!'

That couldn't be good. Her father rarely used her full name.

Narena hopped over the barricade and ventured into the stacks. She was getting better at ignoring edem as it shifted around her like a coiling fog.

'What did you do?' her father whispered when she reached him.

'What do you mean?' she asked.

He nodded to the floor. Narena gasped.

Books were positioned on the ground, spelling out her name in big letters.

'I—' But she came up short.

'You used edem here last night?' her father asked.

'What? Of course not! I've never used edem and I never will.'

'Then who did this?' He gestured to the display before them.

'I don't know!' Narena hadn't been in the library for over a week.

'It's your name.'

'I know.' Was someone playing a prank on her? Who would do such a thing?

'You promise you didn't do this?' her father whispered, looking over to where Marlianne waited. No wonder she had been acting weird; she'd wanted to give them a chance to cover up Narena's involvement before the authorities arrived.

'I promise,' Narena said. 'Why would I write my own name in books?'

Whoever *had* used edem must have fled the scene. But why leave the books behind in her name…

Cursed shadows. It's Cayder! It had to be. But what was he trying to tell her? That he was alive? *That he needed her help?*

'This wasn't me,' Narena said. 'I was home last night. You saw me.'

Her father nodded. 'Of course. I know you would never do such a thing.'

Narena's insides squeezed. She might not have used edem last night, but she had lied to her parents about her whereabouts yesterday.

'We should clean this up before the Regency arrives,' he said. 'We don't want them to get the wrong idea.'

Narena agreed. With the new laws, she'd be thrown into Vardean without question.

'I'll tell Marlianne it wasn't you,' he said. 'It couldn't have been you. You were home with us.'

As soon as he walked away, Narena rushed to the books.

'What are you trying to tell me, Cayder?' she asked them.

The books looked like they had been hastily thrown together to spell her name, as though the person had been in a rush.

Why would he send me a message here? Why not come to my house or the Belch Echoes? Why the library?

Narena picked up a book from one of the stacks and read the cover.

Telene Agricultural Imports and Exports – a History

That didn't mean anything to her. She flipped through the pages, looking for a note, but there was nothing. She went to place the book back down on the pile when she noticed something. An arrow had been drawn on the cover. Pointing to the left.

Elenora picked up the book that sat beside it and saw another arrow on the cover. The next book displayed the same. She continued along the books until she reached the first stack that made up the N of her name. There was an X on the book at the top of the N. Inside the cover, she found an unfinished letter.

Dear Narena,

This is Maretta Broduck. We need your help.

Cayder, Leta and I are stuck on the other side of the veil.

Go to Alain and tell him to get the globe I gave him for his 40th birthday – it should be kept in the dark. The globe contains directions to a defunct Regency base. He needs to set off the weapon that's inside it. He'll need to adjust the settings and remove the fail-safe. That will cause it to implode and create a new tear in the veil. It's the only way we can come home.

Make sure that

Narena stared at the words as though they were written in another language.

Maretta was dead. What did she mean about 'the other side of the veil'? It didn't make any sense. And why hadn't she finished the letter? What did she need to make sure of?

Narena didn't have time to think it over as her father approached. She quickly slipped the book into her bag.

———

After helping reshelve the rest of the books, Narena headed over to the *Telene Herald*. Farrow sat at her desk; her pale skin was almost translucent and her usually bright green eyes were dull and flat. Although she sat at her typewriter, her hands on the keys, she looked as though her mind was miles away.

'Hi,' Narena said, sitting beside her.

Farrow startled. 'Where have you been?' She turned to Narena accusingly. 'It's lunchtime.'

'The library.' Narena placed the book on the table for Farrow to read.

Farrow scanned the letter. 'Who's Maretta?'

'Cayder and Leta's mother. She died seven years ago in an edem-fuelled accident. Although Cayder thought the Regency might have been involved.'

Farrow sat up. 'I'm listening.'

'I think the Regency sent Leta and Cayder to the other side of the veil as some kind of punishment. A kind of purgatory.'

She expected Farrow to laugh in her face, but she tapped a finger against her chin. 'Why do you think that?'

'Cayder has disappeared. He was supposed to break Leta and the princess free of Vardean, but there's been no word since the riot. And now this message appears – from his mother, who is supposed to be years dead.'

'I hate to say it, Narena. But Cayder and Leta might be locked up in Vardean, and that's why you haven't heard anything.' Farrow grimaced. 'Or worse.'

'Then what about this message? Why was my name spelled out with books after edem was used in the library?'

Farrow shrugged – a favourite gesture of hers, Narena had noticed. She was beginning to notice all of Farrow's gestures.

'Leta believed there was an entire world beyond the veil,' Narena said. 'And I know the hullen are real. What if this is where the hullen and the creature that stalked your grandmother came from? Don't you want to find out?'

Farrow huffed. 'You know I do.'

'Then we need to talk to Alain.'

Convincing her parents to have dinner with Alain Broduck was easy. All Narena had to do was mention how lonely Alain must be right now.

That night, the wrought-iron gates of Broduck Manor were left open to receive Narena and her parents. And although the sun wouldn't set for a few hours, Narena shivered as she walked through them.

As a child, Narena had run through the immaculate grounds, chasing Cayder and Leta through Maretta Broduck's prized blooming heart bushes. Their home had always been a happy place to visit, but without the Broduck siblings, the stone structure was as imposing as Vardean.

To announce their arrival, Narena's mother lifted the heavy doorknocker and let it go, releasing a loud clang throughout the manor.

'Re-Re,' her father said, his hand on her shoulder. 'You're shaking.'

Narena crossed her bare arms. 'It must be remnants of the bug I had yesterday.'

Her mother raised her brows. 'Must be.'

The front door swung inward.

'Welcome.'

Alain Broduck had always been intimidating, even though he'd been nothing but nice to Narena over the years. Perhaps it was his large stature, or his position as a senior district judge. Today, however, Narena wasn't daunted by the person in front of her. She felt nothing but sorrow, for he was a sliver of the man he'd once been.

Even though it had only been a week since Cayder and Leta disappeared, and a few weeks since Alain was deposed, he seemed to have lost weight – his skin hanging from his large frame, his cheeks sunken and ashen.

Alain shook hands with Narena's parents and stepped aside for them to enter. 'Come on in.'

Narena felt the pressure of Maretta's message hanging heavily on her shoulders as she walked into the house. Alain didn't know Narena had helped Cayder sneak into Vardean to break Leta free, but like everyone, he likely assumed she knew more than she let on.

The silence of Leta and Cayder's absence whispered through the manor. Even though she knew they weren't there, Narena glanced up the staircase, expecting both siblings to be waiting on the third-floor balcony, ready to welcome their friend into their home.

Tears prickled at the back of Narena's eyes.

'Thank you for having us on such short notice, Alain,' Narena's mother said. 'It's nice to see you, despite the circumstances, of course.'

Narena's father nodded. 'We think of you and your family every day.'

Alain stood stiffly. 'I had the cook prepare tonight's meal. I hope you enjoy it.'

He led them into the formal dining room, where a polished mahogany table sat in the centre, reflecting the twinkling chandelier that dangled from above. The chandelier was mostly decorative; a muted light emanated from ornate sconces on the walls to keep edem at bay. The sconces were twisted iron in the shape of flowering stems, and the glass was the shape of a blooming heart.

A chill crawled up Narena's spine. She had never set foot in this room. Whenever she'd visited, she would retreat to either Cayder or Leta's room, or they would eat their meals in the kitchen.

Alain took a seat at the head of the table. Plates of food were already set; the entrée was a leaf salad with pickled torlu berries and purple-vine tomatoes. Narena's parents sat on one side and gestured to Narena to sit on the other; a gulf of mahogany divided them.

Narena didn't know when to start – *how* to start. She had brought them all here and yet she couldn't find the words to begin. Her parents' gaze was upon her, waiting.

Be brave, Narena, she thought. *For Cayder.*

'Mr Broduck,' Narena said. 'I have something I must tell you.'

Her mother let out a long breath. 'Finally.'

Finally? Her mother knew about Maretta's message? Narena hadn't told her parents, as she had worried they would dismiss it before she had time to bring it to Alain.

'I'm sorry,' Narena said. 'I wanted to tell you all together.'

Alain scoffed. 'Is this some kind of game to you?'

'No!' Narena twisted her hands together. 'I wasn't sure how you would—'

'Where's my son?' Alain thundered, slamming his fists onto the table, shaking the salads. A tomato rolled off Narena's plate and onto the floor.

Narena flinched back. 'That's what I'm trying to—'

'Where were you yesterday?' Narena's mother's brown eyes were narrowed and her mouth set in a firm line. Narena had seen this look before – when her mother was prying the truth from a source. 'We know you weren't sick, Narena. You snuck out.'

Narena's mouth popped open. 'What?'

'It's best you tell us the truth, Re-Re.' Her father's voice was cautious, as though Narena might bolt. She *was* thinking about it.

'Did you see Cayder?' Alain asked, his voice sharp. 'Where is he?'

'You think I was with him yesterday?' Narena asked her parents. Her mother frowned and her father glanced away. Anger burned inside her.

'We don't know what to believe,' her father said. 'After this morning's incident at the library, we know you're involved in something you're not telling us. We were lucky Marlianne called me before the Regency.'

'You and Cayder told each other everything,' her mother said, her look pointed. 'Surely you know where he's hiding.'

Narena gritted her teeth to stop the angry and sorrowful tears. 'I haven't seen him since the day before he went missing. If I had, I would tell you, I promise.'

'Did you know he was going to Vardean?' Alain's fierce expression didn't waver. 'Did you know he planned to break Leta out?' Narena closed her eyes, her head searing with guilt. '*Yes*,' he said, answering her unspoken question. 'I know he was there the night of the riot. He left me a message. A letter to say goodbye.'

She opened her eyes. 'Where did you find the letter?'

'Vardean. The superintendent gave it to me. She lost her job that night, did you know that?' Narena didn't know who he was talking about. 'She saw Cayder, Leta and a few other prisoners trying to escape. Later, she found a letter from Cayder. Soon after, she was escorted out of Vardean, never to return. She thought *I* knew about Cayder's plan. Did *you*?'

The only way for them to trust her, was to tell them everything.

'I did,' Narena admitted, her voice barely above a whisper. 'And I helped him. I wrote an article about the Regency, the existence of the hullen and what happened in Ferrington. Cayder knew Leta would never go free – so he took matters into his own hands and tried to break her out. But that's all I know.'

Her mother gasped. 'You *helped* him? You helped a seventeen-year-old try break his sister out of prison without telling us?'

Her accusation hung heavy in the room.

'You don't understand—' Narena began.

'No, I don't,' her mother cut in. 'You promised you wouldn't be involved in Leta's case after Cayder asked you to lie about the Regency.'

'It wasn't a lie!' Heat rose to Narena's face. 'The Regency *were* behind the fire in Ferrington! I didn't take the stand because I was trying to protect you both!'

Her father's brows were raised high, wrinkling his forehead and aging him more than his forty years. 'Protect us from what?'

'From the Regency!' Narena threw up her hands as though it was obvious. 'Leta was set up. I knew it, and the Regency threatened our family. I did what I had to.'

'I don't know what to say,' her mother said. 'I thought we could trust you. I thought you were smarter than to keep secrets from your parents and place your friends in danger.'

'You *can* trust me!' Narena said. 'I've been trying to help!'

'Your help resulted in my son's disappearance.' Alain's voice was low and dangerous. His eyes were bloodshot and sweat beaded on his brow.

He was blaming her? 'No. That wasn't, I mean – I didn't. I was only trying to—'

'And no one at Vardean will tell me about my daughter,' he

continued. 'I have no idea where either of them are, or even if they are alive.'

'No,' she said again. 'I have a message. It proves everything Cayder was saying was correct.' She grabbed the book from her bag and slid it across the table.

'*Please*,' Narena begged. 'Read the first page. The message is from your wife – it explains everything.' Well, not everything, but enough for Alain to believe her.

Alain stood up, his chair screeching against the polished marble floors. 'Is this some kind of joke?'

Narena shook her head, her entire body trembling. She hated conflict; avoided it at all costs. But she couldn't run away from this situation, much as she might want to.

He *had* to listen to her. 'Please. Just open it. Your wife—'

'Stop!' Alain picked up the book and threw it across the room. 'How dare you mentioned my wife!'

'We're terribly sorry,' Narena's father said, placing his hand on Narena's shoulder. 'Narena has a habit of getting carried away.'

That wasn't true.

'Both my children were lost to this...' he waved his hands '...veil *nonsense*. Do not drag the good name of my late wife into it as well.' Alain's voice was suddenly weary. 'Do you know where my children are or not?'

Narena looked at her book on the floor. She didn't know, not for sure. All that she had was a message from a dead woman claiming to be on the other side of the veil. Perhaps it was a cruel joke after all.

'No,' Narena admitted. 'I don't.'

CHAPTER 22

ELENORA

Death was dark and quiet.

After years of being denied the dark, it was a relief. No pain. No sorrow. No thoughts. No dreams. Nothing but night.

Elenora had dealt with far too much death and loss in her seventeen years. Losing her parents at such a young age had torn her world apart, and then she'd lost the one person who managed to keep her from crumbling.

After Erimen's disappearance, there hadn't been time to process what had happened – she'd been carted off to Vardean moments later. But she had never planned to learn to live without him.

She had never accepted his 'death'. And whether that was because of the strange way he'd disintegrated in front of her, or because of her refusal to accept a world without him in it, she would never find out.

Now that she was gone, how would people mourn her? Perhaps they would never even know she was dead.

CHAPTER 23

LETA

When Leta and her mother landed at the entrance to the underground compound, Erimen was sitting by the waterfall, awaiting their return.

He rushed forward. 'I tried to stop them.'

Leta's mother jumped off the hullen before the creature had even knelt to the ground. She helped Leta down. 'What's happened?'

'Erithe.' Erimen said. 'She called a townhall while you were out. Everyone has gathered to vote.'

'Vote on what?' Leta asked.

Her mother strode towards the cave's opening. 'I can't believe she would pull this the minute I left the compound!'

Leta thought Erithe was a friend of her mother's. 'What's going on?'

'It will be fine, Leta,' Erimen said. His red curls were tousled around his face, as though he'd been running his hand anxiously through them. 'Your mother will sort this out.'

Narena struggled to keep up as they both flew down the icy black stairs. 'Sort what out?'

Her mother didn't turn around. 'Don't worry, Nettie.'

'Don't worry about *what*?' Leta grabbed her mother's hand. A sick feeling swirled inside her. 'I'm not a child anymore, Mother. You can tell me.'

'We don't have time to explain.' She pulled away from Leta. 'I need to get to that meeting.'

Leta had not come this far only to be shut out. 'I'm coming with you.'

'No.' Her mother fiddled with her long, greying braid. 'You head back to the lab.'

'*No*,' Leta threw back at her. 'You can't make me.'

Okay, so *that* sounded childish, but Leta couldn't help reverting to the younger version of herself who hated being left out of things: Cayder and Kema's games, and her mother's secrets.

'Whatever it is,' Leta said. 'I can handle it. I survived a month in Vardean.'

Her mother shuddered to a stop. When she turned around, her eyebrows were knitted together. While she might not like the reminder of how her disappearance had impacted her children's lives, she couldn't hide from it.

'She should come, Maretta,' Erimen agreed. 'It might help to humanise the situation; a face to a name and all that.'

A face to whose name? Leta wondered. *Mine?*

'All right,' her mother relented.

The canteen was crowded; the tables were packed and people lined the walls. King Erimen was right: the entire compound was here, although Leta couldn't see Jey or Dezra among the throng. The room fell silent when they saw the late attendees enter.

Erithe stood at the front of the room, her arms crossed over her chest.

'Hello, everyone,' Leta's mother said with a tight smile. 'Sorry I'm late.'

Leta still had no idea what was going on, but if her mother was angry, then she was too.

People whispered among themselves. Leta felt like she was back in court. Everyone's eyes were on her. Judging.

Erithe let out a frustrated breath, but she stood to the side to allow Leta's mother to be front and centre. Erimen had hung back by the entrance.

'I'm here now,' Leta's mother said. 'You may continue with your vote.'

The room was heavy with tension; those sitting at the front tables squirmed under Maretta's fierce gaze.

'Nothing to say?' she asked.

'Well,' Erithe began, her voice a little shaky. 'I thought it was best to bring the situation to everyone's attention. You've always said that our compound is a democracy, so I thought everyone should have a vote.'

'Of course,' Leta's mother replied. 'Everyone is equal here.' Erithe raised her fair eyebrows at that. 'But as I've pointed out before, we're not merely voting on what rations we have for the week – this is someone's life.'

'It's *all* our lives,' someone from the crowd yelled out. 'This is not just about him!'

Him? Leta looked at her mother but she wouldn't meet her gaze. *Surely they weren't talking about—*

'We have always placed decisions about health and well-being above all others,' her mother replied. 'That's not going to change now.'

'He's not one of us,' another person shouted from the gathering.

Oh no. Leta knew exactly who they were talking about.

'And *who* are we,' her mother replied, 'if not a group of people brought together by circumstance? Just as he has been brought to us.'

'You know it isn't the same,' Erithe said, shooting Leta a sideways glance. 'This is different.'

Leta's mother shook her head. 'How?'

'Because of who his father is!' Erithe hissed.

Leta sucked in a shuddering breath. There wasn't enough air in the room. It was too hot. Too many people. Too many eyes on her.

'She wants to kick Jey out?' Leta croaked.

'No,' Erithe said. 'Of course, I—'

'She wants to stop his treatment,' her mother said with a cutting glance to Erithe.

'But that would...'

Kill Jey.

'Yes.' Her mother nodded.

'Are you kidding?' Leta demanded of Erithe. 'What is wrong with you? Jey is not his father!'

'It's not about that,' Erithe argued, as though she hadn't just mentioned Jey's father as a reason to deny treatment. 'Do you know how much edem will be needed to keep your boyfriend alive? Do you know how many crops that could generate?'

Leta didn't. And she didn't care. This was a person's life! Even if it wasn't Jey they were talking about, Leta could never agree with what they were proposing.

'Months' worth of crops.' Erithe's expression was imploring. '*That's* what it will cost us. Months of food for the entire compound!'

'This is not Jey's fault.' Sweat trickled under Leta shirt and down her back. 'He didn't ask to be shot.'

She couldn't believe she even had to have this conversation. Erithe had been kind to her, but all this time she had been waiting for Leta and her mother to leave the compound, so she could condemn Jey. Was being here not hard enough without her trying to cut Jey's time even shorter?

'No,' Erithe agreed. 'He didn't, but it was his decision to jump through the veil. We—' she gestured to the crowd, 'didn't choose this.'

'You think I'd rather be here than home?' Leta laughed humourlessly. 'We didn't have a choice; we were trying to survive. We didn't know where we were going to end up – but whatever my dreams of this place once were, I never would have thought it would be full of people who were willing to sacrifice a person's life for food!' Leta's voice resounded throughout the room.

'Food *is* life,' Erithe said, her voice quieter – more apologetic. 'You're too young to understand. All you see is your beloved boyfriend. You haven't lived here for more than a week, what do you know?'

'*I* have lived here for seven years,' Leta's mother said with a pointed look. 'I know the pain and suffering we all face. But denying someone treatment is not the answer.'

Leta had seen her mother hold court at parties, always the centre of a crowd. But this was a different woman. This version of her mother was hardened and strong. Leta was proud to stand by her side.

Erithe's mouth twisted into a scowl. 'Then *what* is the answer?'

Leta expected her mother to tell her about the message they'd left Narena, but she only replied, 'We continue to search for a way back home.'

The crowd erupted; some people shouted that there was no way home, and others asked for more information. Some merely wailed in despair.

Leta wanted to clamp her hands over her ears, but she couldn't. This was the world she was living in, and there might very well not be a way back.

'Enough!' a voice boomed from the back of the crowd.

King Erimen marched to the front of the room to stand by Leta. 'When I arrived here, I told you that I was one of you, and that you weren't to treat me any differently. But if I must, I will pull rank.' He squared his shoulders. 'You will not deny this boy his treatment.' He nodded curtly to Erithe. 'I will take a cut from my rations to help ease the burden on our supplies. And we will do our best to ensure this does not impact our future.'

The room held a silent breath.

'Are we all in agreement?' His harsh tone ensured there would be no follow-up questions.

A few people muttered from the crowd about democracy, but no one disagreed.

'Good,' Erimen said. 'This townhall is adjourned.'

Leta couldn't stop shaking. How dare these people plan Jey's demise! Their lives were not more important than his!

'Are you okay, Nettie?' Leta's mother asked after the crowd had left. 'I didn't want you to know about all this.'

'I'm glad I do.' And she was. 'Now I know who I can trust.'

'They're not bad people, Nettie.'

'No, they're not,' Erimen agreed. 'People make poor decisions when desperate.'

Jumping through the veil wasn't the greatest idea in hindsight, although she had been reunited with her mother.

'I have more news,' Erimen said. 'It's not great news,' he added.

What else could there be?

'The missing hullen has been found,' Erimen said.

'Cayder's?' Leta asked.

'We believe so. It was found near the foothills of the west mountains.' Erimen grimaced. 'Dead, I'm afraid.'

Leta covered her mouth with her hand. 'No.'

'That doesn't mean they're in trouble,' he said. 'It could just mean they're on foot.'

Leta's mother squeezed her shoulder. 'It will be all right, Nettie.'

'It will,' Erimen agreed. 'The team have restocked and will continue to search for any signs of—'

'Life?' Leta asked.

Erimen closed his eyes and Leta reminded herself that his sister was missing too. 'We'll find them.'

How could he be certain?

'We can't get too close to the western port,' Erimen explained. 'We've had issues with them in the past and now they attack on sight.'

'You think that's where they are?' Leta's mother asked. 'In the city?'

'It's possible,' Erimen said. 'We're going to send in a team to see if they can find them.'

'I need to go see Jey.' Hot tears ran down Leta's cheeks. While Cayder was still missing, she needed to remind herself that Jey was still here. And that he was safe.

'I think you should wait,' her mother said. 'You're too emotional right now. He doesn't need to know about the townhall meeting and what was discussed. For the time being.'

Leta's mouth fell open in disbelief. 'They're threatening his life! And you want me to hide this from him?'

'It's for his own good,' her mother said. 'Stress works against the body's ability to heal. It's best if he doesn't know.'

Keeping secrets from Jey never ended well.

'Dezra is looking after him,' Erimen said. 'You can trust them. No one will hurt Jey on their watch.'

Leta hadn't even considered that.

This was worse than Vardean.

CHAPTER 24

NARENA

The trolley ride home was quiet. Narena's parents hadn't said a word since they left Broduck Manor.

Regency agents flooded the streets as night closed in. The daytime crowds had dwindled and the remaining stragglers fled at the sight of the Regency's silver cloaks and the sound of their heavy footfall. Narena imagined herself trying to outrun them, but she knew she would always get caught. The day could never outrun the night.

She wasn't a rebel. She knew that her relationship with her parents had forever changed; she was no longer the good girl who caught and rescued birds that had accidentally flown into the library and had gotten lost within the labyrinthine halls. She wasn't the conscientious student who studied every evening and turned in every paper on time. She wasn't the girl who made the traditional Meiyran dinner every Sunday and told her parents her truest feelings and darkest secrets.

Narena stared at her hands, expecting them to look different, but she hadn't used edem to break the law. She had only used the love for a friend. She had done what she thought was right, but she had been wrong. She'd hurt her parents and Alain had suffered.

She wished she could go back and change everything. More than anything, she wished Cayder was here.

———

Her parents said a quick, cold goodnight before Narena carried her weary body up the stairs. She felt a bone-deep tiredness that she had never experienced before and the constant sting behind her eyes threatened to break her fragile resolve.

She hadn't cried for Cayder and Leta since they went missing. Her hope had kept her going. But there was nothing keeping the tears at bay any longer. Her strength had been eroded away.

She pushed her bedroom door open, ready to collapse onto her bed.

But she didn't have time to weep. Farrow was waiting for her.

'You're back!' Farrow jumped up. 'I was wondering if you were going to make it before sundown or if you'd have to stay over at the Broducks'.'

Even the sight of Farrow's bright green eyes and flushed cheeks didn't spike Narena's energy.

'How did you get in here?' Narena asked. Farrow didn't appear to register the defeat weighing down Narena's entire body.

'Window.' Farrow pointed behind her. 'You told me to meet you back here, remember?'

'Oh.' Narena vaguely remembered saying that earlier today, but it felt like a lifetime ago. Narena had been a different person then. Most importantly, she had been a child whose parents trusted her. She had been the person they had raised her to be.

Not true, a little voice said. *They knew you were lying yesterday.*

And perhaps for even longer; Alain had suspected her involvement with Cayder's disappearance from the beginning.

'What's wrong?' Farrow asked.

Narena sat down on the bed and covered her face with her hands. She didn't want to cry. She really didn't want to cry.

Farrow's warm hand pulled Narena's away, but rather than dropping Narena's hand immediately, she held onto it. 'What happened?'

'They didn't listen to me.'

'What?' Farrow's eyes flashed. 'Why not? Did you bring the book?'

'I did, but Alain refused to read it. He thought I made it up.'

Farrow scoffed. 'Why would anyone make this up?'

'He knows I helped Cayder. He blames me for the riot and Cayder's disappearance.'

'*None* of this is your fault.' Farrow was adamant. Narena wished she could borrow some of Farrow's ferocity.

Narena detangled herself from Farrow's grip. 'It is, though. I shouldn't have helped Cayder. And I shouldn't be helping you.'

'What?' Farrow flinched back, wounded. 'You don't want to help me anymore?'

'That came out wrong,' Narena said. 'I *do* want to help, but this is dangerous. Everything about the veil is dangerous. We've been taught that since we were little. Cayder and Leta both suffered for their curiosity. I don't want you to suffer too.'

'Curiosity?' Farrow laughed coldly. 'You think I'm *curious* about my grandmother? About the fact that I've had to lie about who my family is my entire life? You don't want me to suffer?

Well, I hate to break it to you, Narena, but I *have* suffered. And I *am* suffering.'

Narena played with the wrinkle in her skirt and avoided Farrow's intense gaze. 'I know. I want to protect you from getting hurt, that's all.'

Farrow's voice was like a shard of ice slipped between Narena's ribs when she answered, 'I never asked you to protect me.'

'I've already lost my best friend,' Narena said. 'I don't want to lose you too.'

'I'm not Cayder. I'm not his replacement.'

Narena chanced a look at Farrow's face. Two angry red splotches had appeared on Farrow's lily-white skin. Was that what Farrow thought? That she was trying to replace him?

'That's not what I'm doing,' Narena insisted.

'What *are* you doing then?' Farrow pushed off the bed. 'Are you going to help me, or what?'

'Will you ever let it go?'

Farrow blew out a frustrated breath. 'That isn't an answer.'

'I can't go behind my parents' backs again. We tried to get the message to Alain but he wouldn't listen.'

'The man can't find his own children,' Farrow snapped. 'I'll pass on his assistance, thanks.'

'Doesn't that tell you that we're out of our depth?' Narena asked. 'Alain was a senior district judge and he's lost everything. What hope do we have to stand against the Regency?'

'None, if you sit at home protected by your parents and pretend that nothing is happening. *I* don't have that luxury.'

'I'm not pretending,' Narena muttered.

Farrow leaned in close and Narena sucked in a breath. 'You. Are.'

Narena didn't know what to say. But she knew she had to make different choices. She couldn't repeat the same mistakes that she had with Cayder.

'You pretend to help,' Farrow said, 'but you let other people tell you what to do. You allow them to move you around in their game for their own use. You're a pawn, Narena! Cayder used you to get what he wanted. He didn't care about the consequences to you or your family. He used you like you don't matter.'

'That's not true! Cayder was – *is* – my best friend and I helped him because I care about the Broducks. Like I care about you!'

'Not enough to defy your parents.'

'I told you; I did that already and it didn't help Cayder, did it? We shouldn't be taking this on alone. You could ask your mother—'

'Stop.' Farrow held up her hand. 'Just stop. Why do you think I came to you? You certainly weren't my first choice.' That hurt, but Narena gritted her teeth to stop tears from forming. 'My mother won't even entertain the conversation with me. *You* were my last chance.'

'Are you going to give Mr Grotherman my article?' Narena asked. 'Are you going to expose me?'

'You're really asking me that?' Farrow shook her head sadly. 'You don't know me at all.'

She turned on her heel and headed for the window.

Narena could have sworn she saw tears on Farrow's cheeks as she scaled down the side of the house and into the night.

CHAPTER 25

ELENORA

Life came back in pieces.

First, there was pain.

Elenora's shoulder felt as though her arm had been ripped from its socket. *Surely death erases all pain?* she thought.

Next came touch.

Something soft moved across her forehead. *Are they preparing my body for burial in the royal tombs? How did I get back to Telene?*

Then came sound.

Someone whispered her name. *Cayder's voice – but he isn't dead, is he? Unless we both fell off the cliff.*

Elenora opened her eyes.

Finally, her sight returned.

Cayder's blurry face hovered above her. She blinked away the darkness, but it didn't completely retreat.

'Elenora!' Cayder cried. 'You're awake!'

'What happened?' Her voice was hoarse, throat sore.

'You jumped,' Cayder said, 'and I pulled you towards me.

You must have passed out from the pain in your shoulder. You've had a fever.'

She remembered the pain – so much pain. There was still so much pain. And heat. Her body felt like it was on fire. Cayder wiped her forehead with a scrap of damp material.

She took in her surroundings, realising the darkness was not due to her poor vision.

'Where are we?'

'A cave,' Cayder replied. 'The wind started to pick up again and I thought it was best to find shelter while you recovered.'

'How long was I unconscious?'

'Two days or so – I'm not sure.' She could tell from the tightness around his mouth that he had feared the worst keeping vigil.

'I'm sorry.'

He looked appalled. 'Why are you apologising? You're the one who's injured.'

'I didn't mean to make you worry.'

'When you care about someone, you share the weight of their worries. Do you think you can move?'

'I'll try.' Perhaps her head would stop spinning if she sat upright.

Cayder placed his arms around her waist and propped her up against a wall. Even though he did his best not to jostle her, the movement caused a wave of pain down her arm. She leaned to the side and dry retched.

'We need to reset your arm.'

She was so sore she couldn't wipe the spittle that ran down her chin. 'What?'

'We need to put it back into the socket.'

She squeezed her eyes shut. She wanted to return to that quiet place of darkness and no pain. She didn't want him touching her arm.

Cayder's thumb circled around her uninjured arm in soothing motions. 'It's the only way, Elle.'

She knew he was right. At fourteen, Erimen had dislocated his knee. He had been chasing Elenora through the castle and had slipped on a rug and had fallen to the unyielding stone tiles. Elenora had felt guilty for weeks.

'Drink this first,' Cayder said. 'You need to hydrate.'

He held the water canteen up to her lips. She took a small sip, waiting to see how her stomach would react. When she didn't immediately feel the need to bring it back up, she drank some more.

'How do you know what to do?' Elenora asked.

'We had a choice of playing sports or studying sport medicine at school.' Cayder smiled wryly. 'I was never much for team sports.'

'Then you've done this before?'

'Not exactly,' he admitted. 'But I've read about it.'

She couldn't breathe properly, let alone climb in this much pain. This was the only way. But how could she survive the pain when Cayder's gentlest touch sent searing spikes down her arm and up her back and neck?

'It will make it feel better,' Cayder said. 'Promise.'

'I trust you,' she said.

He moved her arm out in front of her and she bit down on her lip to stop from crying out. The metallic taste of blood filled her mouth.

'Deep breaths,' Cayder said.

She was in too much agony to reply.

He continued pulling on her arm until it was straight out in front of her. The reprieve was instant as the ball of the arm rolled back into its socket. Tears of relief fell down her cheeks.

Cayder folded her arm across her chest so her hand was resting over her heart. 'That's it,' he said. 'You did it.'

Elenora laughed. '*You* did.'

'You'll have to keep it in a sling for a while to let it heal.' He wrapped a torn section of his cloak around her arm to keep it in place.

'Thank you.' She pushed to her feet with her free hand. It wasn't impossible, but it also wasn't easy. 'I don't think I can climb like this.'

'I don't expect you to.' He shook his head. 'We're already two days behind schedule. We'll head back to the meeting point and find Kema and Rusteef. They can continue searching for Dr Bueter here.'

Elenora hated being the reason they had to go back, allowing Dr Bueter to get further away from them – or return home.

'The cave continues through the mountain,' Cayder said, picking up his pack and hers and slinging them on his back. 'It travels downward.'

'What if there's a dead end?' She didn't like the sound of walking through a cold, dark cave.

'It's our best way down with your arm like that.' He nodded to the sling. 'I'm sorry, Elle. I'm not strong enough to carry you.'

Elenora placed her free hand on Cayder's arm. 'Didn't we agree to stop apologising to each other?'

He gave her a soft smile that made her want to kiss him. So she did.

'Let's get off this mountain,' she said.

CHAPTER 26

JEY

Jey managed to convince Dezra to let him visit Leta in the lab after she hadn't spent the night by his side. He needed to see her.

Both Leta and her mother were hunched over a desk. The whir of the edemmeter gave him pause, reminding him of the last time he saw his father. He had thought – and hoped – it would be the last.

'Hello, Nettie.'

Leta leaped from her chair and ran to him. He could tell she wanted to throw her arms around him, but reconsidered after eyeing the pouch of shadowy liquid attached to his side.

'You're up!' Leta forced a grin.

Her large, usually bright eyes were dull. It looked like she hadn't slept. He hoped she hadn't spent the entire night working.

'How do you feel?' she asked.

'Better,' he said. 'Doc says my vitals are strong, so they gave me a day pass to see my two favourite Broducks.'

Maretta pushed her thick black-rimmed glasses to the top of her head. 'Don't tell Cayder that.'

'Oh, that wouldn't surprise him.' Jey grinned.

Leta tangled her fingers with his, her warmth grounding him. He could almost forget about the world falling down around them.

Almost.

'What have I missed?' He shuddered as he took in the room – it looked so much like his father's office. Would he ever be free of him?

'I flew on the back of a hullen yesterday,' Leta said matter-of-factly.

'Really?' Jey asked.

'Leta was a natural,' Maretta said, pride in her voice.

This surprised Jey. As much as he loved Leta, she wasn't the most coordinated person. There was a reason why she was always covered in scratches and bruises after sneaking out of her bedroom to come and meet him.

'Any word on Cayder and the others?' Jey asked.

Maretta and Leta exchanged a worried look. 'We believe they might be in the city.'

There's a city?

'Not to sound ungrateful,' Jey said, 'but why are we living down in an ice cave if there's a city we could be calling home?'

'It's a small city,' Maretta corrected, 'more of a town than sprawling Downtown Kardelle.'

'Oh-kay.' Jey was lost, which wasn't something he usually liked to admit.

'We're not welcome there,' Maretta explained. 'The city was built by those who were born here.'

'They're the people you've clashed with in the past?' Jey asked.

'That's right. Erimen is sending in a team to see if he can find Cayder and the others without causing any further conflicts.'

The city would be a good place to start searching for his father.

'And how's, ah—' he waved his hand toward the edemmeter, 'the experiments going?'

Maretta scrunched her nose, looking very much like her daughter. 'We don't know yet. Unfortunately, our research has involved a lot of trial and error. And patience.'

'We sent a message to my father,' Leta said, some colour flaming across her pale cheeks. *She's hopeful.* 'We're trying to create another tear.'

'When one simply isn't enough,' Jey said, 'you must have another.'

Maretta chuckled. 'I like you, Jey.'

To which Jey replied, 'Most people do.'

Jey glanced down at Leta to find her brown eyes sparkling with unshed tears. 'You okay, Nettie?'

She smiled up at him. 'I never thought I'd have my two favourite people in the same room together.'

'Don't tell Cayder,' Jey joked.

Maretta rose from her desk to wrap her arms around her daughter. 'I'm happy too, honey, despite everything.'

'I hate to break this up this beautiful moment,' Jey said. 'But can I steal Nettie?'

'Of course, steal away,' Maretta said with a wave of her hand. 'I've been trying to get Leta to see more of the compound.' She gave her daughter a sad smile. 'It's not all doom and gloom down here.'

Jey led Leta to the orchard. His mission was twofold: steal food supplies and inform her of his plan.

'Wow,' Leta said, taking in the domed room full of lush green trees. 'This place is beautiful.'

'Dezra gave me a tour the other day. I thought you might like it.'

Leta held out her arm to touch the leaves as they walked along the rows of iridescent trees. 'Have you ever seen colour like this?' she asked.

Jey shook his head. 'It's unnatural.'

'Or magical,' she suggested with a smile. 'I wish I had my paints with me.'

'Here—' Jey pulled off his coat and laid it on the hazy dark earth. He lowered himself to the makeshift blanket, careful not to pull at the tube in his arm. Edem swirled around him with its curious tentacles. 'Sit with me.'

Leta didn't move. 'What's going on, Jey?'

He lifted his shoulder. 'I thought we were due for a date night. It's been a while.'

'It's never night here.'

'A day date, then.'

'Come on, Jey.' Leta placed her hands on her hips. 'Out with it.'

Jey tilted his head back with a sigh. 'Can't I just do something nice for you?'

'No.'

Jey laughed. Of course she saw through him; she always had. She was too smart, and that was one of the many reasons he loved her.

'Fine. I will tell you everything if you sit down and enjoy my picnic.'

'Fine,' she repeated. She slumped to the ground and shoved a purple torlu berry into her mouth begrudgingly. 'Delicious. Now tell me.'

'I need to find my father.' He set his jaw, ready for her rebuttal.

'Why would you want to do that? I thought you didn't want to see your father again?' Leta's nose crinkled as though she smelled something bad. At least now she could talk about his father without retreating into herself. She had moved on from that night in his father's office, although she still subconsciously hid her echo-marked hands in her long shirt sleeves.

Jey fished for her hands and latched onto them. 'Because my father is the only way out of this mess. And I don't mean just me and my whole situation here.' He nodded to the bag of edem.

'Mother and I are working on it,' Leta said. 'We sent that message to my father.'

'That plan involves a lot of waiting and hoping. Forgive me if I'm a little impatient to get back home.'

Leta jutted out her chin, pulling her hands free. 'You think I don't want to go home?'

'I know you do, but I could be helping. Me lying in a bed is not helping anyone.' Especially not Jey. He couldn't rest while everyone else was doing everything they could to return home.

Leta's expression softened. 'I know this must be hard for you, Jey, but you don't need to be the one running off to save us. Remember what happened the last time you tried that?'

He huffed a laugh. 'If we're keeping score: I remember *both* of us ending up in Vardean.'

'You can't go gallivanting around, hoping you'll run into your father.'

'First of all, I don't gallivant,' he said, 'I strut with purpose. Secondly, I'm not hoping to run into him, I *will* track him down.'

'Oh?' She raised an eyebrow. 'And how will you do that?'

Edem be damned. She had a point.

'I'm not sure yet. But this city your mother mentioned is a good place to start. As you're aware, my father loves to conquer other people's cities.'

'Jey…' she leaned into him, pressing a kiss to his cheek. 'You need to rest. You're wounded.'

'And that's not going to change.' His tone soured. 'No amount of rest will heal this wound, remember?'

Leta appeared crestfallen. He didn't want to pull the pity card, but he would if it helped her understand. He lifted up his shirt to show the veins across his chest, now also black.

'We promised to tell each other the truth,' he reminded her. 'And I'm telling you that I can't lie in that bed and wait for help to come. I need to do something. My father is the key to all this. He knows the way out of here. He can help us.'

Leta chewed on her bottom lip. 'What makes you think he would? After everything that's happened?'

'I'm still his son. Much as he might want to pretend that I'm not. If he sees me like this,' Jey pointed to the edem pouch, 'he'll help.'

'The man who was happy to leave you rotting in a cell?' She

shook her head. 'I don't know, Jey. I don't want him to hurt you again.'

'He can't hurt me anymore.'

Leta pressed her lips together sceptically.

'I don't care what he thinks about me. But I care about you. I care about going home.'

'And *I* care about you staying alive.'

Jey tapped the pouch of edem strapped to his side. 'With this, I'm all set.'

A fearful expression crossed her face.

'Nettie?' he asked.

'Hmm?'

'I'm telling you the truth,' he said, 'but have you been telling *me* the truth?'

She glanced away. 'What truth, exactly?'

Jey's stomach twisted. 'The whole truth.'

'Well—' She considered him. 'Maybe not the *whole* truth.'

'I know.' He gave her a grim smile. 'Nobody wants me here. They don't want me using their precious edem.'

Leta sucked in a breath. 'Who told you that?'

'Aside from the fact that people practically boo and hiss when they see me?' Jey laughed humorously. 'Doc told me.'

'I'm sorry, Jey. Mother and I didn't want you to worry about it. And you don't have to – Dezra has your back. So does King Erimen. Nobody is going to hurt you.'

'I know,' he said. 'After all, I'm used to being unwanted.'

She shifted closer, carefully avoiding the edem tube. 'You're wanted here with me.'

'I can't stay. Not with this stuff in my arm. I thought I'd solve two of our problems: leave *and* find a way home.'

'Oh, Jey.' She sighed, running her hand along his jaw. 'I can't talk you out of this, can I?'

'No.'

Her expression changed instantly. 'Right then. When are we leaving?'

'We?' He shook his head. 'You're staying here with your mother. You've got your tests to run.'

'Are you kidding?' She looked like she wanted to shake him. 'You're not going out there on your own. I'm not leaving you again.'

'Nettie,' he said soothingly. 'You already killed my father once; I doubt asking for his help with you by my side is the best plan.'

She pouted but didn't argue.

Jey lay on his back and pulled Leta down with him, tucking her into his uninjured side. They stared up at the black tangled roots above them. Light from outside penetrated through the gaps and looked like stars streaking across the night sky.

'It's okay here,' Leta admitted. 'But only because I'm with you.'

Jey didn't like hurting Leta, but this was something he had to do. Not only for her. But for himself.

'I'll be back. Promise.'

Leta leaned over him, her face obscuring the lights above. 'That's not a promise you can make.'

'If I don't try,' he said, swallowing sharply, 'I'm going to die here.' It wasn't a question. His wound would never heal. When all edem disappeared from this world, he would be the first to go. And he couldn't continue to ask everyone to sacrifice edem that should be used on their crops, just so he could survive. But he also wasn't a martyr.

He would do this. He would go off on his own. He would find his father. And he would make this right.

'I can't lose you,' Leta whispered.

He cupped her cheek. 'You won't. I'll be annoying you for many years to come.'

Her tears fell onto his face as she leaned over to kiss him.

'I love you, Jey.'

'I love you too, Nettie.'

CHAPTER 27

CAYDER

The long days Cayder had watched over Elenora's prone body were among the worst of his life. He couldn't leave to find help, knowing she would likely die without his care. Her body's shuddering and shaking as she fought the fever had been his only tether to sanity; she was alive and he would ensure she stayed that way. He barely ate or drank and he didn't sleep. He watched and waited and begged the universe to give her back.

He had done his best to help her break the fever, using nearly all their water to keep her cool, waiting for the moment she would open her grey eyes and bless him with her smile once more.

When she finally stirred, he had wept in relief. Before her eyes were fully open and focused on him, he quickly composed himself. He didn't want her to know how bad it had been, and how close he'd been to breaking. Knowing Elenora, it would only make her worry. Now, his only focus was to guide her safely out of this mountain and get some proper medical attention.

Cayder and Elenora moved slowly through the cave that tunnelled downward, hand in hand. It wasn't the best plan, but Cayder was out of ideas. They moved carefully in the dark, Cayder out in front to spot any obstacles ahead. He didn't want Elenora to knock her arm; he recalled that the first few days, even weeks, were vital for healing, and that the shoulder could easily be dislocated again before then.

Cayder hated seeing Elenora in so much pain. Every wince, hiss or yelp was like a needle to his heart.

'How are you feeling?' Cayder asked over his shoulder.

'The same as the last four times you asked me,' Elenora replied with a chuckle. 'I'm fine.'

'Let me know if—'

'I will.'

He swallowed his concern. If only she knew how many times he thought he'd lost her. Every time her body stilled for too long, or she took in what sounded like a final rasping breath. He would forever be haunted by those days in the cave. He was changed. He would never take Elenora for granted again.

He cared for her more than he thought possible. He'd realised that he might in fact love her.

But he couldn't tell her that. Not now. They needed to focus on getting out of there.

They continued, only speaking when Cayder needed to inform Elenora of a rock to step over or a low-hanging boulder to manoeuvre around. The wind whistled through the gaps between the rocks as another storm picked up outside. Cayder wished they had listened to Rusteef and steered clear of the mountains.

'Shall we take a break?' Cayder asked.

'Yes.' Relief was evident in her voice.

He turned around in the tight space, handing Elenora her canteen. Her eyes were large in the dark, her hair wet with sweat. He wanted to pull her close and never let her go. Instead, he pressed his hand to her forehead. 'You're hot.'

'I'm fine.'

He shook his head. 'You need something for the pain.'

'I'm not in pain.' But she winced as she said it. 'My arm feels better.'

'But not good.'

She gritted her teeth. 'No.'

If he were to guess, they were about halfway down the mountain. Their descent was slow as the tunnel wasn't very steep.

'Do you feel faint?' he asked. She couldn't lose consciousness again. He wouldn't survive it.

'Just warm.'

He wasn't sure that was a good sign. The book he'd read had only instructed how to relocate the shoulder; he couldn't recall anything about how it should feel afterwards. Although he was fairly certain the book advised seeking proper medical care as soon as possible.

Elenora handed her canteen back to Cayder. 'We should keep going.'

'Before we do,' he said, 'there's something I have to – er – go and do.'

Elenora tilted her head. 'Are you blushing, Cayder Broduck?' She chuckled. 'Goodness, I hope you weren't holding on because of me.'

'No.' Although he had been.

'I won't look, promise.'

Cayder was more concerned about the lack of ventilation and echoing in these caves, but now wasn't the time to worry about his dignity.

'Right,' he said. 'I'll go do that then.'

Elenora chuckled again. 'Ouch,' she said. 'Stop making me laugh.'

He moved quickly, not wanting to leave Elenora by herself for long.

A part of the tunnel split into a fork and Cayder moved deeper into the mountain for some privacy. He hadn't realised how desperate he had been; his mind was starting to play tricks on him. He imagined he could hear the trickle of water. He turned one more corner before stopping to relieve himself.

Something dripped down the back of his neck.

He hadn't imagined the sound of water.

Behind him was the darker space of another tunnel opening. It curved off to the right before broadening into a vast cavern carved into black ice. Light streamed in from a crack in the rocky ceiling, shining down into a pool of shifting black liquid that seemed to have melted from the ice.

Edem.

And around the pool were dozens of hullen, their eyes glowing in the dark like bats.

'*Oh,*' Cayder said. 'Hello.'

The hullen remained still, regarding him with their curious pearlescent eyes. Their razor-sharp talons gripped the lip of the pool as they drank the dark liquid.

Huh, Cayder thought. *So that's what the hullen eat.*

'Cayder?' Elenora called from down the tunnel. 'Everything all right?'

The hullen bristled in response to Elenora's voice. The closest creature let out a thunderous hoot, shaking shards of ice loose from the walls. They splashed into the edem pool.

Cayder placed his hands up. 'It's okay.'

These hullen didn't look like the creatures that had helped them in the past. They looked angry. As though he had stumbled into their home and pissed on their doorstep.

'I'm sorry,' Cayder said, abashed.

The hullen snuffed frosted air from their snouts. The one closest to him unfolded its silvery wings to block the entrance to the pool.

They're guarding it, Cayder realised. *They think I'm here to take their edem from them.*

He took a step backwards. 'I'm sorry,' he repeated. 'I'll go now.'

'But you just got here,' a familiar voice said.

A tall, pale man with blond hair appeared from an adjoining passageway. His usually neat beard was scruffy around his sneering face.

Dr Bueter.

He held a drawn bow that looked like it had been constructed from a branch and some wire. The arrows had been fashioned out of sticks with sharpened tips.

Thwick!

Dr Bueter released the arrow into the hullen. The hullen screeched, and scrabbled over each other to flee.

Thwick!

He sent another arrow into the pack, clipping the wing of one of the creatures. The hullen took flight, spiralling around each other within the cavern. One took to the sky through a small gap in the ceiling, knocking shards of ice free to tumble into the edem pool below. The others burst through the ceiling and away.

'Dumb birds,' Dr Bueter muttered. He turned to Cayder, his bow by his side. 'You thought you'd find salvation on this side of the veil?' He chuckled darkly. 'You're a fool.'

'Where's my mother?' Cayder growled. 'Where are you keeping her?'

'As I told you back in Vardean: I don't know where she is.'

'I don't believe you.'

'That's up to you,' he said. 'It doesn't make any difference to me.'

Cayder huffed. 'Don't you care about anyone?'

'I care about my nation.'

'If that were true, then you would stop what the Regency is doing,' Cayder said. 'You would stop the use of edem altogether.'

'Look around you, boy,' Dr Bueter said with a sneer. 'Do you think I can do anything from here?'

'Can't you cross back over?'

'I already told you; there needs to be a part of you still in Telene to bring you back through. When your sister tried to kill me using edem, my team brought me back before I completely disappeared.'

Jey had told Cayder that his father was nothing but bone fragments when he fled the scene.

'This time, your friends destroyed my base and all my weapons,' Dr Bueter said bitterly. 'My team took me to the Kardelle County hospital, but no normal medicine can stop the progression of an edem wound. And here I am.'

Realisation dawned. 'You've never been here before.'

'You can only be in one place at one time, after all.' Dr Bueter gestured to the cave.

'There's no way to go home,' Cayder said, feeling ill. 'You're stuck here.'

Dr Bueter shouldered his weapon. 'As are you.'

'But we need to make things right,' Cayder urged. 'We need to fix this. Save our worlds.'

'What are you talking about?' Confusion wrinkled Dr Bueter's forehead.

He doesn't know.

'This world is ending,' Cayder explained. 'And if it does, so will ours.'

Dr Bueter waved his comment away. 'This world has existed for centuries. It's not going anywhere.'

The Shadow Queen was right; the Regency had passed down the secret of the veil world throughout the years, plotting for the moment they could use edem again.

'You sent the royal fleet to meet with the other nations, pretending to discuss the reopening of the borders, but the Regency is under your orders to attack once on shore.'

'Who told you this?'

'The Shadow Queen.'

'You've met her?' He raised his fair brows. 'I thought she was a myth.'

'Just like a world on the other side of the veil is a myth,' Cayder said contemptuously. 'The Shadow Queen is the only person who can fix the veil. And you need to dismantle the Regency. But we need your help to get home.'

Dr Bueter shook his head. 'I wish you'd listen to me; there's no way back.'

'That can't be true.'

'Maybe if I had my team and my weapons.' He held out his bow. 'But I only have *this*.'

'There has to be a way. Come back with me and speak to the Shadow Queen.'

Dr Bueter scoffed. 'I'm not going anywhere with you, boy.'

'What's your plan, then?' Cayder asked. 'Wait out the end of the world?'

'*This* is my plan.' Dr Bueter waved his hand at the edem pool. 'Those pesky hullen keep edem all to themselves.' He pulled some seeds out of his pocket and placed his hand in the pool. He closed his eyes, his lips mumbled something unintelligible. When he pulled his hand up from the black water, he was holding a bushel of carrots.

'Carrots? Are you kidding me?'

Dr Bueter took a bite out of one of them. 'I can't exactly pull a roast chicken out of here now, can I?'

Of course! Edem controlled time – allowing Dr Bueter to grow the carrots from his seeds in the blink of an eye.

'Where did you get the seeds?' Cayder asked. His stomach grumbled at the sight of the bright orange vegetables.

'I know of a place,' he said.

Clearly, he wasn't going to share the details.

'What are you planning to do with me?' Cayder asked, gesturing to Dr Bueter's bow.

Dr Bueter laughed. 'You think I'm going to kill you?'

'Um…' Cayder had assumed so; now he wished he hadn't suggested it.

'You're just a kid,' Dr Bueter said. 'Younger than my son. Worthless.'

'You're going to let me go?'

'You're nothing to me. Just like Jey.' Dr Bueter's face contorted when he said his son's name, and Cayder realised he didn't mean it. Not completely.

'Your son jumped through the veil with me.' Cayder knew better than to mention Elenora.

Dr Bueter let out an exasperated sigh. 'Of course he did. He never could keep out of trouble.'

'Don't you care about him at all?'

Cayder hadn't had a great relationship with his father since his mother died, but he knew that his father loved him regardless and would be worrying about where he was right now.

'My son causes more trouble than he's worth,' Dr Bueter said bitterly.

Cayder was glad Jey wasn't here; he didn't deserve to be spoken about so callously, especially by his own father.

'As nice as this chat was,' Dr Bueter said, 'it's time for you to leave.'

Cayder needed Dr Bueter to come with him. 'No.'

'Go!' Dr Bueter gestured with his bow. 'Get out of here before I change my mind.'

He dismissed Cayder as though he was nothing.

Cayder wanted to make the man in front of him pay for everything he had done, especially to his mother. But he couldn't force Dr Bueter to follow him and he had no leverage.

'Fine,' Cayder said. 'But this isn't over.'

Dr Bueter huffed. 'I think you'll find it is. You destroyed your only chance of freedom when you destroyed my base.'

CHAPTER 28

ELENORA

Elenora had thought it was sweet that Cayder wanted privacy, but enough time had passed that she began to worry. Then she heard the screech of the hullen.

Elenora moved as swiftly as possible with her arm in a sling. Without Cayder to guide her, she tripped and scraped her shoulder against the wall. But there wasn't time to lick her wounds.

The tunnel opened up into a wide cavern where she found Cayder and Dr Bueter – a rudimentary bow in his hands. Cayder stood with his back to her and she could see the tension in his shoulders. She knew how he felt; he wanted retribution for his mother, and although Elenora could relate, there was much more at stake.

The Shadow Queen needed Dr Bueter alive.

Dr Bueter didn't appear to notice her arrival. She slunk out of sight behind hanging onyx stalactites and crept to the other side of the glittering black pool. Her shoulder screamed at her as she moved. She would deal with the consequences later.

Cayder was talking about Jey when Elenora approached Dr Bueter from behind. She glanced around for something to use, wishing she still had the weapon she'd stolen from Regency headquarters, which was now lying on the ocean floor.

Fortunately, some fractured rocks had fallen from an opening in the ceiling. Elenora picked up a black stone in her free hand. It was cold as ice. She closed her eyes and pictured Erimen, standing on the castle isle's pebbly shoreline.

Let's see you beat this! he would say, before whipping his rock across the water's surface.

Elenora opened her eyes, weighed the rock in her hand and cocked her wrist back, like her brother had taught her so many years ago. She let it fly.

The rock hurtled through the air and struck Dr Bueter in the back of the head. Elenora had only planned to distract Dr Bueter so Cayder could run, but the man fell forward in a heap.

'Lucky I'm left-handed,' she said to Cayder with a grin.

Cayder rushed to her side. 'Are you okay?' His eyes roamed all over her body, searching for additional injuries.

'I'm fine. Are you?'

'I am.' He nodded to Dr Bueter on the ground. 'Thanks to you.'

'We protect each other, right?'

He grinned and grabbed Dr Bueter's bow and arrows.

While Dr Bueter was unconscious, they tied his hands together with some rope from their packs. Elenora had to admit it was satisfying tying up the man who had imprisoned her in Vardean.

Cayder shouldered the bow and placed the arrows in his pack. He pulled on the rope, jolting Dr Bueter awake.

Dr Bueter groaned and opened his eyes. His gaze locked on Elenora. 'Great,' he mumbled. 'You again.'

'Trust me,' she said, gritting her teeth. 'The feeling is mutual.' She had hoped never to see the man's face again, especially when she had yet to find her brother.

Dr Bueter noticed the bow in Cayder's hands. 'What are you going to do to me?'

'You're our ticket home, remember?' He yanked on the rope and Dr Bueter was forced to stand.

'I told you,' Dr Bueter said with a shake of his head. 'You can't go back. None of us can.'

Elenora looked at Cayder for an explanation and Cayder shrugged. 'He said we can't return as there's no part of us on the other side. He's lying.'

Dr Bueter had made the same claim back at the Regency headquarters when Elenora demanded he rescue her brother.

'I'm not,' Dr Bueter replied. 'Why would I be here if that wasn't the case?'

'Let's see what the Shadow Queen says about that.' Cayder prodded Dr Bueter in the back with the edge of the bow. 'Now walk.'

Dr Bueter led while Cayder and Elenora followed behind. They returned to the fork in the tunnel and headed down the other path. It didn't take them long to find the cave's exit; they had been closer to the ground than they'd realised.

They walked for half an hour before they spotted the crawler in the distance. When they reached it, it was covered in sand, but overwise it was just as they left it.

'It only fits two people,' Elenora said. 'What do we do with *him*?'

'We could always tie him to the back,' Cayder suggested, a devious gleam in his eyes. 'Make him run behind us.'

He deserves worse, Elenora thought.

'I thought you need me alive,' Dr Bueter said.

Cayder rolled his eyes. 'Let's tie him in the trunk.'

After they were certain Dr Bueter couldn't break free, Cayder brushed the sand off the crawler's console and jumped into the driver's seat. He pushed the lever down as far as it could go. While each bump pained Elenora's shoulder, she enjoyed Dr Bueter's yelps as he knocked about in the back.

'How are you feeling?' Cayder asked.

'I'll survive,' Elenora said. 'Don't slow down.'

It took a few hours to return to their meeting spot with Rusteef and Kema. The ocean stretched out before them, and Elenora felt some weight lift from her bruised shoulders. Now that they had Dr Bueter for Myrandir, they could focus on finding her brother and the others.

'Over there—' Cayder pointed to Kema and Rusteef's crawler. A tent was erected beside it. Elenora wondered how late they were; it was impossible to tell the time in the ever-present day.

Kema bounded out of the tent at the sound of their arrival. Her face split into a wide grin.

'Boy Wonder and the princess return!' Kema hollered.

Cayder stopped the crawler in front of the tent. 'And not empty-handed,' he said.

Kema's eyes widened when she saw who was tied in the back. 'No kidding. And here I was about to give you a talking-to for being late.'

Cayder ran around the crawler to help Elenora out.

'Oh no!' Kema exclaimed, noticing her sling and bandaged cheek. 'What happened?'

'It's a long story,' Elenora said. 'I'm fine.'

'She dislocated her shoulder,' Cayder said with a shake of his head. 'She's not fine.' He placed his hand on her non-injured arm. 'She needs to see a doctor.'

There was something different about the way that he'd looked at her since she woke up in the cave. An intensity that made her stomach swoop and palms sweat.

'Oh.' A slow smile spread across Kema's face as she looked between the two of them. 'Now I see why you were late.'

Cayder's cheeks reddened. 'Where's Rusteef?'

'He was worried about you two,' she replied. 'He walked back up to the cliff to see if he could spot your crawler. He should be back soon.'

'He was worried about us?' Elenora was surprised; she'd never seen anything but a snarl on his face.

'Sweet, right?' Kema said. 'He's a real softy once you break down his walls – or in my case, spend days asking incessant questions until he caves.' She shrugged. 'He's a good guy.'

'Poor Rusteef,' Cayder murmured.

'I think you mean, poor Kema,' she retorted. 'I drew the short straw while you two were off on a romantic journey of discovery.'

This time Elenora's cheeks warmed. Was it that obvious what had transpired between them?

'Elenora dislocated her shoulder and Dr Bueter shot at me,' Cayder said.

'I didn't shoot at you,' Dr Bueter argued. 'I shot at the hullen. Now,' he struggled to sit upright, 'get me off this infernal contraption!'

Kema leaned forward, her expression fierce. 'A bit uncomfortable, are we? How inconvenient it must be to be held against your will.'

Elenora was glad Dr Bueter didn't have access to his weapon; his gaze was deadly enough. 'You're the guard who helped these misfits escape Vardean.'

'Misfits?' Kema shook her head. 'I prefer crew. Better yet: *League*. And you bet I helped them. They were wrongly imprisoned.'

'Even Leta Broduck?' Dr Bueter spat. 'She tried to kill me.'

Cayder rounded on him, his eyes aflame. 'Too bad she failed.'

Elenora grabbed Cayder's hand in her free one. 'Don't bother, Cayder. He's not worth it.'

'And you, Princess, are the worst of them.' Dr Bueter locked her in his icy gaze. 'I was worried about your brother and all this time I should have been worried about you.'

'We don't need to listen to this,' Cayder said.

Elenora agreed. They had fulfilled their end of the deal. Rusteef could take Dr Bueter back to Myrandir.

Kema held Dr Bueter down while Cayder tied another strip of his cloak around Dr Bueter's mouth. 'There,' Kema said, patting his chest. 'Much better.'

While they waited for Rusteef's return, Kema cooked Elenora and Cayder some food.

'Hate the taste,' Kema said, serving them a small cup of fish stew each. 'But it's better than an empty belly.'

Elenora didn't mind the fishy flavour. It was the gelatinous texture she couldn't get used to. But as Kema said, it was better than nothing.

'Here, eat this.' Kema offered a green roll to Elenora. 'This is the last one we have, but you need it more than we do.'

Elenora took a bite. It was crumbly and tasted similar to seaweed, but it wasn't too dissimilar from a bread roll back home.

'Thanks, Kema,' Elenora said.

Her face lit up. 'It's quite fun to order a royal around.'

'I'm not really a royal,' she replied, to which Kema raised an eyebrow. 'Not here. I'm just like you.' Elenora chuckled. 'Actually, I'm nothing like you. Where do you get all your energy from?'

Kema shrugged. 'I've never needed much sleep. When I was a kid, my dad would give me a puzzle before bedtime so that when I woke after a few hours, I had something to do. As I got older, I snuck out of the house. It started as a game to see if I could avoid the Regency agents, then it turned into something else.' Her expression fell. 'Can I check your shoulder? I had to do some medical training at Vardean. I might be able to help.'

'Of course,' Elenora said.

Kema carefully untied the sling and pain flared down Elenora's arm.

Kema noticed her grimace. 'Hold your wrist to your chest.'

Elenora closed her eyes and took deep breaths as Kema's fingers skimmed across her collarbone.

'It's very bruised, but that's not unexpected considering the injury.' Kema pressed carefully around the joint. 'The arm is sitting in the shoulder socket. Well done, Boy Wonder.'

Elenora opened her eyes to see Cayder watching her intently. He let out a relieved breath. 'I was worried I might have done more damage,' he admitted.

Kema clapped him on the shoulder. 'You did the right thing, considering you were out on your own.'

Cayder nodded and his brows pinched together, the warmth to his ochre eyes dimming. Something had happened in the cave while she was out that he hadn't told her.

'Cayder was amazing,' Elenora added as Kema retied her sling. 'He was so calm.'

'Me?' Cayder huffed in disbelief. 'Elle's been in so much pain but managed to bring down Dr Bueter with one rock.'

Dr Bueter grumbled around his gag as though he wanted to dispute it.

'Thank you, Kema,' Elenora said.

Kema's expression soured and she glanced away.

Concern clutched at Elenora's heart. 'What's wrong?'

'Kema?' Cayder asked, trying to get his friend to look at him. 'Is there something you're not saying? Is Elle going to be okay?'

'Yes. Yes, of course,' she replied. 'This is not about Elenora's shoulder.'

'Then what is it?' Elenora asked. 'You can tell us.'

Kema chewed on her bottom lip and Elenora thought she was going to deny her request.

'I will, Princess. I owe it to you. However, I just want to say that I really like you, and I hope you remember that.'

Elenora was confused. 'I like you too, Kema.'

'You might not after this.' Kema held out her arms, criss-crossed with echo marks.

Elenora had wondered how they came to be, but there hadn't been the opportunity to ask. She grabbed one of Kema's hands to reassure her. They had all used edem in the past, not knowing what the consequences for this world would be. It wasn't Kema's fault.

'As I said, I was a restless child.' Kema pressed a fisted hand to her mouth as though it hurt her to continue. 'And when I started sneaking out, I ran into some other like-minded people.'

Elenora understood the desire to escape; she had felt the same way living on the castle isle. She nodded for Kema to continue.

'But then I fell in with the wrong crowd,' she said. 'The rebels.'

Elenora stopped breathing.

'I was there. The day your parents died. I—' Kema glanced away. 'I helped the rebels. I *was* one.'

Elenora was sure even her heart stopped beating.

Kema had been a part of the day that had forever altered Elenora, taking away a piece of her that she could never get back.

'Sorry doesn't even begin to cover what I did,' Kema said. 'But I am. So very sorry.'

At some point, Elenora had dropped Kema's hands.

'Your echo marks?' Elenora asked, her voice hushed with shock.

Kema nodded once. 'Death echoes.' The fractured lines on her arms were a reminder of how the cobblestone road had shattered when the rebels had tried to control edem at the same time. Kema's death echoes were those of Elenora's parents.

Elenora's mind spun. 'Is that why you helped us escape Vardean? Because *you* should be locked away?'

'Partly,' Kema said, exchanging a look with Cayder. 'And because I knew it was the right thing to do. I didn't join the rebels to hurt anyone. I thought *we* were helping Telene.'

'By breaking my parents' laws,' Elenora said.

Kema's brown eyes glistened with unshed tears. 'I never would have joined the rebels had I known what was going to happen.'

'People always say that,' Elenora muttered. 'Hindsight doesn't erode culpability. *You* joined a group that was actively working against the royal family, *you* used edem knowing the results were dangerous.' Elenora's body went rigid, twinging her injured shoulder. 'It was my birthday. You turned what should have been a joyous day into a nightmare. A nightmare that I have never woken from.'

Kema clasped her hand over her mouth. 'I'm so sorry.'

Elenora couldn't look at her any longer. All she could see was blood spilling across the floor of the trolley as she watched the life fade from her parents' eyes. She whirled around to Cayder. 'Did you know this?'

'I'm sorry, Elenora,' Kema said.

'*Princess*,' Elenora corrected. 'I'm still your princess. And without my brother, I will be your queen.'

'Come on now,' Cayder said. 'Kema didn't mean to hurt—'

'Then you *did* know.' Elenora sucked in a shaking breath. Shock didn't mar his handsome face, only remorse.

Cayder had known and he hadn't told her! He had known something important about the most devastating moment in her life and had kept it a secret. They had promised to look after each other. How could he?

'I did,' he said carefully. 'But Kema has devoted her life to helping those in Vardean. She's helped us. And she regrets everything that happened.'

Even with anger coursing through her, Elenora knew Kema was not a callous person. In fact, Elenora thought she was truly one of the most impressive and lovely people she had ever met. When Elenora was younger and planned to attend university on the mainland, she hoped to befriend someone like her.

But now...how could they be friends when she couldn't even look at her?

'I can't,' Elenora said, glancing around, looking for an escape route.

She needed space.

Where was Erimen? She needed her brother now more than ever. Only he would understand the pain this revelation and betrayal caused.

'You found Dr Bueter,' Rusteef remarked. He had returned to camp while they were distracted. 'Well done.'

Elenora pushed herself to her feet with one hand, ignoring Cayder's offer to help.

'Take Dr Bueter back to the queen,' Elenora said. 'It's time to find the others.'

CHAPTER 29

NARENA

Narena hadn't slept at all after returning from Broduck Manor and her subsequent fight with Farrow. When she stumbled downstairs for breakfast, she found her mother poaching fowl eggs. Narena pulled a chair out from the table; the sound of its screeching across the stone floor reverberated in her head, sending sparks of pain through her temples – the beginning of a migraine.

'Morning,' Narena mumbled.

Her mother was studying the eggs as though they held some kind of secret message.

She glanced up. 'Did you say something?'

Narena's heart squeezed. The distant look in her mother's eyes told her that her mother was still angry.

Narena sighed dejectedly. 'It's nothing.'

Her mother placed some eggs on Narena's plate. 'Your father left early for library. He still has some loose ends to tie up with the Regency about the break-in.'

Great.

Her mother didn't want to talk with her and her father was avoiding her.

The eggs were like rubber. Her mother never ruined poached eggs; it was one of her specialties. Still, Narena said, 'Delicious. Thank you, Me-Me.'

After a few minutes of silence, Narena couldn't take it anymore.

'When will you forgive me?' she asked.

Her mother paused at the stove but didn't reply.

This was worse than she thought.

'I'm so sorry.' A tear fell down Narena's cheek. 'I understand if you never want to speak to me again.'

'What did you say?' Her mother abandoned her eggs and approached the table.

'I just wanted to know when you might forgive me – even if it's years – just so I'm prepared.'

'Oh Narena—' Her mother wrapped her arms around her daughter. 'I have forgiven you.'

'You have?'

'Of course. Your father and I were surprised, that's all. You're so . . .' Her voice trailed off.

'Horrible?'

'No, Re-Re!' She scolded then chuckled. 'The opposite, actually. We're used to you doing the right thing. Sometimes we forget you're only seventeen.'

Narena studied her mother's light brown hands on hers. 'What does that mean?'

'You *will* make mistakes; you will get in trouble. That's part of growing up. But we've been so lucky that you've always made the right decisions. We've all made mistakes at your age – in fact, I still make mistakes!'

Narena pressed her lips together, unsure if her mother was joking. 'You never make mistakes.'

Her mother nudged her chin with her hand. 'Of course I do, Re-Re. And I know you've been struggling since Cayder went missing. It's my fault; I should have checked in with you more.' Her expression fell.

'What's wrong?' Narena asked, fear creeping up her spine. 'Did they find Cayder?'

'Alain's house was broken into last night.'

'What?'

How could that be? They were just there.

'It happened early this morning,' her mother said. 'I'm going over to help. Alain's alone in that big house of his, and now he's not only lost his children, but a sense of security. After everything that happened with Leta and Cayder, he doesn't even want to call the authorities. He doesn't want the Regency coming around.'

Who would do such a terrible thing? 'What did the thief take?'

'Not much,' her mother said. 'Just an item of personal value. A gift from Maretta.'

Oh no...

'It's strange,' her mother continued, 'the thief broke in and walked past all the expensive silverware only to steal an antique celestial globe.'

Narena knew exactly who that thief was.

Narena headed to Farrow's house before work. It wasn't a market day and Penchant Place was quiet. Still, Regency agents stood guard, in case of any trouble. Narena scurried towards the flaking red door.

Narena knocked and waited for the sound of footsteps.

'Farrow?' a voice called out.

The front door flew open and Narena was faced with a woman shorter than her, greying auburn hair in curls around her pale face. Her eyes were brown, but a familiar shape.

Mrs Pedec. Farrow's mother.

Mrs Pedec's face fell when she saw Narena at her door. 'Who are you?' Her expression transformed from disappointment to suspicion.

Narena knew what she looked like: a journalist-in-training – her notebook under her arm, a pen in hand. She shoved them into her backpack and softened her features, which could come across as shrewd when she was on a mission.

'I'm Narena Lunita. I work with your daughter.' Yesterday, she would have introduced herself as Farrow's friend, but their friendship seemed elusive now.

'You know my Farrow?' Mrs Pedec's expression changed again in a flash. She grabbed Narena's elbow and pulled her inside. 'Where is she?' Her brown eyes were both pleading and fierce. Narena could see where Farrow got her intensity from.

'What do you mean? I came here to see her.'

'She didn't come home last night.'

A hot stone landed in Narena's stomach. Narena assumed Farrow had gone from her house to Broduck Manor to steal the globe, but what had happened then? Narena's mother hadn't mentioned Alain catching the thief.

Which meant what?

'Farrow's missing,' Narena said. It wasn't a question.

Mrs Pedec nodded. 'Do you know where she is?'

'No.'

'I went looking for her this morning in all her usual places. But she wasn't there. She – she must be—' Tears flooded her words. She covered her face with her trembling hands.

'I'm sorry.' Narena was apologising a lot lately. And her friends kept disappearing.

This was what Narena had feared. This was what she had wanted to protect Farrow from. But Farrow was already in too deep, even before they met. Narena hoped Farrow hadn't been caught sneaking home by the Regency agents. If she had been, she would be in Vardean by now.

'If you see her,' Mrs Pedec said, 'tell her to come home. I don't know how long her supplies will last.'

Wait a minute… 'Supplies?'

Mrs Pedec let out an exhausted breath. 'She took food from the pantry, but not much. Enough for a few days.'

Hope flared inside of Narena. Farrow had *planned* to go missing. She must be out looking for the Regency base that Maretta's message had mentioned. But where?

'What else did she take?' Narena's hand automatically strayed to her backpack, itching to take notes.

'A change of clothes,' Mrs Pedec said with a shrug. 'Some books.'

Farrow wouldn't go anywhere without her books.

'And her bathing suit.'

Ah.

Narena knew exactly where to go.

———

Narena didn't tell Mrs Pedec about her theory of Farrow's where-abouts in case she was wrong. She found herself boarding the trolley to Rusterton rather than heading into the *Telene Herald* office. She would go to the houseboat, find Farrow, and bring her home before the end of the work day. Her parents didn't even need to know.

She might not be able to find Cayder, but she *would* find Farrow.

The walk from the trolley station out to the houseboat took longer than Narena had remembered. Her mind was spiralling with the possibilities of what she might find at the lake. A shadow creature. A body. Or worse.

Nothing.

What will I do then?

Narena focused on putting one foot in front of the other and not allowing her dark thoughts to latch together like a spider-web, tangling in her mind.

The road through the bush was dusty and dry. There hadn't been any rain in the area for weeks and the ground cracked and crumbled underfoot. This time, Narena wore sandals and a wrap dress over her bathing suit, ready to enter the water if she needed to. Not that she *wanted* to.

By the time she reached the pier, her heart was shuddering inside her chest.

'Farrow?' Narena called out. 'Are you here?'

She listened for a reply, but the only response was the sound of birds and the gentle lapping of the water against the mooring. The wood creaked as Narena approached the houseboat, careful to avoid the missing planks.

'Farrow?'

Narena really didn't want to climb into the houseboat by herself. She peered through the broken window.

'Farrow?'

Something splashed behind her. Narena spun around, ready to face whatever creature had emerged.

Farrow's flash of red hair appeared before she arose from the depths like a sea siren.

'Narena?' Farrow wore goggles on that made her green eyes appear twice the size. 'What are you doing here?'

Narena forced her hand from her heart and laughed to release the tension from her body. 'I was looking for you!'

'Congratulations,' she muttered. 'You found me.'

Farrow ducked her head back under the water and swam to the pier. She scaled the ladder as though Narena wasn't even there. Narena followed Farrow through the window and into the houseboat; she was surprised to find it littered with burning lanterns.

'Are you living here now?' Narena asked, noticing a blanket draped over a chair, which had been turned upright since her last visit.

Farrow huffed. 'Like you care.'

'You know I do,' Narena said. 'What are you doing here?'

'I thought that would be obvious. Aren't you the one who wants to become a journalist?'

Narena ignored the gibe. 'We didn't find anything in here.'

Farrow pulled a long dress over her wet bathers. 'Not yet.'

'You can't wait around and hope that something changes.' She wanted to shake some sense into Farrow.

'I don't have anywhere better to be.'

'You have a job!' Narena said. 'Not to mention your mother is worried sick.'

'Go home and tell her I'm fine.' She crossed her arms over her chest and cocked an eyebrow.

'I'm not leaving you alone.'

'Funny. You were happy to kick me out of your house last night, and now you want us to stick together?'

Narena dragged her hands down her face. She had never met anyone so vexing. 'I want what's best for you.'

'Well, Narena.' Farrow spread her arms wide. 'Take a look around. This is it.'

Unfortunately, Narena didn't have the strength to forcibly drag Farrow out of the houseboat, so instead, she righted a dining chair and sat down. 'If you're staying, I'm staying.'

'Do whatever you want. I don't care.'

Narena hoped that wasn't true. She found herself caring more and more about what Farrow thought. More than she had ever worried about another person, aside from her parents, of course.

'About last night...' Narena ventured. 'Did you go to Alain's house and steal his globe?'

'Who's asking?' Farrow tilted her head. 'You or Alain?'

Narena couldn't believe she was asking that. 'Me. Your friend.'

Farrow stood and headed into the kitchen. When she returned, she was holding a metal globe the size of a beach ball. 'Take a look for yourself.'

Narena studied the map of Telene carved into its surface. There were no obvious unusual marks.

'I don't see anything,' Narena admitted.

'I didn't either,' Farrow said. 'At least, not immediately. But when I got home, I remembered Maretta's message about it being kept in the dark, so I threw a blanket over the globe and something caught my eye.' Farrow turned off all the lanterns until they were surrounded by darkness. This time Narena was too distracted to worry about the edem around them. The globe was illuminated, as though a light source was hidden within. Something Alain never would have noticed in his office due to the permalamp, but in the dark, there was no denying the sketch of a building in the middle of Lake Rusterton.

'The old base is *here*?' Narena asked. 'Where?'

Farrow tapped the goggles on top of her head. 'That's what I've been trying to find out.' She traced her fingers over the globe. 'The markings are not to scale – so the building could be anywhere within the lake.'

'You think it's underwater?'

'Doesn't it make sense?' Farrow's green eyes glowed from the globe's illumination. 'What haunted my grandmother was in the water. Perhaps the Regency base is also there and they unleashed something during one of their experiments!'

'Why would Maretta hide the location of the base on the globe?'

'As a back-up, in case someone needed to find it. Maybe her kids *did* find it!'

Another reason *not* to go searching. Cayder and Leta had never returned. But Narena couldn't abandon Farrow now.

'Fine,' she said. 'Let's go swimming.'

———

They spent the remainder of the day searching the lake for a hidden doorway, a cave or anything to indicate a secret base. Aside from rocks and the occasional shoe, the bottom of the lake was surprisingly bare – only some fish and a few weeds.

Narena headed back to the mooring when she couldn't bend her wrinkled fingers.

'Where are you going?' Farrow asked, surfacing from another deep dive.

'To get something for us to eat.'

The sun was soon to set and Narena had a choice to make: return home or stay the night, further provoking her parents.

Narena found two nut butter and torlu jam rolls in Farrow's bag. Farrow was waiting for her on the mooring when she returned. They sat with their legs dangling over the pier.

'I don't think you brought enough food,' Narena said, handing over a roll.

Farrow took a big bite and spoke with her mouth full. 'I wasn't expecting company.'

Narena returned the roll to the paper and offered it back. 'I'm sorry—'

'Stop it.' Farrow pushed the roll towards her. 'I'm glad you're here.'

'Really?'

'Really,' Farrow said with a nod. 'And I'm sorry I called you a pawn. You're not. You're a good friend.'

'Thank you.' Warmth spread through Narena's chest. 'I'm sorry I said you were blackmailing me.'

Farrow bumped her shoulders against Narena's. 'I was, so fair call.'

Narena laughed. 'At least you're honest.'

'Honesty is the key to a good relationship,' Farrow said. 'Don't you think?'

A piece of nutty roll got stuck in Narena's throat. She swallowed it down. 'Relationship?'

Was Farrow saying what Narena thought she was saying?

'Yeah,' Farrow said with a shrug. 'You have to be able to trust your friends.'

Friends. Usually, Narena liked Farrow's careless shrugs and nonchalance, but this time, it stung.

'Of course,' Narena mumbled into her bread. 'Friends.'

She shouldn't have expected Farrow to think any differently. No one paid attention to her, aside from Cayder, and they had always been more like family. They had kissed once – when they were fourteen and neither of them had kissed anyone yet – just to see what it was like. Cayder was handsome, and a good friend, but there had been no spark – no urge to do it again. Narena hadn't felt anything similar to what her mother's romance novels suggested – the ones Narena had stolen to read at night under her reassuring permalamp.

Narena hadn't felt the urge to kiss anyone since then.

But she wanted to kiss Farrow.

'Hey—' Farrow said, bumping Narena's shoulder again. 'Something wrong?'

'I'm fine.' Narena tried her own careless shrug. 'Just tired from swimming, I guess.'

'Are you sure that's it?' Farrow twisted to face her, rather than staring out at the lake as the sun set beyond it.

'Yes.' But she didn't mirror Farrow's position.

Farrow's fingers found Narena's chin and gently turned it to hers. When their eyes met, Farrow was close. So close.

Close enough to kiss.

Narena's heart thudded as she leaned forward and pressed her lips against Farrow's. Farrow returned the kiss, tangling her fingers in Narena's waterlogged locks.

When Farrow pulled away, she smiled. 'I've been wanting to do that since we met.'

'Really?' Narena's entire body was pleasantly warm and tingling. She definitely hadn't felt that when she'd kissed Cayder.

'There was more than one reason I wanted to be your friend,' Farrow confessed. 'Your connection to that Regency article was a good excuse to talk to you at work.'

They kissed until the sun went down.

CHAPTER 30

JEY

N ow that Jey had Leta's blessing – or as close to it as he was going to get – he needed to escape the compound. While he wasn't *actually* being held hostage, he knew Dezra would try to stop him – for his own good, of course. And Dezra was still wary of Jey, for which he couldn't blame them. After all, Jey *was* lying.

Jey had picked apples from the orchard with Leta – only a couple, as he knew supplies were low – and hoarded some bread from lunch – tucking it into his sheets rather than tucking *in*. If anyone were to pull back Jey's blankets, they'd find an assortment of objects: food, rope, and a backpack Leta had given him.

Now he needed to find himself some transportation to the city.

After another one of Dezra's check-ins, Jey shoved his stash into the backpack. He unhooked his edem pouch from the machine, tucked it into the front pocket of the backpack and slid it onto his back. He threw his coat over the top, concealing the backpack underneath.

As he headed out the door and into the corridor, he nearly ran straight into a young girl. She couldn't have been more than six years old.

The girl scuttled backwards, her mouth agape. 'You're him!'

'I am,' Jey replied.

'The boy from the other side,' she whispered, her brown eyes large. 'What's it like?'

'You were born here?'

The girl nodded, her curly pigtails bobbing either side of her round brown cheeks. 'Yep!'

'It's like this place,' Jey gestured around him, 'but less icy and dark.'

'*Ohhh*,' she said, as though that answered all her questions.

How odd, Jey thought. To this girl, Telene was the mysterious land on the other side of the veil.

'Right,' he said. 'I'd better be off. Got to go save the world and all that.'

The little girl giggled. 'You're funny.'

Jey smirked. '*I* think so.'

Even though Jey had been unconscious when he'd arrived at the compound, Dezra had unknowingly pointed out the exit during their tour when they told Jey that the kitchen was connected to the entryway. Jey had stored that bit of information for later use. And that time was now.

Jey passed through the empty canteen and into the kitchen. A Meiyran man with hair slicked back into a bun stood at a wood-fuelled stove, stirring what looked like mashed root vegetables. The smell made Jey homesick for his mother's cooking.

'May I help you?' the man asked.

'You may,' Jey replied with an innocent smile. 'I was just wondering what's on the menu for tonight?'

The man rolled his eyes. 'You're already taking our edem, now you want more of our food?'

Okay, wrong question.

'Never mind. I'll just leave, shall I?'

'Wait!' the man ordered. 'Don't move.'

The cook brandished a cutting knife in Jey's direction and blocked the way out.

Jey threw up his hands. 'I'm not going to hurt you.'

The cook pointed at Jey's short sleeves and the tattoos visible on his arms. 'Your echo marks say otherwise.'

Jey was really starting to regret getting inked. 'Calm down, mate.'

He wasn't in a position to fight someone, but he knew from his experience in Vardean that he couldn't show any weakness. He looked around for a weapon and spotted a collection of branches behind him. Grabbing one, he spun towards the cook, gritting his teeth through the pain.

'Let me pass,' Jey said, his voice low.

The cook didn't stand down. 'You're not meant to leave.'

Jey huffed. 'I thought you didn't want me here? Make up your mind.'

'Pass that over,' the cook gestured to Jey's edem pouch, 'and you can go.'

'No deal.'

If the man thought Jey looked like a threat, then Jey would become a threat. He drew himself up to his full height, ignoring the pull in his side, and lifted the branch. Jey wasn't planning to hurt the cook, but he didn't need to know that.

Jey could see the fear flick across the man's face as he closed in. The cook ducked out of the way.

'Smart choice,' Jey said.

He pushed through the door and into the foyer. He had to be quick now, before the cook sounded an alarm that Jey was on the loose like some dangerous beast.

Jey slipped the thin branch into the side of his bag and bounded up the stairs. It was the most energy he had exerted for days, and sweat collected on his brow. When he reached the lip of the cave, he blinked into the light like a nocturnal creature seeing the sun for the first time.

A hullen stood by the edge of the waterfall. Its translucent feathers shifted as it took in Jey's appearance, and it stomped its taloned feet. Jey didn't have time to question his good fortune; he would take anything he could get.

'Hey, strange bird.' Jey held his palms up to show he meant no harm. 'Want to go for a ride?'

The hullen bristled and let out a hooting noise into the sky.

'Shhh, mate,' Jey approached the creature with hurried but quiet footsteps. 'Don't you remember me? You saved me and my girl.' He held out a hand for the creature to sniff. 'We're friends.'

The hullen leaned its scaly snout towards Jey's outstretched hand, and he wondered briefly if the creature would take a bite out of it. Instead, it reached towards Jey's back, nudging the hump under Jey's coat.

'You hungry, mate?'

Jey pulled off his coat and grabbed an apple from his backpack.

'I guess I can sacrifice one. For you.' He held out the apple on his palm.

The hullen lowered its snout to the apple, sniffed it, then knocked it to the ground.

'Hey! What did you do that for?'

Jey knelt down to pick up the apple and the hullen took the opportunity to knock over Jey's backpack, spilling the contents across the ground.

'You are a creature of pure chaos,' Jey said pointedly. 'Normally, I would cherish that about you. Today, I need you to step in line.'

The hullen picked up the branch in its mouth.

'Um...I don't have time to play fetch, mate.'

The hullen let out an aggravated snort and stepped closer, pushing the branch into Jey's hands.

'Okay, okay!' Jey took the branch from the demanding creature.

'It wants you to feed it,' a voice said from behind him.

Jey turned slowly, his hands – and branch – in the air. It was King Erimen, his fiery red hair a wild mess around his pale face, his blue eyes narrowed.

'The hullen eats wood?' Jey was too confused to realise he'd been sprung. And by the king, no less.

'Break the branch,' King Erimen said.

'Sure.' *When the king asks you to break a branch, you break a branch.*

Jey cracked the thin branch in two over his knee. The tube in his arm was pulled by the action, but he was too distracted to worry about the pain.

'Edem,' Jey murmured as a smoky liquid oozed out.

The hullen seized the branch from Jey and then spat it to the ground.

'That's why you have a collection of branches,' Jey said. 'It's food for your feathered friends.' It also explained why the hullen hung around this place.

'And what about your collection?' King Erimen nodded to the food on the ground.

'Would you believe me if I said I came out here for a picnic?' Jey asked. 'Your Majesty?'

'Erimen will do, and no, I don't believe you, Jey.'

'You know who I am?' That couldn't be good.

'It's hard not to,' Erimen said. 'You stand out.'

If Jey couldn't talk his way out of this predicament, perhaps he could talk his way *into* it.

'I'm trying to help,' Jey explained. 'I'm actually a good friend of your sister's.' Best not to mention he *actually* hadn't been a fan of Elenora's, especially after she betrayed them.

'I heard.' Erimen didn't look convinced.

'Then you know who my father is?'

Erimen pressed a hand to his side – where *he* had been shot. 'You and I have a few things in common, yes.'

Right. They had both been shot by edem weapons. What a wonderful, exclusive club to be a part of.

'The truth is,' Jey admitted, 'I'm trying to find my father. I'm going to bring him back here to help us find a way home.'

Erimen's eyebrows rose. 'Why do you think he'll help?'

'Why does everyone keep asking that?'

Erimen cringed. 'Your father doesn't have the best reputation.'

'Isn't that the understatement of the year.'

'I can't let you take the hullen.' Erimen gestured to the creature, who was quiet and content after sucking the edem from the branch. 'You understand.'

'I do. But I'd like you to reconsider.'

'The hullen keep us connected to Telene,' Erimen explained. 'We need them for our supply runs. We need them to survive this place.'

'I'll bring it back. Promise.'

Erimen stroked his fingers through the creature's translucent feathers as he pondered. 'You think you can find your father?'

'I think I have a better shot from the sky than from a hospital bed,' Jey said.

'And then what?'

'I force him to return us to Telene. He did it once, he can do it again – for all of us.'

Erimen glanced at the pouch of edem, which had fallen out of Jey's backpack when the hullen knocked it over. The edem pouch was half full.

'I have a built-in ticking clock.' Jey picked up the pouch and tucked it into the band of his pants. 'I *have* to come back.'

'All right then,' Erimen said. 'Let's go find your father.'

'You—' Jey pointed to the king, 'want to come?'

Erimen nodded. 'Your father and I have some unfinished business.'

After being in the dark compound for a few days, Jey's eyes stung as they flew across the vivid sky.

'Where to first?' Erimen asked from behind him.

'I thought he might be hiding out in the city,' Jey said. 'As you mentioned, supplies are low. He'd have to find food.'

'We can't get too close. The Shadow Guards will shoot us down if they catch sight of us. We'll have to land outside the city perimeter and then sneak in.'

The king placed his hand against the side of the hullen's head, closing his eyes briefly. The hullen veered away from the black forest and back across the inlet that Jey and Leta had flown over when they'd first arrived.

Once they reached the ocean, the hullen flew along the turquoise coast.

'Where would a maniacal power-hungry Regency General hide?' Jey mused.

'He wasn't always that way,' Erimen said.

'I'm sorry?' Jey baulked. 'I thought I heard you defending my father, but that can't be right.'

'My parents had me sit in on Regency meetings before they died. Your father was only a Regency lieutenant at the time, but he was optimistic. He thought edem could be harnessed for good.'

That must have been while Jey's parents were still together.

'My father thinks weapons will force the other nations to open their borders,' Jey said. 'Oppression is his idea of good.'

'I'll admit that he lost his way.'

Jey wondered how exactly that had happened. Was it because he got power hungry? Or when he divorced Jey's mother?

'Did you know about this world?' Jey asked. 'Before you arrived here?'

Jey thought perhaps Erimen hadn't heard him. When the king finally responded, his voice was solemn. 'I did.'

'When did you find out? After you became king?'

'My parents told me a few years before they died. They wanted me to know the truth; they thought it was important in understanding the tough laws they enforced. They wanted me to have all the information I would need when I became king.'

Jey wished he'd been given such insight from his father. 'What was your reaction?'

'I was angry,' he admitted. 'And I didn't completely agree with the decisions my parents and the Regency were making. In fact, the last meeting with your father – before he shot me – was about finding a balance. Back then, I didn't know the dire state this world was in and how our actions in Telene impacted the people here. I thought that if we allowed some usage of edem, people would be happier.'

'Meanwhile, my father was using edem to create weapons to attack the other nations.'

'Yes,' Erimen said. 'We were both wrong.'

Jey couldn't believe the king was putting himself in the same category as his father.

'Except you didn't hurt anyone,' Jey said. 'You were trying to help.'

Erimen's reply was lost in the wind.

CHAPTER 31

CAYDER

Rusteef and Kema drove the crawler with Dr Bueter tied in the back, leaving Cayder and Elenora alone together for the long drive back to the port. She wouldn't talk to him – she wouldn't even look at him. He didn't blame her. He felt sick for causing her more pain. He wanted to be the person she went to when she needed reassurance.

'I'm sorry,' Cayder said again – he'd lost count how many times. 'I only found out two days before we broke out of Vardean. There wasn't a moment to tell you.'

She surprised him by replying, 'And since then? What stopped you?'

He swallowed hard. 'We weren't on the best terms.'

'You withheld the truth because you were angry at me?' She turned to look at him and he wished she hadn't; her face was both furious and heartbroken.

'No.' He tried to take her hand but she snatched it away. 'That's not it. To be honest, there was so much going on here, I didn't think to—'

'You forgot.' Her voice was low and dangerous. 'You forgot to tell me that Kema killed my parents.'

He hated to admit it, but he had. He'd had other things on his mind. Even in the days she was unconscious in the cave, he hadn't thought about what Kema had told him. He had only worried for her well-being. 'Kema didn't—'

'She did!' Elenora threw up her free hand and then winced as she shifted her injured shoulder.

'Are you okay?'

'No,' she murmured. 'I am not okay. Remember how you felt about Hubare Carnright?'

How could he forget? Cayder had spent seven years hating the man that had supposedly killed his mother. The sound of his name still sent a spike of anger through his body, even after seeing him locked in Vardean and finding out that he hadn't been responsible for his mother's accident.

'I do,' Cayder said. 'But you *know* Kema, you know she's a good person. And she's going to live with guilt and regret for the rest of her life.'

'That's what makes it worse!' Elenora said, her voice cutting. 'You were my friends and you both kept this from me. I thought I could trust you!'

Friends. Everything Cayder and Elenora had built over the last week had come crumbling down. They were back at square one. Worse. Now it was Elenora who didn't trust him.

'You can, Elle.'

'Can I?' she fired back. He hadn't seen Elenora this heated since she'd set the Regency headquarters ablaze.

'Of course.'

He waited for her to snap at him. To make him call her Princess Elenora. But all she did was close her eyes and let out a slow, shaking breath. He wanted to wrap his arms around her, tell her how much he cared for her, but he knew she needed space.

'I'm sorry,' he said again. He didn't want to hurt her any further. She was already in pain from her injury, and the added betrayal had taken its toll. He would wait for her.

He would always wait for her.

———

'We're almost there!' Rusteef called from the crawler ahead.

Good. It had been a long day of driving and Cayder couldn't take much more of the terse, silent journey.

'It's nearly over,' Cayder said. He wasn't sure whether he was referring to the drive, their promise to the queen, or the opportunity for Elenora to leave the crawler and him behind.

Once they reached the port, they would split up. Elenora would take her own crawler to find her brother and Cayder and Kema would take another. Rusteef would bring Dr Bueter to the queen.

'What's that?' Elenora asked; she was staring at the sky.

A streak of silver shimmered above them.

'The hullen!' Cayder said.

Rusteef increased speed as the hullen's shadow loomed overhead.

'What is he doing?' Cayder asked, mostly to himself.

Cayder pushed the lever down to keep up. The creature pulled ahead, twisting in mid-air to land on the road in front of Rusteef's crawler. Cayder let go of the lever to keep from running into them.

Two figures dismounted from a saddle that was strapped on the back of the creature.

'What do you want this time?' Rusteef growled, reaching for Dr Bueter's bow.

'Wait,' Cayder said. 'That's Jey and—'

A man just shy of Jey's height, with bright red hair and tattered clothing, walked towards them.

'Erimen?' Elenora croaked, her voice thick with emotion.

Cayder helped Elenora out of the vehicle. As soon as her feet touched the ground, she took off running.

'Elle!' King Erimen exclaimed.

'Eri!' Despite her injury, she threw herself at her brother and he caught her in his arms.

'You're here!' she said through her tears. 'You're really here!'

'I missed you, my dearest Elle. What's happened to your arm and your cheek?'

'I thought I'd never see you again.' Elenora burrowed her face into her brother's neck and sobbed.

'So—' Jey opened his arms wide. 'Where's my hug, mate?'

Cayder laughed and gave Jey a hug, before realising the most important thing. 'Where's Leta? Is she okay?'

The corner of Jey's mouth quirked. 'She's with your mother back at the underground compound.'

Much about that sentence didn't make sense, but the main thing was that Leta had been right; their mother was alive.

Jey grinned and Cayder hugged him again. 'It really *is* good to see you.'

'Ouch,' Jey said. 'Careful, mate. I'm a fragile flower these days.'

'What happened to you?' Kema asked.

Jey opened his coat to reveal a pouch of edem tucked into his pants. 'One of the Regency weapons gave me a big, long, lingering kiss.'

'What?' Cayder asked. 'When did that happen?'

'As I jumped through the veil.'

Kema grimaced. 'Are you okay?'

Jey shrugged but his face didn't hold its usual candour. 'I'm alive.'

'What are you doing out here?' Kema asked. 'Not that we aren't happy to see you.' She exchanged a confused look with Rusteef, who was glowering at Jey and Erimen. 'Although I can't say the same for our friend here.'

'We were heading to the city to look for my father,' Jey explained. 'We found you instead.'

'I have some good news.' Cayder gestured to the back of the crawler. 'You also found your father.'

'Well, isn't it my lucky day?' Jey's grin wavered as he stepped over to the vehicle. 'We meet again, Dad.'

Dr Bueter's heated response was garbled by the gag, his face blooming red. He struggled against his bonds as his son stood over him.

'Hmm,' Jey said, plucking at one of the ties. 'Why didn't I think of that?'

Rusteef bristled as though he worried Jey might free his father. 'We're taking the Regency General to the Shadow Queen.'

'The Shadow Queen?' King Erimen asked, pulling away from his sister and moving closer. 'How can she help?'

Before Rusteef could reply, Kema interrupted. 'Meri?' Her eyes widened as she looked Erimen up and down. 'Is that you?'

'Who's Meri?' Elenora glanced between Kema and her brother for an explanation.

Erimen ran his hand down his face, the tips of his ears flushing. 'I am.'

Why had Kema never mentioned she had been friends with Erimen? 'You know the king?' Cayder asked.

'You're the king?' Kema shook her head. 'I – I don't understand.'

Cayder didn't either.

But rather than explaining himself to Kema, Erimen placed his hands gently on his sister's shoulders, leaning down to meet her gaze. 'I didn't want you to find out this way.'

Elenora's entire body was already trembling. 'What are you talking about?'

'Kema and I were friends from before I was crowned,' Erimen explained. 'Before – before Mother and Father died. I used another name as I didn't want anyone to know who I really was. I just wanted to be known as me.'

Kema looked like she wanted to climb under the crawler and hide.

'Oh,' Elenora said, but her brow was furrowed, knowing there had to be more to the story.

'We met through mutual friends,' Erimen said. A frown

tugged at the corners of Erimen's mouth. 'We had similar interests. We wanted the same things.'

Cayder's stomach sank as he pieced together what Erimen was trying to tell his sister.

Oh no.

He wanted to reach for Elenora, knowing this news would destroy her, but he knew she would push him away.

'What things?' Elenora hadn't come to the same conclusion. Not yet.

This wasn't fair. Not after everything Elenora had been through. Cayder wanted to shield her from more pain, but the worst was yet to come.

'We wanted balance,' Erimen said, glancing up at the black vein in the sky and the connection back home. 'We thought there could be some kind of usage of edem where—'

Elenora gasped. 'You were with the rebels?'

Erimen didn't need to confirm Elenora's suspicions; the answer was written all over his forlorn face.

CHAPTER 32

ELENORA

Elenora couldn't believe it. This had to be some kind of mistake; her brother wasn't a rebel!

'Why?' her voice was a breathless whisper. 'Why would you be involved with the rebels when you knew they were working against our parents?'

'It's complicated,' Erimen said, eyes flashing to Kema.

It wasn't complicated to Elenora. Good was good and wrong was wrong. And the rebels had always been in the wrong. They refused to comply with the law. They refused to compromise. They were anarchists. They were traitors.

They had killed her parents.

'When did you get involved with them?' she asked, her breath coming in short gasps. Her head felt disconnected from her body.

'I was young,' her brother said with a meek shrug. 'Younger than you are now.'

'Did you know they were going to be there on my birthday?'

Erimen closed his eyes as though he was reliving that day. It had been the last time their family was whole. It was the day

Elenora had gone from being a daughter, and the royal spare, to an orphan.

And in the same moment, her brother had changed. He was no longer the jovial boy who wanted to play games and sing bawdy songs around the castle, but a sixteen-year-old king with the burden of a struggling nation upon his shoulders. She had thought the sudden change in his nature was due to his grief. Now she questioned whether there had been more to it.

When Erimen opened his eyes, they were full of unshed tears. 'I'm so sorry, Elle.'

Oh no. No. No. No. No.

'You—' she began before her breath caught in her chest.

'I had no idea was what going to happen that day,' Erimen said, his palms up, pleading. 'I promise you that.'

'We were just trying to put on a display of what edem could do when controlled,' Kema added. 'It wasn't supposed to—'

Elenora glared at the guard. 'Don't you dare speak right now. Erimen,' she nodded to her brother, 'did you tell the rebels where to be that day?'

'Elle—' he tried to reach for her, but she stepped back. 'I'm sorry.'

He's not denying it.

'You killed our parents,' she said, her voice firm and deadly. '*You.* Their beloved son.' *My wonderful brother. The perfect king.*

Elenora glanced at the people surrounding her.

Kema. Cayder. Jey. Erimen.

She couldn't trust any of them. They were all liars. Where she might have accepted Cayder and Kema's involvement over time, this truth she could not swallow.

'It wasn't like that.' Erimen's face was red and splotchy. 'Nothing bad was supposed to happen.'

'Our parents trusted you!' she screamed. '*I* trusted you!'

She had known Erimen to be rambunctious and playful, but never a traitor. And even after her parents had died, he had still wanted balance. She had sat next to him when he tried to rationalise his beliefs to Dr Bueter. For years, she had believed a group of faceless rebels had killed her parents. Now all those rebels had the same face.

Her brother's.

Was that why he kept up the tradition of wearing a mask? To ensure no other rebels would recognise him after he was crowned? There would have been riots in the streets if the rebels had come forward with the claim that the new king was one of them.

'I can't believe I wasted time trying to find you,' she said, seething. 'If I had known the truth, I never would have come here.' She would have taken the opportunity to escape Vardean and never looked back.

'With all due respect, Princess,' Jey said, 'nothing has changed. We have to get out of here. This world is still on self-destruct mode.'

'Nothing's changed?' she demanded.

'Okay, okay.' Jey threw up his hands. 'Maybe things *have* changed.'

'Come with me, Princess,' Rusteef said. 'The queen will fix everything.'

'No,' Erimen disagreed. 'We need to take Dr Bueter back to the compound to see Maretta. You can't trust these people, Elle – they've been fighting against us.'

'We can't trust you!' Rusteef bared his teeth in anger. 'You steal our supplies!'

Elenora looked between her brother and Rusteef. 'They're the radicals the Shadow Queen was talking about? The ones who shot at our hullen?'

Rusteef nodded. 'They force the queen's hullen to do their bidding. The hullen are her creatures, not theirs.'

'We're trying to survive,' Erimen said with a sad shake of his head. 'And you won't help us.'

'Because you're not meant to be here!' Rusteef roared.

Elenora couldn't believe it. Her brother had been a rebel in Telene and now he was a radical, fighting against Myrandir – their ancestor.

'I'm coming,' Elenora said, climbing into Rusteef's crawler. 'I don't care what the rest of you do.'

'We can't let you take him.' Jey jerked his thumb to his father. 'As much as he might not like it, he's ours.'

Rusteef pulled the bow from the back of the crawler and aimed an arrow at Jey. 'I will do whatever my queen needs me to do. Don't think I won't let this arrow fly.'

Jey put his hands up. 'Easy, mate. I don't need another hole in me.'

Rusteef placed his hand on the panel to start the crawler.

'Elle,' Erimen's voice was pained, 'don't do this. Only Maretta can get us home. You can't trust them.'

'And I can trust you?' she asked.

Erimen glanced away.

At least he wasn't lying to her anymore.

'Go,' she ordered Rusteef.

The crawler launched, jostling her arm, but she didn't flinch.

Physical pain couldn't hurt her. Not after the betrayal she had endured.

———

'You made the right decision,' Rusteef said as they continued towards the port. 'The queen has kept us safe for centuries. She will take care of you.'

Elenora didn't reply. She was tired of people telling her what to do. Actions spoke louder than words and everyone – including Cayder – had proven their word was nothing but dust.

The *Levisial* was awaiting their return at the dock. Rusteef untied Dr Bueter and marched him onboard. Elenora expected Dr Bueter to put up a fight, but he went willingly, although he took every opportunity to shoot daggers at Elenora.

She didn't care. She was on a mission now. Get home. Take the crown. Shut down the Regency.

Her brother didn't deserve to rule.

She had jumped through the veil as a way back to him, back to normal. But now she knew there was no going back. And 'normal' had been a fabrication.

Even when their parents were alive, Erimen was not who he appeared to be. He had been one of the rebels, planning and plotting against the crown. And what was worse, he had cried with Elenora when they buried their parents. He'd pretended he hadn't been involved. He had made Elenora rely on him, believe in him.

He had tricked her.

No one would trick her again.

CHAPTER 33

ELENORA

Myrandir was waiting below deck when Elenora, Rusteef and the general arrived onboard the *Levisial*.

'You have returned,' she remarked. 'Although not all in one piece.' She gestured to Elenora's arm. 'Are you all right? Where are the others? Your friends?'

'Gone.'

Myrandir seemingly floated towards her, appearing less human than the last time they'd met. She reached out and captured a tear from Elenora's cheek with her grey fingers.

'I'm sorry, child,' she said. 'But you need not fear. I will protect you.'

'I completed your request,' Elenora said firmly. 'That's all that matters.'

Rusteef pushed Dr Bueter forward. 'The Regency General is here, my queen.'

Myrandir disappeared for a moment in a cloud of smoke, only to reappear centimetres away from Dr Bueter's nose. He flinched back; shock in his blue eyes.

'Regency General,' her voice was a sigh. 'Welcome.'

Dr Bueter mumbled something around his gag.

'Remove it, Rusteef,' Myrandir said with a wave of her hand. 'I must hear what the man has to say.'

Once he was free of the gag, Dr Bueter said, 'You must be this Shadow Queen everyone is talking about.'

'It's a pleasure to meet you, General,' Myrandir replied.

'I'm not sure I can return that sentiment,' Dr Bueter grumbled. He gazed up at her. 'What do you want from me?'

The queen leaned in close, her hair swirling around her grey face as she studied him with her pearlescent eyes. 'I need to return to Telene. And I hear you created a way to send people to this side of the veil and back with ease.'

'If you consider getting painfully shot and disintegrating *ease*,' Dr Bueter shrugged, and for a second, Elenora could see his son, 'then yes, that's true.'

Myrandir nodded vigorously. 'Your weapons are incredibly powerful.'

'That's why you brought me here?' he asked, looking around the vessel.

'You set this in motion,' Myrandir said. 'The moment you decided to use your weapons against the other nations. Send me to Telene and I will fix the tear in the veil and return all my power to where it belongs.'

'Why should I?' Dr Bueter asked.

'Because our futures are tethered together,' Myrandir explained. 'It's not just my world at stake, it's yours. If your boats reach their targets and detonate their weapons, you will wipe us all out. My power is not meant to be used so far from the source – from me. It's far too dangerous.'

'*Please*, Dr Bueter.' Elenora didn't even want to look at him, but they needed his help. 'Our lives – all our lives – are in your hands.'

'If you send me to Telene,' Myrandir said, 'then I promise to bring you with me. Once I'm on the other side, I can build a pathway to bring you along.'

Dr Bueter ran a hand over his mouth. 'I'm not sure how you think I can help. My weapons are a temporal adjustment that shifts objects from one side of the veil to another. In order to bring something back, there needs to be a fragment – a trail – of where the object used to be. Even I cannot return.'

Elenora didn't feel sorry for him. If they were trapped here, then she was glad he was too.

'Part of me remains in Telene,' Myrandir said. 'One of the creatures I created when I was young. It is a part of my power. A part of me.'

The hullen, Elenora thought.

'Yes, but I'm *here*,' Dr Bueter said, 'and my machines are *there*.' He gestured to the ceiling and the sky above them.

'I need to go back.' Myrandir's body vibrated with frustration. 'The future depends on it.'

'I can't help you.' He shot a glare at Elenora. '*She* destroyed my base.'

'Using one of your weapons,' Elenora said.

Dr Bueter fumed, his face reddening. 'Now's not the time to gloat.'

But Elenora wasn't gloating. She had used one of Dr Bueter's weapons against him, and then jumped through the veil with it in her hands...

'I know where we can find a Regency weapon,' Elenora said, hope blooming within her. 'I dropped one into the ocean after falling through the veil.'

The Shadow Queen turned to Rusteef, her dress dispersing as she spun. 'Tell the captain to set sail. We must find that weapon!'

CHAPTER 34

NARENA

Even though Narena knew her parents would be worried about her, she didn't return home the following day. If she told them what she was doing, they would ground her. They might even call the Regency. And she certainly wouldn't be allowed to see Farrow.

Narena knew they were close to the truth; she could feel it like a vibration in her body, propelling her through the water. But by the end of the day, their food supplies had dwindled and they were no closer to finding the hidden base.

'I should go home,' Narena grumbled. She was slumped over on the couch. She was tired of being in the water. Tired of the relentless swimming and searching. But not tired of spending time with Farrow.

Farrow fell onto the couch beside her, equally exhausted. 'But we haven't found anything yet.'

'Perhaps there's nothing left to find. The Regency might have covered their tracks, like they did in Ferrington.'

'There's still so much of the lake to search.' Farrow smoothed

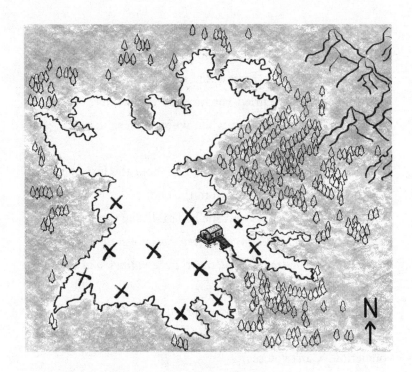

out a map she had drawn of the lake; the areas they had searched had been crossed out.

'My parents will be furious.' She was sick of the sight of the map and the empty spaces that taunted her.

'They'll already be furious, what's a few more days?'

'We have no food,' Narena pointed out.

'I'll go into town tomorrow and buy some.'

Farrow would stay out here until she was proven right.

'Don't turn into your grandmother,' Narena said before she could stop herself. Farrow sucked in a sharp breath. 'I didn't mean it like that,' Narena clarified. 'I just meant that your grandmother tried—'

'And failed,' Farrow said bitterly. 'Yes, I'm well aware.'

Narena reached out to touch Farrow's hand and she didn't flinch away. 'I'm sorry, Farrow. I'm exhausted.'

'I know.' Farrow curled her fingers into Narena's. 'I am too. But we can't stop now. Not when we're so close to piecing this all together.'

Narena's mother had once told her about the lure of a story, and the desire to see it through to the end.

It can be easy to lose yourself, she had said. *And forget who you are and why you even started investigating. Sometimes the journey to the truth isn't worth the cost. Not all stories have endings, and more often than not, they're not happy ones.*

'I don't want to see you lose yourself to this, Farrow.'

'I'm already lost.' Farrow's voice was low, losing its usual conviction. 'Can't you see?'

That was what hurt Narena the most: she *could*. She couldn't pull Farrow back from the edge; she was already submerged.

Narena had stayed with Farrow because she cared about her. She had helped Cayder because he was her best friend. She had done what she could to support them and yet, she hadn't been able to help in the end. As much as she didn't want to admit it, she *was* a pawn. She helped other people, but when had she made a decision to help herself?

'Where are you going?' Farrow asked as Narena left the couch.

'To make my first move,' she said over her shoulder. She wouldn't be a pawn any longer.

Farrow followed her out of the houseboat. Light from the vessel's permalamp radiated out for around fifty metres. Beyond that was darkness. And edem. But Narena couldn't swim one more stroke to reach it. Narena approached the lamp.

'What are you doing?' Farrow asked.

'I'm tired,' was all she said, as though that would explain everything.

Narena lifted her torch and swung it at the lamp. The globe smashed and the light buzzed out. Edem rushed in from the distance like a wave pushing to shore.

'Narena! You're scaring me.'

Narena didn't think Farrow *could* get scared. 'Don't you want to find out the truth?'

The side of Farrow's mouth lifted. 'Is that a trick question?'

'Then trust me.'

Farrow didn't hesitate. 'I do.'

Narena had never considered using edem before, but she didn't waver as she reached towards the shimmering darkness. The edem had heard her call and swathed her fingers in black.

'Show me the way to the hidden Regency base,' Narena said, her voice firm.

'I can't believe you're doing this,' Farrow whispered.

'Neither can I,' Narena whispered back.

Their chuckles were cut short as edem retracted from Narena's hand. With the permacloud obscuring the moon, the lake was barely distinguishable from their dark surroundings.

A gurgling sound echoed from somewhere out on the horizon, like water going down a drain. The houseboat rattled, the boards splintering underneath their feet.

'Run!' Narena cried, jumping from the houseboat onto the mooring.

Farrow followed, landing beside her.

The houseboat collapsed to the lakebed below and crumpled in on itself.

'I'm so sorry!' Narena cried, seeing the destruction. 'I didn't think...'

But Farrow wasn't listening. Her mouth was agape, her pale arm pointing towards the lake.

Except the lake was gone. The water had disappeared, leaving a muddy gulf behind.

CHAPTER 35

LETA

Leta understood Jey's desire to have his father display some kind of human decency, but she worried it would only end up hurting Jey more. And yet, she was relieved Jey had left the compound. She had feared Erithe would sneak in and cut off Jey's edem supply while he slept. Now all Leta had to worry about was finding their way home, and trying not to dwell on what would happen to everyone if she failed.

Leta pushed her mother's notebook away; she couldn't concentrate on formulas right now. She grabbed a blank piece of paper and a pencil. She hadn't drawn anything for weeks. She needed to feel like herself again.

She began drawing the hullen: not the nightmarish creature she had sketched in Vardean, but the *real* hullen. Creatures of protection. Creatures of edem. Creatures of magic.

'That's beautiful,' Leta's mother said from over her shoulder. 'You always loved to draw, even before you knew how. I could never pry a crayon from your hand. You'd draw on everything – sometimes your brother.' Her mother let out a sad chuckle.

Maretta had missed so many meaningful moments of Leta's life. She had only been half-formed back then; her childhood dreams and desires were rough outlines. Now Leta's dreams were fully realised drawings with colour and texture.

And all she wanted was to unite her family and return home.

There was no way of knowing if Narena had received her message and taken it to her father. It was a waiting game, and Leta was losing patience.

Leta's pencil paused on the page and her mother placed her hand on her shoulder.

'Hope,' she reminded her daughter. 'There's always hope.'

Before Leta could reply, a voice called from the doorway. 'Mother?'

The two Broduck women turned to find an exhausted and scruffy-looking Cayder. His shirt was torn and his dark pants were covered in sand, dust and dirt.

'Cayder!' their mother cried, running to him. 'My little ray of sunshine!' She grabbed his hands, tilting her head up to look him in the eye. 'My goodness! You've gotten so tall!'

Cayder's forehead fell against her neck, his body trembling as he cried.

'It's okay, my baby,' she said, wrapping her arms around him. 'I'm here now. We're all here.'

As much as that shouldn't have been a good thing, Leta couldn't help but break into her own happy tears.

'Come—' Maretta said, holding her arm out to her daughter.

Their mother's arms were strong around them as they allowed themselves to be taken by a wave of joy and grief. They might have lost seven years, but they were together now.

Leta felt her heart stitch itself together inside her chest. Now they needed to find a way home.

Eventually, they released one another. Cayder's face was red from crying and his dark hair was a matted mess, but otherwise, he looked well enough.

'Where have you been?' Leta demanded.

'It's a long story,' Cayder replied. 'The important thing is that I found my way here.'

'How?' she asked.

'I guess that's where I come in,' Jey said.

Leta wasn't sure how long he'd been standing behind Cayder, but he gave her a sheepish shrug. 'Lost my dad but found your brother, so I'm calling it a win.'

Leta was careful not to touch Jey's injured side as she embraced him. 'You came back!'

'Didn't really have a choice.' Jey jerked his thumb at Cayder. 'This one was pretty insistent.'

'What about your father?' Jey hadn't been gone very long.

Jey glanced at Cayder, but Cayder was still staring at his mother as though she was a ghost.

'He's being held captive,' Jey said, 'which I suppose is another win.'

'By whom?' Leta's mother asked.

'Rusteef and—' he scrunched up his nose, 'the princess.'

'Elenora?' Leta didn't understand. 'She betrayed us again?'

'It's not that simple,' Cayder said. He wiped his face with his hands, tears disappearing.

'It never is with her,' Leta muttered. 'Why would she do that?'

'She felt betrayed by her brother,' Cayder said, his dark brows furrowed. 'Apparently, he was one of the rebels that caused the accident that killed their parents. I don't blame her.'

'You don't?' Jey asked. 'Well, I do. My father was our only hope of getting out of here. Without him, we're stuck. No offense, Maretta.'

'We're doing the best we can,' she replied.

'We've been working on trying to communicate with the other side,' Leta informed her brother.

The rings around the edemmeter started spinning, silencing the room.

Leta approached the globe. 'Someone's using edem!'

'A lot of it,' their mother said as the rings flew around the globe's surface faster and faster. They watched as the rings halted, crossing over each other and pinpointing the location of the source with a resounding *clang*.

She exchanged a knowing glance with Leta.

Could this be it? Could this be what they were waiting for?

There was only one way to find out.

———

They gathered as many branches as they could carry from the compound's supply room and collected Kema and Erimen from the canteen on their way to the surface. A group of hullen were hanging out by the waterfall. They packed the hullen's saddles with the branches and paired up, each couple taking a hullen. Leta's mother and Erimen led the way.

'There's nothing here,' Cayder said, jumping off the hullen once they were back on solid ground. Kema dismounted beside him. She looked like she had been crying, her eyes red and watery. Leta wanted to ask if she was okay, but Kema kept her eyes downcast.

'Nothing?' Their mother smiled, holding her arms out wide. A large lake that was tinged ruddy brown stretched out before them.

'This wasn't here before?' Cayder asked.

'No,' she said. 'This lake is from Telene.'

Their mother's excitement was contagious. Leta approached the bank, Jey's hand clasped in hers.

'That's a lot of water,' Jey said, looking out over the reddish expanse. 'If we swim out to the middle and the lake shifts back, will we go with it?'

'Living matter can't pass through the veil,' Leta reminded him. 'Only the hullen can.'

'Okay then.' Jey raised a brow. 'Then why are we so excited about this gross-looking lake?'

'We are hoping to create a new tear,' Leta's mother explained. She cupped some water in her hands and took a sip. A slow grin spread across her face. 'Could it be?'

The anticipation buzzed beneath Leta's skin. The water looked normal to her; nothing out of the ordinary, aside from the reddish tinge.

'What are you thinking, Maretta?' Erimen asked. His freckled face was gaunt, the hollows under his eyes pronounced. The vibrant man who had greeted her in the compound over a week ago was now weathered and broken. Even his red hair appeared muted.

'Leta and I had a theory,' Maretta replied with a nod to her daughter. 'While only objects shift back and forth, we wondered if we could manipulate those objects to send a letter.'

'To whom?' Erimen asked.

'That was the problem,' Maretta admitted. 'We couldn't choose where the message would go as we can't control where the objects shift back to. But Leta had the ingenious idea to write a letter that Narena couldn't ignore.'

Cayder looked over at his sister and she grinned back at him.

'Do you think she found it?' Cayder asked their mother.

'Someone did,' she replied.

Cayder glanced at the lake, confusion pulling at the corners of his mouth. 'How do you know?'

'Because this is Lake Rusterton.' In that moment, she looked like the mother Leta remembered. Young, vibrant, happy. 'The largest body of water in Telene.'

'Hurray,' Jey said without humour. 'The delicious muddy waters of Lake Rusterton.'

'Actually,' Leta's mother said. 'I think you'll find the water tastes quite sweet.'

Jey raised an eyebrow but bent down to taste for himself. 'Weird. It *does* taste sweet.'

'That's due to the high levels of lead in the water,' she said. 'It also causes the lake to appear red.'

'I'm thinking that's not actually a good thing.' Jey looked as though he regretted drinking it.

'Not for Telene, no,' Maretta said. 'Which is one of the reasons we don't use the lake for our drinking water. But for us – *this* is good. This means our message was received.'

'I don't understand.' Cayder raked a frustrated hand through his hair – Leta knew that look. He didn't like being left out. 'How does this help us?'

'Lake Rusterton is the location of an old Regency base,' their mother explained.

'Our message was for Narena to tell Father to find the base,' Leta said to her brother. She had to admit she enjoyed lording the information over him. 'The fact that the lake is here, means that Father received our message and is attempting to help us.'

'There's a machine at the old base that when detonated, should use enough edem to break through the veil,' their mother said.

'Machine?' Cayder asked. 'You mean a *weapon*.'

Maretta nodded reluctantly. 'It wasn't built as a weapon, but when it malfunctions, it explodes.'

'How do you know it will work?' Erimen asked.

'Because it's based on the weapon that created the original tear,' Maretta said.

Cayder locked eyes with Leta. The question was clear in the rise of his brow.

Did you know?

Leta glanced away. Now wasn't the time to question their mother's choices. And if it sent them back to Telene, what did its origins matter?

'Great,' Cayder muttered. 'We hope Father sets off a dangerous weapon and then what?'

'We use our edem stores to weaken the veil from this side,' their mother answered with a smile. 'Then we finally go home.'

'What about the boats?' Cayder asked. 'The Shadow Queen said once the Regency reaches the shores of the neighbouring nations and set off their weapons, our worlds will end.'

'We'll send the hullen to stop them,' Maretta said. 'Orders direct from King Erimen should be enough to turn them back.'

'And my sister?' Erimen asked. 'We can't leave her here with Dr Bueter.'

Leta wanted to argue that Elenora had made her choice, but she held her tongue. Despite what had happened back in Vardean, she knew Elenora meant something to her brother.

'Once we're back,' Maretta said, 'I'll talk to the Regency. Ensure that all our resources are focused on bringing her – and everyone at the compound – home.'

Something inside Leta's chest tightened.

'Why would the Regency listen to you?' she asked her mother. 'You were just one of their employees. You did as you were told.'

Her mother grimaced and looked out over the lake. 'I was more than just an employee.'

Leta found it difficult to swallow. 'What were you?'

She let out a long breath before she began, 'I started off as a research assistant. I was hired for my skills in molecular biology. My mission was to harness edem. But I was successful – too successful. Van promoted me to Lieutenant General of their weapons team.'

'Lieutenant General?' Leta repeated. 'But that means…'

'I led the weapons program, yes. They were my design.'

This was not what she had told Leta before: her mother had claimed she was simply doing her job – forced to fulfil Dr Bueter's narcissistic desires. Leta closed her eyes for a moment and saw her mother, the veil of mystery and childhood memories lifted. Underneath her mask was a guilty woman.

Her mother had always seemed so ethereal, so beautiful. She was as magical to Leta as the fairytales she used to read to her at bedtime. But now every memory of her mother distorted with this new revelation. Every party she had held at Broduck Manor was a sinister gathering, each conversation full of lies.

Their mother wasn't all sunshine and smiles. She was corrupt and cold-blooded.

'You're as bad as Dr Bueter,' Leta said.

'That's not true,' Maretta argued. 'I never wanted to hurt anyone.'

'What did you think your weapons would be used for?' Cayder asked. Leta was surprised to hear his voice was as hard as hers.

'Come on, now,' Erimen said, his palms raised to keep the peace. 'We know who the good guys and bad guys are here, and your mother is one of the best. She made some mistakes, but haven't we all?'

'No. We haven't.' Leta turned to the king. 'Jey, Cayder and I have been fighting for what's right. We've been trying to expose all the lies.'

'Nettie—' Jey started, reaching for her.

'No.' Leta shrugged him off. 'I'm tired of all of this! I'm tired of always waiting for the other shoe to drop.'

'I'm so sorry, Nettie. I'm sorry I failed you,' her mother said. Her forehead creased. 'I got caught up in what I was creating, I didn't think about the consequences. I didn't think about the lives my weapons would impact. For years, I've looked at this place as penance for what I willingly created. I deserved the punishment – but you,' she nodded to Cayder, 'and your brother never did.'

'Why didn't you tell us?' Cayder asked.

'I would like to say it was because I was ashamed, but that wasn't it. I didn't tell you because I didn't think I was doing anything wrong at the time. I had Van in my ear, telling me the entire nation would crumble if we didn't force the borders to reopen. I had already lost the opportunity to say goodbye to my father in Delften. I wanted change, just as much as he did.'

'And you were willing to force that change upon them,' Jey muttered.

'It was a mistake. The worst mistake of my life. And while I can argue that Van would have found another way to make his weapons without me, I'm intrinsically linked to the hurt they've caused. I built the underground compound to help those displaced by edem and I've done everything in my power to try to make things right.'

Tears formed, blurring her mother before her. She wasn't a faded photograph of the woman she'd known; she was an entirely different person. 'Why can't you be who I thought you were? Why can't you be the mother I loved?'

Matching tears filled her mother's eyes. 'Don't you see,

Nettie? I *am* the mother you loved. I've always been this person. And I've always protected you. Nothing has changed.'

Maybe that was all true. Which meant that she had never known her mother at all.

CHAPTER 36

NARENA

Narena and Farrow descended into the crater that had once been Lake Rusterton, torches in hand. They started searching the empty areas on their map. The earth underfoot was gluggy and stuck to the bottom of their shoes.

'Bet you wish you had my pink gumboots now,' Narena said with a forced laugh.

'This is disgusting.' Farrow's feet squelched in the foul-smelling mud. 'If I had known this was underneath the water, I wouldn't have been swimming in it.'

'It's the presence of bacteria,' Narena remarked. 'I don't think it smells too bad.'

'Why couldn't edem have brought the Regency base to us,' Farrow moaned after half an hour of walking.

'We're lucky it worked at all. The results of using edem are always erratic. It could have been a lot worse.'

'I guess,' Farrow admitted. 'I can't believe you broke the law and used edem for me.'

Narena's cheek's flushed warm. 'It wasn't just for you. It was for me too.'

They continued hand in hand. The bottom of the lake sloped downward, until the bank was over three storeys above them.

The chasm was deadly silent. Nothing lived down there, and any animals near the lake had fled when the water disappeared down an invisible drain. Narena was wondering if the animals had the right idea when something moved in the dark.

Narena spun, her torch landing on a rock ahead. 'What was that?'

Farrow moved her torchlight in the direction of Narena's. 'Did you see a building?'

'No. Something is moving out there.'

'Like an alive something?'

Narena hoped so. She didn't like the idea of a dead something running around.

'What do we do?' Narena had stopped.

'We can't go back now,' Farrow said. 'We've come too far.' She shone her light behind her and screamed, dropping her torch.

'What?' Narena's torch searched the muddy banks. 'What is it?'

'...I saw something.' Farrow retrieved her torch, wiping the muck off the glass with shaking hands.

Narena didn't want to ask, but she knew she had to. 'What did it look like?'

Please don't let it be teeth. Rows upon rows of teeth.

'I don't know,' Farrow said. 'A tail?'

That wasn't much better.

'Let's keep moving.' She hated to admit it, but Farrow was right: they were too far from the mooring now. And if there was something back there, it was best they moved forward. Fast.

Something *swished* behind them, like a tail being dragged across the ground.

Or a tentacle of some hideous sea creature.

They picked up their pace, dropping each other's hands so they could jog. But the mud was insistent on slowing them down, suctioning their shoes to the ground.

Narena slipped and fell onto her hands and knees, spraying mud up into her face and hair.

'Are you okay?' Farrow helped her up.

Narena nodded. 'Let's keep going.'

There was a *cracking* sound, like a rock crunched underfoot.

Narena couldn't deny it any longer: they weren't alone down here.

'Run!' Narena said, refusing to glance behind.

As soon as they started running, they heard the sound of pursuit. Something slid along behind them, crushing stones in its path.

They slipped and slid across the muddy ground, their torch beams bouncing around in front of them.

Narena's muscles were already weary from swimming all day, and her body protested the further exertion. She had never been into sports at school, and her lack of fitness was showing. Narena was slowing. Meanwhile, Farrow had pulled ahead.

When Farrow realised, she called back. 'Narena! Where are you?'

Narena searched for Farrow in the darkness. Instead, she found the *thing* that had been following them.

It wasn't the hullen. It wasn't anything Narena had ever seen before.

A reedy creature with black coral lumps protruding along its back stood in the dark. Instead of arms, tentacles hung long from its shoulders. The face was flat and fish-like, with large, bulbous, glowing eyes. It opened its mouth wide to reveal thin black teeth.

It stood a hair's breadth from her, ready to devour her whole.

Narena let out a shriek.

'What is it?' Farrow yelled. Her light flashed, highlighting the creature. Her light made the creature dissipate like smoke. Or edem in the light.

'It must be made of edem!' Narena shouted. 'Keep using your torch!'

They flashed their torches behind them as they ran. The creature followed, disappearing as light hit its body, then reappearing across the lake bed. The creature slithered smoothly across the mud while Farrow and Narena struggled to stay on their feet.

'We can't outrun this thing!' Farrow wailed after taking another fall.

'We don't have to. We just have to get to the light. It can't survive in light.'

'What light?' Farrow asked.

That was a good question.

Something wrapped around Narena's ankle and pulled. Narena slammed face-first into the muddy ground. The wind was knocked out of her, and she couldn't move.

'Narena!' Farrow lunged for her, but she wasn't fast enough.

The tendril around Narena's ankle dragged her across the wet earth, filling her eyes, nose and mouth with muck. Narena thrashed, trying to free herself from the creature, but it was too strong.

This was how Krenin died, Narena thought. *This was the creature that killed him. Krenin was dragged to the bottom of the lake and never seen again.*

The creature devoured anything that entered the water. And now it was going to devour her.

But Narena didn't want to become another legend of Lake Rusterton. She twisted onto her back and shone her torch onto the tendril around her ankle.

The tentacle dispersed. She was free!

She sprinted towards Farrow's torchlight.

'Narena! You're okay!' Farrow wrapped Narena in her arms.

Another swish sounded from behind them. They flashed their torches to dissipate the creature.

They continued to struggle across the bottom of the lake. Then one of their torches illuminated something else. Something reflective. Metal.

A dome rose up ahead.

The hidden Regency base – it had to be!

They ran for the entrance, still pursued by the creature.

Farrow pushed open a heavy metal door while Narena shone her light wherever she heard a sound. The creature disappeared and would then reappear somewhere else.

Closer. And closer.

'Come on!' Farrow pulled on Narena's arm. 'Get inside!'

Narena flashed her light at the creature one last time before jumping through the opening.

'Close it! Close it!' Farrow screamed, pushing on the metal door.

Narena dropped her torch to the ground to help her. The creature flew at them, its tentacles outstretched.

BANG!

The creature hit the door as they slammed it in its face.

Farrow slid to the ground. 'What in burning shadows is that thing?'

'I have no idea. But we made it.' Narena held a hand to her chest, feeling her heart pound uncontrollably.

'That thing was after my grandmother,' Farrow said. Her face was white as a sheet of paper. 'Why?'

Narena wasn't sure.

'This must be the airlock from when the Regency entered and exited the building.' Narena pointed to the scuba equipment hanging on the walls.

The adjoining room opened to the metal dome they'd glimpsed from the outside. Rows upon rows of desks with buttons and dials – still flashing – encircled an edemmeter.

'Wow,' Farrow said. 'I can't believe they abandoned all of this equipment here.'

'Perhaps the creature forced them to.' Narena picked up a notebook from a nearby desk.

'Or they set up this base *because* of the creature,' Farrow suggested. 'After what happened to Krenin.'

They decided to split up and search the building for Maretta's weapon.

'Does this look like a weapon to you?' Farrow indicated a contraption that lit up when she touched it.

'I don't know. Maybe?' Narena wished Maretta had had time to complete her letter.

She approached the edemmeter. While she had never seen one up close, she had learnt about how they worked in school. Normally, the rings moved constantly along the surface as it detected the use of edem, whereas this edemmeter remained silent and still.

Perhaps the Regency had abandoned this base because it was broken.

The dome groaned above Narena. The metal plates shifted as the lake went from empty to full again in an instant.

'And now we're stuck underwater,' Farrow said.

Something wet hit Narena's face.

'Oh no,' she said, peering up. It wasn't a big leak, but it would eventually fill the dome with water.

A screeching sound came from above, like fingernails on a chalkboard.

'The creature!' Farrow cried. 'It's trying to get in through the crack!'

'It can't,' Narena said. 'It's too bright in here. It won't survive.'

'We need to find another way out of here. I'm not going back out into the lake with that *thing* waiting for us.'

Narena glanced down at her hands, which glowed with warmth. A dark pattern had appeared on her amber skin like the ripples of water.

'How did it feel?' Farrow nodded to Narena's hands. 'Using edem?'

'Strangely normal.' Narena had felt powerful. In control. She could see why some people continued to use it, knowing there could be deadly consequences. She wished there was some way she could use it to help them find the weapon.

They continued searching around the building and found an emergency exit: a set of stairs leading to an underground tunnel that eventually, according to the sign, led to the surface at the edge of the lake.

'At least we know how to get out of here,' Farrow said, nodding to the staircase.

As much as Narena wanted to fly down the stairs and get as far away from the creature as possible, they still had a job to do.

'What do you think the weapon looks like?' Narena asked.

'It could be anything,' Farrow said with a shrug. 'Everything looks like a weapon in here.'

Farrow was right – on each table there was a console with dials and knobs and blinking lights. Any of it could be the weapon Maretta referred to.

Unless...

'*This* is the weapon,' Narena said, her voice hushed.

Farrow glanced around. 'What is?'

Narena stretched her arms wide. 'Everything.' She dashed along the circular rows of desks, flipping on all the switches that were blinking.

'What are you doing?'

The room buzzed with electricity.

'Turning everything on,' Narena said matter-of-factly.

Once all the equipment was on, the edemmeter opened, splitting into two halves. Beneath the metal covering was a globe of swirling edem. A button on the console closest to the sphere blinked green.

Narena reached out to touch it.

'Wait!' Farrow grabbed Narena's hand. 'We don't know what will happen!'

It was true. This weapon could take down the entire building, and them along with it.

'The fail-safe!' Narena said. 'Maretta said we needed to turn it off so that the weapon would implode, not explode!'

They searched the nearby consoles and Narena found a red switch with fail-safe written underneath it. She flicked the switch down and the entire room began to flash and wail in warning.

'That doesn't sound like a good thing,' Farrow remarked as Narena returned to the blinking green button. 'Perhaps we should take cover in the airlock, just in case.'

'Maretta wouldn't have asked us to do this if she thought it was unsafe,' Narena said.

'Maretta didn't ask us! She asked her husband! I don't know if we should do this.'

Narena knew that she could never be sure either. She didn't want to die. But she also didn't want to walk away.

'We can wait till sunrise,' Narena said. 'The creature will be gone and you can take the tunnel out of here. You got your answers, but I still need to get mine.'

Narena didn't want to help her friends from the periphery anymore. She wanted to be in the centre of the action. She would be brave, like Cayder had been. Like Leta.

Farrow studied the ground. When she looked up, her expression was fixed.

'We started this together,' she said. 'We'll finish this together.'

CHAPTER 37

CAYDER

Cayder couldn't blame Leta for her outburst. They had been betrayed by the memory of their mother. They'd spent seven years mourning a woman who could do no wrong – and had been taken away from them due to a terrible accident. But that was all a lie. Her death was due to her own appetite for power. The reality was too difficult to digest.

When the lake disappeared, leaving behind a huge crater, Leta had stormed off with Jey in tow. Cayder could see from a distance that Jey was attempting to bring her around, but Leta refused to back down; her arms were crossed over her chest.

Maretta sat on the stony bank with Erimen. Both were silent, looking out over the crater. Betrayal had burrowed beneath Cayder's skin; he wasn't ready to speak with his mother. Not yet.

'Hey,' Kema said, pulling at Cayder's ragged shirt. 'Sit with me.'

He sat on the hard earth beside his friend.

'How are you holding up?' she asked.

He rubbed a hand behind his neck. 'I should be asking you that.'

She traced her echo-marked arms absent-mindedly, as though she could erase the past. He hated seeing her so broken. Even her bouncy white curls looked lacklustre. 'I've been better.'

'We all have.'

Kema pressed her lips together in a frown. 'But you can make things right. I can't.'

'You wouldn't wish harm on anyone; Elenora will realise that.' Elle was a good, kind person. She would understand Kema owned her mistakes. It would just take her some time.

'Sometimes that's not enough. Sometimes we don't get forgiveness, as much as we want to earn it.'

Cayder put his arm around her. 'You don't have to earn anything, Kema. We know who you are.'

'Thanks, Boy Wonder.' She rested her head on his shoulder.

They sat together like that, waiting for a sign that Cayder's father had found the weapon. Eventually, Leta returned with Jey. She sat on the bank next to Cayder but remained silent.

After what felt like hours – it was impossible to know with the sky never shifting – a blast echoed from the middle of the crater. The ground shook underneath them and the dry earth splintered. The hullen shrieked and flapped their wings, though they didn't fly away.

Cayder's mother leaped to her feet, her arms out to calm the hullen. 'It's the weapon,' she said. 'It's been detonated.'

Well done, Father.

Erimen mounted one of the hullen. 'Let's go!'

Erimen and Maretta took the lead once again as they flew across the crater. The ground had splintered, creating a deep circular groove with spiderlike fractures extending out from the middle. They landed towards the centre of the fracture, where a shimmering black scar had appeared.

They'd done it! They'd created another tear!

The hullen flapped their wings in agitation, hooting at one another as though they were communicating back and forth.

'I can't believe it,' Leta said, climbing down from her hullen. Some light had returned to her eyes. 'It worked!'

'Stand back!' their mother said. 'Let me check it's stable.'

She approached the veil and bent down to place her hand through the darkness.

Her hand knocked into the veil. 'As I suspected; we can't go through.'

'Just like the other tear,' Erimen said.

Maretta nodded and headed back to her hullen. 'Get me all the branches. Quick!'

Cayder and Kema unloaded their hullen's saddle and added the branches to the pile Maretta was building on top of the tear.

'What now?' Jey asked, eying the stack of branches dubiously.

'We set it alight.' Maretta held up a lantern and lit the wick before throwing it at the woodpile. The lantern shattered and lamp oil leaked out. The small flame sprung to life, catching on the lamp oil and flaming across the branches.

It didn't take long until the brittle wood began to fracture, releasing edem.

Once the pyre had burned itself out, Maretta placed her hand in the coiling black fog that covered the tear.

'Come.' Maretta held her hand out for her children. 'Help me break through to the other side.'

Leta avoided her mother's eyes as she approached. Cayder grabbed onto his sister's hand and gave her a determined smile. 'Let's go home.'

Erimen, Jey and Kema hung back as they stepped forward, edem snaking around their ankles.

'What should we create?' Cayder asked his mother.

'A door,' Maretta suggested.

They closed their eyes and touched smoky substance.

Create a doorway home, Cayder thought.

He opened his eyes and saw the edem began to solidify and stretch into long planks of wood, covering the tear. A brass door-knocker arose from the centre. It looked like the front door to Broduck Manor.

Cayder looked at his sister. Her brown eyes were large with anticipation.

'You do it,' Leta said, nodding to the doorhandle.

Cayder grabbed the handle and pulled the door upward. Beneath it lay the black tear. He stepped forward.

'Edem be damned!' Cayder cursed as he met with the veil's resistance. He slammed his fist against the tear. It was like touching warm, unyielding black glass.

They weren't going home. They'd failed. Again.

He tilted his head back and let out a ragged groan.

'No!' Desperation flared red on Leta's pale cheeks. 'We have to get home!'

'It's okay, Leta,' Cayder said. 'Maybe we need to use more edem?'

Leta thrust her hands in her hair and stormed off.

'We could send the hullen through,' their mother suggested.

'Can we attach another message for Father?' Cayder asked. Kema stood silently beside him. Seeing his usually vibrant friend so dejected made the failure even worse.

'No,' Maretta replied, shoulders slumped. 'Like the other tear, only something made of edem can pass through.'

Cayder's father would never know how close they were.

'Something made of edem?' Jey asked, breaking the terse silence. 'Or something *with* edem in its veins?'

Leta glanced at her boyfriend. 'What are you talking about?'

'My mate here,' Jey patted the pouch strapped to his side, 'has been pumping edem into my system for days now.' He pulled up the sleeve of his uninjured side. Dark lines spiderwebbed across his tawny skin. 'How much edem do you think you need to make it through?'

Jey raised a black-veined hand towards the veil.

CHAPTER 38

JEY

Jey had never been so tired. Between the whiplash of recent events and the wound that was intent on sucking the very life out of him, he was dead on his feet.

Not *dead*-dead, but also not far off.

Perhaps he wasn't thinking that clearly, but he knew his days were numbered, so why not risk his life to help his friends go home?

Jey could feel the warmth radiating from the veil as his hand drew closer to the juncture between worlds. He held his breath and inched forward, prepared to meet some resistance...It wasn't until his hand disappeared in front of him that he realised he hadn't met any.

He quickly snatched his hand back and was thankful to find it in one piece.

'It seems my experiment was successful,' Jey said, wiggling his fingers. 'Guess that makes me a scientist like my dad.' He placed his hand to his heart. 'He'd be so proud.'

'No—' Leta grasped his arm. 'You can't. We don't know what will happen to you on the other side.'

Jey held up his pouch, which was half full. 'I've got time.'

Days, not much more. But if he stayed, they would all die when the Regency boats reached their destination.

'What do you think?' Cayder asked his mother.

'It's risky,' Maretta replied. 'But Jey might be our only option.'

'He's not going,' Leta was firm, her chin jutting out. 'Absolutely not.'

'Hello?' Jey waved. 'I'm right here and very capable of making my own decisions. I'm going through. The question is, what do you want me to do once I'm on the other side?'

Maretta and Erimen exchanged a glance.

'There's only one way someone has moved back and forth between worlds, and that is via the edem weapons Dr Bueter created,' Maretta said. 'Find one and send it back to us.'

'Right,' Jey said. 'Simple.'

'Don't do anything rash,' Leta said.

'Me? Never.'

She pulled him down to her and pressed a heated kiss to his lips. 'I'll see you...' She squeezed his hand, unsure *when* they would see each other again.

He nodded. It was a good enough farewell, for now. 'I'll see you.'

'Good luck, Jey,' Maretta said.

He squared his shoulders, ignoring the tearing pain in his side. He was going to fix what his father had broken. He stepped through the doorway and down into the veil. It felt like submerging in a pool of warm liquid; the same feeling he'd had when he had jumped from the platform at the Regency headquarters.

Then, he was on the other side.

And the other side didn't look so good.

CHAPTER 39

JEY

Unsurprisingly, it looked like a bomb had gone off. Char marks marred the room in a circular pattern. Twisted, melted fragments of metal were scattered across the floor. It took Jey a moment to realise what he was looking at.

An edemmeter. Or what was left of one.

He reached out to touch a piece of the machine.

'Yowch!' The metal was burning hot.

'Who – who are you?'

Jey turned to find two girls around his age. One of them held what looked like the leg of a table above her head as though she planned to strike.

'Hang on,' Jey said, holding his palms up. He realised his raised black veins made him look like some kind of monster. 'I come in peace.'

'Who are you?' one of the girls repeated. She was a pretty Meiyran girl with long plaited black hair.

'Where's Alain Broduck?' Jey asked, scanning the room as though he might be hiding behind some metal fragment.

The girl shook her head. 'He's not here.'

'Are you Narena?'

The girl – who Jey was pretty sure was Narena – glanced at her friend. 'How do you know my name?'

Definitely Narena then. 'I'm Jey Bueter; a friend of Cayder's.'

Her eyebrows shot to her hairline. 'Really?'

'I mean,' Jey said with a shrug, 'mostly friends. Sometimes I think he hates me, other times I think we're on the road to friendship. But it's a long and winding road and I'm not sure we'll ever reach the end.'

Narena let out a squeak and ran to Jey. Jey thought she was going to throw her arms around him, but then changed her mind at the last minute.

'He's alive?' she asked, bouncing on the balls of her feet. 'You've seen him?'

Jey jerked his thumb to the black rip he'd just stepped out of. 'He's right there, actually.'

When Narena moved towards the veil, Jey pulled her back by the shirt. 'Nope. You don't want to do that. Not unless you want to get stuck over there.'

'Stuck where?' the other girl asked. Her bright green eyes were curious but wary. But she had lowered the table leg, which Jey took as a good sign.

'The other side of the veil,' Jey said as though that were obvious. 'And you are?'

'Farrow,' she replied. 'Do we trust this guy, Narena?'

Jey blinked. 'I risked my life to come over here.'

Farrow narrowed her eyes. '*We* don't know that.'

'Wow,' Jey said, looking around the exploded room. 'Tough crowd.'

'We trust you,' Narena said firmly. 'You know Maretta?'

'Of course. She's the mother of my girlfriend.'

'*Oh!*' Narena's face split into a grin. '*You're* the new source.'

Source? Source of what?

Farrow approached and began circling Jey like he was a specimen to study. 'What happened to your—' Farrow gestured to Jey's hands.

'It's a long story,' Jey said. 'But it's not dangerous.' Not to them. 'Promise.'

'Hmmm,' was all Farrow replied.

Doesn't trust easily, this one, he thought. And he knew there would be a good reason for that.

'What happened to Alain?' Jey asked. 'Maretta was expecting him to be here.'

Narena tugged at her plaits. 'He didn't believe me, so we came instead.'

'That was very brave of you. Okay, team, time to focus; I need to find a weapon. It's about this long,' he held his arms out wide, 'and has a chamber of edem inside. Seen anything like it?'

'Why would we give you a weapon?' Farrow asked, a brow raised.

'Stop it, Farrow,' Narena chided.

'I need the weapon to help the others,' Jey said, nodding to the tear behind him.

Farrow's eyes had not un-narrowed. 'Why didn't they come through with you?'

Jey puffed his chest out. 'I'm special. And trust me, the only way for them to come back is to find this weapon.'

'There are no other weapons here. Only the faulty edemmeter.' Farrow pointed to the metal fragments behind him.

That couldn't be right. Maretta had said there would be weapons here. But Maretta had also been 'dead' for seven years.

'Are you sure?' Jey asked.

Despite the life-saving edem plugged into his veins, he was beginning to feel faint.

'Yes,' Narena agreed. 'We searched the entire facility before setting off the edemmeter. There's nothing else here.'

There goes his grand heroic gesture.

He had come up empty-handed. Like his father had always told him, he was useless. He was best quiet and forgotten.

Just when Jey's thoughts couldn't grow any darker, the world around him dimmed. There was a small leak in between the metal plates above and the trickling water appeared to turn black. From the top of the metal dome, darkness fell – like paint dripping down the walls. Tendrils of black stretched towards the floor.

'Has this happened before?' Jey asked. 'Because this doesn't look good.'

'No,' Narena said. 'It hasn't. But...' She exchanged a look with Farrow.

'It can't be.' Farrow shook her head. 'That *thing* is stuck outside.'

'What kind of thing are we talking about?' Jey asked. 'I'm guessing it's not a good thing.'

The darkness continued to run down the walls until the entire room was pitch black. Edem shifted in the shadows like curling fingers, calling to them. The hairs on Jey's arms stood on end and it felt like someone – or some*thing* – was breathing down his neck. Darkness peeled back from the walls and began congealing in the centre, like a whirlpool. Gradually, it knitted together to form the outline of a person.

When the shadows settled, a woman wearing a black dress of smoke with grey skin and glowing eyes appeared in front of them.

CHAPTER 40

ELENORA

The *Levisial* sailed to the section of water that sat directly underneath the tear in the veil and Myrandir sent out divers. While there was nothing Elenora could do to help, she refused to go below deck and rest. Time ticked away like a pulse beneath her skin. The Regency would soon reach the neighbouring nations and detonate their weapons. Even Dr Bueter paced the deck, worried for tomorrow – if there would be a tomorrow.

It took a few hours for them to locate the weapon on the ocean floor. Dr Bueter was swift to recalibrate the settings, but there was only one way to test it; on the queen herself.

'Do it,' Myrandir ordered. 'Now isn't the time for uncertainty.'

When the black flame struck Myrandir in the stomach, sinking into her shadow form, she didn't scream or even flinch. The flame simply dissipated into her.

Elenora thought the weapon had failed until the queen held up her hand. The shadows falling from her fingertips had stopped. Then her grey fingers began to fade away.

'Come,' she beckoned Elenora and Dr Bueter forward.

Elenora stood close to the queen as she disappeared, leaving behind a black stain on the pearlescent deck.

'What do we do now?' Elenora asked.

Dr Bueter opened his mouth to reply, but a black tendril wrapped around his foot and dragged him down *through* the deck. Elenora was next. An obsidian rope tied around her body and pulled her down into the darkness.

Elenora couldn't breathe. She couldn't see. She felt all the blood rush to her head as though she was spinning upside down. A pressure pushed against her chest.

Then, the pressure and darkness were gone.

Elenora was inside some kind of metal dome. Dr Bueter stood on the other side of the queen of shadows.

'Where are we?' Myrandir asked the general.

Dr Bueter looked around the room. 'It appears to be the defunct Regency base in Lake Rusterton,' he said.

Lake Rusterton? Did that mean they were back in Telene?

There were two girls she didn't recognise, standing alongside Jey. Jey looked different from when Elenora saw him last, his usual broad stance was lopsided, and black veins ran up the sides of his neck.

'How did you get here?' Dr Bueter asked his son. 'I thought you jumped through the veil?' He shot a heated look to Elenora as though she and Cayder had lied to him.

If Jey was here, where was her brother?

'I conducted my own experiment,' Jey said, nodding to a slash of darkness behind him. 'But the others are still stuck.'

Elenora's heart leapt; she *was* back in Telene! She was home! Dr Bueter had done it!

'Wonderful!' Myrandir's laugh trilled. 'Well done, Dr Bueter.'

'And you must be the Shadow Queen that I've heard so much about,' Jey said with an exaggerated bow. 'These are my friends Narena and Farrow.' He gestured to the Meiyran girl and a pale redheaded girl. 'Although Farrow is not quite sure about me yet. But don't worry, I'll win her over.'

Narena and Farrow had their hands clasped together, fear in their eyes. Elenora had forgotten the impact of Myrandir's presence. It was not unlike when Elenora had first seen the hullen fly through the veil and to tear the Regency headquarters apart. A mixture of shock and awe.

Myrandir closed her brilliant eyes. 'It's morning. And yet I cannot sense any shadows.'

'That's due to the permacloud,' Dr Bueter said. 'The Regency built a machine to block any harsh light and prevent dark shadows from forming.'

'I am trapped here until night-time?' Myrandir cocked her head to the side. 'You tricked me?'

'No,' he replied. 'I didn't know where we were going to end up. I set my weapon to bring you back to the location you were last in Telene. You led us here, not I.'

Myrandir flicked her hand as though she were batting away a bug. 'Dr Bueter, you will turn off the permacloud so I can roam free.'

'We can't,' Elenora said. 'It's part of our power plant; if you turn it off, the entire city will go dark at night. And anyone will be able to tap into edem – your magic.'

'She's right,' Dr Bueter said with an exhausted sigh, as though agreeing with Elenora pained him. 'You will need to wait till night-time before you can leave here and fix the veil.'

'I have waited long enough.' Myrandir pointed to Dr Bueter, shadows dripping from her fingers like blood. 'You will not keep me caged in this lake like you have one of my pets.'

Narena gasped. 'That creature belongs to you?'

'Yes.' Myrandir grinned. 'My family used to have a home by the lake, but even all the way out here, they made me hide who I was. I was forced to create my own friends for company.'

'Your creature tried to kill us!' Farrow said. 'It killed my grandmother's friend and destroyed her house!'

'Nonsense,' Myrandir said. 'The creature would only be trying to defend itself. Your Regency,' she looked at Dr Bueter and anger simmered behind her glittering eyes, 'have tried to kill it many times.'

'That's why the base is here!' Narena said. 'It was to track the creature. We were right!'

Farrow nodded. 'And that's why it tried to kill my grand-mother; she was trying to expose it!'

'What are they talking about, Myrandir?' Elenora asked.

Myrandir's eyes glimmered with merriment. 'I think it would be best to show you...'

She dispersed back up the walls, towards a small gap in the sheets of metal above them.

Elenora heard the sound of a door opening.

'The airlock!' Farrow exclaimed.

Narena started repeating a Meiyran prayer for safety over and over.

That wasn't a good sign.

When Myrandir reappeared, she was not alone. A hideous creature with tentacles for arms and thin elongated legs stood beside her. Like the Shadow Queen, the creature had luminous eyes and a wide mouth of thin jagged teeth. It was monstrous and smelled of deep murky waters.

Myrandir scratched the creature under its slimy chin. 'I wanted a friend who could live in and out of the water.' She shrugged. 'It doesn't look exactly like what I had in mind, but then again, my creations rarely do. Do they, Pet?'

'What about the hullen?' Elenora asked. They were beautiful in comparison to this ghastly mistake of a life.

'They disobeyed me,' she replied with a sneer. 'They turned against me when my family tried to stop me from using my power.'

Something bitter rose in Elenora's stomach. 'You said *you* wanted to stop – and that they abused your power to the point of your death.'

'They did!' Her voice sounded like the screech of a thousand people. 'They made me wear a mask to hide who I was. They punished me every time I created new life. If my creatures were not to their liking,' she gestured to the monster beside her, 'they killed them. But not the hullen – oh no. They liked those stupid feathered beasts.'

Elenora felt like she was going to faint. 'I don't understand.'

Myrandir shook her head in disappointment. 'When my family could no longer control me and my power, they tried to kill me. I created the veil and my world to escape. And I took their beloved hullen from them.'

'*You* shot down our hullen,' Elenora realised. Not the radicals. Not her brother.

'I didn't know it had you in its grasp, child. I didn't know you were one of my kind.'

Elenora might share some of Myrandir's blood, but that was where their similarities ended. 'Was anything you told me true?'

'Of course,' she replied. 'Our worlds *will* end if I don't stop the Regency's weapons, but there's only one way to do that.'

Elenora was afraid to ask. 'What are you going to do?'

She held her hands wide. 'I will tear down the veil and draw all my power back to me.'

That would remove all edem from Telene's shadows. No more edem, no more edem weapons.

'Then I will rule Telene as I always should have.' She reached out and stroked the neck of her creature. 'And I will create whatever I want.'

The monster beside her snickered happily.

'What will happen to us?' Jey asked. 'To everyone in Telene?'

'That depends on whose side you are on,' Myrandir said. Her monster took a step forward, baring its teeth in a snarl.

Elenora felt ill. The Shadow Queen was dangerous. She had been a prisoner of the veil, and they had released her back into Telene.

How could Elenora have made such a crucial mistake? Was it merely the title of 'Queen' that had led Elenora to believe she was good? Had she not learnt by now that a title didn't mean anything? It didn't mean people were good, or right, or even kind.

'If you won't help me,' Myrandir said, tossing a lock of shadowy hair over her shoulder, 'then I will destroy the permacloud myself once the sun sets. And thank you for the tip on the power plant, Princess. After I destroy it, I will be able to roam freely both day and night.'

Then Myrandir could do whatever she pleased. Not only in Telene, but across the entire world. She could create as many deadly creatures as she desired and kill anyone who stood against her.

'Why did you bring her here?' Narena was looking at Elenora for an answer, as though this was all her fault.

'Your princess has summoned the future,' Myrandir said. 'You should be thanking her.'

Oh no.

When they had first met the Shadow Queen, she had told them that she saw the future, and the end of both their worlds. She had claimed she would protect everyone from that outcome, but it was clear now that the future was caused by her arrival. And Elenora had made it happen.

'I won't let you do this!' Elenora said. 'I won't let you go free.'

'No,' Dr Bueter agreed. 'We won't.'

He raised the edem weapon to send Myrandir back to the other side of the veil. But before he could shoot, the creature's tentacle flew out and wrapped around Dr Bueter's neck. Dr Bueter's face went red. His eyes bulged. He clawed at his throat, making a guttural, choking noise.

'Stop it!' Jey ran to his father's side. 'Let him go!'

Another snake-like tendril extended from the creature, wrapping around Jey's throat and preventing him from reaching the gun his father had dropped.

'My pet is very protective of me,' Myrandir said with a chuckle.

Jey and Dr Bueter thrashed in the creature's grip.

'Do something!' Narena cried.

But what could she do?

'Please don't do this!' Elenora pleaded with Myrandir. 'We can rule this world together. We don't have to hurt one another!'

Myrandir's grey lips quirked. 'I have tried that before; it doesn't work. Step in line, Princess.'

Elenora shook her head. 'I won't.'

'So be it.' She whipped her hand through the air and launched a lasso of shadow towards Elenora.

'Don't—' Elenora began, but her windpipe was crushed. She couldn't breathe. She fell to her knees.

Dr Bueter had already passed out and Elenora was well on the way. As darkness smothered her vision, Elenora's thoughts returned to her family. She hated that she could never make peace with Erimen, and that she would never get to tell Cayder or Kema she understood why they kept their secrets.

Most importantly, she was sorry.

She didn't think about the pain. She didn't care about what happened next.

She just wanted another chance.

CHAPTER 41

NARENA

Narena watched as Jey, Dr Bueter and the princess were starved of air. She crouched behind the tables so the Shadow Queen couldn't see her. She pulled Farrow down with her. Dr Bueter had already passed out – or worse. Jey and Elenora would be next.

'We have to get out of here!' Farrow whispered.

But Narena couldn't move. Nor did she want to. She couldn't allow the queen and her monster to kill three people in front of her, and then go on to kill countless others.

'We can't leave them,' Narena said.

Farrow's face was paler than usual. 'What can we do?'

'Do you still have your torch?'

Farrow held it up.

'You stay here,' Narena said. 'Use your torch when I signal.'

Once Narena reached the other side of the room, she jumped up from her hiding spot. 'Now!' she shouted.

Farrow swung her torch towards the tendril that wrapped around Elenora's neck. The tendril fragmented into smoke and Elenora dropped to the ground with a groan.

Meanwhile, Narena flashed her torch towards Jey's neck. The monster released Jey with a thud. He was hurt, but alive.

'If you think that will stop us,' the Shadow Queen said, 'you're mistaken.'

This time the creature's tentacles came for Narena and Farrow.

Narena tried to ward it off, but as soon as one tentacle disappeared, another would replace it. A tentacle wrapped itself around Narena's middle and squeezed. Her hand was trapped underneath: she couldn't lift her torch. Farrow wasn't in any better shape – her hands were restrained behind her back.

'A shadow may disperse in light,' the queen said with a slow blink, 'but it always comes back. You cannot kill the dark.'

'I'm sorry,' Narena shouted to Farrow. They should have run.

Farrow shook her head. 'You have nothing to be sorry for.'

Narena wished she could hold her one last time. She wished she had done things differently. She wished a lot of things had been different—

'Get off me!' the queen cried.

Three hullen had appeared through the veil and begun attacking the queen and her pet. One hullen ripped at the queen, tearing shadowy chunks from her body. Another tore into the monstrous creature, splitting it in two. The tentacle loosened around Narena's waist and she flopped to the ground.

'Stop!' the Shadow Queen cried as her pet was devoured by the hullen. 'No!'

Another hullen latched onto the Shadow Queen's back and ripped at her hair.

The queen dissipated into a curtain of shadows. She twisted

around the room, dodging the reach of the hullen, but they were relentless.

The queen flew up towards the small crack between the metal plates above them and disappeared into the shadowy recesses of the lake, where she would be safe in the dark.

The hullen let out a series of hoots then disappeared back through the veil.

Farrow ran to Narena and pulled her to her feet. 'Are you okay?'

'Yes.' Narena rubbed her stomach. There would be some bruising, perhaps even a cracked rib, but she was alive. 'Are you?'

Farrow threw her arms around her. 'I was worried I was going to lose you.'

Narena pressed her face into Farrow's neck. They were safe.

'Sorry to interrupt,' Jey said letting out a wheeze. 'While the queen is gone, I don't think we can call her forgotten. We need a plan.'

'I agree.' Elenora said, propping herself up against a broken piece of edemmeter. 'She said that shadows can't be killed, just dispersed.'

Jey approached his father's slumped form and felt for a pulse. 'Much like my dad, it seems,' he said in relief, sagging down next to him.

'The queen will be trapped in the shadows of the lake until sundown,' Farrow said. 'Then she can do whatever she pleases.'

'We have to stop her,' Elenora said.

'Agreed,' Jey said. 'If it weren't for the hullen, we'd all be dead.'

'But even the hullen couldn't kill her,' Narena pointed out. 'Only annoy her.'

'She did seem mightily annoyed,' Jey said.

Narena rubbed her temples while Elenora stared up at the ceiling. Jey poked his father to make sure that he was, in fact, still alive.

'So what? We give up?' Farrow asked. 'Allow her to take over Telene? Allow her to populate the world with her flesh-eating beasts?' Farrow's eyes were wild, her cheeks flaming. Narena could see she wanted revenge for her grandmother and the person who had created the beast that had led to the end of her life.

'No one wants that,' Jey said. 'Not even my dad, and he's the worst.'

'You're Telene's queen, aren't you?' Narena asked Elenora. 'What can we do to stop her?'

Elenora shook her head. 'I'm just the princess; my brother is the one in charge and he's still on the other side of the veil. *I* can't do anything.'

'Don't sell yourself short,' Jey said. '*You* destroyed the Regency headquarters.'

'I'm just the royal spare,' Elenora argued.

Jey shrugged. 'And I'm just a thorn in my dad's side. That doesn't mean I'm useless.'

'Or helpless,' Farrow added. 'I'm a Pedec. A truth seeker.'

'Exactly!' Jey pointed at Farrow as though he knew what her declaration meant. 'We can do and be whatever we want.'

'I want Cayder,' Narena admitted. Farrow and Elenora both looked at her; Farrow's brows were crumpled in confusion. 'I want to *see* Cayder, I mean. He'd know what to do.'

'Only the hullen can travel through a tear in the veil,' Elenora said.

'Or someone with a lot of edem in their blood,' Jey offered, holding out his black-lined arms.

Narena tugged on one of her plaits as she pondered. 'Maybe bringing down the veil isn't such a bad idea.'

Jey baulked. 'It might be the recent lack of oxygen to my brain, but it sounds like you agree with the Shadow Queen.'

'Narena is right,' Elenora said. 'If there's no veil, the worlds will be one again. The hullen will be on this side. With us.'

'Then what?' Jey asked.

Elenora and Narena exchanged a look.

Elenora grinned dangerously. 'We fight.'

CHAPTER 42

CAYDER

Cayder knew something had gone wrong when the three hullen dove through the doorway and into the veil, leaving them behind. The hullen were drawn to the use of edem, and to protect people from its power.

Whatever was happening on the other side wasn't good.

They came back only minutes later, one after another.

'What happened?' Cayder asked his mother as she placed her hand on the creature's head. Maretta and the hullen both closed their eyes.

'The Shadow Queen is on the other side,' she replied, her eyes flicking back and forth beneath her eyelids. 'The queen and one of her creatures attacked the others.'

'What?' Cayder asked. Why would she do that?

Cayder reached up to touch the hullen's scaly face and shut his eyes.

Show me everything, he commanded in his mind.

The darkness behind his lids morphed, shifting like edem in shadows. He saw the black of the veil as the hullen approached and a sudden shift to light as it arrived on the other side. Everything else was sketched in grey.

This must be how the hullen see the world.

The Shadow Queen stood in the centre of a circular room; she had something wrapped around Narena's middle.

Where's Father? Why is Narena here?

Jey and Dr Bueter were also under attack, but from a hideous gangly creature. Then he saw Elenora—

Elle!

His heart thumped wildly in his chest as she fought for breath.

He should have been there! He should have been fighting by her side. He never should have let her go.

The hullen fought the creature, tearing it to pieces, and the Shadow Queen disappeared. The hullen then retreated through the veil, leaving everyone behind.

Cayder opened his eyes and sucked in a stabilising breath.

Everyone is safe. For now.

'Why would the queen attack?' Cayder asked breathlessly, his heart still pounding. He felt disorientated, the world around him too harsh and too bright. 'It doesn't make sense.'

'Because she wants Telene for herself,' Jey said, as he stepped out of the veil through the door. 'She's been lying to you.'

'Jey!' Leta ran to him, searching for additional injuries. 'Are you okay?'

'I'm fine, Nettie.'

'What about the others?' Cayder asked, glancing at Erimen. 'Elenora?'

'Everyone's a little shaken up,' Jey admitted. 'But we're okay. We have a plan.'

Cayder grimaced. When there was a plan, there was the chance for something – or *everything* – to go wrong.

'Out with it, Jey!' Leta said in exasperation. Cayder liked that his sister kept him in line.

'The Shadow Queen is planning to tear down the veil tonight,' Jey explained. 'That will bring our worlds back together. She is going to go for the power plant and destroy the permacloud so she can roam free during the day. And she plans to get rid of anyone who stands in her way. But we're going to be ready for her.'

'We've seen what she can do,' Kema said, 'and we're no match for her and her power.'

'Even the hullen didn't kill her,' Cayder added.

Jey pursed his lips. 'I didn't say it was a perfect plan. But if we band together, along with the hullen, then we have a chance. Maretta, Erimen – do you think everyone from the compound will join our fight?'

Maretta looked to the king and he nodded. 'Of course,' Maretta said. 'They all want to go home.'

'They're going to get their wish,' Jey said, 'but if we don't stop the queen, they're not going to like what's waiting for them on the other side.'

'We should also warn Rusteef,' Kema said.

'Why would he be on our side?' Cayder asked.

'Because he's a good man.' Kema crossed her arms over her chest. 'I've spent time with him and there's no way he would know what the queen's real plan is. There are people in the city who need to be protected.'

A fire had reignited in Kema's eyes, and Cayder knew his friend needed this mission to atone for what had happened with the rebels.

'Mother?' Cayder asked. 'What do you think?'

His mother frowned. 'It sounds like we don't have a choice. The worlds are going to reunite, and we have no idea what to expect.'

'Expect chaos and creepy creatures,' Jey offered helpfully.

'Where is the queen now?' Erimen asked. Cayder could see the boy slipping away and the king rising to the surface.

'She disappeared into the lake,' Jey said. 'She'll be trapped in the shadows until sunset, just as she's been held a prisoner here due to the persistent daylight.'

A prisoner...

A missing puzzle piece clicked into place.

'We need to find a place that has constant diffuse light,' Cayder said. 'Somewhere she can't escape from. And somewhere that isn't connected to the power plant.'

'What are you thinking?' Leta asked.

'We may not be able to destroy her,' Cayder said, 'but we can *contain* her.'

'Of course.' Kema grinned in understanding. 'Vardean.'

———

As soon as they arrived back at the compound, Cayder's mother communicated a message to the hullen to gather as many of their kind as they could.

It was lunchtime down in the compound and the canteen was full.

'I'll check to see if anyone's missing,' Erimen said.

Kema nodded. 'I'll help.'

The pair took off down the icy corridors.

Cayder's mother headed towards the front of the room; a few people glanced up as she passed, while others muttered their grievances and continued eating.

'I'm calling an urgent townhall,' Maretta called out, lifting her voice above the hubbub of the room. 'I'll begin in five minutes. Make sure your family are all accounted for.'

A few people looked scared; most were curious.

'I told the hullen to return in six hours,' Maretta said to them quietly. 'We have time to prepare everyone for battle.'

'With what weapons?' Jey asked.

'Illumination is our only form of protection. We have torches and lanterns. We can attach them to the hullens' saddles.'

'How will we know where to find the Shadow Queen?' Leta asked.

Cayder pulled the maps Rusteef had given him from his bag. He layered them on top of each other and flattened them onto the nearest table, pushing aside bowls of food.

'*Here*—' Cayder pointed to a spot along the Unbent River. 'We know she'll attack the power plant, so we need to be in the same location.' He lifted the top layer to show the corresponding point on the map. It wasn't far from the mountain range that Elenora and Cayder had tried and failed to climb.

Kema and Erimen returned with some stragglers, and they were ready to begin the meeting.

'Thank you for your attendance,' Cayder's mother said to her assembled audience. 'This is the moment we've been waiting for.

We are going home!' She tried to smile, but concern still lined her brow.

'You found a way back?' a man questioned from the crowd.

Maretta shook her head. 'Our way home found us, but it's not going to be easy.' She nodded at the king.

'We need your help,' Erimen said, his shoulders already squared for battle. 'The veil between here and Telene is soon to dissipate and our worlds will become one.'

The crowd chattered among themselves.

'There's no need to fear!' Maretta exclaimed. 'We are fore-warned and therefore we can protect ourselves. And our best form of protection, as always, is the hullen.'

'There aren't enough hullen to protect all of us!' a woman said, standing from her table. 'How will we decide who will be protected and who won't?' She glowered at Jey for a reason Cayder did not understand.

'We are gathering as many hullen as we can, Erithe,' Maretta replied. 'We can fit two people per hullen – or three children. Our best bet is to be in the sky when the transition comes, as we do not know what will happen on land.'

'We cannot stay here,' Erimen said with a firm nod. 'You have a few hours to pack your things, but then we must depart.'

'What about the people who have lived here their entire lives?' another person asked.

'I'm sorry,' Erimen said, clasping his hands together. 'This was not a choice we made – but it's a choice we can make the best of.'

'I choose to stay here,' someone called out. Others mumbled their agreement.

Cayder had thought everyone would be happy to return home, but for some, this had always been their home – or had become it.

'This world is ending,' Cayder said, standing next to his mother. 'And it's happening whether we like it or not. If you stay here, you'll die.'

'And what promise can you make us if we leave with you?' Erithe asked.

'I can promise you a chance,' Cayder said. 'That's all we can ever ask for in life.'

CHAPTER 43

ELENORA

Elenora didn't have the opportunity to rejoice in being back in Telene. Time was against them. Jey had returned briefly to fill them in on the plan to lock the Shadow Queen in Vardean, and while it took some convincing, Dr Bueter agreed to evacuate the prison in preparation.

They escaped Lake Rusterton's Regency base through the emergency exit and parted ways with Dr Bueter. Elenora headed to the *Telene Herald* with Narena and Farrow; they needed to warn everyone for the fight ahead.

The offices were quiet when they entered.

'We've missed this morning's one a.m. print run,' Narena explained. 'We'll have to write for the special Sunday afternoon edition.' Narena shoved paper into the typewriter with shaking hands.

'Here—' Farrow took the pages from her and fed them into the machine. 'I'll type.'

'What should we write?' Narena asked.

For centuries, the people of Telene had been lied to. People weren't ready for the truth. 'We don't want to scare them, but we need their help,' Elenora said.

Farrow nodded. 'We'll tell them enough to intrigue them.'

'Curfew starts at eight,' Elenora said. 'But what time does it actually get dark?' It had been months since she'd seen the sun dip below the ocean from her bedroom on the castle isle. Her life before Vardean was hazy like a dream.

Narena ran to a stack of this morning's newspaper and flipped to a map of Telene on the back page.

'Nine-o-two,' Narena informed.

'And what time does the office open today?' Elenora asked.

'Ten a.m.,' Narena said with a tense nod. 'We only have an hour before this place is full of people.'

'Don't worry,' Farrow said, settling into the chair. 'I type quickly.'

THE TRUTH BEHIND THE VEIL WILL BE REVEALED TONIGHT!

By Narena Lunita and Farrow Pedec

For centuries, we've been lied to. Our history hidden. The truth buried. But tonight, all will be revealed.

If you've ever wondered why the call of edem is so strong, you are not alone. If you've ever wished to examine the dark, we see you. If you've been calling for balance, we hear you.

Our world is about to change and we call upon you to be there to ensure we survive another day.

This evening, the Regency General has cancelled curfew and requests your presence at the power plant before nine p.m. Bring any and all forms of illumination that you can.

And be prepared to fight the darkness once and for all.

They printed the article and waited for the Sunday staff to arrive. Elenora helped Narena and Farrow slip the article into the Sunday afternoon newspaper as it came off the presses.

'I can't believe I'm doing this again,' Narena said. 'My mother is going to kill me.' They were hiding in the back of the publishing plant to ensure no one recognised them.

'She will understand,' Elenora said, sliding another article in between the pages. 'I'll make sure of it.'

Narena looked uncertain, but it was too late to turn back now. They needed everyone's help if they had a chance at defeating the Shadow Queen.

———

At eight-thirty, Elenora, Farrow and Narena took a trolley to the Unbent River with their supplies; they had ransacked the *Telene Herald*'s lantern reserves and packed as many lanterns and lamp oil containers that they could in their bags.

The trolley pulled to a stop in front of the power plant, which was pumping clouds into the atmosphere with a hiss. A small gathering of people stood in the street, holding burning candles or torches.

'There's only a couple of hundred people here,' Farrow lamented.

Taking down the power plant would provide the Shadow Queen with a perfect playground of darkness. With no perma-cloud in the day, she could roam free in the shadows and wreak havoc in the night. This world would be hers.

Narena pulled the lanterns out of her bag and began lighting them. 'We did everything we could,' she said.

Elenora wondered if that was true. She had always been a monarch behind the scenes, behind the shadows and behind a mask. If she wanted her people to join her – believe her – they needed to *see* her. Trust her. Know her.

She took one of the lanterns and wove her way through the crowd.

'Where are you going?' Narena asked.

'To save my people!' Elenora called back over her shoulder.

A concrete blockade separated the crowd from the power plant. Elenora placed the lantern on the top of the blockade and used her uninjured arm to pull herself up. She looked out to the brave citizens of Telene who had answered their call. They clutched their torches and candles with uncertain hands, eyes darting about.

'Thank you for coming!' Elenora called out, holding up her lantern to her face so everyone could see her.

The crowd bristled in confusion and outrage.

'*You* wrote the article?'

'You're just a kid!'

'I knew this was some kind of joke!'

'I am Elenora, Princess of Telene!' Elenora proclaimed. 'Sister to King Erimen. I need your help to save our city!'

'The Princess is dead!' someone shouted. 'How dare you impersonate a royal!'

Elenora glanced at Farrow and Narena. How could she prove she was the princess?

'What she says is true,' a man said from below her – *Dr Bueter*. He climbed onto the blockade to stand beside her. Elenora's breath escaped her. He came to help?

'It's the Regency General!'

347

The crowd scattered.

Hundreds of Regency agents sauntered into the street, their silvery cloaks flapping behind them. They encircled the crowd in a protective barrier.

'It's a trap!' a man cried out. 'They're going to lock us up for breaking curfew!'

'Calm down!' Dr Bueter shouted to the restless mass. '*She* is your princess.' He handed Elenora the bejewelled mask she'd left behind in Vardean. The lumanite stones glittered under Elenora's lantern, shining streaks of light across the crowd. 'And you should heed her warning!'

Dr Bueter had worked against them for so long, and while he had agreed to evacuate Vardean, she didn't expect him to stand alongside her tonight.

'You need all the help you can get,' he gruffly muttered to her, as though he didn't actually want to be there.

'What made you change your mind?' Elenora asked.

He laughed, but not unkindly. 'I haven't. I still believe in what the Regency has done.' He held up a hand before she could argue. 'We have always fought to uncover the truth.'

That was ironic, considering what the Regency had done to cover up their involvement in both the Ferrington fires and her brother's disappearance.

Dr Bueter shrugged. 'I've seen what the Shadow Queen can do, and I have always wanted to protect Telene, despite what you may think.'

'Let's agree to disagree,' she said. They had more pressing matters.

Elenora put her lantern down and ran her hands over the horns on either side of the luminescent mask. She raised the mask to place it over her face, but hesitated. Her mother had worn this mask, like her mother before her and hers before that. In the beginning, this mask was worn by the Shadow Queen, to hide her face and the power pulsing beneath her skin. But Elenora didn't want to hide. Not this time.

She held the mask up so the crowd could see it. 'This is the mask of the royals. It has belonged to my family for generations, and for generations we have worn it to signify our title and protect ourselves from the dark. And I always thought it was the dark we should fear, however this mask did not only conceal my identity, it concealed the truth of our world. Tonight, I want you to see my face as I tell you the truth that has been denied from us for too long.'

The people in the crowd still fretted, but were silent. She had their attention.

'An entire world lives beyond the veil. It was created by the Shadow Queen, a banished, powerful royal. When the tear was created, her power seeped through from the other side. And this is the power we tap into in the shadows. When something disappears from edem, it is sent to this other world. A world in limbo. And then it returns to us. The veil between our worlds makes the use of her magic unpredictable, but trust me when I say she has full control over her power and it is deadly.

'Tonight, the veil will fall, combining these worlds. The Shadow Queen will attack the power plant to cut off our electricity and destroy the permacloud so that she is free to reign.' She pointed to the structure behind her. 'She will kill anyone who stands against her. This is why I have called you here. Will you help save Telene from her attack?'

Elenora couldn't do this alone. None of them could. They needed each other for this to work.

Elenora held up her hands to the sky. 'Will you help me fight back against the dark?'

The crowd was silent until someone shouted out, 'I will!'

It was Narena, waving her torch from the crowd.

Farrow chimed in, 'So will I!'

'And all of the Regency will be of assistance tonight,' Dr Bueter added.

Elenora might not like the general, but she did need his help.

The Regency agents each called out, starting a wave among the crowd. It wasn't the number Elenora had hoped for, but it would have to do.

'Thank you all!' Elenora said. 'I need you to use any form of light to protect yourselves and—'

The bell for the curfew began tolling from a nearby clocktower.

It was nine o'clock.

'We need to work together!' Elenora cried, her heart thumping wildly. 'We are stronger as a group. We can defeat the dark once and for all!'

Elenora found Narena and Farrow amongst the horde.

Two minutes, Narena mouthed.

Elenora nodded, holding her mask tight in her hand.

This is it.

They had one chance to defend the power plant from the Shadow Queen.

As much as Elenora wished Erimen was with her, she knew it was her time to take her place as a royal. She had been in every meeting with Erimen, she had learnt the ways of their people and their wants and needs.

She wasn't just the spare. She was a leader just like Erimen.

Elenora was the beginning of a new way to rule, where the people would know the truth to every decision they made.

She was ready.

The last of the sunlight disappeared from the sky. The streetlamps encircled the crowd in a bubble of light, separating them from edem. Everyone was silent, waiting for the attack. Elenora wondered how long it would take for the queen to travel from Lake Rusterton before she—

BOOM!

The crowd jumped. Cracks appeared in the funnel of the power plant behind them and the hiss of the permacloud stopped abruptly.

She was here.

The streetlamps around them flashed then popped, one by one. Darkness fell. Screams came from the crowd.

'What do we do, Princess?' a woman shouted out from the dim.

'Stay calm!' Elenora declared. 'And raise your lights!'

'That's adorable.'

Elenora turned to find the Shadow Queen behind her, her eyes flashing like a cat's in the night. She loomed against the broken power plant tower – seemingly larger than at the old Regency base. More powerful. And much more frightening.

'You think that will help?' the Shadow Queen asked. She waved a couple of fingers and blew out all the candles in the crowd.

People screamed and fled for the nearest cover.

'Stay strong!' Elenora shouted to those who remained. 'Keep together – hold up your lanterns!'

The Shadow Queen knocked Elenora and Dr Bueter off the blockade with a wave of her hand, pushing a wall of darkness towards them.

'The princess is not your ruler,' the Shadow Queen's voice thundered, her crown of shadows trickling down her forehead. '*I* am.'

Elenora pulled herself up from the ground. Her arm was hanging at an odd angle and pain shot up her neck and down her spine. She had dislocated her shoulder again, but she didn't have time to wallow in pain.

'Don't listen to her!' Elenora cried out. 'She will kill anyone who stands in her way!'

'Then don't stand in my way.' The queen appeared in front of her, knocking her down with another wave of her hand.

'Use your lights!' Elenora screamed.

'Be quiet!' the queen ordered. 'While I may not be able to extinguish all of their lights, I can snuff you out.' She brought her grey foot down on Elenora's chest.

Elenora couldn't breathe. She flapped around, desperate for something to fight back with. Even edem eluded her grasp. Then her fingertips reached something familiar. With her last breath, she took hold of the mask and pulled it towards her. She held it up and light from the lanterns refracted from its surface onto the queen. She tried to angle it strategically—

The queen knocked the mask out of Elenora's hand with a snicker. 'You think that's enough to hurt me? You're just like my parents.'

Elenora's heart sank. That was her only line of defence.

The queen stepped on the mask, smashing it to pieces. Her mother's most prized possession was gone. And soon Elenora would follow her parents into the everlasting dark.

And yet, the Shadow Queen quivered, her body shuddering. She whirled around to find the crowd had encircled her, led by Narena and Farrow.

'You cannot kill me!' the queen exclaimed. She tried to snuff out a lantern close to her with a wave of her hand, but her shadowy fingers had turned a pale pink. She was reverting to her human form.

'Don't be afraid!' Narena called out to the crowd.

They lifted their lanterns and stepped closer to the queen, creating a bubble of warmth and light. Elenora could feel the heat warm her skin, reassuring against the dark.

The Shadow Queen looked back to Elenora, her face twisted in rage. 'Your efforts are futile.'

'No.' Elenora pushed up on her side. 'The fight for freedom never is.'

The queen huffed then jumped skyward, fleeing into the night.

'Are you all right?' Narena bent down to help Elenora up.

'Yes,' Elenora wheezed. 'I'm fine.'

The Shadow Queen floated above the crowd. Her eyes blazed; two twin suns in the starry sky.

'Can't you see I'm trying to save you?' the queen roared. 'It's your Regency who wants to destroy our worlds. Only I can stop them.'

She closed her eyes and threw her arms out wide. The ground trembled underfoot. Anyone who still had some form of light held it up to ward against the queen, but her power was far too strong.

The edem that swirled around in the dark was drawn towards her, wrapping around her arms, legs, hair and neck. The queen threw her head back in delight as it became a part of her.

More and more edem whipped through the air, so thick that Elenora could barely see.

She stumbled as the cobblestones cracked underfoot. Someone grabbed her uninjured elbow to stop her from falling.

'We have to get you somewhere safe.' It was Dr Bueter.

Elenora shook her head. 'We have to stay. The others will be here soon.'

Then the sky exploded.

White streaks appeared overhead as the veil began to falter.

A tree shot up from the earth, bursting through the roof of a nearby building and branching up to the sky.

'Oh no,' Elenora whispered.

More trees sprouted from the ground as the two worlds collided. The front of the power plant was obliterated as half a mountain appeared where it had stood moments ago.

This was worse than Elenora thought. She should have used the article to tell everyone to stay home!

The sky flashed glaringly white, illuminating the streets. For a moment, the Shadow Queen was a jet-black ink blot against the bright sky, her head thrown back in elation.

And in a flash, all light disappeared and the world was dark.

CHAPTER 44

JEY

At eight p.m., everyone from the compound headed to the waterfall, finding around a hundred hullen awaiting them. The creatures flapped agitatedly, as though they could sense the approaching danger. Jey wondered if they could see the future, and what his might look like. He forced himself to focus on the plan. He'd worry about his injury on the other side of this – literally and metaphorically.

Maretta asked the creatures to evacuate the children and the elderly first; taking them to the coastline where it would be safer when the worlds merged. Kema headed to the *Levisial* to warn Rusteef of the dangers coming their way, and to evacuate their city. Anyone who wanted to stay and fight took a hullen towards the valley that matched the coordinates of the power plant's location.

Leta rode with Jey. She held onto the back of his shirt, careful not to touch his wound.

The sky flickering dark was the first sign of the veil coming down.

'Launch!' Erimen commanded, and the flock of hullen sailed into the sky.

The side of one mountain was the first thing to crumble like a kicked sandcastle. In its place stood the remnants of the power plant.

'It's happening!' Leta spoke into Jey's ear. 'We're going home.'

But what's going to remain of it? Jey wondered.

The field below turned grey, as cobblestones sprung from the earth like blooming flowers. Lampposts unfurled along the streets like dominoes falling in reverse. A narrow section of land that wound around the mountain range dropped down to form a deep riverbed. Murky liquid rose like a bathtub filling with dirty water, forming the Unbent River – a sight Jey would have been happy never to see again.

The hullen fluttered their wings as the world around them transformed piece by piece. A middle section disappeared between two mountains as though someone had erased them from the map; in its place stood the Kardelle County hospital. Another building appeared, and another. A dark smoky haze blew in across the earth below and when it cleared, a hundred or so people were standing in the streets.

Their screams were louder than the rumbling of the earth.

Then someone turned off the lights.

The hullen let out a unified screech.

'And we're back,' Jey said.

Some buildings had crumpled to the ground in the merge; large pieces of stonework littered the streets. A throng of people were running and screaming in despair. Jey didn't blame them.

'Remain calm!' Jey heard Elenora shout from the ground. 'The veil is gone and our worlds are now one.'

Jey swooped down towards her. Farrow and Narena were holding her up; Elenora's arm was at a strange angle.

'Where's the Shadow Queen?' he asked, scanning the inky sky for her blazing bright eyes.

Elenora looked up. Pain was written all over her face, but she seemed determined, not scared. 'She disappeared once the veil came down.'

Another hullen pulled its wings in tight and landed beside Jey.

'Elenora!' Erimen jumped off his hullen to reach her. 'Are you—'

'I'm so sorry!' Elenora flung one arm around his shoulder. 'I never should have left you!'

'It was my fault,' he said. 'I should have told you the truth years ago. I don't blame you for being angry. I deserve it.'

They held onto each other.

'What do we do now?' Jey asked the royals. The hullen were descending, returning people from the compound to the ground, which was only causing more chaos among those in the streets.

'We have to find the Shadow Queen.' The fire had returned to Elenora's eyes, and this was the princess Jey knew not to mess with.

'Any ideas where she might have gone?' Erimen asked his sister.

'Her home,' Elenora said with a grim smile. '*Our* home. She wants to rule.'

'What should we do?' Narena was clutching so hard onto a lantern that her knuckles were white. Her dark eyes flitted about.

The Shadow Queen could be anywhere in the darkness. But Jey couldn't see anything moving. Not even edem...The darkness was still. Edem was gone.

Jey didn't have time to worry about what that meant for him and his condition.

Elenora nodded to Narena and Farrow. 'We'll find her. You two go home to your families and lock your doors. You've done enough.'

Narena exchanged a look with Farrow and she nodded. 'We're staying,' Narena said, raising her lantern. 'This is our fight too.'

Elenora couldn't argue against that. 'Find a hullen,' she instructed. 'And head to the castle isle.'

The king and princess climbed onto a hullen and returned to the sky.

Jey leaned forward to touch the side of his creature's face. *Find the Shadow Queen*, he thought. *Please and thank you.*

The creature hooted and launched upward. A swarm of others followed behind.

Leta leaned her chin on Jey's shoulder as they soared across the unobstructed night sky, the hullen's eyes like stars surrounding them. If they weren't in the middle of a battle, it would have been beautiful. 'How are you feeling?' she asked.

'My bag's almost empty.' And he felt it. The wound had begun to burn, as though it were growing...

'We'll fix it,' Leta said. 'When this is all over.'

Her voice cracked. They both knew it was unlikely. Edem was gone from this world, and he didn't think the Shadow Queen would want to share her power to keep him alive.

Leta pressed a kiss to the side of his face. 'I love you, Jey.'

'And I love you, Nettie.'

'No matter what happens,' Leta said. 'Just know that I'll never let go.'

Jey knew she wasn't talking about the battle. He wished he could see her face. He swallowed hard. For once in his life, he didn't know what to say, and he knew that staying silent would mean more.

The hullen traversed the ocean until they reached the castle isle. Jey could see darkness swirling within the top of one of the turrets, like smoke from a blaze.

'Should we knock?' Jey asked.

'Let's surprise her.'

The hullen dove towards a stained-glass window that ran along one side of the turret. The creature let out an ear-splitting scream as it rammed, taloned-feet-first, into the glass, smashing it into colourful fragments.

Inside the turret, the Shadow Queen sat up on a platform, darkness cascading from her dress onto the floor. The room was gloomy; only a sliver of moonlight cascaded in through the broken window.

The queen languidly raised her head as though their presence were a mere inconvenience. 'Why won't you leave me be?'

'Seriously?' Jey asked with a scoff. 'You tried to kill us and plan to take over the world, and you expect us to take it lying down?'

The queen's bright eyes flashed in warning. 'I want what is rightfully mine. What I deserved the day I was born.'

Another hullen landed behind Jey's. Cayder and Maretta rode in on its back.

'This world isn't yours anymore,' Cayder said. 'Times have changed.'

'That may be true,' she replied. 'But I have the power to change it back.'

'And populate it with your flesh-eating creatures. How wonderful,' Jey said sardonically.

The queen pushed to her feet, her shadowy hair vibrating in anger. 'How can you argue against me while riding one of my creations?'

'You hate the hullen,' Leta said. 'Why? Is it because they care about us? Protect us? Instead of kill? Like you do.'

The queen's lip curled into a snarl. 'You're not worth protecting. *I* was born with this power. *I* should have been protected!'

The opposite stained-glass window exploded as Elenora and Erimen crashed through it. Jey shielded his eyes from the spray of glass.

'You're trapped,' Erimen said, lifting his chin. 'We have you surrounded.'

'It's over,' Maretta agreed.

The queen set her beaming eyes onto Maretta. 'I thought you of all people would understand my desire to control this world.'

Maretta's face flamed. 'I don't know what you mean.'

The queen looked amused. 'You have hurt more people than I have, Maretta Broduck.' She stepped slowly down from her platform as though she had all the time in the world. 'I have seen everything you have done.'

She's playing with us, Jey realised. *She doesn't see us as a threat.*

Maretta shook her head. 'It was a mistake.'

'Because you got caught in your own crossfire.'

'That's not true.' Maretta glanced at her children and Jey grabbed Leta's hand. She squeezed it back. 'It was a mistake from the beginning.'

'And yet you still made it,' the Shadow Queen said with a tilt of her head.

'We've all made mistakes,' Elenora said from the other side of the room. She gave Erimen an understanding smile. Their hullen clicked across the polished marble floor on its wide taloned feet. 'It's by recognising them and vowing to do better that we show the kind of people we truly are.'

Cayder put his arm around Maretta. 'You and my mother are nothing alike,' he said to the queen. 'You refuse to see the error of your ways. You won't back down.'

The Shadow Queen smiled. 'Yes. That is true.'

'You still have time to do the right thing,' Erimen stated. 'Surrender and we can come to some arrangement.'

'An arrangement where I don't rule?' She shook her head. 'I must decline your considerate offer.'

She closed her eyes and a black haze filled the room. While Jey couldn't see, his body screamed in pain. He felt torn, fragmented. His side burned as though he'd just been shot.

When the haze faded, two monsters like the one from Lake Rusterton stood guard between the hullen and the Shadow Queen.

How could they defeat her when she could create an army with a snap of her fingers?

One of the monsters lunged for Cayder and Maretta, while the other launched itself onto Jey's hullen's back, snarling and biting at him with its spindly black teeth.

'No, you don't!' Leta cried. She whacked the creature in the head with a lantern.

The creature was startled for a moment before snapping at Leta instead.

Jey's hullen spun away, flicking the monster backwards with its talons. The monster hit the ground and fell onto its back. Rather than rolling up to its feet, it morphed, its head pushing through its own body so that it was facing their direction, teeth bared.

Jey shuddered. 'I will never unsee that.'

Jey's hullen shrieked and flew at the monster. The monster flailed, its arms reaching for Jey and Leta. But their hullen was bullish in its attack. It bit into the monster's shoulder. The royals' hullen rushed forward and grabbed the creature's legs. The two hullen pulled in opposite directions. The creature was torn in two. It gurgled then fell into a lifeless lump on the marble floor.

'I will create more,' the queen snarled. 'You can't stop me.'

'We don't need to,' Elenora replied. 'We just need to corral you.'

Then their hullen leaped, propelling itself headfirst into the queen and sending her flying out the nearest broken window.

Outside, a flock of hundreds of hullen waited. Each creature was ridden by someone from the compound.

'Use your lanterns!' a voice called out from the flock. It was Narena. She was riding a hullen with Farrow sitting behind her.

Everyone held up their torches to create a ring of light.

The queen twisted, dispersing into dark tendrils.

'Don't let her get away!' Elenora cried.

The flock tightened around the queen. In the warm light, she began to return to her more solid form. She couldn't escape. Not now.

Jey urged his hullen forward and out the open window. But it wouldn't budge.

He twisted around to find the other gangly monster had a tendril wrapped around the hullen's talons.

'Let go!' Jey growled.

Another tendril launched towards Jey and Leta smashed it with her lantern. Before he could stop her, she jumped from the saddle.

'Go!' she held the lantern up towards the tendril to free the hullen. 'Help the others!'

Jey shook his head, but didn't argue. He wouldn't take on Leta Broduck. She was fire personified. She wielded the lantern like a sword, barrelling towards the monster.

'You heard her,' Jey nudged his hullen forward. 'Go!'

Outside the castle was chaos – and not the kind Jey enjoyed. The Shadow Queen had created more of her spindly monsters and most of the hullen were busy fighting them off. A few hullen still encircled the queen. Elenora and Erimen held out their flickering lanterns with doomed hope, Narena and Farrow fought beside them. Their numbers were dwindling and soon the light would follow.

'I created you!' the Shadow Queen spat at the hullen surrounding her. 'I will destroy you!'

She lashed out, throwing a wall of darkness towards them, propelling the hullen backwards. The circle of light around the queen dimmed. As the hullen were scattered across the sky, the queen returned to her more elusive form. Soon she would once again disappear into the shadows.

Their plan wasn't working; the queen was too strong. To end this, Jey would have to do the one thing he hated – he would have to improvise.

'I need a light!' Jey cried out as he flew across the sky. Hullen and creatures battled each other below. It was a nightmarish scene and one that would haunt Jey for all his days to come.

'Here!' Narena yelled from somewhere below.

Jey grinned as she threw a lantern and container of lamp oil towards him. He caught them, but not without feeling like he was being torn in two.

Keep it together, Jey. You can fall apart when this is all over.

First, he had to light up this witch.

'Don't let her see you,' Jey whispered to his hullen, his hand against its neck. 'Stay in the dark. Stay quiet.'

Jey understood the hullen's desire for the Shadow Queen's blood, but the winged creatures were too obvious in their attack. They would need to sneak up on her to gain the upper hand. Now was not the time to be bold and boisterous. Like his father always wanted, Jey would be quiet.

The queen had her back turned to him as she tackled the other hullen, fighting them off with wave after wave of darkness.

'Hi,' Jey announced. She hadn't noticed his approach.

She spun around, her eyes flaming. 'You again,' she snarled. She eyed the pouch of edem against his side and reached for it with smoky fingers.

Jey yelped as the needle was ripped from his arm. Although the pouch was nearly empty, he immediately felt the loss of the minute amount of black liquid that had been trickling into his veins.

'Just like your father,' the queen said, nodding to the pouch in her hand, 'taking what's not yours.'

Jey slumped forward on the hullen, spent. There was nothing more he could do. He had one small lantern against the immense power of the queen. And no other hullen would come to his rescue; they were busy fending off the monsters the queen had released upon them.

He could barely keep his head up to see his oncoming demise.

He wished he could tell Leta he was sorry. He even wished he could see his father one last time. After all, he was all that he had left of his family.

The Shadow Queen tipped what edem remained in the pouch into her mouth, her eyes flaming bright as the edem returned to her body.

Which gave Jey an idea...

'Get in nice and close,' he whispered to the hullen.

The hullen let out a hoot and dove directly for the queen. With trembling hands, Jey unscrewed the lid of the lamp oil container and took a large mouthful. He pushed himself upright, ignore the searing pain in his side. He held up the lantern's flickering flame and sprayed the oil towards the queen in one big breath.

The blaze was immediate and intense. Lighting up the sky and scorching the night.

The Shadow Queen screamed as the light transformed her into her human form and engulfed her body in flame. The other hullen were quick to act, closing in on her and grabbing her solid arms, legs and hair in their mouths and with their feet.

We got her, Jey thought.

'Well done, mate,' he said to his hullen, slumping back down.

———

Jey's chest tightened once they reached the prison's gates. He wasn't sure if it was due to the sight of the building, or his dwindling health. Perhaps both.

He managed to keep himself upright as they flew across the water, the Shadow Queen trapped within the flock of the hullen. Even though darkness crept in at the edges of his sight, he wasn't going to miss this.

'Over here!' Kema called. She had the doors to Vardean open.

Kema dove out of the way as the queen was forced into the building.

The diffuse light inside Vardean surrounded the queen, keeping her body in her human form. While her skin turned pink, her veins remained black as the darkest night.

'You cannot kill me!' she bellowed. Her eyes were like bottled lightning.

'We're not planning on it,' Kema said, pulling a lever.

The central elevator in the foyer began to lower.

The Shadow Queen threw out an arm, but nothing appeared. Her power was diminished by the light.

'You have nowhere to go, Shadow Queen,' Elenora said, sitting high on her hullen as though she were the crowned queen. '*This* is your home now.'

'But I'm your blood!' the queen roared.

Elenora glanced at her brother behind her. 'You've had your chance to rule,' the princess said. 'Now, it's our turn.'

Once the elevator had lowered, the hullen closed in, forcing the Shadow Queen to step up onto the platform.

'There are lots of sleeping options,' Jey said. 'Take your pick.'

'You can't keep me in here forever!' the queen shouted.

'I think you'll find that we can,' Jey replied.

The elevator rose into the prison sector, cutting off her howls of rage.

CHAPTER 45

CAYDER

Cayder's mother stood in between Leta and himself as they approached Broduck Manor, their hands linked. He wasn't sure who was shaking. Perhaps they all were.

He couldn't believe he was finally home, and with his mother. It felt too good to be true. A dream he hoped never to wake from.

'What if your father isn't happy to see me?' Maretta asked. Her cheeks were wind-burned from flying on the back of the hullen.

'Why wouldn't he be?' Cayder asked.

She glanced at Leta and twisted her mouth into a grimace. 'Because of everything I've done.'

'Father knows who you really are,' Leta said with a nod. 'Just like we do.'

Their mother had made a mistake helping create the Regency weapons; and she had spent the past seven years paying for it. Now it was time to put the past in the past and embrace their future.

Tears formed in her eyes. 'Thank you. Both of you, for being so gracious.' She gave them each a kiss on the cheek.

It was still early in the morning and the sun had not yet completely risen behind Broduck Manor, which stood, thankfully, in one piece. Because most of the Shadow Queen's world had disappeared over time, the damage to Telene during the merge had not been too catastrophic, aside from some industrial buildings around the Unbent River, which had been empty at nighttime. And there had been no casualties, thanks to Narena and Farrow's article and the help of the hullen.

'Are we going to stand on the porch all day?' Leta asked. 'I want to see Jey soon.'

After they trapped the Shadow Queen inside Vardean, Dr Bueter had taken Jey to the hospital; his wound looked worse once the queen was locked away. Elenora and Erimen had returned to the castle isle to order the return of the royal fleet, dismantle the Regency and begin the business of restoring their nation. Cayder had wanted to stay with Elenora and tell her how he felt, but he knew it wasn't the time.

Maretta fussed with her braid and her dress's collar.

'You look beautiful, Mother.' Cayder gave her hand a reassuring squeeze.

She smiled and sucked in a deep breath. 'Here we go—'

Maretta lifted the heavy doorknocker and released it. When there was no response, Maretta rapped her knuckles on the door.

'Go away!' Cayder's father bellowed from inside. 'Can't you see it's a state of emergency!'

Maretta chuckled under her breath. 'Your father hasn't changed.'

'Nope,' Leta said with a grin. 'If anything, he's worse.'

Cayder nodded in agreement. 'Father, it's us! Open the door!'

Cayder held his breath as he waited.

The door opened and there his father stood, dressed in his silk pyjamas. Cayder had never seen his father in anything other than a well-pressed suit. Even on weekends.

'Cayder? Leta?' He swallowed a few times, blinking as though he was staring into the sun. 'Maretta?'

'Alain.' Maretta dropped Cayder and Leta's hands so she could embrace her husband. 'I'm home.'

He staggered back, as though Maretta was a ghoul intent on his destruction. He clutched a hand to his chest. Leta and Cayder exchanged a worried glance. Was he having a heart attack?

'Father...' Cayder said, approaching cautiously. 'Take a deep breath. Everything is all right.'

'Don't tell me what to do!' his father snapped. And with that, he turned and stomped back into the house as though nothing had happened.

'That was suitably weird,' Leta whispered to Cayder.

'Agreed,' Cayder whispered back.

They followed him into the foyer and found him collapsed in a chair by a painting of a blooming heart, his head in his hands.

'Well,' he said, 'it's over. All those years of studying for nothing. No job. No family. No mind.'

'What are you talking about, Father?' Cayder asked. Why on earth was he worried about his studies at a time like this?

'You haven't lost everything,' Maretta said, her eyes brimming with tears. 'We're here, Alain. All of us. Together.'

'Miserable delusions,' he muttered. 'Leave me alone!'

'*Father.*' Cayder was firmer this time. 'I can assure you that you are *not* hallucinating.'

'Sure. And then I'll wake up like I always do,' his father murmured, lifting his head from his hands. His eyes were red-rimmed and glassy.

His father had been dreaming about them. Leta and Cayder's absence had hit him harder than Cayder could have imagined.

Suddenly Cayder found it hard to breathe.

'Alain, my love.' Maretta crouched so they were eye to eye. 'You are not dreaming now.' She placed her hand on his.

His eyes went wide. 'No. No. No. No. No.'

'Yes,' Maretta said with a smile. 'We're here.'

'Really?' He looked between the three of them, as though someone might disagree.

Maretta nodded and he pulled her into an embrace, finally letting go of his tears.

Then he opened his arms for his children.

CHAPTER 46

NARENA

Narena was grounded for a year. She considered that to be a fair settlement, considering she'd thought she was going to be grounded for life. Unfortunately, that meant she couldn't see Cayder. *Fortunately*, Farrow already knew how to sneak into Narena's room.

'Hello,' Farrow said, climbing in through the window.

'Hello.'

Farrow sat down beside her. It felt different having Farrow in her room now that they were together. Anticipation hummed along Narena's skin.

'How's your mother?' Narena asked.

'Better after I told her what really happened in Lake Rusterton.'

Three days after the Shadow Queen had been imprisoned, the *Telene Herald*'s editor-in-chief, Mr Grotherman, had approved a tell-all from Farrow's perspective. Since the veil had come down, there was an unquenchable appetite for any news on the Regency, edem and the veil. Farrow's story covered all three.

'What about you?' Farrow asked. 'How are your parents taking everything?'

After capturing the Shadow Queen, Narena headed home and had nearly been knocked out with a pot and pan upon walking into the dark house. Luckily, her parents had recognised her voice before attacking.

'King Erimen and Princess Elenora wrote to my parents to explain that I'd been helping them on official royal matters.' Narena grinned at her *girlfriend* – she got to call Farrow that now. 'They couldn't exactly argue against the rulers of Telene.'

'But you're still grounded.'

Mr Grotherman had offered to pay Narena to write a series of articles on the hullen and the edem monsters they had battled. The world was equal parts terrified and fascinated with the creatures and Mr Grotherman wanted an insider's perspective. The assignment would involve spending time at Vardean, where the hullen stayed to watch over the Shadow Queen and were subsequently sustained by her power as it dispersed into the atmosphere.

The series would set up Narena's career; she would become a household name.

But she declined. She wanted to enjoy her final year at school with Cayder and see how she felt after graduation. She wasn't in a hurry to become a journalist or study at university. With the veil gone and the borders reopened, the world was hers to explore.

But for right now, she wanted to enjoy being reunited with her best friend and spend time with her girlfriend. The rest of the world would have to wait.

'Does that mean you can't come to the royal celebration next week?' Farrow asked.

'My parents couldn't deny a personal request from the king,' Narena replied with a grin.

Farrow's green eyes sparkled. 'Great. Because I need a date.'

Narena leaned over and pressed her lips against Farrow's. 'You got me.'

'And you've got me.'

'There's something else I got you.' Narena leaned over to pull the present from under her bed. She handed the rectangular box to Farrow.

'Why?' Farrow looked at the box as though it might bite her.

'Because I wanted to?' Had Narena gone too far? Were they not at the gift-giving part of their relationship? It *had* only been a week since they'd become official girlfriends.

'Good answer,' Farrow said. She opened the box and gasped.

Inside was the portrait of Farrow's grandmother that Narena had ripped.

'I had the painting fixed for you,' Narena said. 'I thought you might like to have it.'

'Narena—' Farrow shook her head. 'I don't know what to say.' She pulled the framed painting out from the box. 'This is wonderful.'

Narena's heart squeezed. 'Your grandmother would have been so proud of you.'

'Thank you.' Farrow threw her arms around Narena. 'Thank you for helping me uncover her story.'

'Thank *you*,' Narena said, 'for helping me embrace mine.'

374

CHAPTER 47

LETA

Leta sat by Jey's bedside as his vitals began to fail. Jey's father paced around the hospital room, muttering, swearing and antagonising anyone who came close to him. Leta allowed him to stay, because his presence meant he cared about his son. And that meant everything to Jey, especially now.

'Do something!' he shouted at Dezra. As the leading specialist in edem wounds, Dezra had started working at the hospital after the veil collapsed. Leta could tell Dezra had a soft spot for Jey, and was doing everything they could to make him comfortable in these final moments.

Cayder and Kema were also there; though Leta was pretty sure Cayder was watching over *her* rather than Jey. Kema stood in the doorway as if she was guarding the room.

'The family is back together,' Jey whispered, nodding to their friends, new and old.

'It's a twisted family,' Leta whispered back, tears clogging her throat.

'It is.' Jey smiled. 'But it's ours.'

It wasn't fair! Leta's family was finally reunited, but now she would lose Jey. And this time there was no coming back. There was no other side of the veil. No hope. No edem. Nothing.

Leta had tried not to cry over the past week; she wanted to be strong for Jey, who continued to be annoyingly upbeat for someone who was soon to die.

'We did it!' he kept saying. 'We came home. We caught the bad guy. We saved the world.'

That wasn't enough for Leta. She wanted to be home *with* Jey. She wanted to relish in having her mother back, without having to exchange one grief for another.

Maretta wasn't at the hospital; she was helping Erimen and Elenora restructure the Regency, and overseeing the dismantling of their weapons.

'Do you regret it?' Leta had to ask.

'Getting shot?' Jey pulled a face. 'Of course I do.'

Trust Jey to make light of the situation. 'Do you regret meeting me, knowing where it led us?'

Jey rubbed circles on the back of her pale hand. Leta's death echo had disappeared when the veil had broken down. 'Do I wish things had gone a little differently? Sure. Do I wish I had never met you? Absolutely not.' The dark veins had reached his jawline, but he was still the most handsome boy Leta had ever seen.

A tear escaped and ran down Leta's cheek.

'No, Nettie. Don't.'

Leta knew if she broke down, she wouldn't be able to stop. And they would waste their last moments together.

'We never got to pick up our rendezvous in the Vardean elevator,' she said with a hiccup.

'Well…' Jey waggled his eyebrows. 'I'm here now, aren't I? But you might want to clear the room first. We have an audience.'

Leta laughed through her tears. She would miss this, miss him, miss everything he stood for, and how he supported her. Loved her. How he was always just *Jey*. The world was brighter with him in it.

'Our time together wasn't long enough,' Jey said. 'But when something is good, when is it ever?'

Leta nodded; she knew she'd burst into tears if she replied.

'Sorry, Dad,' Jey said. 'I know you'd rather be out doing something else – *anything* else.'

'No,' Dr Bueter replied, giving his son a rare grin. For the first time, Leta could see where Jey inherited his smile from. 'There's nowhere else I'd rather be.'

Jey locked eyes with Leta and she knew what he was thinking: Jey had to lay dying for his father to finally be there for him.

The machine monitoring Jey's vitals started beeping. Leta clasped Jey's black-veined hand. His father grabbed the other.

Jey let out a pained groan. As hard as this was going to be, Leta wouldn't leave him. Just as she promised.

'Dezra? What's happening?' Leta asked, fearing the answer.

'The edem infection is spreading,' Dezra replied. 'His organs are failing.'

Jey released another groan and began trembling.

This is it. This is the end.

Cayder placed his hand on Leta's shoulder, lending her his strength.

Jey let out an agonised wail and then went still.

Leta sucked in a breath, waiting for the rise and fall of his chest to falter. The room fell silent and Jey took a final painful gasp.

'*Wait!*'

Maretta dashed into the room. She carted a small machine behind her. She placed it beside Jey's bed and held out a needle attached to a thin translucent tube. 'Insert this into his veins!' she instructed. 'Now!'

Dezra looked to Jey's father for permission and he nodded. Dezra inserted the tube into Jey's black veins.

'What are you doing?' Leta asked.

But her mother didn't reply. She pressed a button on the side of the machine and it started whirring.

Rather than pumping fluid into Jey's veins, black liquid was drawn out. It was removing edem!

'What's happening?' Leta asked. Her voice thick with emotion.

'I have a theory,' her mother said. 'There's no more edem and no more veil. When Jey was shot, he was between worlds and more edem was the only way to keep him in one place. But now, *here*.' She gestured to the hospital room. 'There's only Telene. And I think having *too much* edem in his system caused his vitals to shut down. What was once keeping him alive, is now killing him.'

Jey's hand was cold, lifeless. Leta squeezed it, wishing she could give him her strength.

'Everyone's blood contains small traces of edem,' Maretta explained. 'I've spent the last few days working on a way to draw it from my own blood, so that I could use it on Jey. I didn't want to tell you in case it didn't work.'

Jey let out a moan and stirred, his eyes flicking behind his lids.

Maretta smiled at her daughter.

'Looks like it works.'

CHAPTER 48

ELENORA

Elenora contemplated hiding away from the night's festivities. She was exhausted. She'd spent the past two weeks in meetings; first with the Regency, then with everyone who'd been transported from the other side of the veil, and finally with foreign dignitaries from around the world, to explain what had happened. Then there were the plans to rebuild the power plant – minus the permacloud, of course.

Elenora was sick of the sound of her own voice; she had never spoken so much in her life. But she knew she couldn't hide out any longer – Erimen would drag her from her room if she didn't make an appearance. After all, it was her eighteenth birthday party.

Elenora twisted her golden hair onto the top of her head and pinned it with a jewelled clasp. The edem mark on her neck had faded, although she would have worn her hair in the same style even if it hadn't.

She dusted her eyelids with a glittering grey and donned a dress with ruffled black layers and a silver lining. When she moved, the dress shimmered – a nod to edem and the magic that had been a part of their world for so many years. She had the royal seamstress make a sling for her arm out of the same material.

'I hope I made you proud,' she said to the lumanite mask on her dresser. She had retrieved it after the Shadow Queen was imprisoned and had it repaired.

'Of course you have.'

Erimen watched from the doorway; he wore a blue and silver striped suit. His red curls were gelled into an elegant wave over his forehead. 'Though there was never any doubt about that.'

Elenora smiled at her brother. 'I miss them.'

He closed his eyes briefly. 'I do too.'

She moved to wrap her unrestricted arm around his middle. 'They would have been proud of you, too.'

He nodded, although guilt wrinkled his brow. Now there were no secrets between them, he could start to forgive himself.

'Are you sure you're up for this?' He nodded to the doorway and the commotion as the staff prepared the castle for their visitors.

Her birthday was never an easy day, but for the first time, she was happy to celebrate it, *and* she had friends expecting her. Her younger self would be delighted.

'I am.'

The castle ballroom was already bustling with people by the time Erimen and Elenora entered. The room had been lit with hundreds of candles sitting along the stone windows, dripping white wax down the walls. In the centre sat a cluster of round tables with colourful spreads of foods from all over the world – gifted from the foreign dignitaries who had travelled to Telene to discuss resuming trade.

The royal siblings walked arm in arm and greeted each of their guests. The party was designed to allow everyone to mingle, with a few lounges clustered in the dim corners of the room. Telene was learning to embrace the darkness.

'Happy birthday, Princess Elenora.'

Elenora turned to the familiar voice of Graymond Toyer, looking dapper as ever.

'Oh!' A flood of memories from her time in Vardean threatened to take her to her knees. She dug her fingernails into her palms to stay in the present and left her brother chatting with the Delften Queen.

'Mr Toyer! Thank you for coming,' she said.

'I should be thanking you.' He nodded to Kema, who stood by the entrance of the room, checking people's names off the list as they entered. Rusteef stood on the other side, looking his usual gruff and irritated self. No one would get anything past those two.

'You didn't need to give my daughter a second chance, but you did.'

Elenora reached out and squeezed Graymond's hand. 'I *did* need to, and I wanted to.'

He shook his head with a smile. 'I never thought I'd see the inside of the castle.'

'Well? What do you think?' She leaned in and whispered, 'Tell me the truth.'

Graymond considered it for a moment before admitting, 'It's cold and draughty.'

Elenora chuckled.

'But I'm more than happy to be here.' Graymond lifted his glass. 'Thank you for the invite.'

'I might need my lawyer in case I get into any trouble tonight.' She winked.

'I'm here for anything you need, Princess,' he said with a bow. 'Always.'

Elenora spotted Leta and Jey over by the Delften food table.

'My mother's is better,' she overheard Leta say as she took another bite of a sugar-coated deebule.

'I'll be sure to tell the Queen of Delften that her deebule is not up to scratch,' Elenora whispered in her ear.

'Princess!' Leta's hand flew to her chest. 'You startled me!'

Jey had powdered sugar on his chin. 'Don't listen to Nettie – these are delicious. And happy birthday, Princess.' He raised a gooey pastry to her.

Elenora grabbed her own deebule and tapped it to his. 'Thank you, Jey. It's truly wonderful to see you. I'm so sorry that I couldn't be at the hospital last week. It's been an incredibly busy time.'

'You didn't miss much. The whole incident was very anti-climactic.' He shrugged. 'Spoiler alert: I didn't die.'

'Jey!' Leta admonished, her brows in a firm line.

'Too soon?' he asked.

'Forever too soon.' Leta pursed her lips, which made Elenora laugh.

'How *are* you feeling, Jey?' Elenora asked. 'I've been so worried.'

'Much better, see—' He pulled back his sleeves to show his tattooed arms – the dark veins had receded. 'Maretta created a way to draw the edem from my blood. I only have to visit the hospital once a week for treatment until there's no more edem in my system.'

'I'm so glad.' She squeezed his hand. 'Is Maretta here?'

'Yes,' Leta groaned.

Elenora glanced around the room; she spotted Narena and Farrow together on the dancefloor, but couldn't see Maretta.

'If you see a couple of old people acting disgustingly in love, that would be my parents,' Leta said.

'More disgusting than us?' Jey asked, peppering kisses along Leta's neck while she pretended to bat him away.

'No one is more disgusting than you two,' Cayder said, appearing by Elenora's side.

Leta rolled her eyes at her brother. 'Funny.'

Cayder was wearing a crisp black blazer with a black shirt and chrome buttons. His dark hair was slicked back from his tan forehead. In the low light, his amber eyes sparkled like burning embers.

He looks so handsome, Elenora thought.

'Hey, Elle,' he said with a bow of his head.

'Hi,' her reply was barely above a whisper.

'Let's go join Narena and Farrow on the dancefloor, shall we?' Leta grabbed Jey's arm.

'Why?' Jey asked, then looked between Elenora and Cayder. 'Oh, yes. The dancefloor is calling my name. Have a good night!'

But Elenora couldn't tear her eyes from Cayder.

'Happy birthday.' Cayder stood strangely stiff. 'You look beautiful, like a star cut from the night sky.' He grimaced. 'Wow. That was incredibly cheesy.'

Elenora smiled. She liked this shy version of him. 'Thank you, Cayder.'

He held out his hand. 'Can we go somewhere?'

Elenora looked at the guests around her, laughing, chatting, dancing. Everyone was having a wonderful time. Everyone was safe and well.

'Yes.' Elenora took his hand; it was warm and reassuring. 'I'd like that.'

Elenora led Cayder down to the pebbly beach. The castle behind them hummed with music and voices. Without the permacloud and streetlamps, the stars glimmered brightly. It was a beautiful night.

'I'm sorry, Elle,' Cayder said as soon as they reached the waterline. 'For everything. I should have told you about your parents as soon as I found out.'

'No,' Elenora shook her head. *I'm* sorry. I never should have gone off on my own. I released the Shadow Queen on Telene. I'm the one to blame.'

He hadn't let go of her hand. 'You thought you were doing what was right. You trusted her – and so did I. And in the end, it was because of you that we're here. You brought us all back together.'

Her heart felt full, her chest buoyant. She never wanted to lose this feeling.

Cayder brushed a stray hair from her face. 'How are you?'

'I am—' she was going to say 'great' but decided Cayder deserved the truth, 'absolutely exhausted.'

His eyes were soft and understanding. 'Of course you are. Everyone is looking to you and Erimen for the answers about our future. That's a lot of pressure.'

'It's my duty.'

'Is it?' He tugged gently on her hand so they were facing one another. 'Is this what you dreamt of when you were locked in Vardean?'

Most nights she dreamt of him, but she couldn't voice that. Not yet.

'Maybe not,' she admitted. 'But I can't leave my brother to take on this burden alone. Not now that we're finally back together.'

'Why not? He's the king.'

It was a fair question, and it wasn't like Erimen had asked her to stay. She had assumed that he wished to have her by his side, but she knew he would support her in whatever she chose to do.

What did she *really* want?

A flutter began to build inside her chest; hope begging to break free. 'What would I do instead?' she asked.

He ran his hand down her cheek and rested it against her neck, where her echo mark used to be. 'Whatever you want, Elle.'

She could go to school with Cayder. She could travel abroad. She could learn a trade on the mainland, or work to replant the torlu trees in Ferrington, or help Graymond and Alain on the pardons for those imprisoned for edem usage, or study the hullen – she had loved the freedom of flight.

She could always come back to her brother and her royal duties when he needed her.

'What about you?' she asked. 'Are you still planning to become a prosecutor?'

'I think I've had enough of the law.' Cayder chuckled, dimple flashing. 'But I have time to figure out what's next. And we can figure it out together.'

Ever since the days in the cave, Cayder wore that same look of intensity on his face when he looked at her. Her heart skipped a beat and a shiver danced along her skin.

She felt safe. She felt loved.

Elenora might not know exactly what her future held, but she knew what she wanted to do next.

She leaned forward and kissed Cayder.

ACKNOWLEDGEMENTS

For years, I've wanted to write a sequel to one of my books, and I'm immensely thankful to Allen & Unwin for giving me that chance with Shadows of Truth! I always saw the story crossing two novels and I've loved exploring what lies beyond the veil – I hope you did too!

Many thanks, as always, to my supportive friends and family. In particular, lots of love to my parents for their unconditional love and support. And to Andrew, who brightens the darkest of days. I love you.

Allen & Unwin have been the perfect home for my books in Australia and New Zealand and are continuously supportive of my writing career. Working with Kate Whitfield was an absolute pleasure and she pushed me to make this the best book it could be. Thank you to Jodie Webster, Eva Mills, Reem Galal, Simon Panagaris and the entire team at Allen & Unwin – you're the best creative partners an author could ask for! And a huge shoutout to Debra Billson for creating the stunning cover that I fell in love with the instant I saw it!

Being an author can often feel like a solitary, lonely endeavor, but I'm so lucky to be a part of the wonderful YA community in Melbourne. Many thanks to the incomparable Amie Kaufman for her wisdom and friendship. Huge hugs to Katya De Beccera, Adalyn Grace, Sabina Khan and Mel Howard for helping me ride the ups and down of the publishing industry.

Big cheers to my literary managers at Gravity Squared Entertainment, who continue to fight the good fight in getting my books translated onto the big or little screen. And to my wonderful agent Sarah Landis who always dispenses the perfect blend of encouragement and sage advice.

Publishing a book is like sending a piece of your heart out into the world and hoping it won't get crushed. So thank you to all the readers out there who continue to let me know what my books mean to you. It's because of you that I keep coming back and doing this thing called writing all over again.

ABOUT THE AUTHOR

Astrid Scholte is the internationally bestselling and award-winning author of *Four Dead Queens*, *The Vanishing Deep* and *League of Liars*. When she's not writing, she works in film and animation production. Career highlights include working on James Cameron's *Avatar*, Disney's *Moon Girl* and *Devil Dinosaur*. She currently works at Industrial Light & Magic on the latest blockbuster.